ADVANCE PRAISE FOR UNDER A SECRET SKY

Under a Secret Sky

Author David Madsen brings 1952 in California back to life. Written in the third-person narrative from the perspective of a strong female character, the reader is privy to her most personal thoughts and feelings. The character descriptions are phenomenal, and the characters are likable and relatable. The reader's senses are constantly stimulated with descriptive phrases that bring the scenes to life. With a prevalent theme of secrecy from multiple sources throughout, this undeniably enhances the mystery. I loved how intricately this novel was plotted and the slow reveal of one secret after another. This kept me engaged and wanting more. Anyone who loves a bit of Cold War history and government conspiracy will quickly devour Under a Secret Sky. Filled with raw human emotions, the delicate structures of relationships, and outstanding character growth, this book is a must-read!

—Readers' Favorite 5-star review

Praise for Madsen's previous books, U.S.S.A. and Black Plume

This is a unique, very clever, and disturbing look at America and Russia in the near future.... Superb, sinister, shocking and a little too believable.

—Nelson DeMille, Author of "Plum Island", "The Gold Coast"

The setting for this totally beguiling thriller is so clever it could stand without the plot.... irresistible.

—Kirkus Reviews Starred Review

This superior thriller owes something to Tom Clancy, but much more to Raymond Chandler.

—Publishers Weekly

Strong, suspenseful plot and colorful characters, some of whom we wouldn't mind getting to know over caviar and a bottle of Stolichnaya... audacious originality.

—The Baltimore Sun

David Madsen has invented a fresh setting for his novel of the near future, and he exploits it well. Bottom line: One of the most unusual mysteries of the year. One of the best, too.

—The San Diego Union

A first-rate thriller with plot, action, characters and social extrapolation expertly combined.

—Ellery Queen Mystery Magazine

The Finns who know the Russians and Russia better than most people, were very impressed by Madsen's excellent knowledge of the country and its people.

—Licht Agency, Finland

A stunning 'what-if' fantasy.

—Houston Post

U.S.S.A.'s setting is the near future, in a Russia conquered by the U.S. after WW III, which ended not in Armageddon, but with the failure of Soviet missile systems to function. Madsen (Black Plume) convincingly depicts an occupation more entrepreneurial than military. Yesterday's enemies are today's customers: Golden Arches and the Goodyear Blimp, American Express and 7-11, all have emigrated; a Disneyland is under construction in Moscow. Private eye Dan Joplin, a CIA agent whose job disappeared with victory, walks mean streets from booming downtown Moscow to a Siberia devastated by nuclear attack, where survivors are kept in strict quarantine. To solve the novel's puzzle he must understand a spectrum of a well-drawn characters, Russian and American, caught in a vortex of change that has made previous knowledge irrelevant, and living in a new order emphasizing buying and selling, better able to supply consumer goods than value systems. This superior thriller owes something to Tom Clancy, but much more to Raymond Chandler. BOMC and Mysterious Book Club alternates.

—Publishers Weekly Review

"Poe enthusiasts will certainly enjoy this warm homage, discovering that Poe's ominous spirit echoes forever more."

—Los Angeles Times

"Madsen's ability to see the world through funeral lenses in impressive. The voice, the mood, the violent, grisly crimes - all these evoke Poe at his most full blown. Madsen's bizarre thriller would make Poe roll over in his grave and grin."

—Seattle Post-Intelligencer

"It's a must for fans of inventive gaslit amusement."

—Kirkus Reviews

"Not only is it an engaging murder mystery, it captures Poe's rollicking sentence rhythms and mixture of horror and hoaxing."

—Library Journal

UNDER A SECRET SKY

DAVID MADSEN

KONSTELLATION
PRESS

Published by Konstellation Press, San Diego

www.konstellationpress.com

Cover design: Scarlet Willette

ISBN: 979-8-9908181-0-1

To my mother, Dorothy Green Madsen:
As I wrote this adventure, I asked myself what you would have done and followed your lead.

PROLOGUE

They weren't hidden because no one was looking for them. They weren't secretive because they had nothing to conceal.

Only a few select outsiders knew what went on in the tiny, second floor suite of offices in an unfashionable neighborhood of Washington, and the organization felt no need to enlighten anyone else. Question the neighbors, and you might hear "Oh, they're a charity for Korean orphans," or "they offer oil painting correspondence courses; a racket, if you ask me." They had no name and those who worked there had no official titles. But no one used an alias, the phones were always answered, and mail came directly to the office delivered by a postman, not a furtive, late-night courier.

The pet project of an idealistic, but morally blackened one-term congressman, whose self-professed sins were never explained, whose name and district were forgotten by the rest of the country, the organization had been slipped into the budget on the last day of the 73rd Congress in 1935 and routinely approved on the first day of the next. Their operating expenses were so paltry and their mission so vague, that everyone with accounting knowledge of the government's inner workings assumed they were someone else's department, so year after year their budget was approved—never growing, but never shrinking either. They had served under two presidents, endured Depression and war, and last month mourned the death of actor John Garfield. Now, in June 1952, their budget had been reapproved at a crucial moment.

They were reclusive, but by choice, not by charter. It was generally accepted that if people ever found out what they did, they would be laughed at, scorned, or at best praised by a few independent souls. But the overriding reaction to their existence would probably be indifference. They saw themselves as scholars and researchers, pursuing their work in an ignored corner of the capital far from the disputatious halls of power. They weren't threatening, and no one threatened them. When the Director gathered the staff together on a seasonable June day, the windows of their second-floor offices thrown open to the breeze drifting off the Potomac, they expected his usual unruffled, parsed words of assurance.

The Director was a thrifty New Englander who dressed accordingly in off-the-rack suits, highlighted by identical blue neckties which he rotated once a week. His only indulgence were his eyeglasses; he carried several pairs, which he changed frequently according to lighting and environment. No longer a young man, he also had several upgrades, purchased at a discount, pre-selected for the coming months or years when his vision would worsen. He sorted through the collection on his desk, settling on his most serious pair at hand, dark brown rims devoid of trim or flourish.

He began his talk by tying together stray threads of dubious intelligence and established fact into a plausible narrative, his strength as a former lawyer. He spoke of phone tips corroborated by back up phone calls, newspaper stories which required readers to read between the lines that were between the lines, a skill in which they excelled. A stack of letters from like-minded citizens across the country, who they had cultivated during the last few years. A few telegrams, which they had originally treated as "alarmist."

As he talked, the Director's voice tightened, acquiring a tense, clipped tone his staff had never heard. He patted a wall with his fists. "Here, in these quiet rooms, it's easy to think we don't matter." He walked to the new researcher's desk, smacked it with an open palm, startling her backwards in her chair. "Here, seated at these dusty desks, we imagine we are jousting at lost causes, with books and paperwork our only lances." He spread his arms to take in the entire office. "Underpaid, overlooked, we barely figure in the rush of history."

He walked to the tallest of the open windows. If someone were watching from the street—as someone assuredly was – the Director would appear as just another Washington bureaucrat of indeterminate age and rank. He turned his back to the window, a calculated gesture of indifference. "Today, that is all about to change," he said, as his staff of seven edged closer. "We may have to develop new skills and talents. We could be called upon to transgress bureaucratic boundaries. Most of all, we will have to toughen ourselves to be at once elastic and steel." He waited for them to absorb this message with its unaccustomed urgency. Their flat expressions told him they were skeptical. He needed to press harder.

"We are not spies, but we may become spies."

That connected. They were startled, glancing at each other, wondering if they had misunderstood. And now, one more thrust. "We have no true enemies, but in the weeks ahead, we may make some."

Down on the street, the trim, austere, blue-suited, bow-tied man in frameless glasses watching the second-floor offices from the back seat of a Lincoln Cosmopolitan, could not have agreed more.

1

She would tell him tonight. You didn't keep secrets from your husband. *Ladies Home Journal* insisted that an aura of mystery was the most important weapon a woman possessed. But the editors of those magazines, whose recipes she clipped but whose advice she never took, lived back East, not in California, rode elevators to work, dined out every night, and generally dismissed life as it was led in the rest of the country. It took hard work to be mysterious and energy to cover up.

"Bogey, two o'clock!"

Jimmy pointed to a flashing light twenty degrees to the northeast of the aircraft beacon on top of Black Mountain, the gentle sloping peak that overlooked the Bay Area peninsula.

"Approach speed estimated at one hundred, fifty-six knots, bearing one two, seven degrees. Still unidentified," he said. "Mom, did you hear me? This could be it."

Jean looked at this eleven-and-a-half-year-old boy, so charged up with enthusiasm and arcane interests. His blue eyes were forever focused on horizons she couldn't see. His blond-brown hair, dusted with a summer day's adventures, straggled across his eyebrows; the only grooming techniques that worked on him were applied once a year by the school photographers. He was short for his age, so he had become a jumper, leaping up to grab at things that were out of his reach — canned goods on the top shelf, the ridges of doorframes, the flags their neighbors flew on holidays. Someday, perhaps, he would feel tall enough and stop jumping. That would be a sad day, she thought.

"Just a Liftmaster. Heading for Moffett Field," Jimmy sighed.

"Guess tonight's not the night."

She felt his disappointment, as though it were her own.

"Tomorrow we'll start before it's dark, "Jean said. "After all, the Arnold sightings were in broad daylight."

Jimmy frowned, preparing himself for the short, sad trudge toward the dinner table. Jean squinted up at the sky. "Hold on. Hand me the binocs." Jimmy passed her his Army binoculars (coated optics as he often reminded her). She scanned the crestline of the hills, then swept her gaze from north to south, east to west.

"What is it?" Jimmy demanded.

"Thought I saw something."

"Something?"

Jean nodded, handing him back his binoculars. "Let's give it another half hour."

"Dinner'll be late," Jimmy said.

"Yep. Dinner'll be late."

As Jimmy prowled the skies with fresh expectation, Jean turned her attention to Echo Lane, a two-lane road that led straight to their garage, like a runway. At the far end of Echo, they could watch the commuter trains of the Southern Pacific as they flashed up and down the Peninsula. Between the 7:30 southbound from Millbrae and the northbound to San Francisco, Robert's Plymouth would appear at the far end of Echo and seem to accelerate, even though he always drove below the speed limit. He'd cut the engine and coast into the driveway, proud of the little maneuver that gave his nightly homecomings their trademark.

The kitchen. The woman's command post. Another thing the magazines got wrong; a kitchen was also a hive of potential disappointments. She washed lettuce in the sink, which looked out on the driveway. The kitchen seemed designed to be an observation post so she could keep an eye on Jimmy. She'd seen him ride his first bike from this vantage point, slap his first coat of paint onto the redwood fence that bordered the lawn. Would she still be spying on him as he took his first drive, drank his first beer, kissed his first girl? She looked away and let him play unobserved. "Jean Vale, you're not thinking today," she said to herself.

Scotch taped to the underlip of the drain board tile was a small note written in shorthand: "Presidents Backwards." She slipped the scrap of paper into an apron pocket. Glanced out the window—no sign of Robert yet, Jimmy lying prone on the driveway, peering through binoculars. Normandy invasion.

"Truman, FDR, Hoover, Coolidge."

Jean dashed into the front room. Another piece of paper taped to the underside of the davenport: "Shopping list by category."

As she whirled through the house, recovering the hidden notes from inside the fireplace, from below the base of the pole lamp, she recited by memory the challenges written on each scrap: "Whitecliff Market—items in Aisle Five"; "List of San Francisco Radio Stations"; "Co-workers, alphabetized"; "Islands recaptured from Japan, reverse order".

She put the notes up in the morning after Robert left for work, and used them during the day to settle her nerves. He ate lunch at work and always returned home at seven, so she took them down at 5:30 to give herself plenty of time. Jimmy knew about them and had once hurried to hide them when Robert came back to the house to pick up some paperwork he'd forgotten. She'd grown comfortable with the process and with her cover story if she were ever caught: "I'm planning on entering a radio quiz show." She looked out the front room window; darkness at last, Jimmy still prone infantry style, but now, headlights were streaking his face. Maybe Robert on his way.

She ran into the hall. Bedroom first, or bathroom? Bathroom—a note taped to the toilet tank. Bedroom—three notes stuck to the back of her dresser this morning at 7 a.m., as KYA broadcast Bay Bridge traffic conditions.

But there were only two notes.

Robert must have found the third note. Why didn't he say anything? Because it's in shorthand—no man she'd ever met knew shorthand. So maybe he took it to work, and asked Shirley to translate it. "Count all the tines on all the forks," Shirley would've read. Then given Robert a look. "Is Jean still having problems? It must be difficult for you ..." But then her hand curled into her apron, and she found the note. She'd forgotten that she had already retrieved it. I need a list to keep track of my lists, she thought.

The kitchen timer dinged. Pot roast done. Cooked all by her lonesome. Almost. She checked the clock, seven-thirty. The man who was never late was half an hour late. She ladled out the salad and the whipped potatoes, kept the pot roast warm in the oven. Jimmy came in, dribbling gravel from his shirt, head now buried in the Norton Star atlas which they'd given him for Christmas.

"Do you think a flying saucer could hover in place long enough to fool us into thinking it's Polaris?"

"Did your father say anything about being late tonight?"

Jimmy shook his head, washed up as always without being prompted, sat down, picked the sliced radishes out of his salad.

They waited. Jimmy made notes in his star atlas. Jean glanced at the afternoon paper: July 15, 1952: Palo Alto boy injured by highway construction explosives, the war in Korea, photos of the new Queen Elizabeth, of President Truman playing piano. Every few seconds, her eyes strayed to the front window.

"This salad's pretty good".

"You hate salad." Jean studied Jimmy, seeing in his face what she felt. She picked up the phone, dialed Robert's work.

"Manufacturing Specifications, please."

"I'm sorry, they've all gone home."

"What about the janitors?"

"They can't answer the phones."

"Can't you ring anyone on the floor?"

"Sorry, ma'am. I'm happy to leave a note for the department for tomorrow morning." A snooty tone had entered the operator's voice, as though she didn't want to be there and knew she wouldn't be for long.

Braden Enright was an electronics company coming on strong, like dozens of companies on the Peninsula. Its founding during the first year of the Depression was legend: Carl Braden, a broke engineering student with no head for business, met Merritt Enright, a business student who could barely plug in a toaster. With money cadged from aunts, uncles, and cousins, they rented space in a bankrupt bank, using the tellers counter as their workbenches. Eventually, Carl Braden learned to balance the books and Merritt Enright learned his way around an oscilloscope, and they invented equipment that tested other equipment that measured aspects of the visible and invisible world that no one had thought to—or wanted to—measure before. Though it could seem egg-heady, Robert said it boiled down to "nuts and bolts" when he brought home parts of wave analyzers for Jimmy to play with. "B.E." was outgrowing their original plant, stuck between a plating factory and a dental supply warehouse in downtown Palo Alto. They were moving up Page Mill Road to the golden-fleeced hills, easy rolling land that breathed in nourishing fog at night and exhaled it into gauzy California sunshine by dawn. Robert had driven them up there when the move had been announced, and paced out the area that would be his office. "Louvered windows, skylights. And get this: DuPont "easy eyes" color engineering." Robert had smiled at the phrase, bending down to pick foxtails out of his socks. Memories of that day were suddenly so vivid, everything poised, bright and alert.

"It's the switchboard, right?" Jimmy asked. "I know that building. It's on the southwest corner, right next to where dad parks."

"Operator, can you go to the window and tell me if there's a green 1948 Plymouth four door parked in the lot?"

After a put upon sigh, the operator reported back.

"No ma'am, no green Plymouth."

"OK, thank you." She hung up. "Jimmy, I'm going to lie down a bit."

Jimmy frowned, looked away. He knew what lying down often meant.

She sat on the edge of the bed, looking at the wedding photograph displayed on the "his" of the matching walnut dressers. Robert in a dark jacket and tie, a perfect match for his perfectly parted black hair, his deeply set eyes a bit mysterious, his broad forehead set above narrow, angled cheeks carrying traces of his mother Marie and his father Henry, both Northwesterners, Scandinavian heritage mixed with Merrie Olde England. His smile was more aggressive than the photographer had asked for, an expression not just of happiness, but of accomplishment. He'd wound his way through life and a dozen jobs, down from Portland to the Bay Area where he'd "landed" a Californian. Jean had always thought of herself as plain: wavy but not luxuriant hair, full lips, true, but they required daily doses of ChapStick to thrive, hazel eyes that did their job—her vision was 20/20—but Robert had never said he could lose himself in her eyes. "Plain." That was her mother, Alma, speaking with a Modesto native's ingrained modesty. I look good in this picture, she thought. Not Dietrich exotic, not Goddard glamorous, more Jean Arthur, ready for anything. Not bad for a city hall photographer. Their wedding was the perfect expression of a guiding force in both their lives—don't make a fuss. "I do's" spoken to a distracted judge, gifts to help them on their way, an alarm clock (purchased with Green Stamps; she recognized the brand) for the groom, a cookbook for the bride. In and out, fifteen minutes, tops. There was a war coming and government officials were in a hurry.

She felt her grip tightening on the bottle of pills in her hand: isoniazid, brand new, developed as a tuberculosis medication, now useful for people with neurotic, reactive depression. She hadn't dared to try them; maybe she was hoping that by simply possessing them she would feel better. Pills were the ultimate confirmation, the physical evidence of her diagnosis. If she told Robert... No, she couldn't imagine telling him. Not yet. Maybe it was a blessing that he wasn't home yet. Worse, maybe he already knew and didn't *want* to come home.

She was already out the door, heading for the garage before Jimmy could catch her.

"I'm coming."

"You're going next door. Grandpa Tamarkin can entertain you until I'm back."

"Until *you're* back?"

"I'm going to retrace his route home in case there was an accident."

She got to the Nash, opened the driver's door. Jimmy kept coming.

"Jimmy. No!"

Usually, she followed her firm "no" with a softer "no" modified with an explanation: "We can't afford the Raleigh, just the Schwinn." But this "no" came from the chest and was more commanding than anything in Robert's arsenal. Jimmy retreated and she backed out of the driveway.

She sped through quiet streets of single family homes, ranches and split levels, that were springing up among apricot and peach orchards. Los Altos was not a town anyone was from—incorporated only months ago, it hadn't been around long enough for that—but it was a town many aspired to. It was a carefully considered place, meant to transform home front into home, a soothing refuge after years of war. There were no sidewalks or businesses or advertising billboards. As the boosters who wrote the chamber of commerce brochure boasted, "The ugliness and tumult of the industrial world do not intrude upon the serenity and beauty." During the day, the red blooms of pepper trees and freshly planted emerald lawns gave the streets the look of a child's coloring book being gradually filled in. At night, as the planners envisioned, the locals relished their private lives. They stayed off the streets and out of bars and had people "over."

No sign of Robert, but no accident scenes, either. She drove north on El Camino Real, the Peninsula's principal north-south thoroughfare, passing Rick's Swiss Chalet, Dinah's Shack, scanning their parking lots for Robert's car, even though he was not a man who stopped on the way home for martinis with the boys.

She slowed down at Engineer's Row—a dozen buildings, many reconfigured from Quonset huts, their lobbies discretely lit, patrolled by yawning night watchmen. Inside, they worked on the future. Occasionally, Robert dropped by to talk shop, but he was not there tonight.

When she reached Braden Enright, a half moon was out. In its wan light, the empty parking lot looked vast, the administration building with its saw tooth roof line felt inhospitable. She parked in a spot designated for Robert's department, Manufacturing Specifications. She sat in the car for a minute, waiting for the courage to enter the lobby she'd passed through a thousand times. It had been seven months and nine days since she'd left the job she loved in the purchasing department; her pension was shame, embarrassment and bitter memories of her last day on the floor. She felt the stabbing that had become so familiar since then, knives inside her chest, piercing vents into her body, letting the "bad" out. Or letting it in. The isoniazid called to her from inside her purse, "take me, I'm your courage." Not yet, she told the pills.

She knocked on the glass lobby doors. The glass was smudged, spider-web cracks here and there. The Braden Enright trademark—the letters B.E. swept back like jet wings, electricity sparking between them—was fading and flaking.

A watchman she didn't recognize came to the door. Tall and pale, eating a piece of chiffon pie.

"I'm Jean Vale. Mrs. Robert Vale. My husband works here."

He motioned that he couldn't hear her through the glass.

"Is anyone in there?"

Again, he just shook his head. Jean motioned for him to open the door. As he unlocked it, she saw shadows flitting through the lobby behind him before they disappeared.

"Sorry, ma'am, my hearing's pretty well shot. Year and a half a bomb loader for the 504th."

"I just want to see if my husband's here."

"Sorry, can't let you in."

"But someone's here. I saw them."

"Janitors, ma'am."

"Can I just come into the lobby to make a call. I'm awfully worried, he was supposed to be home hours ago."

The watchman hesitated. With a wedding-ringed hand, he maneuvered the slice of chiffon pie to his mouth.

"Your Missus worries, doesn't she? I bet you call her twice a night."

A weak smile from pie crust coated teeth. He unlocked the doors.

"Phone's on the receptionist desk. Dial 9 for the switchboard. Make it snappy."

Jean nodded, went toward the desk. The lobby was dingy and neglected—uncomfortable steel framed chairs, a coffee table with overflowing ashtrays—the janitors may be hard at work, but they hadn't been here. A collection of electronic instruments in display cases with typewritten labels. On the walls, photographs of Carl Braden and Merrill Enright beaming proudly as the first 709 Oscillators came off the assembly line. The same pictures had been there since Robert started work for B.E. six years earlier. Next to the cigarette smoke-stained American flag had been the so-called "patriots wall," photographs of those B.E. employees who had served in the armed forces. But they were all missing, leaving dusty squares on the wall. Even Lawrence Cutler was gone; he had been the centerpiece, posing in an Army Air Force uniform on a runway somewhere in England. He'd been a bomb group commander during the war, and his dashing good looks in a flight jacket had helped him advance through the ranks at B.E. Following the death of Carl Braden, Cutler had become president of the company. Of course, it didn't hurt that he was married to Carl Braden's daughter, Frances.

"Mrs. Cutler took 'em to the new building, I think," the watchman said. "Going to have her own office up there too, I hear."

Jean picked up the phone, gave the B.E. operator the number.

"He's a good man, Mr. Cutler. Hired me even though my ears are shot," the watchman said.

Yes, a good man, Jean agreed. Despite everything.

"Shirl, it's Jean Vale, I'm really sorry to call you so late but—"

"That's OK, hon, just me and Daphne duMaurier. How you doing, anyway? I worry, you know."

Shirley Lane was Robert's secretary, his first, a potent symbol of his ascension from assembly line to desk. She was a blunt, determined South Dakotan who'd pressured the Boilermaker's Union to let women into the Richmond shipyard work force during the war, personally sent one thousand books to troops in the Pacific ("those fellas love Lady Chatterley") and landed her job with Braden Enright the day after VJ Day when everyone else was too hung over from celebrating to think about applying for work.

"I was just wondering what time Robert left work this evening."

"This evening?"

"Yeah, what do you mean?"

"He left after lunch."

"What? Did he say where he was going?"

"No, but I just assumed."

"Assumed what?"

"Well, he had that glimmer he gets."

Robert? Glimmering?

"He gets it sometimes when work's going well, or when he's talking about you or Jimmy, and then he gets it when ... Well, I don't know what causes it."

"Ok, today's particular glimmer. What triggered it?"

"Honestly, you don't need to get snippish. As I say, I don't know."

Yes, she was snippish. She was worried, suspicious and a little jealous that Shirley knew more about her husband's "glimmering" than she did.

"You have no idea, not even a hunch?"

"OK, OK. I thought maybe you two were sneaking away for a little afternoon rendezvous, no kids, no signal generator blueprints for him to go over."

Jean smiled. Shirley was a good soul. She was not one of those who'd watched with disdain or gossipy curiosity as Jean left the building that last day of work. There was no reason to tangle with her.

"Hon, are you saying Robert hasn't come home yet?"

The guard was waving at her to wind up the call. Jean heard footsteps approaching from behind the swinging doors that led to the assembly floor.

"They won't want to see you here, Mrs. Vale."

His pie-eating folksiness had been replaced by a stiff, almost frightened concern. For her or for himself? He held open the front door and Jean moved through it without looking back.

The parking lot seemed to expand as she crossed it, her car growing smaller and farther away. She thought she heard footsteps coming after her, the flick of a Zippo lighter—or maybe it was just the ticking of her bracelet watch, magnified by silence and darkness. She didn't look back, didn't want to recognize anyone if they were after her. She felt silly now; you didn't run away from the men who paid your husband's salary. She checked her rear-view mirror; just the night watchman stared at her from the lobby. Alone with his pie and a thermos of coffee.

THE CITY FATHERS were expecting a lot of crime in Los Altos. Or they were expecting a flock of new residents who expected a lot of crime. They had scraped up the funding to hire a prominent architectural company to design a police headquarters that was all roof, as if two aircraft carrier decks had been seamed together and hinged toward the ground, heavy overhangs that obscured windows from passersby, casting eternal shadows on the freshly seeded lawn.

Jean had driven by the house—no sign of Robert's car—then headed for the station, twenty miles over the speed limit, straddling the center line, hoping a cop would stop her so she could file her report on the spot. There were four brand new Chevy police cars parked parallel to the station entrance, their whitewalls spotless. Jean slipped in behind them, then hurried to the reception area, passing a bicycle rack holding a single Schwinn Black Phantom. It was Jimmy's.

The lobby was still a building site, ladders leading to wires that coiled through the unfinished ceiling, plaster dust coating new benches where no one waited. Jean had expected to hear pistols cocking and radio chatter, breathless young men speaking in clipped, coded phrases. But the only sound was a "whooof" as a duty officer blew sawdust off a Motorola radiotelephone that he had just unpacked.

"Yes?" he said irritably, as he began to study the instruction materials that were strewn across the Formica reception desk

"I'm here about my husband. Well, my son, too, actually."

"What about them?"

Jean scanned the lobby, hoping that one or both of the men in her life were here, sharing the night's harmless misadventures with a sympathetic policeman.

"I—well this may sound silly, but I can't find them," Jean said. "I'm afraid they're missing."

The duty officer, a puffy, slope shouldered man who seemed very comfortable with the slow pace of late-night work, looked her over, sharpened a pencil, broke the point with the first letter he wrote, re-sharpened it.

"Name?"

"Vale, Robert. That's my husband. Son's name is Jimmy."

"*Your* name."

"Jean Vale, 543 Kensington Drive, phone Whitecliff 8-5612."

The officer smiled, relaxed.

"We've got him here, your boy. Whipped me at twenty questions twice already." He spoke quietly into an intercom, and a moment later Jimmy emerged from a side door, eating a waffle cone, accompanied by another cop.

"What are you doing here, young man? I told you to go to the neighbors, not gallivant around town in the middle of the night."

He didn't answer. Jean knelt, held him firmly by the shoulders.

"Jimmy, what's wrong. What is it?"

Jimmy turned away, licked at his cone.

"Is it about your father? Has something happened to him? Has there been an accident, or—" Jean looked at the duty officer. "My husband, Robert, he didn't come home from work."

"The boy filed a complete report." The officer read from a clipboard. "Robert Jensen Vale, age 38. 5'9", black wavy hair, left hand part. Burn scars on left thumb and left index finger from soldering iron. Employed at Braden Enright, 298 Page Mill Road, Palo Alto. Last seen wearing white, long sleeved Arrow shirt, red tie with right upward angled striping, gray slacks, and lace-up boots. Does not wear glasses but may have a pair of safety goggles in shirt pocket. Note: boots, NOT loafers or those shiny black shoes that businessmen in movies wear."

The duty officer smiled at Jimmy, who smiled back.

"That's a very observant boy you've got there, Mrs. Vale. We could use a man like him in about ten years."

"And my husband?"

"We've been on the phones. Checked hospitals in Santa Clara and San Mateo County. No one by that name admitted, no major accidents tonight. We're distributing an alert for the car, green 1948 Plymouth P-15 four door, California plate 6X1-352."

"OK, that's a start. I just came from Braden Enright. Things didn't seem right. The night watchman was ... off somehow. I phoned his secretary. She said Robert left work at 1 p.m. That means he's been gone for over ten hours!"

"Did his secretary, Miss—"

"Lane, Shirley Lane."

"Did this Miss Lane give any indication as to where your husband might have gone, or his state of mind? Was he fearful, did he seem in some sort of trouble?"

"No, nothing like that."

"I don't mean to be rude, but ... is Mr. Vale the type of man to run away from his problems? I'm married myself. I know how dicey things can get."

Jean felt a tremor in her jaw and shoulders, a memory she

had tried to sequester and forget because there was nothing to it.

Jimmy whispered to her. "Mom, I need to talk to you."

"No. He's a stand-up husband, a good father. He would never ..."

Well, that one time, maybe, the so called 'missing week.' Ten years ago. But no. That had been fully explained, Jean's jealous suspicions laid to rest.

She knew the duty officer was waiting for more, but she was unable to grasp that she was sitting in the brand new, Los Altos police station because her husband was missing. Bed sounded nice about now, sweet, curtained gloom.

She let Jimmy lead her to a bench. The officer wanted no part in the family drama he sensed was coming. He went back to his new Motorola.

"Mom, dad was here last week. I was riding bikes with Tommy Miyaki and I saw him."

Jean heard, didn't react.

"I watched him through the window. He talked with a desk guy, not this guy, but someone else. Then dad saw me. He gave me a look, a look that said, 'Don't tell mom'."

Jean stared at her son, who was old enough to keep Robert's secrets without being scolded or told to do so, who could sense the meaning behind a look and hold it easily within himself.

The police radio squawked at full volume.

"Eureka!" shouted the duty officer, before turning it down to a scratchy background murmur.

Jimmy scooted closer to Jean and whispered roughly in her ear. "I told them. The guy on duty, and the other cops tonight. They say there's no record of dad ever being here."

SHE TURNED on all the lights and put on the coffee pot, longing for the friendly drip and hiss of the percolator. She had thanked the police officers, loaded Jimmy's bike into the trunk and driven home in silence. Wondering what else Jimmy knew that he hadn't shared with her.

Now, at the kitchen table still laid with dinner, she asked for it all. He wouldn't volunteer, so she took it piece by piece.

"What time of day was it?"

"About 4:30."

"Was anyone else with him?"

"No".

"How did he look? Embarrassed? Angry? Scared?"

"Busy. Determined. Like when he showed me how to shingle the roof."

"Did he have anything with him?"

"A picture, I think. A note pad, maybe ..."

"Did he talk to you about it? Tell you anything else?"

"No."

"I need the truth, Jim! Your father may be in trouble!"

Jimmy tugged at his t-shirt hem, the sign he always gave when he bowed to parental authority that he recognized was for his own good—as long as she didn't tell him it was for his own good.

"That's everything. And that's not breaking a promise to dad."

Jean flinched. It was a pinprick response that said, "I won't reveal *your* secrets, either."

She turned on the front porch light and they dragged to their bedrooms. Jean made a few calls to Robert's co-workers, was greeted by sleepy annoyance, followed by "I don't know" leading to concerned, "Call me tomorrow." She lay on the bedspread, stretching out on Robert's side, trying to absorb his recent presence, summoning him back home. She heard Jimmy in his room at the end of the hall, throwing his bedclothes onto the floor, "bivouacking" as he called it, with flashlight and code-books, and Classics Illustrated.

"Jim, do you want to sleep in here tonight?"

"Need to secure the backyard perimeter, mom," he called.

"Front yard perimeter needs patrolling, too."

She heard rustling as Jimmy broke camp and moved into their bedroom. He took up his post on the floor beside the bed. She waited for the whispered breath that meant he was asleep and falling into the dreams he would tell tomorrow at dinner time. The windows were open and, out front, sprinklers fizzed, bringing their freshly sodded lawn to life.

2

The first second of wakefulness can contain an entire morning's impressions: the caws of mockingbirds; the squeal of the paper boy's bicycle brakes; the grinding of gears on the Peninsula Creamery's delivery truck; the clatter of milk bottles as they are dropped onto the front porch. The cramp in her left hand that had clutched the bedspread all night; the sounds of Jimmy bustling in the kitchen; the smell of coffee and toast; the love she felt for his role as early morning caretaker. And the voices ...

Theirs: You understand the possible side effects.

Hers: Yes, I've read the documentation.

Theirs: It falls to me as the supervising physician to review them aloud with you. Many but not all patients experience psychomotor agitation, periods of detachment, weight gain, sleep disorders. Nausea, vomiting, anemia, abdominal pain, and memory impairment may also be encountered.

Hers: I know. I've heard it all.

Theirs: However, many patients also report increased vigor, sociability, and elevated mood, which is where you come in, because from what we understand, your husband has not been—

Hers: He tries. He means well. His gentle jokes, he cooks dinner every now and then, does some of the marketing so I can relax as he calls it, but it's too much for him.

And the phone on his nightstand—how long had it been ringing? "Robert?"

"Am I speaking with Mrs. Robert Vale?"

"Yes, yes, have you found him?"

"Ma'am, this is Sergeant Revell of the Monte Vista police."

"Have you found my husband?"

"We think we've found his car. Green 1948 Plymouth—"

"Yes, that's it. But no sign of him, of Mr. Vale?"

"Not that I've been told."

MONTE VISTA WAS three towns to the south, in the opposite direction of Braden Enright. Not even a town really, a Flying A gas station and a diner that boasted "America's Champion Plate Spinning Waitress." But the hills –studded with oak trees casting wide pools of shade, and the best views in the Bay Area.

Jean drove up a narrow, paved road towards the ridge, following the directions given to her by Sergeant Revell. Jimmy scanned the horizon with his binoculars, treating the day like an adventure. The pavement ended. She pulled into a turnout, throwing dust onto two police cars that were already there. A hundred feet off the road, in a sea of wild grass and poppies, as though it had been air-dropped out of the sky, was Robert's car.

Here? He drove it here?

And then she was running, pounding over the trampled ground, tearing away from the arms that grabbed for her. When she got to the car, she reached out to touch the fender, the metal hot in the morning sun. Cops surrounded her as she tried to yank open the door.

"Mrs. Vale, he's not there. We understand your fears, but you need to let us finish up."

She looked into the face of a Monte Vista cop—early thirties, eyes that radiated both weariness and empathy. Jaw working hard on a double dose of Wrigley's, posture upright and unperturbed. A veteran, she decided. He'd probably seen things that made a hysterical housewife with a possibly missing husband seem like a treed cat. 'Officer Fielder' said his nametag.

"I need you to verify that this is your husband's car, ma'am," he said.

She nodded, slowly circling it, peering through the windows, monitored by another uniformed cop. The car was neat as always, no tools or coffee mug or hamburger wrappers, an empty plastic litter bag from the local dry cleaners dangling from the radio on-off knob.

Jean gazed down at the valley, a patchwork of homes and downtowns that was rapidly erasing the last few open spaces, backing all the way up to the vividly colored salt evaporation ponds of the Bay.

"It's a signal," she said.

"Pardon me, what do you mean by that?"

The other cops hovered, sensing that the morning might prove more interesting than filling out the paperwork on a stolen vehicle.

"Do they have to be so eager?"

Fielder nodded at his buddies, and they backed off. Jimmy cornered one of the cops, who-succumbed to his boyish interest in his badge and gun. Soon, Jimmy was pinning the badge onto his shirt, with a knowing glance at his mom.

"We used to come up here during the war. Even during the black outs. We didn't need headlights, we knew the road so well. We'd spread out a picnic, right about where that manzanita bush is now. Robert liked to watch the planes at Moffett Field. And those giant blimps heading out on submarine patrol. He found them soothing somehow."

Fielder nodded, waiting for more.

"Half those houses weren't built yet. We'd dream about

building our own down there, narrowing it down by neighborhood and street. No matter what was going on in the world, this is where we could peer into the future. That's why he left the car here, to tell me everything's going to be fine."

Fielder flipped through his notebook. "It's just that we believe we have two sets of footprints leading away from the car, ending up at the pavement."

For a moment, the sun felt unbearably hot on her skin, like an interrogation lamp in a cop movie. "So, you're suggesting—"

"I'm not suggesting anything. There are no signs of a fight, so probably whoever was here with your husband was a friend."

"Jean?" A familiar voice called to her from the road. Lawrence Cutler was stepping out of a new Chrysler Imperial, gleaming and beaded with water, as though he'd already washed it this morning. He locked it, despite the police officers present. He'd had to struggle for the things he had, she recalled from one of their conversations, so he took good care of them. Marriage to the founder's daughter didn't seem to have changed him and she had always liked that.

In his early 40s, Cutler was about five-nine and slight, but skilled at making himself seem bigger. In a group setting, he positioned himself on higher ground, or he spotted those with slumping postures and stood upright next to them. His suit clung to him a tad too tightly, emphasizing a robust physique that he had not let soften since the war. He kept his bristly brown hair in a military cut. He had heavy John L. Lewis eyebrows which he punctually trimmed, and when he shaved, he made it an art form. A man who knew that appearances were half the battle.

He strode down to her and grasped her by the shoulders.

"Jean, I came as soon as I heard."

"Thank you, Lawrence, but that wasn't necessary."

"Still, Robert is employee badge 99, and we take care of

family." He turned his attention to Fielder. "So, what's the latest?"

"Sir, the car was found early this morning by a couple of nurserymen who were out gathering poppies."

"I know that. In the last hour, I mean. Any updates?"

Fielder looked annoyed. He probably felt that he had been building a rapport with Jean, and here comes a bulldozing civilian to interrupt his questioning. But he deferred to Cutler, an enlisted man still taking orders from a commanding officer.

"I was just telling Mrs. Vale here that based on indentations in the seat cushions, and trampled grass patterns leading away from the passenger side, that Mr. Vale was not alone."

"Anything in the trunk?"

It was an oddly specific question.

"The usual—spare tire, jack, couple oil cans, two pairs greasy overalls, one adult, one child."

"One of Robert's attempts at father-son auto mechanics." Jean smiled. Neither of them cared the slightest about working on cars, but it was a manly rite of passage that had to at least be attempted.

"And I imagine there was no personal identification left behind, either belonging to Mr. Vale or this mysterious other party?"

"Sir, my sergeant obviously cleared you to come up here, but that doesn't mean I need to bring you into this investigation." The other cops edged closer to back up Fielder.

Jean grew uncomfortable, literally standing in the middle between her husband's boss, who had the power to discipline Robert for not showing up to work today, and the police who she had entrusted to find him.

"Lawrence, did Robert say anything at the office recently ... about, I don't know, personal troubles, man-to-man stuff. How was work going?"

"Up to snuff as always, Jean. Which is one of the reasons I

was alarmed to hear last night that you had been to the plant expressing your concerns about Robert's whereabouts."

Cutler had known since last night?! It was not her place to call him, but why hadn't *he* called her? Expressing his own concern, maybe asking a question or two?

"Do you think this has anything to do with your—?" Cutler asked, lowering his voice.

"With my—?" Jean asked.

"Departure from the company. That can't have been easy on Robert."

Wasn't a lot of fun for me, either, Jean wanted to snap. But she kept her peace. This was not the time to stir a stale pot of soup.

"Mr. Cutler, please let me finish with Mrs. Vale and we'll get to you in due course," Fielder said.

Cutler seemed to be assessing the resolve of the cops as they squinted into the rising sun, shifting back and forth on their feet, brilliantly shined boots grinding into the dirt. He then looked at Jean, realizing that his take charge approach was not going to be effective.

"We'll talk later Jean. Wherever he's at, we'll get him back, I promise."

We'll get him back? Meaning Braden Enright will get him back? Had they driven him away in the first place?"

Cutler took a last look around the scene, searching for whatever he'd hoped to find there. Hawks circled above, a small whirlwind scooted fallen laurel leaves across the hood of Robert's car. Cutler shook his head and returned to his pristine Chrysler. Fielder waited until Cutler had started his engine, then took her aside.

Jean looked around for Jimmy. He was in the front seat of a police car, a Monte Vista cop showing him how to operate the radio. A cop car, a boy's idea of a fun house, but Jimmy wasn't interested, and he seemed to be interrogating the cop, not the other way around.

"Can I show you something?" Fiedler asked.

He led Jean behind a stand of oak trees that shaded the car. She jumped back with a shiver—a human figure was hanging from a low branch. After a second, she realized it was only a suit of clothes.

"Do you recognize these?"

It was a black suit, with a white shirt, a charcoal tie and a black petaled boutonniere. She ran her hands over the fabric, inexpensive, but brand new. She checked the label; it had been purchased at the Palo Alto Penney's. Size 44—Robert's size. She dug through the pants' pockets—no wallet or loose coins, no B.E. pocketknife, a prized possession he carried everywhere.

"We found this in the trunk."

"But you told Lawrence—"

"Mr. Cutler is not family, ma'am. He doesn't need to know you and your husband's business. His reaction doesn't interest me at the moment; yours does." He shoved another stick of Wrigley's into his mouth, until his cheek bulged like a tobacco-chomping pitcher.

"I've never seen this before."

"Was there a death in the family recently, a close friend maybe? Someone whose funeral your husband would want to attend?"

"Without telling me?"

"Well, you know, husbands and wives ..." Fielder's words trailed off into a sigh. As though married couples were foreigners, whose inscrutable culture a bachelor could never understand.

"OK, let's just get these last few questions under our belt, and we'll have you on your way." Fielder lowered his voice. "Please understand I have to ask these. Does your husband have a drinking problem, a gambling habit, excessive debts—anything like that?"

"No, no, he's steady as she goes."

"Any personal or business conflicts? Anyone wishing him harm?"

"No one."

"No unexplained phone calls, people you don't recognize showing up at the house?"

"No."

"And none of his friends or neighbors had reported anything out of the ordinary, anything that would hook your attention?"

Jean kept shaking her head 'no' as Officer Fielder worked his way down the Monte Vista Police's official list of vices and human frailties until he reached, she assumed, the W's.

"Any, well ..." he blotted his forehead with a handkerchief he'd pulled out of a black leather case clipped to his belt. "Any other women in his life that would be cause for your concern?"

"Do wives whose husbands disappear usually answer that question?"

"If they're angry or jealous enough."

"Ah! And then the wife becomes suspect number one."

"There are no suspects here, Mrs. Vale. We don't even know if we have a crime."

Jean felt woozy, dazed. Why would Robert drive up here, if he hadn't intended to signal that everything was OK? Why was he slipping off to attend secret funerals? And with who? Who had he been with that he trusted more than her? No matter what disturbances boiled inside her, she could always prop herself up against Robert. Who could steady her here this morning? The police? Lawrence Cutler, with his proprietorial inquisitiveness? Jimmy?

Yes, Jimmy.

SHE COULDN'T GO into the house. She sat in the Nash, studying Robert's car in her rear-view mirror. She had driven home, followed by an officer driving the Plymouth, and a squad car which took him back to Monte Vista police headquarters. So a small convoy, under police escort, had driven down Echo Lane and stopped in front of their house. Watched by the kitchen window housewives of Los Altos. She'd heard their lilting, gossipy tones as she grocery shopped the Purity aisles. "*I haven't even been in her house once, have you, Ellen?*" "*We're all on a budget, but she could make an effort to look more put together*" "*Letting her boy cavort with that Russian fellow. Could be a Commie for all we know.*"

Well, now they would have a good story to tell over dinner.

She couldn't bring herself to search Robert's car, apprehensive about what she might find, but also terrified she might find nothing. She listened to a news broadcast—reports that England was soon going to have the A-bomb—then switched to music, sleepy Percy Faith, violating one of Robert's personal credos about draining the battery by playing the radio when the engine wasn't running. Jimmy hadn't wanted to go back inside either, so she'd released him to the care of the Gilletts next door. He would probably be telling all sorts of wild tales now, but she didn't care. The Gilletts, with their muddled national backgrounds and honest to goodness live-in Russian spy were the only neighbors she trusted to listen, to help, maybe even to dismiss her concerns with a friendly "c'est la vie," but never to judge.

"YES, yes that's it! A simple but smart cipher, which replaces Russian letter with an English 'w.' Not every time, but every five times, and even this pattern changes from message to message."

Grandpa Tamarkin sat next to Jimmy on the couch, a cracked, leather notebook opened on his lap, sipping tea from a glass as he proofread Jimmy's "homework." Tamarkin was a Russian of the last century, grudgingly adapting to life in suburban California. His high collared white shirt bore hot dog relish stains. His beard, once unruly and flowing, was being clipped back year by year, like an overgrown yard yielding to a determined gardener, and recently Jean had spotted him sunning himself on the Gilletts' front lawn, wearing sunglasses. He was studying the California driving laws, and often late into the evening Jean could hear him crunching through the gears of Helen's car as he backed in and out of the driveway. He hovered in his mid-seventies; he had not aged a day in the five years he had lived next door, but he never looked younger, either. "I have reached the age for which I was made, and I intend to stay here," he liked to say. Jimmy had taken to Tamarkin, who had returned the affection by teaching him the "secret codes of the Tsars."

Jean and Helen Gillett huddled at the other end of the long living room, their voices absorbed by Navajo rugs and wall hangings. Helen was French, her husband Frederic was Belgian. Their lives had been restless, driven by professional migration until they settled in the Peninsula where Frederic—a certified genius according to Robert—had found work as an electronics engineer. Neither was Russian, but somehow via a network of relationships that Jean still didn't understand, they had welcomed Grandpa Tamarkin into their family, and now he lived in a back room, where he worked on mysterious memoirs and yelled through the venetian blinds at workmen digging the neighborhood's first swimming pool.

"I don't know what to say, Jean. Well, I do know what to say —it is not another woman, I'm sure of that," Helen said.

"How do you know?"

"Because Robert is—"

"Loyal?"

"Not so adventurous."

Helen was in her mid-thirties, blunt and unpretentious. Her arrival in the neighborhood had inspired a brief Frenchification among the other wives, who began to appear in tight-waisted, V-collared dresses presented as Parisian, but sewn from patterns Jean had seen on sale at Sears. Helen had responded by slouching around in gardening overalls. Jean felt that she had found an ally, someone who was not obsessed with fitting in or climbing the ladder. Helen had been a good friend when Jean lost her job, and an even better friend on those late afternoons when Jean hid in her bedroom, shades drawn, far from the kitchen. Helen had a card file of Jean's usual recipes which she consulted to cook secret dinners, not so delicious or daring that they would arouse Robert's suspicions, but solid and nutritious, delivered furtively to the back door so that food was on the table when Robert got home, Jean's housewifely duties fulfilled.

"Frederic is not adventurous in that way either." Helen said. "When you are married to a man who is perpetually away on business, you develop instincts where that is concerned."

The missing weekend again. February 1942. Robert had flown by himself up to Portland for his parents' thirtieth anniversary. She had not been able to get time off, but he had put in two weeks of overtime and was granted three days. The prospect of spending time in Marie and Henry's overheated home, dominated by Marie's hand-knitted doilies and teacup collection was not appealing anyway; Henry seemed to be permitted no active male presence in the house, which always depressed her. There had been a real anniversary, though; there was no "cover story." She'd called to offer her congratulations, chatted briefly with Robert about the shifting visibility of Mount Hood, a typical Portland conversation. But when he came back, he was not a son who had celebrated a joyful occasion in his parents' life, but a man who had seen or heard something he wished he hadn't. He came bearing gifts, extra rations of sugar and coffee, a souvenir TWA route map for Jimmy, and everything was supposed to be peachy.

"If he didn't run away, then he was taken!" Jean said. "There are only two explanations."

"A relative or old friend in trouble or a financial matter that he didn't want to trouble you with. Private pressures that he wishes to sort out by himself," Helen replied.

"Then who was the other person with him?"

"The police will find out. I'm sure of it."

Grandpa Tamarkin said something in Russian.

"These are American police, Roman."

Tamarkin grumbled a response, returned to correcting Jimmy's code work.

"I forget how well he can hear," Helen whispered. "And his eyes—they can spy a bird on the roof two houses away and tell you its species and wingspan."

"And the reading of lips," Tamarkin said.

Helen barked back at him in Russian. She translated for Jean. "I said he's talking shit—one of my few Russian phrases."

Tamarkin spoke quietly to Jimmy, who gathered his homework and went into the kitchen.

"I told him the Tsar's assassination codes would be his next job and that he should have head start. Also, where the Tootsie Rolls are kept."

Tamarkin walked deliberately across the Navajo rug, inspecting its patterns.

"Fascinating, the Navajo stairway patterns, no? As though they want to lead you straight into the Earth." Tamarkin's demeanor had changed from grandfatherly storyteller to something harder. "Jean, what I will say to you now is troubling, but important."

"Roman, please, not one of your political speeches," Helen said. "Come Jean, let's go see how they are progressing with the pool. It won't be long before all of you can come over for a swim on a hot day."

"I'd like to hear him out," Jean said.

"Are you aware of what is happening in your country, Jean?" Tamarkin asked.

"I read the papers. I listen to the radio."

"Is that the same thing as to be aware?"

"They got us through the war. Ever hear of Edward R. Murrow?"

"And did they always tell you the truth?"

"Well, sometimes they couldn't say certain things that would harm the war effort. It was for our own protection."

"It's always talked about as for your own protection. When the state wants to hide something, they hide it. When they want something to be found, they find it."

"That's Russia," Jean said.

"That is everywhere."

Helen spoke to Tamarkin in French, he replied with a lengthy, animated burst of French mixed with Russian that brought a frosting of saliva to his lips.

"Please don't talk in front of me so I can't understand," Jean said.

"I said he was upsetting you," Helen answered.

"I *am* upset. I was upset when I got here and I'm even more so now."

"And that is how it should be," Tamarkin said, with a satisfied nod.

"Grandpa Tamarkin, why are you doing this?" Jean asked. "We've always been nice to you, let Jimmy come over here on his own, and now you're trying to scare us both."

"Jean, I understand the need to hurt back those who tell you the facts."

"What are you talking about? What facts?"

"I saw them. Last night, and this morning."

"Roman, you live in fantasy. Please keep it to yourself." Helen handed Tamarkin a handkerchief. "Wipe your mouth. You are like a slavering dog after a bone."

"Quite right, I am an old Russian dog. What can I have to offer?" Tamarkin tied his leather notebook shut. "But like all dogs, sometimes I break off the leash. Perhaps the eyes, peering through the blinds, sharp and seeing, as Helen says, belong to me."

"Grandpa Tamarkin, who did you see?" Jean called.

"Ah, as Helen says, perhaps I live in fantasy."

Back home, Jean fumed. What a cranky old meddler Grandpa Tamarkin was, with his hints of prowlers and conspiracy. The intrigues of a man whose mind was clouding over as he aged. Still, he came from a world where intrigue and spying were his daily bread, so she supposed he saw it everywhere. Meanwhile, back in real life, Jean had a phone call to make.

Marie answered in her tinkly voice, as breakable as the British tea services she collected. "No, Jean, we haven't heard from Robby for quite some time. Is anything wrong?" Jean assured her everything was fine, inquired as to her and Henry's health ("Middling, you know how it is"), and signed off before middling turned life-threatening. Then she double checked the door locks and secured the windows. She drew all the curtains. Though it was barely past noon, she switched on the backyard light. Useless as a safety measure, but action calmed her.

She had wanted to talk to Jimmy, to ask how he was feeling —was he scared, was he angry? But knowing he would never answer, the questions remained bound in her chest. She'd told him to stay indoors the rest of the day, and he had silently acquiesced. Too silently, she thought.

In the bedroom, the door locked, she began what she called "the great ransacking." She and Robert had clearly demarcated private spaces—dressers, nightstands, his and hers sections of the closet. They never needed to enforce the lines of privacy. They were not a nosy couple; they were not questioners of motive or doubters of truth.

And Jean had always assumed that the only household secrets were hers.

An hour later, Jean drooped onto the bed, surrounded by the familiarity of Robert's possessions. Love letters – hers to him. Postcards – Robert to his parents, paycheck stubs, pipes from his smoking days, broken wristwatches, two suitcases, both empty—no cache of money or bearer bonds here. Father's

Day cards, Christmas cards, birthday cards, anniversary cards — one read: "Still some cups and saucers left, we've got a vase or two. Looks like we've had some peaceful years together, me and you." There were no cryptic notes in his pockets, no matchbooks with mystery phone numbers in his folded handkerchiefs. She almost wished she'd found a diary in the Dobbs hatboxes that held only Dobbs hats, a confessional full of rage against the mortgage company or the neighbors, hints of scandalous behavior, a tryst on the B.E. hayride with the saucy new brunette in Purchasing. But there was nothing and Jean felt a bit disappointed by the sheer knowability of the man.

Then she heard it—clanging, the percussive echo of hammer blows on metal. The noise nearly drowned out the ringing phone. Helen was on the line.

"Jean, you should check on Jimmy. In the driveway. Something is happening. I don't know what."

The doors to Robert's car were slung open. The front bumper had been removed. The front left tire was slashed and slowly exhaling. The hood was up, the trunk open. Robert's tool box lay on its side, wrenches, hammers, screwdrivers spilling out of it. She heard a grunt from inside the car, a ripping sound. Moments later, wisps of cotton floated out through the open back seat window.

Jimmy was in the back seat, gripping an X-ACTO knife, peering into the crevice he had lanced into the upholstery.

"What're you doing! Do you know how long your father and I saved to buy this car?"

"It was one of the cops. His idea."

"What?"

"He said a man's car is like a safe. You never know what he's got stashed away in there. 'I'd dig a little deeper if I were you, sonny boy'. I didn't like the sonny boy part, but—"

"We tried to teach you the value of a dollar."

Jean grasped the end of the bumper. "Helped me re-attach

this. I don't want your father to come walking down the driveway and see what you've done."

Jimmy looked up at Jean, tears in his eyes. Feathers from the seat lining clung to his moist cheeks. "He's not coming home today, mom." He wiped his cheeks with an oily rag, giving himself a grease monkey at quitting time look. He slid out of the car. He began to put his father's tools back in the box, arranging the screwdrivers in a row of graduated sizes. Then he stopped, threw open the driver's side door. He rolled the window up, then down, then up again. He slid a screwdriver into the narrow slot where the window retracted, probing for something.

"I need a clothes hanger!"

"What for?"

"I just remembered something."

"OK, but don't tear anything else apart!"

By the time she returned with the coat hanger, Jimmy had removed the arm rest, the window and door handles, and was pulling off the fabric that upholstered the door.

"Jimmy!"

"Help me, come on."

Resistance was useless, she knew. So, she crouched for leverage, and helped him pry the door panel free rivet by rivet, until it flopped onto the driveway, exposing the inner works of the door with its gears and locks and sliders. A large, wrinkled sheet of paper was lodged behind the window springs. Jimmy removed it, smoothed it out on the hood. It was a placemat from Spivey's Drive-in, the kind a waitress sets on your window tray when you get car service. Spotted with hamburger grease and smeared with ketchup, but on the underside, a note in Robert's handwriting: *"Source was right. There are others."*

"We were having cheeseburgers one time, and I saw it get crumpled into the window—by accident, I thought. But now, I don't know."

"What does he mean by 'source?' Who are 'the others'?"

Jimmy shrugged.

Here was the secret message she'd hoped to find, a hint of hidden things that any self-respecting person would leave behind when they vanished. Because she didn't understand it, she felt a little better.

"Well, it's good detective work, no matter how you slice it," she said.

Jimmy looked up at the sky, the morning overcast burned away, a clean slate of a California day. "We have to find him, mom."

"We will, I promise."

"No, *we* have to find him."

"We're just two people. The police, they have dozens of men. Mr. Cutler is very influential—he can help, too. We don't know what happened. Maybe he's hurt, or maybe ..."

"What if I ran away? You'd come after me, wouldn't you?"

It frightened her that she and Jimmy were both edging toward the same conclusion: Robert wanted to be gone, wanted to be somewhere without them. Repairing some past damage he'd never told her about? Tending to his second family? Hadn't some GI's formed other families during the war, in the Pacific, in Europe? But Robert hadn't been overseas. He'd been here. With her, with their young son, with his new job. What did you do in the war, dad? Jimmy once asked. He survived it for our sake, she'd answered.

"Wouldn't you?"

"Of course we'd look for you. We'd send out Patton *and* MacArthur."

"Well ..."

Jean tousled Jimmy's hair, a gesture he only permitted if his hair ended up mussed, not slicked down. He was right. There was no police department or co-worker or official inquiry that could satisfactorily explain what had suddenly happened to their family. Something had risen up inside Robert—from his own thoughts, from the house he shared with them, from the outside world, or from everywhere all at once. It was up to Jean and Jimmy Vale—flying saucer hunters—to find him.

3

"You can't go in there!"

She smiled and kept going. Past the startled receptionist with her beauty parlor sheen and her plastic pearls, through the swinging doors and into the sprawl of the B.E. main offices. She'd practiced at home in front of the closet mirror—the determined pace and the straight-ahead gaze, all to avoid being questioned or badgered into retreat. And for crying out loud, it worked.

A few of the secretaries still wore their hair short, a holdover from the war when the machinery of munitions could clamp onto a woman's hair and pull it out by the bloody roots. Lawrence Cutler's influence no doubt, trying to impose the discipline he enjoyed in the military on office life seven years later. They looked up from their hundred words per minute and their dictated correspondence, leaving out the double entendres their male bosses often included, as a taunt and sometimes as a come on. They watched her beeline through the corridors formed by the desks, to Manufacturing Specifications at the back of the building. "That's her," she heard whispered, the "her" spit out with an emphasis that implied, "The gal they had to let go. The gal with problems."

The desks in Robert's department were spacious to accommodate the technical drawings that he proofread and annotated every day from 8:30 to 4:30. Greg Summerville and Carl Adams, two of Robert's co-workers who she recognized from the annual blood drive—Adams was Type O, same as Robert she recalled—stood up, took turns grasping her shoulders and out-promising each other to "help however I can." She smiled her thanks, then headed for Robert's station. Shirley Lane was waiting, a little heavier than Jean remembered, her blonde hair flecked with grey, her lipstick choice as adventurous as always. Shirley was one of those people whose mission was to impart extra strength to the world around her. She took pride in her ability to manage other people's troubles; her prescriptions to manage "that down in the dumps feeling" ranged from hot baths to cold showers to the music of The Ink Spots and candlelight.

"How you holding up? How's the boy?"

"We're doing all right. Considering ..."

"I've laid out his appointment books, his work schedule for the past two weeks. His dictated memos are this pile. Any correspondence I typed for him is this pile." Shirley's efficiency was well known at B.E. Now, in a time of crisis it rose to the level of prophecy—everything Jean had wanted to see, Shirley had organized chronologically. She pulled out Robert's chair, gave it two counterclockwise swirls to raise the seat and slid it under Jean.

"You take your time. I'll get coffee. We girls have our own percolator now; no longer dependent on the swill the engineers drink."

Shirley edged away as the lowering sun glared through the blinds and faces wandered to the wall clock—4:00. Jean whipped through the paperwork Shirley had arranged. Seeing the last two weeks of his work life laid out so tersely, she was reminded of how boring B.E. could be. She tugged at the top desk drawer—it was locked. All the drawers were locked—tiny metal cages holding ... what? Would he keep the key here? She sifted through the loose junk on the desk top—pens, pencils, a slide rule, a magnifying glass, parts of a disassembled oscilloscope. No key.

"Coffee?"

Shirley stood over her with two B.E. coffee mugs. Her eyebrows arrowed in disapproval.

"I need to get into the desk, but I can't seem to find his key."

"Well, I don't have it."

There was that attitude again—clipped, a part of Shirley that Jean didn't recognize.

"But you must have a duplicate?"

Jean pulled at the drawers again, gave them a loud, wrenching shake until Shirley's hand settled on hers and tightened. Jean felt the blood backing up into her wrist.

"I can't let you in there," Shirley said.

"But you work for Robert."

"I work for B. E." Shirley smiled. "I remember Robert telling me the etymology of the word *secretary*: from Late Latin *secreterius* or confidential officer; then Middle English *secretary*, or a person entrusted with secrets. Braden Enright's secrets, not his."

Jean followed Shirley's gaze to the west side of the floor, where the Braden Enright executives worked, phones cradled on their shoulders, haloed in amber by sun. They made a point of not partitioning themselves behind frosted glass and locked doors. They still knew most of the workers, personally handed out the Christmas bonuses, grilled hamburger patties at the company picnics. They didn't think of themselves as towering industrialists, as entitled or destined; they thought of themselves as lucky. Jean had always liked them, and they had liked her back. They'd inherited their managerial style from Carl Braden, who worked at an ink-stained wooden desk he'd retrieved from the bank building where they started out. The same desk where he died of a heart attack six years ago—God's revenge for forcing out Merritt Enright, some said. As for Enright, he either got out while the getting was good, with a fat bonus, or missed the biggest boom since the end of the war. He had gone back to teaching at a business school at the university at Berkeley. He was bitter or gleeful, depending on who you asked.

"Understood," Jean said. "May I make a call?"

"Be my guest. I'll just finish up at my desk." Jean waited until Shirley had moved out of ear shot, then asked the switchboard to connect her with the house. Jimmy had been at the library looking up recent funeral notices and she was anxious to know what he'd learned.

"Anything?"

"I got four names, mom. Two from the *Palo Alto Times*, two from the *San Francisco Chronicle*. We should get the Chronicle, they carry Batman and Robin."

"We'll see. For now, I just need the names."

"OK, OK. Ethel Hart, born 1897, Danville, Illinois, died June 7 in San Carlos. Myron Gundy, died June 6th in San Jose. Rosemary Tiller, born 1888, Devon, England, died in Alameda June 7, Arthur Merrill, born Albuquerque, died San Bruno June 1."

She didn't recognize any of the names. Not as fellow B.E. workers, not as Robert's friends. "So, nothing in the last week at all."

"Steven Stubbs, born Los Gatos 1949, died June 13 in Santa Cruz."

"My God, just a child. This is getting us nowhere."

"Maybe there wasn't a funeral".

"Or maybe there was, but it was private. They didn't want anyone there who they didn't know."

"Spoken like a real Vale Investigations senior op."

"What?"

"See you at home."

The office chatter increased. There was a closing of drawers, the whoosh of correspondence being whipped out of typewriters, a cheerful bustle towards the exits. Shirley slipped into a coat that was too heavy for summer and waited.

"I think I'll just sit here for a bit, Shirl," Jean said. She picked up the one photo that Robert always kept on his desk: the two of them on the ferry from San Francisco to Oakland, huddled against the wind, the skies slanted with rain, a just married couple united against the elements.

"OK then. Well, behave yourself." Shirley joined the throng to the exit, then looked back, her expression unreadable.

Jean checked her watch. The office always emptied out quickly. Within minutes the floor watchman would begin his rounds. He would check the locks on the filing cabinets, peer under desks, scour every supply room, barge into the men's room, knock on the ladies room door and, if no one answered, barrel right in. She needed a temporary hiding place.

SHE FOUND a perfect hiding spot in the Ozalid room, concealed behind blueprints which hung from ceiling clamps like a load of drying laundry, her nose plugged with Kleenex against the corrosive stink of the ammonia vapor.

Jean thought about how it should have gone. They would've enjoyed a "How was your day? Fine, how was yours?" dinner. Over dessert—Danish Junket, Jimmy's favorite—they would've emptied purses and pockets in search of the rare coins Robert said were still in circulation, which meant any Woolworth's transaction had the potential to make them rich. Maybe spent ten minutes making up imaginary shows on the TV set Jimmy had drawn on cardboard and propped up on the bookshelves between the Literary Guild selections and the *Encyclopedia Americana*. Traded sneaky smiles—a brand new Philco TV was on layaway. Jimmy might have gone out front to play catch with the Burke kids from up the street; Jean and

Robert would have settled in lawn chairs on the half-poured back patio.

"I've decided to seek treatment," she would have announced —no preamble or apology, because talking about it was nearly impossible and she didn't want to get stuck in the niceties that had silenced her before. Robert would have absorbed the news impassively for a moment, reached for her hand and asked, "What sort of treatment?"

"Medicinal at first. I spoke to a psychiatrist. We'll see how it goes."

"Dear, I know things have been grim for you ..." They had always been a "Dear" couple, not a "Honey" couple. "Honey" couples sounded flingy and shallow, "Dear" couples were stable and enduring.

"They've been bad for you, too. For all of us. And we can't continue this way."

"Psychiatrist? You're just sad, you're not crazy!"

Robert knew that "sad" didn't approach the truth, but he was astute enough to realize he could never describe the turmoil in Jean's head, in her organs, on her skin. He would never experience the second mind that seemed to be taking shape inside her skull. It wasn't his fault that "sad" was all he could see.

"What sort of medicine?"

"We'll, it's something new, sort of experimental."

"My wife? Experimented on? *My* wife?"

He would have taken it as a personal failing. So obvious, why hadn't she seen it? When, or if she did tell him, she would have to phrase it differently.

THE LIGHTS FLICKED on and off, the watchman's flashlight clanged against the Ozalid duplicating machine.

"Anyone in here?"

Jean held her breath to avoid causing a telltale ripple in the blueprints. She'd splashed a little extra ammonia developer on to the floor. Thanks to the permanent stink, the Ozalid room was no one's favorite place.

"Jesus Christ." The watchman coughed and moved on.

Jean waited for the watchman's footsteps to fade, for evening quiet to settle. Soon, she could hear the building breathing in and out as the heating and air conditioning systems kicked on and off. She gingerly pulled back the blueprint curtain.

The angry face of a janitor glowered at her.

"What the hell are you doing here?" the janitor demanded. She was a compact woman with short, curly brown hair, wearing a red flannel shirt and blue jeans with the cuffs turned up. A utility belt bristling with cleaning supplies was cinched around her stomach. A cigarette protruded from curled down lips; when the ashes dropped to the floor, she instantly picked them up with a scooper. She called over her shoulder. "Jessie, get in here, I've got something." She pulled a spray bottle out of her utility belt and pointed it at Jean. "This here is no Endust. This is used on B-29s. It's not something you want to have in your face."

Jean held out her old badge, pressing her thumb over the expiration date.

"Just finishing up." Jean crinkled her nose. "You know these boys—when they need a big printing job, they want it done after hours so they can save their sense of smell for the wifey's Chanel welcome home."

The janitor studied the badge with eyes that had been permanently narrowed to slits by years of squinting through a chemical haze of disinfectant and wax strippers.

"Jessie, would you mind?" the janitor yelled again.

A moment later, a tall colored woman entered. She was in her mid-thirties, her hair bundled up in a San Francisco Seals baseball cap. She wore wide-legged pants, belted impossibly high on the waist, Katherine Hepburn style, and a khaki work shirt, sleeves rolled up tightly, revealing a long scar on her left arm. She stared critically at Jean, stroking her chin with a rubber-gloved hand. Then Jean recognized her.

"Jessie Harper, I saw you at the Janitor Races! You too," Jean said to the other janitor. "You're Connie Latimer, you took second."

"It was a tie," Connie Latimer said.

"Depending on the angle you were watching from," Jessie snapped back.

"Well, from my angle, it was a goddamn tie. I heard Frances Cutler at the Christmas party saying I was the actual winner," Connie said.

During the mid-war years, the male janitorial staff had been drafted, and women had been recruited to clean the facilities of the fast-growing company. When the war ended, it was assumed the women would move on to husband hunting and their male replacements would be rehired. But the women were not interested in giving up their paychecks and they refused to leave. And so, on the Friday night before Labor Day —with intended humor—the powers-that-be staged a janitorial war of the sexes, a competition between the female janitors and the male job applicants. The events included window washing, bathroom cleaning (a team event which provoked controversy because the men's rooms had both toilet bowls and urinals, which required separate tools and techniques, so the women's team ran it with a ten-point handicap), blindfolded identification of cleaning chemicals based on smell, floor waxing (judged for durability and sheen) and drinking fountain maintenance. Shortly before 1 a.m., the leader board showed several contestants tied for first, including Connie Latimer and Jessie Harper. Connie was white, and Jessie was colored, so to some in the rooting sections, it became a run-off between black and white. The judges decided on a mop off: six sweating custodial candidates with numbers painted on their buckets, a race that ran from the assembly benches through drafting and into Sales before reaching the finish line at the swinging exit doors. In the final sprint, a trio of janitors—Connie, Jessie and Pete Markowitz, who was rumored to have grenaded twelve Japanese soldiers on Tarawa while nursing a chest wound—scrubbed their way between the desks and chairs, cheered on by a work force whose loyalties were now confused. There were men who wanted additional male janitors to confirm their manly status; there were women who wanted to keep the male janitors on staff for the ogling opportunities; and men who wanted female janitors for the same reason. In the last turn, Markowitz lost traction on a soapy puddle, and fell, fishtailing on his back towards the finish line like a ballplayer sliding for home, so technically *he* was first. Jessie and Connie, the next two finishers, appealed to the judges, who ruled that contestants needed to end the race on their feet. Jessie and Connie kept their jobs, and Pete Markowitz, war hero and graceful loser, gave both women a pat on the rump, took out a G.I. bill loan and now owned and operated two diaper trucks.

"This badge is out of date," Jessie Harper said.

"I just came to pick up some of my husband's stuff. He's sick, but working from home."

The janitors traded skeptical looks.

"At least holster your weapon, Annie Oakley," Jean said to Connie, who slipped her cleaning spray back into her utility belt.

"Come on, I'll show you ... please?" Jean led the two janitors to Robert's desk.

"67 B," Connie said.

Jessie Harper nodded. "A tearer, not a crumpler."

"We don't really pay attention to their names, just desk numbers as they're marked on the grid." Connie waved a laminated map of the office floor. "67 B—your husband is easy to clean up after. He tears his paper into squares, instead of crumpling it, which saves wastebasket space."

Jean pretended to search through her pockets.

"Listen, I think I left the desk key at home. You have a master, right?"

"Yeah, but we're not really supposed to—"

"I bet on you two that day, you know. The odds were stacked against you, but I took a flyer." Jean had never placed a bet in her life. But Jessie Harper handed over the key.

"Five minutes. Then bring it back, we'll be over in the 30's."

With Harper and Latimer safely on their rounds, Jean opened the three side drawers to Robert's desk. They were all empty. She pulled out the double wide top drawer, expecting marked up blueprints, finding a Pine-Sol tainted void instead. She felt queasy; it was as though her purse had been emptied. It looked like Robert's secret, that Shirley so jealously guarded, was that he had no secrets. She dropped heavily into Robert's chair. It rolled on its casters; she didn't try to stop it.

Then she spotted the corner of a piece of paper taped to the back side of the desk behind the center drawer. She slid the drawer out on its runners as far as it would go but didn't see anything. She glanced over her shoulder—Harper and Latimer were lugging buckets up step ladders to reach the transom windows. She slipped under the desk, nearly lying down and extended her arm. She tugged at the piece of paper, and withdrew a legal-size envelope, folded over on itself, wrapped in several layers of Scotch tape.

Using Robert's Grand Canyon honeymoon souvenir pen knife, she ripped through the tape and opened the envelope. It contained a mimeographed copy of the B.E. master personnel records. Over three hundred and fifty names, categorized by department. Address, phone number, year hired. Jean leafed through the names, unsure what she was looking for. On each page, one or two names as well as their contact information had been blacked out. She held the pages up to the light, but the names were illegible. She'd had occasion to see the personnel lists before; when someone quit or was transferred or fired, their names stayed on the rolls for three months, while issues such as insurance or severance pay were worked out. She assumed this was a temporary list, but it was not B.E. business as usual. It was as if these names—these employees—had never existed. She flipped through to the S's. Between Madge Schaeffer and David Slater, one name was blacked out. Next to it Robert had written in pencil: "H. Sirk. Promoted? Where?"

Jean saw that Connie had left the office floor plan on the desk adjacent to Robert's. She scanned it, but there was no desk belonging to anyone named Sirk. Maybe he had worked in the assembly plant where Robert had begun his career with B.E. Silently closing Robert's drawers, Jean slipped through the double doors to the assembly division.

She passed ranks of benches cluttered with oscillators and wave analyzers, taking shape like creations from an adult erector set. The assemblers sat on stools, there was no slouching in roll-away chairs here, no phones, no secretaries. The assemblers' stations were identified by wood laminated nameplates, and their toolboxes bore name tags underlined with deadly threats aimed at anyone daring to borrow their tools. Again, no Sirk. Who was he? Robert had never mentioned the name. He wasn't an outside sales rep because he was listed in the personnel files—until he'd been blacked out. Who the hell was he? At the end of the assembly bench was a stack of phone books from Bay Area cities, their covers dotted with silver drips of solder. Could it be that simple? For once, it could. Harold and Evelyn Sirk lived at 142 Alden Street in Redwood City. Jean hurried back into the offices, returned the master key to Jessie Harper with a million thanks.

THE SIRK HOUSE was at the end of a cul de sac, a wood framed, one story trimmed in blue and white with a wraparound porch. There was a side entrance to a newer add-on that had probably been built during the war and rented out to port workers. No lights on, no cars in the driveway. Jean had called from a payphone outside the Rexall, but the operator told her that the line had been disconnected.

She stood at the edge of the yard. Wind chimes dangled from the branches of a young, spindly Modesto ash. She reached into the mailbox. It was empty. It was like their own mailbox, galvanized tin, with a flat, slotted top where you could screw in a nameplate. She and Robert had installed theirs together, drawing out the moment with a little pomp, toasting bottles of Miller High Life so it felt a bit like a Victory ship christening. The top of the Sirk mailbox was scratched, a rubber shard from a washer clung to one of the empty screw holes. Someone had removed the nameplate.

She stared at the Sirks' curtained front window, trying to imagine who was home, what they were doing and how their lives had unexpectedly intersected with hers. She climbed three steps to the porch, the floorboards worn by afternoon sun and foggy nights. The weathering was uneven, there were darker patches where a set of outdoor table and chairs had once stood. The front door was painted cream, with a fan shaped transom window, a brass knocker in the shape of a lion's head. It didn't really knock—it thudded, echoing inside the house. Jean rapped against the front window.

"Evelyn? Evelyn Sirk? It's Jean Vale, my husband Robert works with Harold at Braden Enright." She turned the doorknob, but it was locked.

She walked to the rear of the house. A row of well-tended fuchsias was shaded by an acacia tree in brilliant yellow blossom. There were strips of wood nailed into the trunk that served as climbing stairs. Built into the lower branches were four walls of pine and the 2x4 frame of a peaked roof—a Fort Apache style tree house under construction.

She peered in through a small window. She saw a bathroom, no towels, no bath mat, an open medicine cabinet that was empty. She could see a wedge of hallway and beyond it, the living room. No furniture, nothing on the walls. Harold and Evelyn Sirk had moved.

Robert had vanished, and now the man he was looking for was gone too.

She tried the back door and the add-on door. Both were locked. She rounded the other side of the house, none of the windows had been conveniently left open. She briefly considered breaking a window—the nozzle from a garden hose would to the job—but the cupboard was literally bare. What could she find in there?

She tried the neighbors. No one home on the house to the left. A teenage boy across the street wouldn't slide out from beneath the car he was working on, so she talked to his greasy jeans. I really didn't know them; they moved; in a moving van, how else? A few days ago, I guess, I wasn't paying attention; I don't know where he worked so I don't know if he got a new job; nope, didn't say where they were going; I hope someone cool moves in. Jean gave up, went to her car but didn't get in. She studied the Sirk house; it didn't feel right. Why had they left the half-finished fort? No mom in the world wanted to risk the wrath of a child yanked away from his favorite playhouse. Then she saw something he hadn't noticed before, black and flat, squashed in the middle of the road. She bent down and pried it up, flapjack style. It was a black boutonniere.

Someone else had attended the funeral that never was.

As Jean got out of the car, she saw a stirring of shadows beneath the front porch light. Jimmy and Grandpa Tamarkin marched toward her, holding up their palms.

"Don't go inside, mom."

"What? Why not?"

"The battle positions have shifted."

"What are you talking about?"

"I told you about it, mom. The troops at the front and back

doors. They've been disturbed ... well, at least the ones at the back door."

Jean looked at Tamarkin, probing for an adult assessment of the situation, but he returned an amused smile.

Jimmy took her by the hand, led her around to the back of the house. Tamarkin followed, lighting up a cigarette.

"Grandpa Tamarkin, this is a blackout situation!" Jimmy snapped.

Tamarkin nodded and stubbed out his cigarette beneath a curly toed slipper. Jean realized he was in a robe and pajamas.

Jimmy opened the back door a notch, enough room for them to slide in sideways. On the floor of the laundry room, between the sink and the wall of dead-end plumbing, waiting for the washing machine they would soon be able to afford, his Army men were arranged in formation—infantry, armor, artillery. The desert-tan uniforms of the Afrika Korps squared off against British green. Jimmy knelt over the battle scene and studied the ranks. "You're looking at the siege of Tobruk, middle of May 1941. Here's the British 3rd Armored, that there is Rommel's 15th Panzers, armed with—"

"Jimmy, get to the point."

"They've moved since I set them up."

Jean flinched. She glanced at Tamarkin whose smile had faded.

"I set them up so if you opened the door, the leading infantry would be knocked over—whomp, a whole line of 'em would go down." He demonstrated by closing, then re-opening the door which bowled over two rows of soldiers. "That's what happened. Whoever knocked them down, tried to set them back up but got the formation wrong."

Jimmy took Jean's hand, led her and Tamarkin through the laundry room and kitchen to the front door. More Army men arranged on the floor, this time supported by fighter planes. "Battle of the Bulge. Not accurate, I know—air power was pretty useless thanks to the weather, but the models are neat.

This set-up, no one touched. No one came through the front door since we left the house this afternoon."

Jimmy loved his battle panoramas, sometimes to the point where it disturbed Jean, but she told herself that toy soldiers and a knowledge of tactics were actually innocence preservers, his version of cowboys and Indians.

"What do you think Grandpa Tamarkin?"

"I think your playful son has signs of becoming clever man".

"Should we call the police?"

"At this point, I think, is mistake."

"But this is crazy! This is not what our lives are like, burglars breaking in and ransacked desks."

"Ransacked? I don't know this word," asked Tamarkin.

"Searched," Jean said. "At work, Robert's desk had been cleared out, like a hospital room emptied after a patient's death."

Tamarkin worked leathery fingers through his beard. His eyes seemed to cloud over for a moment. Jean thought she could see him drifting back in time, then vaulting forward, traveling the mysterious and wondrous turns of history that had brought him from Imperial Russia, a country that had endured hundreds of years, to Kensington Drive, in a house built five years ago, in a town that had been a town for less than six months.

"Jean, would you make please some coffee? I have some vital information to share with you."

"Sure, OK. Wait—what if they're still here?" Jean edged through the house, turning on lights. "Robert, is that you? Are you here?" She checked the hall, the bathroom, both bedrooms. No one and no sign that anyone had been there.

"Jim, are you sure that your little alarm—"

"He is sure, Jean," Tamarkin said. "I saw them."

. . .

"NO SAMOVAR, SORRY," Jean said as she poured them coffee.

"I have become used to the American coffee."

They sat on opposite ends of the Chesterfield, each in their own pale spotlight cast by the pole lamp. Jimmy was monitoring the street through the front window, but he was highly attuned to adult conversation and would absorb every word they said.

"The men you saw," Jean prompted.

"First, so you must know that I am not your usual, peeping Thomas. I was born poor, Jean, in a village that is on no map, far from Petersburg, far from the history of the world. I was soon a runaway boy—a real 'teenager' in search of adventure. And because I was smart and tough and good at being alone, and knew my way around the country, I was hired by government official from a government bureau. And I did well there, in a world of codes and false identities; renaming myself until the village youth with dirt on fingernails was gone. But when revolution came, my many names were on lists—lists are vile things, Jean. Never be on lists. Even now, your country is making lists ..."

"Reds!" Jimmy said, nodding in agreement.

"The new masters didn't know that I would work for them, too. I was not *politicheskim*—political. I wanted to live in a world where I could practice my art; that is how I had thinking of it. Sooner or later, I knew that the list checkers would get to real name, and they could then arrest me. So I flee Russia."

"How did you end up here, Grandpa Tamarkin?" Jean asked.

"We save that for another time. I will just say for now that I am grateful to Helen and Frederic, grateful that I have friends like you and Robert and Jimmy."

Tamarkin finished his coffee and held out his cup for a refill. Then he lowered his voice.

"I am dying from waste here, in my bedroom with the fresh sheets and the cat hair and the always warm heater. Dying from crossword puzzles and Mickey Spillane and library editions of Russian books. So, when I first see them, passing by in their cars at odd hours, not on their way home from anywhere or on their way to an early morning job, I tell myself they are come for me."

Jimmy perked up. "Russian spies?"

"The Soviet consulate in San Francisco is filled with men and women who do different jobs at different times, and the Russian memory is long. It excited me, I admit. To be a target again—wonderful!"

"You weren't scared?" Jean asked.

"For me, no. They can be blunderers, such guys. They would not dare something serious or violent here and, if they did, they would fail. So, I studied them from my nest in the kitchen at night, from the seat in Frederic's car in the driveway. I wrote notes of their age, weight and height, their haircuts, their clothes, cars they drive, the way they walk. They were of course Americans—there's an American walk, you see—and they had not come for me." He sipped his fresh cup of coffee. "Do you have a biscuit perhaps, for dipping?"

Jimmy dashed into the kitchen, did one of his trademark vertical leaps to the top shelf, grabbed a package of Hydrox.

"Jean, I am a man who is always need a task. Not a cause, dear God, no. Causes have done more damage to the world than uncaring. But I have talents."

"Such as?"

"Powers to see things." Tamarkin paused and pulled a Hydrox apart. He scraped out the white filling with a spoon and stirred it into his coffee. "When you shake your dust mop—usually on Tuesdays—you turn your head to the right, shut your eyes and sneeze. You have two aprons, the checky one for dusting day and the blue for incinerator day. When you return home from shopping, you honk horn twice if you need help with groceries. You leave your driving gloves on the gearshift. Jimmy, to tell by the knife carvings in the back fence, I guess that you are trying to teach yourself how to write left-handed. A valuable skill."

"So, you're the neighborhood snoop? And I thought it was Ellen Burke with her driveway gossip and her bifocals." Jean said.

"This is all behavior that is in plain view."

Jimmy sat up, reached into his back pocket.

"Tell mom about the counterfeiting!"

Tamarkin smiled gently. "He means forgery."

"You do that too, huh? Naturally."

"One of the stories of Europe in this century is the story of papers. It has always been good to be from someplace else, another town, another province, another country. Balkans attempt to prove they are Italians, Russians wish to pass as Estonians, Czechs as Hungarians. Travel passes, Displaced Persons Camp Registration Forms, International Refugee cards. Stamps, always stamps, ration coupons, Vichy *Changement de Domicile Cards,* NKVD Pass Allowing Freedom of Movement during Air Attack, and my favorite because it is so German, a Nazi form given by the *Reichsschrifttumskammer.*"

"And a California Driver's License for James Benjamin Vale." Jimmy waved a new California Operator's license, complete with thumbprint. His age was listed as 17, and as far as Jean's amateur eyes could tell, it was a perfect forgery.

"And the men?" Jean asked. "You saw them break into our house?"

"I saw them in your driveway. I assumed the rest." Tamarkin pulled a small notebook out of his bathrobe pocket. "Subject One: 25–30, 1.79 meters—that's five foot, ten inches"—light brown hair cut short, heavy glasses, white shirt, sleeves rolled up, dark slacks, smoked Viceroys. Subject Two: mid-30s, five foot, eight inches, many muscles, a mole to the left of his Adam's Apple—still my favorite English phrase—brown fedora hat I think you call it, with two pencils, or maybe one was compass in the hat band, white shirt, dark slacks. They are driving a black, 1949 Ford two-door with Nevada license plate T-643-J."

"Nevada?"

Tamarkin nodded, closed the notebook with a satisfied snap.

"Do you think these men took Robert?"

"Took? We have no proof. Maybe they are looking for him, too."

Jean went to the front window as the images of the last two days rushed past her, impossible to grasp. Suddenly, she was in the passenger seat of her father's Maxwell Touring car, *Benjamin Maddux, Master Carpenter* hand painted on the doors, propped up on his toolbox for extra height, head thrust out the window into the hot wind as the fields blew by smelling of peach blossoms and grasshopper poison. "Faster, faster!" she'd always squealed. Even in winter, the tule fog low on the ground, the headlights unable to pierce the grey cocoon that enclosed them, she'd demanded reckless, unforgiving speed. When she was four, she'd had a bad few months when she became convinced there were Tule Monsters, packs of beasts who were half-wolf, half-cat, with barbed tails and fangs that grew out of their heads where their ears should have been, waiting out there in the reeds, their sole mission to punish.

"Maybe we should go to a motel." Jean said.

"The Town and Country on El Camino has TV!" Jimmy said.

"You could stay with us," Tamarkin said. "I'm sure Helen will not mind. In addition, Jimmy has fallen behind a little on his code work."

Old man and boy looked at her expectantly. It was the kind of decision she and Robert would have made together.

"Maybe that would be for the best." Then: "No! I will not be scared out of my own house. Robert and I bought this when it was just frame and foundation and put up the rest ourselves.

These walls and these floors are here because of us. Jimmy, put on fresh coffee."

She stood up and tightened her belt—the red French thing Robert had bought for her birthday at the *City of Paris* because he wanted her to have something from San Francisco's most famous European emporium, a shopping excursion that involved a round trip train ticket and two taxi cab rides which cost more than the belt, and briefly burdened her with the suspicion that what he really desired was a teensy-waisted *mademoiselle* rather than the solidly-hipped, aggie-town gal that she was. It was absurd of course to attribute Redbook motivations to her husband's attentions; he loved her for who she was and she loved him for it. And he was no Tyrone Power himself.

"We'll stay right here. We'll stand watch. The three of us. Until the sun comes up."

4

The next morning, Robert Jensen Vale had the honor of being the first official "Missing Person" case to be handled by the new Los Altos Police Department. The duty officer Jean had dealt with the first night became excited as he took down the information. She expected him to reach for his brand-new Motorola radiophone and issue a "Calling All Cars" appeal.

As she was leaving, a door on the far side of the lobby opened and four policemen stepped out of a conference room. They wore different uniforms—khaki, olive drab, black, and dress blue, with badges competing for shininess. A meeting that called together three different departments: Palo Alto, where Robert worked, Los Altos where he lived, and Monte Vista, where the car had been found, represented by Officer Fielder. These were not big city cops with murders to solve and rackets to break up. They were the kind of policemen who returned Jimmy's bike when it was stolen, whose German Shepherds Jean had admired in the Pet Parade. This was surely a sign that they were bringing fresh energy to Robert's disappearance. She was about to stride over to them, when Fielder gave her a subtle shake of the head. She nodded, signal received, and went out to the parking lot.

She waited by the Monte Vista patrol car, but when Fielder pushed out the front door, he angled his chin toward the civilian parking lot at the side of the building. She went to the Nash, swiping pepper tree blossoms off the hood until the Monte Vista car coasted up next to her, Fielder at the wheel, window rolled down. He was agitated, checking his rear-view mirror. He turned up his police radio to full volume, voices and static crackling, masking their conversation. "They're not really taking this seriously, Mrs. Vale."

"What are you getting at? What was that meeting all about?"

He looked straight at her; he couldn't say or wouldn't say.

"Who is taking it seriously, then? Who's in charge of the investigation?"

"Let me restate. If you want to find your husband on *your* terms, you're going to have to get a little drastic. You can't rely on these folks. Good luck." He drove off, the radio chatter following him, then fading. Her blood told her to storm back into the station and tear into those cops one by one, with tales of midnight intruders. Her brain told her to follow Grandpa Tamarkin's advice. The police were not her ally.

Fielder wanted drastic? She would give them drastic.

It was 6:30 p.m. in Washington D.C., 3:30 on the West Coast, when the intercom buzzed in the Director's office.

"We're ready for the broadcast," his secretary said.

He went into the library, a room whose fading mahogany walls were lined with paintings of ships from the days when the offices were home to the Bureau of Navigation and Steamship inspection. A console television had been set up at the end of a conference table. The staff was assembled, sipping coffee, and nibbling on his secretary's durable pound cake. The lights had been doused and the blinds drawn for better TV viewing. Their new researcher, Carmen, a former Library of Congress archivist, was adjusting the television reception.

The Director glided his hands over the smooth varnish of the console.

"A Zenith TV. Can we afford this?" he asked.

"Terrific sales running right now, as they're bringing out the new models. I've become something of a TV and hi-fi expert, if I do say so. You asked us to develop new skills, remember?" Carmen clicked through the channel dial, until she landed on the NBC's lightning-bolted microphone trademark.

"And how are we managing to watch a West Coast program live?"

"It's not completely live," Carmen answered. "It's a kinescope from Frisco, flown to Los Angeles where it was fed into the repeater station system ..."

The Director coughed impatiently.

"It was complicated, but we made it happen," Carmen said.

"Is this legal?" the Director asked. A shrug from his lawyer, "Cardigan" Jack, meaning "no."

"She's on," the director said, relieved that he would not have to endure any further explanation, scientific or legal.

He saw a woman with wavy hair fringed with curls and a set look to her mouth. She wore a light-colored blouse with a high neckline, a lose-fitting business jacket draped over it. She sifted through a pile of papers at a desk, looked off camera, and nodded as someone whispered a last-minute pointer.

"Hello, my name is Jean Vale, of Los Altos." Her voice quivered, and she cleared her throat. "Five days ago, my husband Robert Vale disappeared and efforts to find him have failed. The police say there is no evidence that a crime of violence has been committed, so it is a true mystery that's ..." She hesitated, reading ahead in her prepared script.

"You're doing fine," a male voice said.

"… a mystery that has devastated me and our son, who misses his father. Here is his picture." Mrs. Vale held up a photograph of Robert Vale, a face you would not think twice about. He looked satisfied, even happy to have his picture taken, which was from an identification badge of some kind. "He is thirty-eight years old, with black hair, five foot nine, and weighs one hundred and fifty-five pounds. He was last seen wearing a white, long-sleeved shirt, a red tie, and gray slacks. If you have any information on him, please call me personally at Whitecliff 8-5612. Thank you." The screen went black and an "Everybody Likes Ike" ad began to play.

The Director studied his team, marveling at the research materials—documents, photographs, books, geology reports, news clippings, maps—they had compiled. "So, am I prepared for my trip to the West Coast?"

"Yes, sir," came the answer, in the ragged yet enthusiastic unison the Director valued so highly. No one's voice dominated, no single personality tried to seize the limelight. He turned to his secretary Myrna (she liked Ike). "You remember my air travel preferences?"

"You like the TWA Connie, aisle seat, multiple stops to stretch your legs and take the lay of the land." Myrna preened a bit, smiling. "I've arranged for a private car to drive you to National. Less conspicuous than a taxi, more difficult to follow."

The Director nodded. It had been a long time since he had embarked on a field mission, and he felt both solemn and invigorated. And a little old. "Those of you who know me well may be expecting me to read thematic poetry aloud, or to quote from my arsenal of history aphorisms. But as the time for action, not stanzas from Siegfried Sassoon or Wilfred Owen, is upon us, I'll just say let's deal with Mrs. Vale, shall we?" He gathered the staff's research into his briefcase. "I think we're all curious to see where this leads."

. . .

It was not how Jean imagined the Vale family would enter the television age. She pictured them picking up the television box at Sears, opening it in the living room, Jimmy reading the instructions aloud as Robert set it up, fiddling with the antenna, calling up his entertaining catalog of adjectives: "dad-burned, dumbfangled, bassackwards." Maybe they would splurge on southern fried chicken from Dinah's, including Jean's farm town weakness, pickled pigs feet, then sit down to watch *Burns and Allen* or maybe *You Asked For It,* Jimmy choosing the programs from the television guides he had been collecting. Instead, she was on television herself, before she'd even watched a minute of it in her own living room, a "human interest story," a "housewife's heartbreak," a "mother's heartfelt plea."

With Helen reinforcing her bravado, she had worked her way through the Yellow Pages until a producer at KSJO, a San Jose station, responded to "the angle" of an anguished mom and her son pleading with the public to help find their missing husband/dad. The producer had made a call to "a guy who owes me a favor up in the city," and she was on the San Francisco air waves the next day. Jimmy, Helen, and Grandpa Tamarkin had come along too, offering moral support, but Jean suspected they were most interested in seeing the inside of a television studio.

She had been terrified, her body wandering off from her mind. This was everything she dreaded, compacted into sixty seconds: confession to strangers, public speaking, fear of judgment. The studio lights started blinking, men called out sharp, terse orders. To her shock, it went well. There were no mocking faces leering back at her, no critics hunched in their corners sharing laughter and whispers. And despite the TV floor manager pantomiming tear-stained cheeks, she refused to cry.

“You were very good,” Helen said.

“Natural, I believed you,” Grandpa Tamarkin added.

Why wouldn’t I be believable? she thought. *I was telling the truth.* But she supposed there was no absolute truth in Grandpa Tamarkin’s world, just gradations of lies.

They were in the car, Jimmy riding shotgun, Grandpa Tamarkin and Helen in the back seat. They drove down Van Ness, passing the auto showrooms where the whole family used to ogle the new cars after their rare trips up to the city for road show versions of “The King and I” or the “Ice Follies.” And Jimmy loved the city: the fog, the long coats and hats men and women wore to fend off the chill; the crowds, the unfamiliar faces, Chinatown with its movie set alleys, policemen on horseback, the city’s history of gold rushers and earthquake, so Jean just drove, no destination in mind.

"Hey mom, look at that guy!" Jimmy pointed to a man hopping down the sidewalk on crutches, his left leg severed above the knee.

"Poor man," Jean said. She turned at the next street, hoping to spare Jimmy the sight of the man as his balance trembled, threatening to spill him to the pavement. Just around the corner were more handicapped men, missing arms, legs, hands, faces scarred. Rolling and hobbling in a ragged formation, a parade of the wounded—heading for an American Legion post she realized, a storefront draped with red, white and blue bunting, promoting "Home Cooked Meals" and "Tuesday is Movie Night: *You're In the Navy Now* with Gary Cooper. Jimmy gazed at the men, pressing his hands to the window, as though he wanted to jump out of the car and move among them.

“You know it's not polite to stare,” Jean said. “Especially not at those who are less fortunate.”

Surely “less fortunate” was not the proper phrase, but Jean recognized that she was quoting her mother, Alma, who had always tried to draw Jean’s attention away from the Okie caravans, with their tired, gaunt, hollow-eyed yet determined work seekers. Not because Alma wanted to protect Jean from human misery, but simply so she could later scold her: "You better mind your p's and q's, or else you'll end up like them."

"I've never seen so many before," Jimmy said. "Grady's dad got his thumb shot off, but you never see these guys around town."

It was offered as a comment, not a question—why not? You just didn't see them on Los Altos streets. But they probably were there. Indoors. At private functions for GIs. Visiting hospitals for doctor appointments. Not bragging or showing off. Not complaining. Not on display for her boy's entertainment.

Eventually, Grandpa Tamarkin guided Jean to a Russian neighborhood in the Richmond District, with its onion-domed churches, tea rooms, grocery stores and bakeries. He wrote up a shopping list of groceries—smoked fish, buckwheat, millet and semolina to make kasha, rye *kvass*, homemade *pelmeni* and *piroshki* and handed it to Jean with a wad of cash.

"Don't you want to go in? Hear Russian spoken?"

"I am fine here."

"Those are White Russians," Helen said. "You'll be fine in there too."

"Where there are white Russians, there are Red Russians watching the White Russians, making sure they don't do anything that might make the Red Russians phone their bosses." Grandpa Tamarkin gazed at the Russian writing on the stores, watched parishioners heading to mass at a small, white-washed church. "We were here in California before the Americans, you know. We brought glass windows, and stoves, built the first wood houses. First windmills, first ships. The river at Bodega Bay, the *Slavyanka*, the Russian River you call it, had many sturgeon, the seas filled with otter. We ate sea lion meat, raised beets and cabbage and cattle. We worked side by side with the Indians, with the Alaskans, and with God. An enchanted life, I think it was."

"J. Edgar Hoover thinks you want it all back," Jean said.

"Jimmy knows more about Russia than Mr. Hoover," Grandpa Tamarkin smiled.

Back home, Helen volunteered to handle the phone in case anyone called about Robert, while Jean got some sleep. Too restless to lie down, she wandered out to Robert's car, sliding into the passenger seat, inhaling his absence. How to reorder life—or should she reorder it at all? Wash the car once a week as he always had, using his homemade polish on the chrome? Empty her purse every day, trolling for valuable coins? Do the private, personal things with Jimmy that Robert had done, the boy-man stuff. But what were they? She looked at the driver's side door, which Jimmy had reassembled, although the fabric was scratched and the streamlined chrome accents were buckled.

She burst into his room, where he was reading *Kidnapped* by flashlight.

"When you and dad go on your outings, where do you go, what do you do?"

"I'm reading."

"You've read it twice before. Come on."

"The lumber yard, hardware store. We went to the air show that time."

"I know all that. I'm talking about the stuff you keep between just you two fellas—like when you and I watch the skies for flying saucers."

"I don't know. We just drive around, I guess. He used to let me sit in his lap and steer, but I'm too big for that now."

"Where do you go? Any place in particular?"

"We went to the batteries up at Fort Funston once, the observation bunkers. And sometimes ..." His voice faded. He played his flashlight across the ceiling, targeting a Daddy Long Legs.

"Jimmy, what? Maybe it could help us find him."

"We go to Spivey's, like I said. For milkshakes. We get the car serviced and just sit there, listening to the radio. Maybe we talk, maybe we don't."

"When you do talk, what do you talk about?"

"Mom, that's not fair." Jean saw him blush. Girls? He still played with Army men.

"I withdraw the question, your honor." Jean grabbed Jimmy's pants and t-shirt from the bed, tossed them into his bivouac. "Feel like a milkshake?"

SPIVEY'S on Middlefield Road was a garish, glowing coffee shop, ringed by aquamarine neon, pulsing like a comic book interplanetary power source, the white fluorescence of its dining room streaming out onto the streets, lighting up the empty sidewalks.

"There, third spot from the left, grab that," Jimmy ordered. Jean pulled into a parking spot that was midway around the circular building, with an angled view of the street. "He always parks in the same spot." They ordered chocolate shakes from a flouncy, Toni-permed Mexican carhop named Rosie, then Jean turned on the radio.

"What station do you usually listen to?"

"Opera. If it's at night, we spin the dial and try to find the station farthest away. We even got Canada a couple times."

Jean found a San Francisco classical station re-broadcasting a Metropolitan Opera concert from New York. She checked her rearview mirror, and watched the street. Traffic was light, the windowless, low-slung industrial buildings that housed companies with futuristic names like Teradyne, Aerosphere, and Powermatics were closed, no sign of a swing shift.

"So ..." Jean prompted.

"So?" Jimmy asked.

"Is there anyone in particular? Have I met her? What does dad think of her?"

Jimmy shook his head in anti-mom disgust. "That's not how it usually goes."

"So, instruct me. I'm dad for tonight. Just pretend."

"He'll just sit there, thinking for a while. He may get out and walk around the car, stretch his legs, make a bunch of teenagers mad because he's hogging a parking spot, then he'll get back in and say "When I was your age ..."

"OK, well, when I was your age, I dreamed of being the junior fencing champion of Modesto. I caught polliwogs in the slow-moving parts of the Tuolumne River, tried to feed them to our cat Butch, and when he wouldn't touch them, I ate a couple myself and made myself sick. I'd never seen a talking movie, thought I was ugly as sin and was starting to fall in love with the boy across the street.

"Fencing, really?"

Jean jabbed at Jimmy with her straw, a series of feints and parries that left gobs of chocolate shake on his shirt.

"Really. Now it's your turn—I mean dad's turn."

"He never told me anything real, just made-up stories."

"How did you know they were made up?"

"They were all about him and his best friend, Johno. How they trapped the last wild buffalo in Oregon, tamed it and gave rides to the kids in the neighborhood. How they built a radio and talked to Lindbergh in the middle of his flight across the Atlantic. How they found a secret town of Titanic survivors."

"This Johno, he was real though?"

"Yeah, dad has a word for him. *Hellion.* You know, the type of kid your mom warns you not to play with. Johno's picture is in his wallet. You never saw it?"

"I never met any of your dad's friends."

Up the street, a gate opened in a stretch of chain link fence, two cars drove out, their headlights off. As the cars passed, Jean saw that the headlights were fitted with black-out slits, which deflected the light beams downward. She hadn't seen them in years.

"So meanwhile, back at the ranch ..."

Jimmy squirmed, gulping the rest of his shake, going for the freeze pain so he didn't have to talk.

"Is it Monica Herndon?"

"Nooooo."

Meaning yes, the truth coming out in a flurry of nerves that had Jimmy rolling through the radio dial.

"I'm not spying or prying. You sat next to her in your last two class pictures, so I just thought, well, she's nice, so are her parents. Bill Herndon organizes the sack races at company picnics. Bev's everywhere with her little movie camera. Are you seeing her again ... before school starts, I mean."

Jimmy shrugged, raised his eyebrows, playing it nonchalant —Robert Mitchum without a cigarette. "I think she's going to be at the Cutler *Sunset Magazine* party thing."

"How did you know about that?"

"She told me. I'm not wearing a tie, by the way."

Before Robert had disappeared, Frances Cutler, Lawrence Cutler's stylish, confident and beautiful wife, had invited them to a cocktail party at their stylish, and beautiful new home in Menlo Park. It was going to be a photography session for the editors of *Sunset Magazine*, a garden party theme to showcase the home which had been designed by Cliff May, who was apparently famous down south, and they wanted *real people* to serve as background. Jean was surprised that she and Robert had been invited. At first, she imagined that it was a cruel gesture, paying them back for the dinner they had hosted for Frances and Lawrence, an "impress the boss and his wife" evening that had not gone well. Jean had spent two weeks combing through her cook books, finding nothing that lived up to her notion of a gourmet triumph. She had tried a few things during afternoon trial runs—blanquette de veau, A. Sabella's recipe for oysters Rockefeller—none of which was quite right but ended up providing interesting after-school snacks for Jimmy. With the last of her food budget, she had decided to go basic: filet mignon, scalloped potatoes, string beans and bacon, and making their first appearance in the Vale household, Gilbey's Gin martinis. And it had not been bad; quite good, even complement-worthy. It was Jean herself who had embarrassed the evening and the promise it had held. She'd been tongue-tied at first, then overcorrected, tearing through a recitation of news events that were not dinner table conversation—the crash at the Farnborough Air show which killed twenty-seven people, including the first British pilot to break the sound barrier; the increase in polio deaths; the "Lonely Hearts Killer" dying in the Ohio electric chair. She'd watched the Cutlers' every bite, she'd measured their exhalations and "hmms" on a scale of approval or disdain; she caught herself sweating into her untouched martini; she got up every thirty seconds to "fine-tune the mix." Shapes didn't seem right; plates weren't round, forks weren't straight. Finally, exhausted from the sheer effort it took to sit upright and look at things, she had pleaded a splitting headache and gone to lay down. Although the Cutlers had sent a Thank You card, the anticipated dividend of a promotion for Robert had not appeared and the evening was never mentioned again.

Not even on the day she reached the end of the line at B.E. and Lawrence Cutler, with finesse, tact, and a bonus check "let her go."

And yet, the invitation to the party had come in the mail, signed by Frances Braden Cutler in flawless, feminine script. Thinking about it now, Frances was too poised and correct for a malicious gesture of reprisal; besides, it was an important day for her, why would she risk inviting guests she felt would embarrass her? Maybe to Frances, a headache was just a headache.

. . .

"We'll see, Jim. In the light of everything that's going on now, maybe we shouldn't".

"Mom!"

"We'll go, OK? We'll go."

"No, I mean look."

A blue light on the wall of an industrial building two blocks up began to flash. The same building with the gated chain link fence.

"What's that?"

"I don't know, but it happened the last time dad and I were here, too."

"Did you do anything?"

"Nope, just watched. We finally went home."

"And you always parked in this spot?"

Jimmy nodded. She realized that the car was angled just so, giving them a clear view of the building with the winking blue light. This was a stake-out spot; perhaps the father-son talks had been real, but they had also provided a believable cover, obscuring Robert's real reason for being here.

"That building, do you know what it is? Did your dad ever try to get in there?"

"No, it's just a warehouse or something."

Jean got out of the car. "Stay here, keep the doors locked." Jean crossed the street and walked up the sidewalk toward the flashing light. Two blocks away from the cheerful neon of Spivey's, she found herself in darkness, her footsteps clacking on the sidewalk. A guard dog barked, she heard it straining against its chain leash, metal clanking. As she approached the building, she could hear a faint buzz from the blue light; it seemed to be straining too, about to burn out. Headlights—she narrowed her body behind a telephone pole. A Good Humor ice cream truck rolled by, a cigarette glowing in the cab.

She reached the padlocked gate. She saw two rows of factory-like buildings. A wide alley ran between them, ending in shadows on the far side of the property. None of the buildings had names or street addresses. They seemed deserted, but as she listened to the stillness, closing her eyes, blotting out the world—a practice she had nearly perfected—she detected the thrum of motors, each with a distinctive frequency, and she felt the hair-tickling charge of electrical transformers.

An engine started up, heavy and reluctant, probably belonging to a truck. At the back of the property, a boxy shadow separated from the darkness and drove slowly along the alley. Lights came on; fog lights, not headlamps. Two male figures—guards?—popped out from between the buildings and strode right for her. Jean ducked away as the men unlocked the gate. The vehicle stopped at the open gate, the guards' flashlights illuminating the driver's face as he chatted with the guards. He had cheerful, wide features and he blew a pink balloon of bubble gum, which tinted blue in the pulsing light. It was a modified school bus, re-painted the color of sand with no markings, the windows blacked over.

She pounded on the side. The metal was tinny and giving. Smudges of sandy color came off on her fist—the paint was still wet. She grabbed a handful of change from her purse, threw it at the blacked-out windows. The driver honked a warning, but Jean kept on banging

"Robert, are you in there?" she yelled. The bus driver revved the engine, but he couldn't t shake Jean off. Her veins were coursing, her night vision perfect. "Robert, it's me. Robert!"

A window was lowered part way down, the upper half of a woman's face appeared, obscured by shadow, suspicious eyes peering over the blacked-out glass.

"Is Robert Vale in there? Are you Evelyn Sirk, I was at your house ..."

"There's no Robert here, ma'am," said the woman. Someone else's hand appeared, started to raise the window back up.

Jean waved the photograph of Robert. "This man, has anyone seen him?" The woman reached out a hand, Jean jumped, trying to pass her the photograph. "Here, take this, show it around. Please!" The hand hesitated a moment, then it was yanked back inside before it could take the photograph, the window slammed up, a lock snapped into place. The bus finally found its power and pulled away with its sequestered cargo, coughing out dirty exhaust as though it were still running on black market wartime gas.

5

Isoniazid.

Not one of Superman's mortal foes. Not a horror movie villain played by Bela Lugosi. An antibiotic, odorless, colorless. Many patients report mood enhancements and increased sociability.

The Cutler home gleamed, squares of spangled light on a shady street of oak trees and ranch houses. A procession of polished stepping stones led through a rock garden planted with miniature Monterey Cypress to walls of glass, framed in blonde wood. The roof was pitched upward and rested on more glass. Photographer's lights glared from inside the living room where party-goers mingled in loose groups. Absolute hell.

Maybe half a dose. One pill ...

She and Jimmy sat in the car down the street from the house, waiting. For courage. For a game plan. She wore her favorite light summer slacks, a short-sleeved yellow blouse, and what the magazines called "sensible shoes." Jimmy, in jeans, Keds, and a striped t-shirt with a small notepad tucked under the sleeve suggesting a pack of cigarettes, looked like a teenager in the works. When they had first received Frances' invitation, all Jean had wanted was to not make a fool of herself, and for Jimmy to have a normal afternoon talking with a girl he liked. A few careless hours of boyhood. Now, it felt like an incursion into foreign territory where the natives knew more than she did. Last night, they'd fielded a few incoming phone calls—men vaguely fitting Robert's description had been spotted threatening to jump off Hoover Tower, passed out drunk in a Southern Pacific commuter train, stepping in and out of cabs in a dozen Bay Area cities. She didn't pass the tips along to the police.

"I am not looking forward to this."

"Me neither," said Jimmy.

"I thought you wanted to see Monica?"

"I don't know ..."

"It's natural to be terrified of girls at your age. There'll come a day when you're not terrified of them, and then you'll be terrified of them all over again when they're adult women."

"Dad is today's mission."

A hand tapped on her door. "I have checked all the license plates. The Nevada follower car is not here," said Grandpa Tamarkin. He had ridden with them, so he could run a quick surveillance of the Cutler's neighborhood. He would stand watch, as Jimmy said. In his efforts to blend in, Tamarkin was dressed as "American" as he could manage—blue jeans, a violet polo shirt, sunglasses propped jauntily on his forehead. "I know your instinct is to ask them questions, but that will maybe not succeed. So pretend that you know certain things, and see how they answer. In their answers, you may learn something. I will be near." And then he strolled off whistling "In the Mood," just another undercover Russian spy out for his afternoon constitutional.

They walked toward the front door, Jimmy self-consciously carrying a bouquet of discounted violets Jean had picked out at Woolworths. Jean fished into her purse, opened the pill bottle, held her hand to her mouth and faked a cough. Down the hatch.

Jimmy yanked the notepad out from his sleeve, tore off a sheet of paper and handed it to her. Before Jean could read it, Frances Cutler was there, Rita Hayworth hair framing the gentle curves of her face with lush cascades of brown and copper. Her lightly freckled skin radiated health and the tender care of cosmetics handpicked at I. Magnin. She wore a beige, sleeveless something or other that swirled when she moved. She was a few inches taller than Jean, and carried her height like a thoroughbred filly who knows she'll always finish in the roses. Before she was Frances Cutler, she'd been Frances Braden, who'd grown up without a mother within "blood spatter distance of the meat packing plants in South San Francisco, a city with so little ambition they stole their name," as she was quoted in the B.E company history. Gifted at arithmetic as a young girl, she was said to look over Carl Braden's shoulder, offering corrections as he drew up the plans for the company's first products. She hadn't needed college, she'd learned everything about the family business by hovering behind his workbench, or perched on the edge of his desk, reading and memorizing; blueprints had been her "homework." If she had been born a man, perhaps the company chairmanship would be hers by now.

"Jean, you look so summery, so cheery. And you, young man, you're the perfect California boy, aren't you? The photographers are gonna love you. I believe I saw Monica Herndon out back near the barbecue." She winked at Jimmy, who glanced up at Jean. She smiled her OK, and he headed toward the back yard. "Just be yourself. You won't even notice the photographers." Jean spotted two young men in sweaters, cameras dangling around their necks, gliding among the guests, kneeling, leaning, pushing up onto their toes to get their shots.

"Thank you for the invitation, Frances. I figured that with Robert disappearing—"

"I'd renege? Not my style." She lowered her voice. "Lawrence is exercising whatever influence he has with the authorities. His employees are as important to him in peace-time as his aircrews were in wartime. I can't imagine what you're going through, but you are not alone in this. Being among people is one of the greatest tonics I know. And as for the other ..." She paused, a grace note of pain appearing on her face. "You'll bounce back and rejoin the team when you're ready."

Frances led Jean into the living room, a wide-open space with streamlined furniture and floor-to-ceiling glass walls, both front and back; there seemed to be nowhere to hide from the outdoors. Even the fireplace was built into the glass wall.

"We use the other side of the fireplace for outdoor entertaining," Frances explained. "Indoor-outdoor, that's the concept here. Blurring the borders between interior and outdoor living spaces. And given our glorious California light, why not?"

Light like Jean had never seen poured in, spreading some kind of charge, making everyone seem healthy and unnaturally young. It was not the California light she had grown up with. It was even different from the light she lived in now, just a few miles away.

A commotion near the kitchen door caught Frances' attention. She sighed. "He's at it again, even after the magazine people told him not to—the clustering is not photogenic." She handed Jean a chilled cocktail. "Try to enjoy yourself, Jean, but don't force it. I'll understand. I'm off to keep the trains running." Frances headed towards the kitchen, straightening and arranging as she went.

Jean glanced at the notebook page. Jimmy had written down Grandpa Tamarkin's description of the two intruders. She scanned the partygoers in the living room. There were ten or so, the women in sun dresses or pedal pushers, the men wearing Hawaiian shirts or golf shirts and neatly pressed shorts. None seemed a likely burglar or stake-out artist. But what was she expecting, trench coats?

She heard laughter and "oh my gosh" and "would ya look at that" coming from the kitchen and went to investigate. More party guests flocked around a tall man, like teenage autograph hunters. He was a handsome figure in his late fifties, an unruly lock of gray hair dangling onto his pale forehead. He wore frameless glasses which drew attention to black, piercing eyes. He was slender as a telephone pole, wore a gray suit and dark tie, handkerchief squared in his breast pocket, cufflinks glinting on monogrammed white cuffs: "VBC." A cigarette holder dangled from his lips FDR style as he performed what seemed to be a magic trick.

"... so we're facing a scenario where you are trapped behind enemy lines, with no forward communication at all. What to do? Since I presume the Cutlers do not keep carrier pigeons, we will pursue other solutions. Do any of you ladies have a scarf?" A woman Jean recognized from the B.E. sales department took a patterned silk scarf out of her purse and handed it to the man. Their respective wedding rings touched briefly as he gave her a smile that made her flutter. He shook the scarf with a magician's flourish, and pulled an ascot out of his own pocket and held it up to the light. There was a map printed on it. "Western Holland, under German occupation. So, here's your road map. Gentlemen, any of you have a handkerchief?" Greg Summerville handed one over. The man studied it, then shook out his own crisply folded handkerchief. There was a map on one side of it as well. "Western France, with roads leading to coastal extraction airdromes secured by the Maquis—*La Résistance*. There's your escape route." He had an East Coast accent, not the "dem, dese and dose" of the Dead End Kids, but something softer, compelling. A voice and a demeanor that entranced men and women.

"Vann, come on now, my guests need to circulate." Frances said.

"Just a moment, Frances," Vann said. "You're going to need a compass. Any of you ladies have a large button you could part with? Brass, such as a bellhop might wear would be fine, dome-shaped if possible, but given it's a summer's day, I may be out of luck." He was very much in luck as two women produced chunky metal buttons that had somehow wound up in their pocketbooks. Vann nodded, then took a similar button out of his pocket. He twisted it and it came apart, revealing a miniature compass beneath the cap. "The points are marked with luminous paint for night work. With this sewed into your overalls, no one's the wiser. Now for the men, a button from your fly would be ideal, making you almost search-proof." A ripple of laughter. "So, you see, most of us have whatever we need close at hand, should the need to conduct clandestine warfare ever arise." Vann picked up a martini glass from the kitchen counter, took a grateful, generous sip. "Which of course, we hope it never does."

"Vann, please, let me spill something on you, so I can get you to change out of that god-awful suit," Frances said.

"I was just moving on to the creation of a 'dog drag'—how to evade tracking dogs. Would you have any capsicum in your pantry?" Then Vann spotted Jean, and the showman's glow left his eyes.

"Jean, this is Vann Claridge. He thinks he's back home, where every room is the Oval Office or a Congressional hearing chamber and he has to keep listeners entertained with his heroics. Vann, say hi to Jean Vale. Her husband works in our Manufacturing Specifications division."

"Pleased to meet you, Mr. Claridge," Jean said. His handshake was firm, but his arm shivered slightly from the elbow down. Not from the cold surely. Perhaps he had a nerve condition? "Back home is Washington, I assume."

"Where we still know how to drink. What sort of concoction is that, anyway?" he asked, pointing to the cocktail Jean had yet to sample.

"It's a Bali Hai," answered Frances. "White Rum, lemon juice, grenadine, chilled champagne. Fun, don't you think?"

Claridge snorted. Martini in one hand, he took Jean's elbow and escorted her through the room. Now, she sensed people trying not to stare, could hear the whispers, burbling like creek water—"On television, of all things"; "I don't buy her story." The same gossipy voices, just moved up a notch or three on the social scale. No matter what she did, she stood out. So why not go all the way, scream at them: "What would you do if it was *your* husband missing?" She calmed down under Claridge's gallant care, as they threaded through the curious and out the back door.

The outdoor guests were copies of the indoor partygoers, the same laughter at the same jokes, the same shop talk. There were a few kids who seemed parentless scattered around the yard like décor, the girls playing jacks on the lawn where no girl ever played jacks and the boys playing catch with mitts so new, they'd never felt the smack of a fastball. Lawrence Cutler manned a grill, maneuvering steaks and hamburgers, kneeling to study their position, then re-arranging them. A photographer daubed barbecue sauce onto Cutler's apron, then snapped a flurry of pictures of the chef at work. The meat was plastic, Jean realized, the smoke curled up from smudge pots hidden beneath the grill.

They moved to a bar where a middle-aged Filipino man in a red vest was mixing drinks.

"Reuben, why don't you show Mrs. Vale here how it's done," Claridge said.

Reuben pulled out a chilled beaker and a martini glass from beneath the bar, and lovingly poured Jean her drink.

"Reuben's the bartender at the Saint Francis. I believe he served General MacArthur following his ... dismissal by the president, do I have that right, sir?"

Rueben smiled and nodded.

"I hired him when I learned I was going to have to endure one of Frances and Lawrence's casual California shindigs."

"And does Mrs. Claridge join you on your tours of West Coast shindigs?"

"Sadly, my Anne died three years ago. But no, she didn't enjoy politicking, and that's really what all this is," he said.

"I'm sorry to hear about your wife," Jean said. "You still wear your wedding ring. A lot of men wouldn't, and a few women for that matter."

"To marriage, the glue of American life." They toasted, and Jean sipped the martini. She had never been much of a drinker, but today she appreciated the bite of the alcohol, its bitter attack on the throat.

"Were you really a spy behind enemy lines, Mr. Claridge?"

"I spent the war captaining a desk. The glory and skullduggery accrued to others. I just picked up a few parlor tricks along the way."

"And now, you sit in Congress?"

"My stars no. Who in their right mind would elect me? I do seem to do appointments rather well though. I sit on various advisory boards and committees—the life blood of our nation, or so it sometimes seems."

"What do you advise on?"

"Scientific and engineering matters mostly. Occasionally I stray into policy."

"And you advise who?

"Oh, everyone, from small American companies doing pioneering work, all the way up to the top."

"The president?"

"It's been my good fortune to have his ear a few times, yes."

Jean flushed. Was it the martini or the aura of assured power that emanated from Claridge? She realized that she admired accomplished men who carried themselves modestly. Now, she was flat-out blushing.

Increased sociability, no nausea or abdominal pain yet.

"I've never met anyone who's met the president."

The photographer moved towards them, waving his hands. "Act natural, profile turned to the sun when possible," the photographer said. "It's the good life in California. You're soaking it up." Jean turned away. She was not anxious to appear in anyone's close-up.

"Frances assures me that they'll use no more than ten or twelve shots. The chances of either of us being immortalized in print are slim." Claridge prowled off to inspect the landscaping. Jean followed. There was no lawn, just formations of severely pruned shrubs and white concrete planter boxes sprouting spiky, unidentifiable shoots.

"I hear you've been having a deuce of a time," Claridge said.

"It's been rough on my son." Jean said. "Although he hides it pretty well." Jean motioned towards the living room. Jimmy was sitting on the floor next to Monica Herndon, a dark-haired girl in a pink dress, white socks and red sandals, a black scarf draped artfully around her neck, which could not have been her own idea. They were watching a built-in television as another photographer clicked away, moving them closer until their knees were nearly touching.

"Where does the investigation stand at this point?" he asked.

"There's no trace of my husband and I'm a crazy woman spouting wild, improbable theories."

"I'm sure it's not that bad."

"The police are dismissive. No help at all."

"Well, the hell with them. Take steps on your own. You know your husband best."

"Oh, I have." She felt a flare of courage, even recklessness, as the martini and the isoniazid mixed, pulsing an electrical buzz through her arms and legs. "For example, Frances doesn't think I know about the warehouse or factory or whatever it is on Middlefield Road."

"You mean the new office park up in the hills? Lawrence showed me sketches. Impressive."

"No, I mean the unmarked building where the blackout buses are parked."

"That sounds mysterious indeed." Claridge sneezed boisterously. "Pardon me, I seem to be allergic to California. Another round?"

Jean nodded yes. Claridge marched to the bar, and she watched as he and Frances Cutler exchanged a look through the sliding glass door. She thought she detected a subtle nod from Frances. Meaning what?

She looked around for Lawrence Cutler, but he had left the barbecue grill. She strolled through the garden, gliding her hand across the cool plasterwork on the planter boxes. There was a flash of white between the cypress trees. Cutler, still in his chef's apron, slipped around the corner of the house to the side yard. She followed and saw a man striding across the pink flagstone path to meet Cutler. Gangly, bony, wearing a knee length canvas smock, in his late thirties. His face was deeply tanned and weather-worn, a terrain of grooves and lines. His pupils were huge, like a wolf with night vision and they were focused on Cutler. He acted worried, not panicked, but getting there. Cutler planted his hands on the man's shoulders to calm him. Whatever Cutler said, it didn't work, the man pulled away, his arms whirly gigging. He glanced over his shoulder at a gray panel truck parked in the middle of the street, riding low on its suspension, overloaded. Jean edged closer, trying to overhear the conversation, but breezy jazz piano suddenly plinked from outdoor speakers tucked among the eaves. Cutler shook his head 'no' at the man, over and over.

Someone brushed past Jean—one of the photographers, draped in cameras. He snapped a couple of pictures before realizing that he had intruded on a private scene. The gangly man lunged at the startled photographer, yanked the offending camera from around his neck, snapping the strap and dashed it to the ground. There was a motionless second, as if everyone were posing for one of the party shots.

The gangly man edged backwards, those eyes boring into the photographer, making himself memorable which was probably the opposite of what he intended. Then he spun and hurried to the street. The panel truck started up with the roar of a heavy engine and pulled away. Claridge walked up, calm, martini-flushed, and picked up the camera. Jean saw that momentary fluttering of his hand. After a brief glance from Claridge, Cutler guided the photographer back to the party, pulling cash out of his wallet. At that moment, Jean realized that Vann Claridge outranked Lawrence Cutler, president of Braden Enright, husband of the founder's daughter.

Isoniazid, do your stuff. How about another one ... half of one ...

Jean didn't bother to disguise the move, opening the pill bottle, breaking a tablet in half, then—what the hell?—took both halves, washing them down with a swallow of ice-cold gin.

"Who was that fellow? More to the point, who are *you* Mr. Claridge?" She poked him with her index finger, her voice rising. "And what's so all fired important about that camera that a *presidential advisor* needs to get his hands on it?"

"Maybe my martinis are a bit strong for you, Mrs. Vale." He winked at her. "They've been known to knock an assistant secretary of state onto his well-upholstered ass. I see Frances waving at me, so I best mingle as ordered." Claridge headed for the buffet, smiling, nodding, sipping. He plucked the olive from his martini, popped it into his mouth. Then she saw him set the martini down, open the camera and remove the film, holding it up the sun.

"Smile, Jean!" It was Bev Herndon, with the movie camera that seemed permanently attached to her face, husband Bill in her wake like an assistant. Bev wore a plaid shirt knotted at the waist, and khaki trousers. Bill was dressed in a blue jacket over gray slacks. Unlike many couples whose styles gradually merged, Bev and Bill refused to mirror each other. She'd seen

Bill dressed as a beachcomber while Bev was dolled up in costume diamonds and a cocktail dress like Gloria Graham.

"Bev. Great to see you!" Jean roared, pulling her into an embrace.

"Yeah, you too," she said, set off balance. "I'm getting some good stuff with Jimmy and Monica. Kinda cute together. I saw Jimmy giving her pickpocket lessons. Greg Summerville's claiming it was Jimmy who snagged his wallet out of his shorts."

"So, listen, Bev, after gallivanting across post-war Europe for the War Department with that camera of yours, you still do some of the advertising work at B.E. don't you? Short films, that kind of thing?"

"Now and then. They figure if I could make Europe in ruins look good, I could do wonders for the assembly lines."

"Did you ever film down at the Middlefield Road office?"

The isoniazid is very, very, very ... interesting.

"You know, the top-secret location that even we long-term employees don't know about," Jean said. She loomed into Bev, lowering her voice. "Just whisper it to me Bev. We're pals, you can trust me."

"I don't think we have—"

Bev was interrupted by Frances, her hostess smile beaming artificially. The happy faces, the quiet joviality of the guests, the cooing admiration of the Cutler home's "clean lines"—all of it was artificial. Jean was real, the martini was real, the vanished Robert was real.

"Jean, we need to talk," Frances said. The Herndons scampered away, Bev tossing a forced casual wave over her shoulder. "This is a little awkward, but Lawrence and I have a request."

"Shoot".

"We'd like to ask you to clear it with us first, before you make any more television appeals."

"I have to ask your permission to search for my husband?"

"It's not an order, Jean. Just a polite request, friend to friend."

"Why isn't Lawrence here, asking me himself?" Jean said,

"He's waiting in his study." Frances took her by the elbow. "This way." Frances guided them along the side of the house to steps that led down to a door that was below ground level. They moved along a concrete corridor stacked with gardening tools, passing a metal door with a combination lock.

"That where you keep the family jewels?" Jean asked.

Frances laughed. "It's a modified version of a concrete bomb shelter; reinforced with steel for greater flexibility. That seems to be the key. Vented gasoline generator provides power. Lawrence's idea really. The first one on our block, maybe in the entire Peninsula."

"What does he know that the rest of us don't?"

"That his saxophone practice is best done privately. Here we are."

Frances opened a door to a spacious office, its open windows channeled in laughter and shafts of sunlight from the yard. But the view of the partygoers was from the knees down only, a strange, sort of spooky perspective. Lawrence Cutler was seated at a large desk stacked with files and technical drawings. The walls were lined with photographs of pilots and bombers, mechanics and bombers, WACs and bombers. A saxophone rested on an arm chair in front of a music stand. Airplane engine parts decorated the book shelves, pristine and dramatically lit, like museum pieces, not a trace of grease or grit. The place of honor was held by a Colt pistol, the official U.S. military side arm of World War Two.

Big band jazz filled the room until Cutler switched off a speaker system recessed into the wall.

"We've routed our hi-fi system throughout the house. That way Lawrence can practice along with the greats." Frances said.

"Just me and Benny Goodman," Cutler said. "Sorry to take you away from the party, Jean, but this won't take long." He flicked a wall switch and a giant ceiling fan made from airplane propeller blades began a slow, lumbering spin. Jean was startled by the strength of the breeze that filled the room. "Look closely, you'll see a signature on one of the blades. Lana Turner. A week after her visit to the base, Daisy Mae—that was the plane's name—was hit hard over Essen, made it back on two engines. Saint Lana the boys took to calling her."

Outside his window, the garden party was growing louder as the level in the liquor bottles went down. Cutler lowered the venetian blinds. "Lousy damn day for a party, considering the Robert situation. None of us is much in the mood I guess," he said. Jean and Frances took up positions at opposite ends of a couch stacked with National Geographics. Cutler leaned against the front of his desk, like a boss trying to ingratiate himself with the workers on a Friday afternoon.

"I'll be frank. Your public appearances are not helpful at this point," he said.

She laughed. A harsh, scornful laugh that she didn't recognize. "Not helpful to who?"

"We will find Robert. And I have a certain pull with the police."

"I noticed. You used to be in the business of making heroes. Now you make cowards out of our local cops."

Oooh, nasty and attacking ... this feels goooood.

Frances clasped a consoling hand on Jean's. "We understand you're going through a personal crisis. But B.E. is at a very sensitive stage, and we don't feel the focus should be on missing employees right now. It's a distraction."

"And why do you have men outside my house ... *inside* my house like burglars?"

"Jean, please, you and Vann's martinis were clearly not made for each other," Frances said. Jean realized she was still holding her glass, which she drained in a gulp, slamming it down on Cutler's desk with such force that the olive popped out. They watched it roll across a stack of files, then drop onto the floor.

"We have a team looking for Robert," Cutler said. "So, of course it's their business to familiarize themselves with your neighborhood. But burglars? Don't be ridiculous."

"This is my husband we're talking about, and I'll go on the Arthur Godfrey show if it will bring him back. You'd do the same if Frances were missing. Now, you promised to answer a couple of questions ..."

Weight gain, no. Anemia, not yet. Memory impairment? My memory is sharp as a tack, thank you. Feelings of suffocation? No. Well, maybe a little.

She felt hot. Everything in the room was increasing in brightness, the bomber pictures impossibly reflective in their glass frames. Her vision swam to the control panel of the speaker system. A red light was glowing. "Is that two way? Is someone listening in? Is it Vann Claridge?"

"Jean, please—" said Frances.

"Who the hell is he? Some furtive presidential advisor just waltzes into your garden party? The moment I walk in the door, you put me into his care?"

"There's nothing furtive about Vann, at least not since he was a mucky muck in the OSS," Cutler said. "He was instrumental in the post-war recovery of Europe as well. He's a public figure with a biography any of us would envy. And he knows his way around the government purse strings. We're in a very competitive business climate, and he's advising us on a few projects; projects that that will pay for this state's growth— your streets, your sewers, Jimmy's education, all the way through college."

"Tell me about the building on Middlefield Road, Jean said.

"That is one of our facilities, yes," Cutler said."

"I never shipped anything there or took delivery of a single item bound for that address. I never even knew it existed."

"It started up after you left."

"Robert never mentioned it either. Employee number 99, who's given you eight years of his life. And you kept him in the dark."

Cutler sighed, about to give a stern lecture to a stubborn child. "The work we're doing there is taking us in different directions and requires different scientific disciplines. It's an expansion of our business, which has always been to measure and calibrate the physical world and its related phenomena. We have a great deal of respect for Robert, but this work is outside his area of engineering experience—it's sure as hell beyond mine. This will put us in direct competition with the big fellas like Bell, maybe Varian, even Lockheed."

"It puts us ahead of them, actually," Frances added. "As long as we keep it under wraps."

The light was so bright behind Cutler, a piercing halo, it made her squint. *We squint to discern the truth, don't we, to see the fine grains in the bigger picture.* She felt short of breath and, oh boy, here it comes...

""So, are we clear on where we stand?" Frances asked.

No, we aren't clear at all, Jean thought. If Robert wasn't working on the new project, why was he watching the facility from Spivey's? The most disturbing answer was that he was spying on B.E. for another company. Since Robert didn't get the promotion he had expected, had he turned on them to make more cash? Would they do something to Robert if they caught him? Maybe they had already caught him. Maybe the case was closed, now they were covering their trail.

Nausea, abdominal pain, an overwhelming urge to vomit ...

She got to her feet, but the swirling in her stomach slammed her to the side, she listed, like a newsreel battleship that had taken a torpedo. She felt herself falling toward the bookshelves, sensed arms beneath her shoulders, Cutler's arms with hair that tickled through her blouse, Frances' arms that clanked with bracelets. She shook them off, righted herself. "The bathroom is ...?"

Below ground. Windowless. No shiny fixtures, no radiantly-heated floors. No frills, like a service station restroom. Perfect for that houseguest who embarrasses herself. She crouched, grabbing the edges of the toilet as her innards growled and heaved. But nothing came. It was nausea without possibility of relief. She thought of the singing drunk who used to beg for spare change outside the State Theater in downtown Modesto. "Did you ever hear the story of Willie the Weeper, he had a job as a chimney sweeper, he had the habit and he had it bad ..." The first man she had ever seen truly sloshed.

A tapping at the door. "Jean, you all right in there?" Cutler asked.

"I'm fine." She got to her feet. Her stomach still hammered at her, but she forced herself to ignore it. She would apologize to the Cutlers, slink out the side yard to avoid the crowd and never again attend any event billed as "California Entertaining."

Another knock on the door.

"I'm coming. Hold your horses."

When Jean opened the door, Jimmy was there, Cutler standing behind him.

"Your boy caught a glimpse of you through the window, found his way down here," Cutler said. "I'll give you two a moment." Then Cutler returned to his office.

"SOMETHING'S UP," Jimmy said.

He closed the door, turned on the water and flushed the toilet, going into all-out cloak and dagger mode. "Dad sent us mail."

"What?"

"Grandpa Tamarkin just told me."

"He's here? At the party?"

"No, he's in the car. We used the horn code. Four short, three long, one short, so I went out and talked to him."

"What kind of mail?" Jean asked.

"I don't know. He called Mrs. Gillett from the corner to report in and she told him."

"OK, let's vamoose." She straightened her dress, threw water on her face. "How do I look?" Jimmy frowned at the question; moms didn't ask sons how they looked. She eased open the door, but Jimmy grabbed her wrist.

"One more thing." He was smirking with pride, drawing the moment out.

"Well ...?"

"While I was giving Monica pickpocket lessons, I found this. In that tall guy's suit pocket." It was a metal-framed identification badge issued to Vann Claridge, granting him "Authorized access: Calcite Division." A photograph of him posed against a height chart: he was six-foot-two. His signature ran vertically up the left side of the badge, Lawrence Cutler's signature was on the right, dated yesterday, captioned, "Authorizing Officer."

What was the Calcite Division? Where was it? Why had Vann Claridge been granted admittance by Lawrence Cutler? No time to mull or stew—they had to get home to the mail. She and Jimmy went back out to the yard. The party sounded like it was winding down, slurred thank yous and goodbyes. As they headed for the side gate, hoping to slink out unnoticed. Frances called out.

"Jean, Jimmy!" She scurried after them, handed Jean her pocket book. "You left this at the bar."

"Yeah, the bar. My first mistake." She scowled at Jimmy, who still held Claridge's ID badge. He snuck it back into his jeans. "Frances, I'm so sorry. I wasn't the best ambassador for former B.E. employees today."

"Honey, as put together as I like to think of myself, there are more than a few parties to which I will not be reinvited. So please, don't feel bad on our account."

"Well, it was a wonderful time anyway."

Jean shook Frances' hand. They left through the side gate, picking their way across the rock garden. Jean spotted the Nash at the end of the street, which was crowded with partygoers' cars backing out and doing U-turns. Grandpa Tamarkin was leaning against the driver's side door, polishing his sunglasses on his sleeve. When he spotted Jean and Jimmy, he ran up to them. "There was a gray car, no windows, not sure what you call it in English ..."

"A panel truck," Jean said.

"Yes, that. A man ran to it from the house, and drove off very, very fast."

"I saw that man at the party. There was a fight," Jean said. "Did you get a chance to talk to him?"

"No, but I made a memory of the license: 44-907, Nevada."

Nevada again, Jean thought. "Great work, Grandpa Tamarkin. Can you drive us?" Jean asked, as she wilted into the back seat. Jimmy piled into the front.

Tamarkin puffed up, as though he were proud to serve as her chauffeur. "My license is temporary, you know. I must have driving teacher with me."

"I'm your instructor for today. So, home please, and don't run any red lights."

Tamarkin clunked through the gears and jerked into low. As they drove off, Jean twisted to look out the back window. Clouds had gathered above the Santa Cruz Mountains, brushed to a delicate orange by the setting sun, another perfect California twilight. She saw the Cutlers watching her from the doorway of their dream house, Lawrence's hand curled around Frances' waist. For several seconds, her nausea returned.

6

The mail seemed to be looking up at her, challenging her to discover its secrets. Jean had imagined she would tear it open the moment she took it out of the freezer; instead, she laid it on the dining room table, while Helen, Grandpa Tamarkin and Jimmy took seats, as though waiting for dinner to be served.

On the way back home, Jimmy had been unusually quiet.

"What?" she snapped.

"They said you got sick back there."

"The food didn't agree with me."

"I was worried it was another ..."

"Another what?"

"Spell, attack—you know ..."

"I did not have another anything," she said in what Jimmy called her "and that's final" voice. In a couple of years, she knew he would not accept anything as "final," but for the moment, he let the subject alone.

There were three over-stuffed, 8x10 packing envelopes sealed with staples and tape and some kind of extra strength glue. The envelope was addressed to Robert in his own handwriting; there was no return address. The envelopes had been postmarked in Mountain View, three days earlier.

"Do you think it means dad's OK?" Jimmy asked.

"Yes, sweetheart, I do."

Did she? She had no idea what would be inside. Files stolen from B.E.? Some sort of communication to the family? Had Robert written his address voluntarily, or had some band of kidnappers forced him? Jean ran her hands over the envelope, feeling the textures that Robert had so recently touched. It was still cold from the two hours it had spent in the freezer.

"It wouldn't fit in the mailbox, so the mailman left it at your front door," Helen said. "I was watching the house, so I thought I better get it before someone else does. When Roman called, he told me to put it in the freezer. I had no idea why."

Jean clasped Helen's hand in gratitude, nodded a thank you to Grandpa Tamarkin. "Well, here goes." Using a letter opener and a paring knife, she slit through the tape, then pried open the staples. The glue was the last barrier; cutting into it would rip the envelope and risk damaging the contents. Jean glanced skeptically at Grandpa Tamarkin. He wore a satisfied grin, fresh from his triumph behind the wheel.

"It will be good, believe me. Tap it first."

Jean tapped the envelope heavily on the edge of the table. Then using the letter opener, she cut through the flap as the glue cracked off into tiny pieces. Seconds later, she had it open while leaving it intact.

"Wow, neat!" Jimmy exclaimed.

Jean gave Grandpa Tamarkin a kiss on the cheek. He smiled modestly. "I learned to work with what we have—all of Russia is a freezer."

Jean slid the contents out of the envelope. There were stacks of papers—carbon copies of typescripts, blue-tinted mimeos, official looking documents with letterheads.

"Good Lord, there must be a hundred pages here," Jean said. Many of the pages had underlined passages and handwritten notes in the margins. "Step one, I say we try to identify dad's handwriting," she said. "Look for dad's name, too," she added.

"Let's each take a pile," Helen suggested. "And perhaps some coffee?"

Jean got the percolator going as the others started sifting through the papers. "My team" she caught herself thinking, and she felt a funny swell of pride. She'd been a daughter, an employee, a wife, a mother, but never a team leader.

By the time the coffee was ready, the documents had been separated by date and by category. Most of the documents, whether carbon copies or mimeos bore the winged shield letterhead of the United States Army Air Force. These were further divided into papers from individual units of the Eighth Army Air Force in England—the 1st Bomb Wing, 65th Fighter Squadron, the 52nd Fighter Group and so on. The dates ran from September 1942 to January 1944. Jean did a cursory run through of the handwritten notes—she didn't recognize Robert's writing in any of them. The annotations were assessments of damage done during bombing missions. Other notes recommended delaying fuse insertion until just before takeoff. Nothing personal or revealing. Her initial thrill was edged out by disappointment and confusion. What were they looking at? Why had Robert mailed all this stuff to himself? How could it be connected to his disappearance? Robert had never served in the Army Air Force, let alone been to Europe.

"These here are crew lists," Jimmy said, raising a stack of documents that bore the Eight Air Force England and Europe letterhead. "This number at the top is the plane number and nickname: Devil's Daughter 67. This next is the tail number: 134789. And these are the names of the guys assigned to the plane with their jobs. Ten to a plane on a B-17 Flying Fortress—pilot, copilot, navigator, bombardier, ball turret gunner, etc. Last number, the long one, is their Army Air Force Serial number, you know, their dog tags."

"And these are called 'Mission Diaries," Helen said, holding a stack of postcard size forms. Each form had a series of printed categories: Date, Object, Method, Strength, Execution, followed by handwritten entries. The mission objectives were in code; there were no names of cities or even countries, but Jean assumed they referred to bombing targets in Italy or Germany that the planes would have attacked from their bases in England.

"For what are we searching, Jean?" Tamarkin asked. He pulled an expensive looking magnifying glass from his vest pocket. "Zeiss engineering for old men's eyes."

"Well, Robert's name, although I can't imagine it's there since he didn't serve. And Lawrence Cutler. Oh, and Harold Sirk, too."

They fell silent as they sorted through the dozens of lists. She had never realized how quiet their neighborhood was until at that moment when the four of them flipping pages felt like it was the only sound for miles. No cars drove by. No dogs barked. No kids laughed as they kicked a ball around.

It was drudgery and time should have dragged; instead, it whipped by. Jean stood above the table, gazing over the others' shoulders, her glance flicking from stack to stack, her eyes tuned to the word VALE, but she never saw it.

"Here's Cutler!" Jimmy shouted.

"I have it too," Helen said.

Colonel L. Cutler appeared on the crew lists and the mission diaries. He was listed as group commander of the 94th Heavy Bombardment Group of the 4th Bomb Wing, based in Bury St. Edmunds, England.

"Sirk's there too," Jean pointed out over Helen's shoulder. Warrant Officer H. Sirk was a navigator on a B-17 named Dallas Alice, tail number 178986. "Wonder if there's anything for Jimmy Stewart?" Jean asked.

"Mom, he was with the 445th. Although Clark Gable may have been here."

"All right, so I presume each group that Cutler commanded was comprised of several airplanes. Let's pull those crew lists together and see what we have."

They soon had a list of four bomber squadrons that had been under Lawrence Cutler's command—four crews and four backup crews, eighty names. Jean cross-referenced the crew lists and their plane numbers with the mission diaries and found they overlapped in several places. "It looks to me like whoever assembled these documents was focused on one or two particular squadrons, the third and the fourth."

Jean turned over the last page, and there on the back were ten lines of handwriting. Not words, just numbers and letters and random punctuation marks. "This is ... what is this? Mathematical equations?" Jean asked.

Grandpa Tamarkin scanned the page. "They are code, a rather basic one. I see possible substitution or transposition traits."

"Don't we need a codebook? And this is the Army Air Force we're talking about here. Were their codes ever broken?" Jean asked.

Grandpa Tamarkin passed the pages to Jimmy and waited. Jimmy stretched, widening his shoulders, and smiled. "I'll take that java now," he said. Jean frowned but poured him a cup of coffee. He stopped her from adding cream. He drew out the moment, relishing the unexpected dependency of the adults.

"It's a substitution cipher with Morse Code inserts. But mostly just numbers and letters. This is homemade, not military. We can crack this."

"Khoroshiy mal'chik. Good boy," Tamarkin said.

"But why is this page coded, and the others aren't?" Helen asked.

Jean felt something drift through her clouded thoughts, but it refused to settle. As Jimmy and Tamarkin sharpened pencils and began to dig into the codes, Helen got up, headed for the door. "I'll make us some dinner. *Croque monsieurs* for the table?"

Jean didn't answer. An image was taking shape just behind her eyes, but she couldn't get it into focus.

Helen gave up waiting for a response and left them to their work.

"Each line is a different length," Jimmy said. "If we knew what they meant we could begin to build the system."

"Planes? Cities they attack?" Tamarkin suggested.

Then Jean knew. She dashed to the bedroom. From the nightstand she snagged the manila envelope she'd found hidden in Robert's desk at B.E. She tore through the pages of the long personnel list as she ran back to the kitchen, nodding to herself.

"They're names!" Jean said. She laid the pages with the blacked-out names on the table. I can even give you the first letters." She drew her finger down each page, pausing at the blacked-out names, guessing the first letters from the names that appeared on the list before and after them. "A... C... C again... D... G... M... P... R... S—that will be for Sirk—and Y. Ten last names. Ten crew members."

Tamarkin and Jimmy looked impressed.

"So, is this a boy's only club, or do I get my Dick Tracy decoder ring too?"

"Well ..." Jimmy considered. "Maybe a Tess Trueheart derringer. Unloaded of course."

"Jimmy, put on a stack of your dad's records. I need some background music while I watch you men work."

They had a new Crossley record player, red as a fire truck, tucked underneath Jimmy's cardboard television. It could handle both 45 rpms and long-playing albums. As Artie Shaw's cascading clarinet and Helen Forrest's warm vocals filled the house, Jean swayed at the kitchen window, making herself a target for the shadowers, if they were out there. We know more than you think we know, she thought. When "All the Things You Are" came on, Jean trembled. She had never considered herself a romantic—there was no such thing where she grew up. She and Robert didn't have "their song." No love poems; they let the Hallmark Corporation speak their anniversary and Valentine's Day sentiments. But the music and Robert's gnawing absence—neither she or Jimmy had sat in his usual dining room chair since he'd disappeared— worked on her.

"We danced to this the night you were born. The woman in the next bed had a radio. Well, your dad danced, holding my hand in the hospital bed while he cut his usual graceful line. I was still numb on pain pills and sort of shimmied lying down, which is an improvement over my usual dance floor abilities. He had ... he *has* style, that man." Jean pounded her fist on the table and the paperwork jumped. "Even if he has goddamn vanished and left us to figure it out ... to figure *him* out."

The music played, the coffee was drained. Helen's *Croque Monsieurs* had been a hit, Jimmy ate three. Jean paced between the hallway and the kitchen, watching Jimmy and Grandpa Tamarkin at work. Impatient for results even though she had no idea how a list of ten names from back in the war would help them. The hours passed.

Shortly after eleven, Jean saw them. One stood beneath a pepper tree across the street. The other slumped in a car parked up on Echo Lane, his shadowed face streaked with light that must have come from the radio dial. She switched off the kitchen light.

"Mom, we're working here!"

"They're back. Do you recognize him, the one under the tree?" Jean asked Tamarkin. He peered over her shoulder out the kitchen window.

"No, but I am not surprised by that. They will change, so that we may not identify any certain individual."

If there were enough of them for two shifts, why not three, or four? An organized force, tightening the circle around her home and family. Jimmy was scared too; Jean saw it in the way his jaw quivered, and his lips squeezed together. She'd seen that look the day he'd jumped off the roof onto the lawn to practice his paratrooping skills. He had been frustrated that he couldn't match his friends' mastery of a battery of boyhood tricks: blowing on a blade of grass to make it whistle; snapping his armpit until it popped—well, farted. So he had decided to outdo them. She'd spotted him up there, skidding on the shingles, calculating the angle of the jump. She'd called out to stop him, but had been too late. He'd ended up with two twisted ankles and a month of enforced inactivity. The image of him in midair, his face twisted in fear, had never left her.

"They want what we have," Jean said. "They know Robert took this stuff."

"Or they're waiting for dad to come home so they can question him?" Jimmy suggested.

"Well, if they work for B.E., they work for Lawrence Cutler. Whose house I spent the afternoon at. I'm through with all this slinking around. I'm going out there to talk to them."

"And why are you so certain they work for B.E.?" Tamarkin asked.

"Well, who else?"

"We have United States Army Air Force files here. Are they secret? We are still at war, yes?"

"In Korea. This stuff is from Europe."

"Maybe other documents are missing."

"How would I know that?"

"Until you do, maybe not wise to confront them?"

Jean felt her determination flagging. "I don't know, I don't know. This is more your kind of thing, not mine."

"Mom, the guy just got out of the car. He joined the other guy, they're heading this way."

Jean locked the front door. "OK, I'm calling the police." As she reached for the phone, it rang. The clang was as loud as a fire alarm. She had turned the ringer to high after Robert disappeared so she wouldn't sleep through any calls.

"Mrs. Vale?"

"Yes, who is this?"

"It's Jessie Harper, Mrs. Vale."

"Who?"

"The janitor. From B.E."

"Oh, yes, the first-place finisher. Sorry, I didn't recognize—"

"They're still coming!" Jimmy said.

Jean marched to the kitchen window and cranked it open, the curlicue phone line stretching out behind her. "We see you out there! Whatever you've got in mind, you'll never get past this Louisville Slugger. My friends are here too, and they're just as serious!"

Jimmy broke into a grin. Jean was a bit shocked herself.

"Mrs. Vale, are you alright?" asked Jessie on the phone.

"Fine, fine. Just having a little family argument here."

The men had stopped, huddling in conversation at the top of the driveway.

"Well, I'm sorry about that, I'm sure, but—"

"Can I call you back?"

"No, please, it's urgent. I need to speak with you."

Tamarkin tapped Jean on the shoulder. She jumped.

"What concerns me is that they are not taking measures to not be seen," Tamarkin said. "Also, I am trained to recognize when a coat or jacket has a shape—a bulge do you call it—that may hide a gun. These are bad men, Jean."

The men started up the driveway, splitting up to put space between them.

"Jimmy, out the back door. I'll collect the papers. Let's go!"

"Mrs. Vale, are you there?" Jessie's voice was insistent, breathless.

"I'll call you tomorrow."

"No, it needs to be tonight!"

"OK, give me your number."

"Jean!" Tamarkin grabbed her by the shoulder. She jotted down Jessie Harper's number on the crew list, hung up the phone. She jammed the documents back into the envelopes and followed Tamarkin and Jimmy through the laundry room and out to the backyard.

The night was heavy with a humidity that was rare in the Bay Area in summer. Doves cooed from the rafters in the unfinished garage. Moonlight threw the shadows of the framing onto the patio like Halloween skeleton bones.

Jimmy led them across the lawn, around the woodpile to the slatted fence that separated their yard from the Gillett house.

"Jimmy, driving your car was quite enough difficult for me," Tamarkin said. "I cannot climb a fence!"

Jimmy pulled back the pyracantha bush that blocked a section of the fence, careful to avoid pricking himself. He pulled on the woven slats, one by one, then leaned his shoulder into the fence, revealing a small opening that had been sawed into the fence. It opened into the Gillett yard. Jean marveled at her son's secret ingenuity.

"Jimmy, when did you—"

"You take a lot of naps. Me and Frank Burke cut one into the Tremaines' yard, too," he said, indicating the yard directly behind theirs.

Jean nudged Jimmy and Tamarkin through the hidden portal. She followed, pulling the pyracantha back into place to conceal the opening.

In the Gillets' backyard, the pool excavation with its half-cemented walls felt like a dark pit, waiting to swallow them up. They picked their way around it and went in through the sliding glass back door. Helen met them, surprised by their sudden appearance.

"Helen, I need you to call the police. If they know it's me, they won't do anything." Helen nodded and led them into her kitchen. As Helen dialed, Jean and Jimmy and Tamarkin kept watch on the front of the house.

"They're still out in the driveway, mom," Jimmy reported.

"Yes, I'd like to report a burglary at 543 Kensington Drive,"

Helen said. "No, I live next door. Yes, they're in there now!" A pause as Helen listened. "My name?" she said, a prickly tone in her voice. "Helen Gillett—perhaps you've heard of my husband Frederic? He's a prominent engineer and a personal friend of William Shockley." Jean smiled at Helen's rank-pulling. Helen gave her a world-weary shrug, which only a Frenchwoman could pull off.

"OK, fine." Helen hung up. "They're sending a car. Jean, you need a cognac?"

"Booze already did me in once today. My God, was that just this afternoon?" Jean realized she was sweating. She blotted at her forehead with a dish towel.

No more than five minutes passed before a gleaming new Los Altos Police Department Ford Mainline, red light swirling, pulled into their driveway, its powerful, perfectly tuned V-8 announcing itself proudly. Jean saw two officers she didn't recognize get out of the car and walk up the path to the front door, before disappearing from her line of sight.

"I can't see a darn thing."

Helen abruptly went out the front door. They watched her stroll casually down her driveway, cross the street to the mailboxes, probe her hand around inside, raise the outgoing mail flag, then walk back, sneaking glances at Jean's house.

"The four of them are talking at your front steps," Helen said.

"Are they arresting those guys?" Jean asked.

"It didn't seem so."

A moment later, the two cops and the two mystery men reappeared, and went to the police car. One of the officers got into the front seat while the other talked with the two men. Their conversations didn't look confrontational. Nevertheless, the officer's hand rested on his holstered gun. And then it was over. The second officer broke off his chat with the mystery men and got into the car. The red light cut off and the police car drove away. The mystery men smiled at each other like a couple of teenagers who had just talked their way out of a speeding ticket. They walked up Echo Lane to their own car. They got in, then drove two houses closer to the intersection of Echo and Kensington. They parked, cut the engine, and sat there.

"Looks like they're here to stay. My babysitters."

"I do not think they had time to get into the house," Grandpa Tamarkin said. "Even if they did, they couldn't find the files, so they'll wait for you to make a move. To see if you go to any place or meet anyone to pass them the files."

"So, if I go to the cleaners, in their minds I could be on a secret mission. I can't leave the house without them on my tail. Which means conducting my life by telephone."

Tamarkin gave Jean a serious look. She nodded, finally understanding.

"They may have some way of listening in?" she asked.

"It must be considered. Perhaps they put something on your phone when they broke in."

Jean thought of the urgent phone call from Jessie Harper. Had they overheard her call? Were they now sending a team to Jessie's home as well?

She got out the number she'd written down, picked up Helen's kitchen wall phone, and called her back.

"Mrs. Vale, is that you?"

"Yes, it's me."

"Listen, can you come down here?"

"Is there anyone outside your home? Anyone suspicious looking, I mean?"

"I'm not at home, Mrs. Vale. I'm at a phone booth. Across the street from B.E."

Jean felt a ripple of fear in her stomach. "Is this somehow connected to my husband?"

"I think so, yes."

"You're not at the Palo Alto facility, are you?"

"No ma'am. I'm out on Middlefield."

"I'm on my way."

Jean hung up the phone, looked out the kitchen window. The surveillance car was still there, the silhouettes of the watchers shrouded in darkness.

"Jean, you can't go anywhere as long as they are out there. It's not safe," Helen said.

Jean paced, wishing that she smoked, that her hands and fingers and breath could busy themselves, instead of clenching up. "I could go out the back way that Jimmy cut through the Tremaines' yard. You could bring your car around and get me. If I could just borrow it for an hour."

"We're coming with you," Helen said.

"This is my problem right now, not yours. Better if you stay here, keep an eye on those men. Jimmy and Grandpa Tamarkin, you keep working on the code."

Tamarkin nodded. "But Jean, when you reach this place, I insist you call us. There are only three people in the world you can trust at this moment, and they are all here."

"Not counting Robert," Jean said.

Tamarkin simply arched an eyebrow.

Back in their own yard, Jimmy helped Jean remove stacks of wood to reveal the doorway he had cut into the back fence. There was a dense stand of juniper on the Tremaines' side of the yard, which concealed the hole; lights were on in the house. She hugged Jimmy, then pushed through the juniper onto a lawn. At the rear of the house was a half-framed lanai; someone was moving around inside. Jean saw Marilyn Tremaine padding through the lanai, her sleepless newborn daughter blanketed and squirming on her shoulder. Beyond the lanai, in the family room, she spotted Don Tremaine kneeling at a television trying to tune in a signal. Marilyn had bragged about the family room during an over the fence conversation; an extra room soon to be filled with Naugahyde furniture, hi-fi equipment and meat freezers until it was so overstuffed, there would be no room for the family. Jean ducked from tree to tree as she hurried across the Tremaine's lawn and down the side of the yard to the cul-de-sac of Arbolito Way.

Two minutes later, Helen pulled up in her sensible, two-door Plymouth, kept the engine running and Jean slipped into the driver's seat. They nodded and Jean drove off, studying Helen in the rearview mirror. She looked resigned, worried maybe, as she waved in the streetlight's stingy glow.

7

VALE PRIVATE INVESTIGATIONS – Discrete, Dedicated, Deadly

From: Field Operative (F.O.) J. Vale

To: Senior Operative (S.O) J.M. Vale

Subject: Search for Missing Person XYZ.

Time: 022:35

Case Status: XYZ has been gone four days now. Currently following leads. Local police are no help. Not a Dick Tracy anywhere.

Current location: Bivouac at temporary HQ. Assisted by G.Tamarkin and H. Gillett.

Progress Update: Mysterious code found on back of documents submitted by XYZ has been cracked. Solution below:

Line 1 – Neal Boardner Clark, 27, pilot

Line 2 – William Creighton Slansky, 23, copilot

Line 3 – Harold John Sirk, 26, navigator

Line 4 – Randall Manero Ravetto, 24, bombardier and nose gunner

Line 5 – Maxwell Alan Prentice 26, radio officer and top turret gunner

Line 6—Roger Napoleon Duval, 25, engineer

Line 7 – Frank Ramsey Alvarez, 22, waist gunner
Line 8 – Delbert Ian Connelly 25, waist gunner
Line 9 – Preston Banner McHale 21, tail gunner
Line 10 – Morris Ralph Gupman 27, ball-turret gunner
Course of Action: Consultations needed with S.O. Vale

THE FACILITY on Middlefield Road was as closed down and dead looking as the first time Jean had seen it. There was no lobby or entrance, so she didn't know where to look for Jessie Harper. Maybe Jessie had called from Spivey's Drive-In, but Jean saw no sign of her. It was after 10 p.m. and the restaurant was lonely looking. Instead of the usual teenage couples, men and women sat by themselves at booths meant for four, or at the counter with several stools as a conversation buffer between them. Drinking coffee or milkshakes, their taste buds perhaps longing for a Burgie. Jean continued up Middlefield, turned left and saw Jessie Harper standing in the light of a phone booth at a closed post office. Jean parked in the lot. Jessie hurried over to the car and Jean opened the passenger door for her to slide in. She was wearing a crisp white shirt with a Richfield Hi Octane patch over the pocket, like a service station attendant, and a pair of black slacks with gold stripes running down the leg.

"Thank you for coming, Mrs. Vale. It's Connie Latimer, you remember her, we work together? She's in there and she hasn't come out." Jessie said.

"In where?" Jean asked.

Jessie nodded across the street to a windowless, one-story warehouse-style building that crouched dark and mute behind a low cement wall that was capped with chain link. On the roof of the building, antennas of various sizes shot up like needles in a sewing kit.

"Is that part of the new B.E. facility?"

"They call it the South Shop, but it's B.E. all right. Connie's been cleaning in there for the last two weeks. She's got a special clearance to work it. Tonight, she called, said she needed some help, maybe she could get me on for some extra hours."

Jean nodded, unsure where Jessie was leading.

"Connie went in, told me to wait by the pay phone. It's a job, I didn't ask why, I figured she'd have to pave the way for me with her boss. But it's not just that; she's been behaving oddly for a while. Ever since she started in there."

"I don't understand—how does this concern my husband?"

"Well, Connie thinks maybe he was here."

"Why would she think that?"

"Those of us who work after hours, who clean up, we're invisible, but we still have eyes. They try to hide things, make people and God knows what vanish."

"What are you talking about?"

"Wastebaskets. Crumpled paper bearing names. Reports. Memos. They don't think we see as we snatch up the coffee-stained scraps and toss them into our barrels, but we do. We know who works at which desk, we notice when a nameplate, or family pictures, or personally engraved pencils are gone. We notice when men who worked at the plant one day are gone the next."

"Could just be routine transfers."

"That's what Connie thought. But then—"

"Wait a sec," Jean said. "What did you mean by 'he *was* here'?"

"Connie says this is some sort of way station. Transfer here is just temporary."

"Why is any of this Connie's business?"

"That I couldn't tell you, Mrs. Vale. She's just always been the nosy sort."

"How long has she been inside?"

"About an hour and change."

"Could mean anything. Her boss sent her to another building, she's on a break."

"Yes, I suppose that could be."

Jean thought of the blacked-out bus and its hidden passengers. Were they volunteers? Transfers? If this was a way station, what was the final destination?

"Do you know the name 'Harold Sirk'?" Jean asked.

"Rings a bell. He might work in the tooling shop. Yes, I think he's one of them who made the move over here. You got a tire iron in this trunk?"

They got out of the car. Jessie pulled a crowbar out of her slacks. What once would have seemed absurd to Jean, now presented itself as the only natural course. Jean rooted through Helen's trunk until she found a spindly looking tire wrench.

"Can't do much business with that. Go for the jack," Jessie said.

Jean lifted out the jack, which was so heavy her arms drooped. She struggled to lift it parallel to the ground, like a baseball bat.

"There you go, leverage. Real Roy Campanella. And I thought I was gonna have to educate you, Mrs. Vale."

"Jean ..."

"We're not friends yet. Let's see how this goes."

They strode across the street to the wall that surrounded the building. Jean found herself staring at Jessie's strange outfit.

"Yeah, about my get-up tonight. I live above a laundry operated by a friend of mine. You'd be amazed at how many clothes customers never show up to claim that are just my size. Really saves on the wardrobe budget." Jean smiled, recognizing a kindred spirit, someone whose life had taught her to count her nickels and dimes.

A padlocked gate broke up the fence, enough for a single line of workers to file in and out. The South Shop, with its brown, lumpy stucco finish, windowless façade and squat profile, was the ugliest building she had ever seen. Two low wattage light fixtures were impaled in the walls, dingy and useless.

"We have a plan?" Jean asked.

Jessie laughed, turning her face up to the moon, half a pie glowing through the clouds. "The man in the moon's got plans. You and me, we got four arms and a few pounds of iron. So come on, give with it." Jessie nodded at the thick chained pad lock that wrapped around the gate. Jean swung the jack above her head and slammed it down. Her aim was slightly off, but it didn't matter.

"Shit, it was already unlocked," Jessie said, dropping her voice to a whisper. "Somebody must've opened it from the inside while I was on the phone." Jessie slipped off the lock, shouldered open the gate and they ducked through. Jessie reattached the lock, and they headed for the warehouse.

"Hey, hey," shouted an urgent voice. A night watchman puffed after them, a pale figure in dark slacks and a starched gray shirt with black tie and black trimmed pockets. He clenched a nightstick in his fist. Handcuffs dangled from his belt but he didn't appear to have a gun. He seemed agitated, darting glances over his shoulder.

"We're closed. You can't be in here."

Jessie showed the watchman her employee badge. "I'm on the custodial staff, sir. I'm here to meet my co-worker for a special assignment tonight." As the watchman scrutinized the pass, Jean noticed his nametag: "Randy Crane."

"You're OK, I guess. But what about her?"

"She's my supervisor," Jessie answered.

"You got any identification?" Crane asked Jean. She fumbled through her pocketbook with one hand, the jack feeling clumsy and incriminating.

"My car broke down on the way in, and I called her to come get me," Jessie added.

"I'll still need her ID," Crane said.

Jean hesitated. If she revealed her identity and Robert was really here, perhaps even held against his will, would she make things worse?

"OK, I don't like this one little bit," Crane said. "Let's go to my office. I'll make a couple calls and straighten this out." Crane nudged Jessie and Jean toward a walkway that led between the warehouse and the fence. Jessie looked at Jean, asking for help, for ideas, but Jean felt empty. They followed Crane down the walkway. Suddenly, they heard a rumble from inside the warehouse and the exterior lights dimmed.

"Old Sparky, huh?" Jessie joked.

"If you'd really been cleared to work here, you'd know we're shutting it down, not cranking it up. Come one, move it." Crane's face stretched tight, as though it were running out of skin. He seemed like he was considering whether to use his nightstick on a woman. Then Jean went way out on a limb.

"Randy Crane! You were a first sergeant, 305th Bomb Group based at Bury St. Edmonds."

Crane stopped. "And you are who exactly?"

"Dottie Crandall. Maiden name's Sirk, you know, Harold's older sister?"

"Don't know anyone named Sirk. And I wasn't a sergeant and I wasn't in the 305th and I wasn't at Bury St. Edmonds." Jean was dying, flailing as she went down, so why not keep going.

"But you were over there, I'm guessing. You got that look about you."

The vanity of a flier is purer than that of any other soldier, she remembered Lawrence Cutler saying, maybe during the infamous dinner at the house. "I was in the 92nd. Out of Alconbury," Crane said. "We flew the most disciplined combat boxes in Europe. That's why so many of us made it home." Jean nodded, but there was something in her nod and her nervous hands that Crane didn't like. "Or maybe I never left the States and am making it up. You're a pretty brazen goddamn liar, and for that I'll give you credit."

"Mr. Crane, listen—," Jessie began.

"Shut the hell up, both of you." Crane brought out his handcuffs and grabbed Jean by the wrists. "At orientation, they told us the Reds were busy as fire ants recruiting people to dig into our secrets, and I wonder if I've caught me one now." Cuffed to Jean by his left wrist, he clamped a bear-trap grip on Jessie's upper arm. He started to propel them along the path again, when they heard a voice behind them shout "Randy!"

Another watchman stepped out of the warehouse, his posture rigid as a rifle barrel. "I need you in here. Ambulance is on its way. I want the back gate opened. Some of the brass just showed up and their hands are full as you can imagine."

"I've got problems of my own here, Chuck," Crane said.

"Tonight you sneak your girlfriends in? Of all nights?" Chuck hustled back into the warehouse. Crane sighed, orders were orders. He reversed course, trying to drag Jean with him. But Jessie blocked his path. "Double time it," Chuck yelled from inside the warehouse. Crane unlocked the handcuffs, shot the women a murderous look, then ran off.

"Let's see if there's a back door," Jessie said. Jean dropped the jack behind the chain link, and they continued along the path until they reached the rear of the warehouse. Two tall doors that ran on tracks were opened about a foot, like parted theater curtains. Jean and Jesse risked a peek inside.

It wasn't a warehouse.

The floor space was expansive. Lab benches and desks lined the walls. There were several rows of filing cabinets. *The Army Air Force documents*, Jean thought. *Robert got them here.* At the center of the building, a giant cylindrical storage tank, sprouting with pipes and hoses, squatted on a cement foundation. The tank looked large enough to stand in. It was an ungainly, riveted device that seemed to have tumbled from the pages of Jules Verne—it did not look like the product of B.E.'s best engineering minds, or a vision of the future that would lead the company in new directions. Built into the left side of the tank were three small, aircraft-style windows. A camera tripod was set up outside the windows. A short flight of stairs led to a door in the tank. At the bottom of the steps, three men in white shirts and business slacks stood shoulder to shoulder, looking down at the floor. B.E. executives, Jean thought. Their faces were stoic; "bad news faces" she called them, the expression you adopted when a business deal was about to turn sour. Two of the executives broke away and headed off, revealing a shape lying on the floor. The third man, his sleeves rolled up, a stethoscope dangling from his neck, crouched next to it. Jean saw that it was a human figure, covered by a blanket. The contents of a first aid kit were scattered around the body, evidence of a frantic life-saving effort.

They heard a deep mechanical groan, and the heavy doors began to slide open wider. Jean and Jessie ducked out of the trail of light spilling through the doors, and edged along a narrow alley that paralleled the building.

"We need to see who that is!" Jean whispered.

Was it Robert? She'd lain awake, imagining how she would find him: wandering the city alone and amnesiac; at a poker game, indulging a secretive gambling jag; drunk in an alley, a furtive wino all these years; entwined in the arms of some floozy—never a lady, never a true rival. In her fantasies, Robert never rose, he always fell; without her and Jimmy, he never became noble or heroic. What would it mean if he were dead on the floor of his employer's secret facility, shrouded in an Army surplus blanket, the focus of intense, murmured discussion?

They found a grimy, wire-meshed window, and squeezed themselves between two heating units so they could both see in.

A chunky man in shirtsleeves was bustling toward the tank, carrying a camera. He knelt over the body, the lens like a snout, sniffing for blood. The medic lowered the blanket, and the photographer fired way, flashbulbs blazing before they were ejected to the floor.

It wasn't Robert.

"Sweet Jesus," gasped Jessie. "It's Connie." Her eyes were closed, her face was gray and lined with red wrinkles, thin as threads. Her fingernails were an ugly, flecked blue, as though she'd been to a colorblind manicurist.

An ambulance rolled into the building, no siren, no flashing light, the two executives guiding it to Connie's body.

"That machine, that thing, it killed Connie," Jessie said. Tears dotted her cheeks; she quickly wiped them away. "We got to get out of here."

"This is Robert's company! Your company. I used to work for them ..."

"So did Connie. Same thing could happen to your husband if we stick around."

Jessie backed away from the window. She began to dig around in the trash cans like a cat probing for a scrap of food. She came up with a neat roll of cloth, then unfurled it into a full-length janitor's apron.

"This is Connie's," Jessie said. "She wouldn't just throw it away. It's here for a reason." Jessie searched the apron pockets and pulled out a few scraps of crumpled paper, stuffed them into her pants.

Then they ran for it, the night quiet, the streets empty. Jean glanced back, hoping that Robert would materialize to explain everything. But all she could see was a tall rectangle of glaring light, and behind it the silhouettes of B.E. engineers hovering studiously over Connie Latimer, as though she were nothing more than a backfired experiment.

8

All happy American families look alike, the Director mused. Their happiness is driven by a belief in the future's wide-open spaces. Death and darkness have been left behind; chrome-trimmed cars, Orlon and Dacron await them. Even A-bomb tests on television can't slow down the optimism train.

Here we are at war again and the country seemed not to notice.

And here *they* were. His happy Americans. Clipped from the pages of the B.E. newsletter "Measuring Up," the Vales photographed well, genial strivers who smiled, but didn't grin. At a company picnic, the wife in blue jeans and a flannel shirt —the Director suspected hay rides were part of the festivities— the husband wearing a blazer and light-colored slacks, never able to completely relax, his eyes focused somewhere beyond the photographer's lens, the son in a dusty t-shirt, a kid who got into things, but never so deeply that he couldn't get out.

Happy, yes. And perhaps threatened in unique, unprecedented ways.

He tucked the photos into his copy of Michener's *Return to Paradise*—he'd left the Tolstoy at home, preferring light reading when he traveled. He switched out his brown reading glasses for a lighter pair with no lower frames. He looked around the airport, taking comfort from the busy or bored swirl of life around him: kids begging their mothers for ice cream and being denied; white-gloved Pan Am stewardesses laughing as they tried on each other's hats; men at the magazine racks paging through *Life* with one eye, the other on *True Detective*; a Marine lance corporal in uniform, perhaps Korea-bound judging from the tears of the clinging family which he was dragging through the airport like so many overfilled suitcases. The Marine might, if he were unlucky, brush against the familiar darkness, but most people nowadays glided along their narrow paths, stumbling over small bumps and reveling in unexpected joys.

The exit door opened and he heard the revving engines of the TWA Constellation. He briefly considered trying on the sunglasses he had bought specifically for this trip but decided not to make a fashion show of himself. He cast one last look at the photo of at his happy Americans and wondered about them —were they unlikely heroes or heedless fools?

"Officer Fielder, please."

"Officer Fielder is on leave, ma'am."

"On leave? Policemen go on leave? Why?"

"I don't know. I'm just the night shift operator."

"Can I speak to someone else, someone above him?"

"Can I take your name and number ma'am?"

Jean hung up just before Jessie could grab the receiver from her hands. A phone booth outside a bar. The Zoom Room, the Atomic Bomber, something like that—in Cupertino, Sunnyvale, somewhere like that. Their cars parked nose to nose, a six pack of Lucky Lager on Jessie's hood, halfway gone.

"You're acting like a fool, and I don't think you're a fool," Jessie said.

"I know, I know, I just thought ... Officer Fielder seemed so understanding, on my side, it was my last ... I don't know what it was my last of ..."

"Was your last shred of belief, that's what. Mine's been AWOL awhile now, and the sight of Connie back there pretty much slammed the door on it." Jessie punched her fist into the phone booth, which stubbornly refused to shatter, drawing blood from her knuckles anyway. "Connie is my sister-in-law. And a widow at that."

"Oh, good Lord, I ... I'm so, so sorry. I had no idea."

"We kept it under wraps down at the plant. Connie was what you folks call 'broad-minded.' Always agitated about something. Connie the Crusader we called her. I know what you're thinking. Gordon—that's my brother—was another cause for her because he was black and discriminated against. But their love was true, Mrs. Vale, believe me. And you want star-crossed marriage? Gordon, like me, from a little nothing burg down around Houston, Connie from big city Chicago." Jessie rolled up her left sleeve to expose a burn scar that ran from wrist to elbow. "We came up here to work in the shipyards at Hunter's Point. The Army took Gordon and left me to the welding and the wiring. Gordon, he was a bona-fide hero. He was with the 93rd Division, died out there on Bougainville. And now Connie's gone too. No side-by-side burials for them, that's a fact." Jessie looked about to cry, tugged a pack of cigarettes from her Richfield pocket, lit up, offered one to Jean. "I drink Lucky and I smoke Luckies, 'cause God can't do it all. Help yourself, the smoke dries up the tears."

"You can cry in front of me, Jessie."

"Not in front of them I can't." She glanced at the bar, where a group of men stood in the open doorway, drinking, watching. "What a sight for the barflies, huh? Two women—one Negro, one white—angry, frightened, heartbroken or maybe about to be. They can have all that. But tears they're not gonna get." Jessie slid into the front seat of her car, a Desoto, the chrome teeth of its shark-like grill polished and ready to bite. "Let's get the hell out of here and get ourselves situated."

JEAN CRESTED the final hill and swung into the parking lot of Lick Observatory at the summit of Mount Hamilton. Grateful that she still had Helen's car; B.E.'s bloodhounds were probably tearing into her Nash. The lot was empty as she'd hoped. She parked near the overlook, the lights of Santa Clara County strung out below her, so normal, so still. In her rearview mirror, Jean saw the silver dome of the Observatory glistening in the dark, like an egg about to hatch.

Jean waited in darkness, sensing the Isoniazid bottle inside her purse. Her assessment of its effects was mixed—dizziness, feelings of suffocation, nausea, exactly as advertised. Those were the negatives. Increased sociability leading to uncharacteristic aggressiveness—could she define those as positives?

Her "condition" had taken away the one thing she liked most about herself: competence. Her ability to do her job, to get through an afternoon on her feet, without shades drawn; to prepare after school snacks for her son that weren't random items of mismatched food—halves of crackers, stale cookies, unpeeled carrots—to get dinner on the table, unaided. Could a pill bring that back? On her last day working at B.E., when Lawrence Cutler found Jean Maddux Vale, employee badge 88, cowering in the storeroom, hemmed in by towers of oscilloscopes and audio oscillators, and suggested that she needed a "rest cure"—which she interpreted as isolating her so that she couldn't infect her co-workers—Robert had protested, followed Lawrence into his office, intending to plead and cajole. But Jean had stopped him. The one shred of herself she clung to was the power to fight, or retreat from her own battles. So maybe pills, as a weapon. She didn't know anymore, didn't even know how to know.

And could any pill bring her closer to the truth? There were too many threads, too many missing connections for her to see the whole picture. Robert Vale, open, reliable, a man who moved forward, not in leaps and bounds, but by putting one foot in front of the other, who seemed to accept life's limits, felt grateful to be employed, a homeowner, a husband and father had driven off one afternoon into a maze.

His path had somehow intersected with Connie Latimer's and now she was dead.

She cranked down both front seat windows, breathed in the night air. From her purse she pulled out the pieces of paper that Jessie had retrieved from Connie's work apron. They had turned out to be bowling score cards, scribbled with chemistry or engineering equations. They were from Strike It Rich Lanes, Calcite, Nevada. The identification badge Jimmy had pickpocketed from Vann Claridge granted him authorized access to the Calcite Division. But there was no street address, no phone number. She opened the Nevada road map she'd picked up at a Standard station. By the light from the radio, she guided her finger down the alphabetical listing of Nevada towns and cities. There was no Calcite. She scanned the state, north to south, east to west. Aside from Reno and Las Vegas, it was an empty place, the sparse population living in clusters that edged the Great Basin and the Mojave Desert. But no Calcite. A town too small to show on a map. Probably just a filling station and a couple desert rat shacks. Or maybe it was a ghost town.

With a bowling alley? Where anonymous players rolled strikes and spares and performed complex calculations on their scorecards?

Jean heard the hiss of tires as a car entered the parking lot, headlights off. Jessie pulled next to her, Jimmy in the passenger seat. He hopped out and began toting things from Jessie's car. In the flare of the dome light, Jean saw the oatmeal-colored Samsonite overnight case Robert had given her for their fifth anniversary, Jimmy's olive drab duffle bag which held his "tools and weapons." Jimmy stowed it all carefully in the backseat of Helen's car.

"How did it go?" Jean asked.

"Good. Traveling light, traveling prepared," Jimmy said.

"How's Helen? How's Grandpa Tamarkin?"

"OK, I guess. They'll watch the house, they said. For signs of dad."

Jessie got out and hurried to Jean at the driver's side. She passed another pair of Jean's slacks and her dark blouse through the window. "I figured this wasn't a fancy dress sort of trip," she said. "So, here's the lowdown. If Helen or that Russian character need to get in touch, they'll do it through me." She passed Jean a business card for "Lucy's Ladies Only Launderette," with a San Francisco address and phone number. "Number is a pay phone they got on the wall. Call in, and if they have news, they'll tell you. And if you got news, call the number and they'll tell me." She he handed Jean an envelope. "There's five hundred dollars in here. Some from your friends, some's from my personal treasure trove."

"And I've got twenty in quarters. From dad's too-new-to-collect drawer." Jimmy was fiddling with his field glasses, focusing them on the observatory, calibrating them, first the right eye, then the left eye.

Jessie, acting on the predictable instincts of all women and some men, tousled Jimmy's flyaway hair. "Guess there's another man of the house, huh, Mrs. Vale?"

Jean was touched. She felt like sobbing then and there, but knew she had to stay in one—or at least less than a dozen—pieces for her son's sake. "I'll pay you back, every dollar. And surely it's Jean by now, isn't it? After everything?"

"Yeah, that's fine. It is."

"I'm pleased."

"Let's not make a show of it."

"Mom, Grandpa Tamarkin said we should take the car for a hundred miles then just leave it somewhere. Don't call to tell them where it is. The cops will eventually find it and they can tow it home. He says for you to rent something."

There were sparks of excitement in Jimmy's eyes; a real-life detective story was unfolding around him, every boy's dream.

"A woman died tonight, Jim. Did Jessie tell you that?"

Jimmy lowered his gaze, the chastised nod he had perfected. He was a studious observer of adult protocol, and he knew mourning was called for. And he knew this was more than a game. She couldn't use the word "dangerous" to describe the trip they were about to undertake because it would only egg him on, but she wanted him to take their situation seriously.

"We're not going home for a while, you know that?"

Again, the nod.

Jean squeezed Jessie's hand until her own hand grew hot.

"Jessie, I'm sorry about Connie. I don't understand any of it. I know Lawrence Cutler personally. Well, I thought I did. He wouldn't condone this."

"But he would hide it, wouldn't he? Quick insurance payout, a brief, flattering notice in the company newsletter. An industrial accident."

"Maybe that's what it was?"

"You mean she got her Shirley Temple curls caught in the conveyer belt, that kind of accident?"

Jean knew she needed to shake herself free of her notions and her once true beliefs. "If Robert was in any way to blame for this—"

"My belly says Connie and Robert were on the same side, and ran up against the same enemy, whoever the Sam Hill that is. Remember, they don't know we were there, they don't know what we saw. In poker, that's a pretty solid hand."

"I'd like to stop by your home someday," Jean said. "And visit. Like normal people do. Hear more about Gordon."

"I'll make you one of his omelets. He was famous for them in his outfit. Then he got promoted to field artillery, and I bet those guys didn't know what they were missing once he was no longer a cook." Jessie's voice clenched. "He'd have liked you and your young man."

Jimmy slammed the back door shut, climbed into the passenger seat. The decisions had been made.

"Jessie? Calcite, Nevada. It's not on any maps."

"I know. I called the operator. No Strike it Rich Lanes, either."

"A town that doesn't exist."

"Best place to look for a missing man. You find your husband, Jean. Find this young fella's father." She winked at Jimmy, and he blushed. "I'll handle the home front. I've had practice."

THEY DROVE east until shortly before 9 a.m. From the narrow groove of Niles Canyon, the grassy hills rose in shadow to the canyon ledge, lit up by morning light. Jean pulled into a turnout behind a boarded-up fishing cabin. Alameda Creek burbled below them, like a simmering pot of something comforting and tasty. Jean had always found water sounds peaceful, like a cool compress to treat the long, dry summers of childhood. But their situation was far from comforting; it was awful. They had run from home, and were still running, carrying everything they had in Helen Gillett's car. Binoculars and canteen at hand, Jimmy volunteered to "sit the first watch" and Jean, still behind the wheel, fell asleep.

VALE PRIVATE INVESTIGATIONS – Discrete, Dedicated, Deadly

From: Field Operative (F.O.) J.B. Vale

Subject: Search for Missing Person XYZ

Time: 5:45

I'm on watch tonight. Senior Operative (S.O.) Vale is asleep. Still no sign of missing person XYZ, despite repeated efforts. S.O. Vale under strain. Not making her lists; recommend she begins list making again.

Supplies: Full canteen, stockman pocket knife, thumb-focus field glasses (right lens cracked); angle-head Army flashlight, extra leak-proof Ray-O-Vac batteries; cheeseburgers and fries; Wittnauer Military compass; Boy Scout First Aid Kit. Introduction to Russian code Systems—handwritten; pouch holding select engineers tools belonging to XYZ including needle files, telescopic gages.

Road Conditions: Good. Gas tank is ¾ full, oil temperature fine, tire pressure normal at 44 PSI (for one passenger).

Destination: Somewhere in Nevada

SECONDS LATER, Jean felt Jimmy nudge her awake. But hours had passed—the warmth on her eyelids told her the sun was up and in full blaze.

"You were talking in your sleep, mom."

"What did I say?"

Jimmy opened the personalized Russian notebook he'd gotten for his last birthday from Grandpa Tamarkin—it always gave him a charge to see the Cyrillic version of his name on the cover.

"Sounded like 'Wealth, water, contentment, health'."

"We've got water, we've got health. Two out of four ain't bad." She kissed her professionally-equipped night watchman on the forehead. Jimmy wetted his hand and wiped all traces of the kiss away.

She drove out of the canyon into the valley, holding a steady eastbound course, hoping Jimmy wouldn't notice. For two hours he didn't.

"Hey, Nevada's that way," Jimmy said, unfolding the map, gliding his finger to the south.

Jean didn't answer, kept heading into the afternoon as the sun passed over and behind them, driving through brown and furrowed fields flecked with wispy cotton bolls from the recent harvest. In the distance, an almond orchard was a gray-green stripe on the land, wavering in the heat.

"Mom!"

"We're taking a detour."

Jean veered off the highway onto a dirt road. Its washboard ribbing jolted them up and down; something clattered in the suspension. Jean reached a crossroads, two dirt tracks intersecting in the middle of an alfalfa field, no road signs, no directional markers.

"Let's see, I think the road to the left is 147th Lane, the one on the right bypasses the old Gemello place and dead ends at the river." Jean swung right, as Jimmy studied the map, trying to orient himself. The landscape became more hospitable—vineyards, a scatter of valley oaks offering shade. At the top of a gentle rise stood a two-story house that needed paint and love, but was otherwise tough and resilient, like an aging boxer. Jean felt a twinge of memory when she saw the house's porch with its filigreed railings—misty winter afternoons watching her father plane down the floorboards, gathering the fragrant pine shavings he left in his fast-moving wake. He built 'em to last, that's for sure. She turned onto a narrow dirt track that probably hadn't felt the scrunch of car tires in years. The track ended at a shallow, slow-moving river. Jean pulled the car as far off the track as she could before it mired in the thick, clotted dirt. Cottonwood trees arched above them. She hoped they would provide enough cover so the car couldn't be spotted from the turnoff.

"Nature's garage," she said. "Let's go."

"Mom, what's going on?"

"Young man, you are not to ask questions right now. You will do as I say until I say differently."

She didn't wait for an answer. She ripped the registration from the steering column, took the car keys, then grabbed her Samsonite from the back seat. Jimmy picked up his duffle.

"What now?"

"We march." Jean walked to the waterline which was at its summer low and began to pick her way along the stone cobbled sand at the river's edge. "We've got at least two miles to cover."

"Going where?"

"Never you mind."

Jean picked up her pace, Jimmy trudging after her. They followed the bends of the river as the sun speckled the lazy water. A peaceful scene, but it did not calm Jean; the knives in her stomach sharpened, as they hiked closer to their destination. She felt her anxiety prickling out through the back of her neck. Right into Jimmy.

"Mom."

"Not now. Keep going."

"Mom, you need to start a list."

"OK. California counties and their county seats."

"Too easy."

"From north to south. Del Norte, county seat Crescent City; Siskiyou, county seat Yreka; Modoc, county seat Alturas ..."

"And you should do a method for track covering, such as walking backwards or doing a longer stride so your tracks look like a man's."

"I am not walking backwards."

"All right, then I will." Jean felt Jimmy's back bumping into hers. "And we should mix our tracks up—confuses a posse." They kept on, joined at the back like competitors in a picnic race, as Jean set the pace and Jimmy walked backwards, scuffing at her footprints with his hiking boots.

An hour later, they turned away from the river and trekked

across an onion field to a paved road. With their overnight case, duffle bag and sacks of half-eaten hamburgers, they probably looked like modern-day, mother and son Okies, hunting for a spot to bed down. It was a neighborhood of businesses that needed open space: oil equipment storage yards; tractor repair garages; scrap dealers. They passed a dirt track speedway, quiet now, but making big plans for Saturday night when they promised to give away a free 17-inch television. Beyond the speedway was an outdoor auto parts yard that had a few cars for sale: "EZ deals on California Cars."

Jean left Jimmy at the car lot's bent metal gate. "Whitewalls or regular?" she asked. Jimmy shrugged, chomping French fries. He was still there two hours later when Jean rolled out of the yard behind the wheel of a slightly dented 1940 Dodge Coup two door with heat-flaked brown paint and brand-new retread whitewalls. "1940, the last great year for American cars, fantastic trade-in value when you wear it out, although you won't wear it out because it takes a lot of punishment," the hay fever-plagued salesman had promised, after accepting Jean's $200 cash offer, then scooping up another two twenties to let her handle the paperwork herself. She hadn't given him her name or showed her driver's license.

Jean adjusted the rearview mirror and caught herself smiling. She had never been a sharpie, she'd rarely pulled fast ones. Robert had bought their two cars, claiming he'd made "a great deal," although Jean had never heard anyone confess to making a terrible deal when buying a car. She felt a flush of pride, but she knew why she'd cinched the deal: the salesman had recognized her as one of their own, a local who hadn't managed to scrub the Central Valley out of her pores or change the rough cut of her gestures. Maybe it was her clothes or the set of her eyes, permanently narrowed from squinting into glaring sun in summer and cloaking tule fog in winter. He had marked her and helped her—so be it. Feeling accomplished and in charge, she gave Jimmy the bad news. "We're stopping at Nana's."

"What? Why? We have to find dad!"

"Jim, I may be walking into a lion's den. I can't take you with me. You'll be safe at Nana's."

"But that's not the deal!" he barked.

"We're in trouble here. Your dad may be in trouble. I'm not making deals, I'm giving orders."

"It's not fair, though."

"Jimmy, when has the 'it's not fair' argument ever worked for you?"

"Christmas two years ago, when you wouldn't let me have the archery set. Five months later, when I woke up, there it was in my room, gift-wrapped."

"That was for your birthday."

"It was connected."

"You're staying at Nana's. I'm not going to argue."

"But I helped with clues, with the bomber crew lists, I helped us cover our tracks. You need me!"

Jean slammed the brakes—they were more sensitive than she was used to, and their bodies were hurled into the dashboard, then caromed back into their seats. Behind them, a Borden's Ice Cream truck squealed its tires, but honked politely.

"This is not a goddamn adventure out of *Boy's Life*. You are trying my patience, and I am going to need every ounce of it. Do you hear me?"

She grabbed his chin in her palm and tried to force him to turn his head to look at her. He resisted, holding himself stiff and rooted, staring straight ahead. She tightened her grip, he squeezed his neck muscles into rigid cords—he was stronger than she imagined. The straining, grunting contest of wills continued for a few more seconds, until Jean pulled her hand away. Jimmy didn't budge, didn't look at her and Jean drove on.

. . .

The "world famous" Modesto Arch spanned First Street, welcoming drivers with the city's official slogan: "Wealth, Water, Contentment, Health." One night in the middle of the Depression, the lights on the word "Wealth" had burned out—it was either a comment by God or the work of a practical joker. Now, "Wealth" blazed brighter than ever, nearly washing out the words "Water, Contentment, Health." Modesto was modest no more.

As Jean drove along Upper Tenth Street, wealth seemed everywhere; if not wealth, then "get up and go." Women stepped along the sidewalks, fluid and free in summer dresses, purses ready for action. Others in business clothes and severe hats that did nothing to keep off the sun but presented a picture of unfussy competence, whirled in and out of office buildings and banks. Men in summer suits—most men she had grown up around had *one* suit, and it was all-seasonal—greeted each on the sidewalk with 'great to see ya' handshakes, the exchange of business cards, heads bowing to look over a contract or a deal. There were refurbished hotels and name-tagged men huddled in the lobbies. Jean imagined them to be oil equipment sales reps, dairymen, cotton brokers, ranchers. And people were shopping, emerging from Ward's and Penny's, arms spilling with packages, followed by employees who pushed dollies stacked with appliances to car trunks that were open and waiting.

She drove through downtown to the Modesto she recognized, the quiet streets, the shady ash trees, the cottages and two-story houses known by the names of their long-deceased owners. Jimmy hadn't said a word and made no move to get out of the car when they pulled up in front of Alma's house on Oakdale Street. It had been eight years since they had last visited, enduring a long, tense Thanksgiving which Robert, usually diplomatic when it came to her mother, described as "a son-in-law's sentence, a daughter's penance." Jimmy had been three and a half, attracting the occasional clucking "tsk

tsk" from Alma when he blundered into the kitchen, but otherwise he left her unimpressed. The house, originally built by a dry goods merchant, expanded and re-roofed by her father, was a wood-sided two story with a wide front porch framed by white-washed columns set on river stone pedestals. It was mirrored in larger and smaller variations all over town, but theirs was made unique by ornate dormer windows that her father claimed were copied from a banker's mansion he'd seen in Stockton. The windows Jean had spent years of her life looking out of, watching and waiting. When she was a girl, it was always the brightest house on the block, the paint touched up annually during the first week of July, when she and her parents and a few enthusiastically messy neighbors would work late, slathering the walls yellow—Goldenrod, her father always corrected—edging the window and door frames a glossy white as fireworks streamed into the skies.

There had been no painting parties here for a long time. It had gone worn and faded, like a house you'd donate to the Salvation Army if they took houses. It wasn't in bad repair, and it didn't look trashy—her mother would never allow that—but it was unloved.

"She doesn't like me," Jimmy said.

Jean shrugged. Alma didn't know anyone well enough to be capable of an emotion as intense as dislike.

Jimmy stayed in the car while Jean climbed the steps to the front porch. It creaked in new places, sagged in others. She knocked. Peered in through the lace-curtained windows, but saw only vague shapes of lamps, cabinets, furniture. Knocked again, no answer. She went to the back of the house—an empty, sagging clothesline, a dead persimmon tree, a row of exhausted rose bushes. The garden furniture that her father had built—picnic table, three practical but comfortable chairs were gone. The bird house he'd crafted for her and that she had painted, leaned at an impossible angle on its wooden post, as though it lacked the ambition to topple over. Jean knocked on the back door, but still there was no answer.

"Mama, it's me. And Jimmy. We need to see you. It's important."

Jean pressed her ear against the back door—not even the shush of slippered feet inside. Then she heard footsteps and doors thudding shut beneath the house, as though some animal were blundering around down there. Jean felt for the latch that was concealed in the gap where the wooden siding met the cement foundation. It was still there, creaky but it did the job; when she lifted the latch, a few feet of siding separated from the wall, turning on hidden hinges, forming an artfully disguised door. She levered the door open and was punched by a wave of stale, trapped air. A sparrow streaked out from beneath the house, dizzy with sudden freedom. Jean peered into the opening, cement steps descended below ground.

Jean walked down the stairs. The low angle of the sun cast a weak light into a narrow passageway that had been dug below foundation level. The passageway was lined with stained redwood and supported by joists every few feet. It had always reminded Jean of a mine shaft. As a girl she imagined that it spiraled down to the bottom of the earth. After a few feet, the passageway dog-legged to the left and led into a wide, expansive chamber. The sunlight didn't reach here, but it didn't need to—the room was lit by two shaded light bulbs hanging from the ceiling. A whittled pine bar stretched the length of the far wall. Above the bar, shelves were stocked with preserves and pickled beets. The other three walls looked like a wooden honeycomb, designed to hold wine and whiskey bottles. But the honeycomb was empty, just rows of round holes fringed with cobwebs.

In the center of the cement floor sat the garden furniture. Her father had built the chairs in three sizes—Papa Bear, Mama Bear and Baby Bear. On the Papa Bear chair sat her mother, Alma. Who'd never expressed an opinion one way or the other about Jean's career or her choices, who never referred to Robert by name, only as "your husband" and never doted on Jimmy, like the "Grandmother Rule Book" as she called it, seemed to dictate. She simply didn't want to participate in other people's happiness, determined to stew in cranky misery, alone and proudly bitter.

I must be kidding myself, she thought. Coming here for help.

9

Alma had always said it was the wind. The prairie wind that cut into the Midwest from Canada, whistling in through every crack in every wall, burrowing into your ears, your nostrils, breaching your clenched teeth and funneling into your mind. Some folks lost their sense of direction, others couldn't eat or sleep. Thousands abandoned built-up lives and left for good, taking the train, driving, walking—El Dorado was anywhere that the wind didn't blow. It got into a family's roots, into the generational bloodstream, where it just kept blowing, into sons and daughters, grandsons and granddaughters. It caused fatigue, arthritis, temper tantrums and the permanent blahs. The wind had ridden west from Kansas with Alma's grandparents, settled with her parents on a peach orchard in a remote patch of Stanislaus County, and when borers killed the peach trees, moved into the brand new, growing railroad town of Modesto in the fall of 1889. Where, thanks to the wind, Alma maintained, she'd been born unhappy.

"What are you doing down here?" Jean asked.

"New neighbors in the Dalton place. Nosy. Don't like it."

"What could you have to hide?"

Alma just sniffed, not looking up. "One could ask what *you're* doing here?"

"I need your help."

Alma turned her head and studied Jean. It had been years, decades, since those four words had crossed her daughter's lips, headed in her direction. Alma was a small woman, densely packed, although the packing was starting to loosen up with the years. She wore long dresses, long sleeves, and high collars, to minimize her exposure to the elements. She hated heat, dreaded wind, cursed the rain, and in winter, when snow appeared on the Sierras, she would always declare "I suppose it's a blessing that we don't live up there." Her face was wide, which as she aged, gave nature a broad palette to incise wrinkles. Her short-cropped curls were mostly gray, with a few twists of brunette hanging on. Her eyes were pale blue and sharp; she'd never needed glasses and swore she never would.

"What can I help you with that Robert can't?"

"Robert's not here."

"Again?"

In a Christmas morning phone call, years ago, as Robert and Jimmy played with his new toys, crawling across the folded cotton snow beneath the tree, tinsel dangling down their foreheads. Jean, tired, giddy from a sleepless night of gift-wrapping, feeling pride in her family and therefore a little bullet-proof, had mentioned Robert's missing week to her mother. Recognizing her slip, Jean had immediately moved the conversation on. But the fact locked into Alma's mind as negative facts usually did.

"Mama, we need to talk. I don't have much time."

Maybe her mother would not believe her or would not be moved by a confession of trouble—someone else's problem implied that hers did not exist. Jean pictured the gestures she'd seen in movies, when characters' exasperation exploded into action: seltzer sprayed, a grapefruit squeezed into Mae Marsh's face by Jimmy Cagney in *The Public Enemy.* Her props were limited. Maybe she could smash a few bottles of pickled pigs feet onto the floor?

"Wow, what is this place?" Jimmy crept in, his hair frosted with cobwebs. "You have a secret room down here!"

"You should see the interior stairs," Jean said. "Sliding panels, trick handles, hidden staircases. Something out of Houdini."

"You stay right there," her mother snapped. "I will not have you prowling about."

"Go on, Jim, it's just on the other side of the room—the hidden panel."

Jimmy edged closer, trying to decide whether to skitter past Alma to avoid a confrontation, or to stay put and be the polite grandson. He split the difference, scooting past Alma's chair to a recessed panel next to the bar.

"Hi, Nana, hope you're feeling well."

"Right there, Jimmy," Jean said. "Feel that little groove, it's down around knee level."

Jimmy crouched, running his hands across what appeared to be a featureless wall.

"You'll feel an indentation, put your fingers together and press."

"A woman can't even enjoy the privacy of her own home these days," Alma said.

"Go on, give it a go."

"You leave that well enough alone."

"It's OK, Jimmy. I'll take the heat," Jean said in her Bogart voice.

A few more fumblings and the panel slid open on wooden runners, revealing a narrow flight of stairs. A thread of light climbed up the center of the stairs like a road divider, leading to a peephole in a crawlspace door.

"Wow, where's this lead?"

"To the pantry," Alma said. "And I'll thank you to stay out of there."

Jimmy turned back to the cellar. Avoiding Alma's stare, he took in the whole room for the first time. "What is this, anyway?"

"You know about Prohibition, right?" Jean asked.

"Sure. Al Capone. The St. Valentine's Day Massacre."

"Well, even though it was illegal to buy and sell alcohol, people still wanted a drink. And they didn't necessarily want to drink alone. So those who could afford it built home speakeasies, I guess you could call them—secret wine cellars, whiskey rooms. Your granddad, being a carpenter, developed a sideline building these rooms. I guess there are a few still left scattered around the county."

"So granddad broke the law?"

"It was perfectly legal," Alma said. "And it would have brought in more than wooden nickels in its day, too. We were thinking of selling the place, buying some land. If the house had a speakeasy, it would jack up the value." Alma glanced in annoyance at Jean, as though blaming her for the demise of Prohibition.

"Yes, Granddad and Nana drank like sailors," Jean said. "They brewed ten percent beer and bathtub gin down here. Gave it to me instead of milk."

Jimmy chuckled. Alma stood, hunching into the slouch that reminded the world of the many burdens on her shoulders. For some reason, Alma was holding a pair of scissors, which she slipped into her housecoat pocket.

"Well, I can see it's two against one, as usual," Alma said.

"Mama, why does it have to be anybody against anybody else?"

"Because that's the way life is. Or haven't you told the boy that yet?"

. . .

Jean could still move through Alma's house blindfolded. Every stick of furniture, knickknack, rug, and lamp was in the same position they had been in for decades. The same iced tea rings on the walnut coffee table, the same stacks of *Saturday Evening Posts* ending in 1944, piled neatly next to the fireplace. Same old phone she'd always had—heavy, black, clumsy. Even the sunlight-bleached rectangles on the ceiling beams were in the same spots, which meant Alma still opened the curtains to the same width, down to the inch. Every room was polished weekly, the air thick with Johnson's Wax and somewhere in the house, insects had been dispatched with several volleys from a flit-gun. But then her Alma-tuned instincts detected something slightly different. She scanned the living room again—what was it? Before she could investigate further, Alma turned into a whirl of distracting energy. Rolling out the carpet sweeper, organizing her week's darning.

"Mama, listen to me!" Jean said as Alma mounted a Windex assault on glass that already sparkled. Jean peered out the side window—she'd moved the car off the street into the weed-choked driveway and Jimmy was out there, unpacking.

"I need you to take Jimmy for a few days."

"Take him?"

"Take care of him. Feed him, keep an eye on him so he doesn't wander off. Bathe him if humanly possible."

A spray of ammonia, a squeak of rag on glass. "What's going on?"

"Robert is in trouble. I need to help him, and I can't take Jimmy. That's all I can say."

"Oh well, if that's all you can say—"

"I could say a lot more, but you wouldn't believe me. Just do us this favor. Be a grandmother to your grandson."

"A child should be with his mother in times of trouble."

"Well, he can't be, not now. He could be in danger. That's just the way it is."

"And if your man is in *real* difficulty and this is not some tall tale you've cooked up to draw attention to yourself, call the police. I don't imagine there's anything *you* can do about it on your own."

Jimmy clattered in from the side yard, his duffle bag in one hand, her overnight case pressed between his upper arm and his torso, in a bellhop's stance. She nodded him upstairs, and as he passed the walnut sideboard with the decorative legs her father had turned himself, she noticed the photos. There had always been an array of framed pictures set out on the sunburned doilies, anonymous relatives from non-smiling, past generations. One of them was turned face down.

"I'll get dinner started," Alma said, scooping up the overturned photograph and dropping it into an apron pocket.

Dinner was cheerless and strained. Well, Jean and Jimmy felt the strain, Alma the bustling cook seemed fine. Small talk got Jean nowhere, Jimmy's dramatic recitation of Poe's *The Raven*, the only poem he'd ever learned, stirred no reaction. Alma didn't ask about Jimmy's grades or his friends or pose sports questions like a normal annoying Grandmother would. And she said nothing about Robert. Alma had made spaghetti with meatballs, one of Jimmy's favorite dinners. Perhaps realizing she had accidentally pleased him, Alma served boiled asparagus as a side dish, a vegetable that he truly hated. Though her freezer held a quart of Rocky Road, she offered rice pudding as dessert. She cleared the plates, and moved to the sink so she could keep her back to them as she did the dishes. She rinsed off tomato sauce as Jean and Jimmy watched the muscles in the back of her neck tense and relax. And then she started to whistle a tune. Sounded like "Tennessee Waltz." Alma didn't sing or hum and Jean certainly never heard her whistle.

"I guess it won't kill me if you two stay the night."

Jean slept three hours, maybe four, before something in the house woke her. I haven't slept in my childhood room for twenty years, with good reason, she thought. It wants me restless and edgy; it wants me gone. Then she laughed at herself. It's a bed, a room, and a night, like thousands of others she'd lived through and would continue to live through.

But something *had* awakened her.

She sat up, dipped her fingers in a water glass and streaked her eyes.

She focused on the old familiar shadows. *I admired myself in that mirror, she thought, as she caught her sleepy figure reflected in the tilt mirror that stood in the corner. I preened, puffing myself up, then I heard the neighbor's dog barking through that opened window —the dormer window that was good enough for the best banker in Stockton. Then she'd heard the approaching rumble of the Maxwell touring car, a noise to which she had tuned her heart and her expectations during those dedicated, solitary school day afternoons with hammer and saw. I ran, vaulting down the stairs, faster than I had ever run before, faster than I've run since. If only I'd been slower ...*

She checked on Jimmy, curled asleep under blankets on the circular hooked rug that had been here since before she could remember. Her freshman year in high school, her first drinking party with the older kids out at Enslen Park, she'd staggered home and thrown up two bottles of Billy Franklin's dad's home-brewed ale on that rug. But if anyone could scrub out every last stain and trace from a rug, it was Alma.

She descended the stairs, moved into the kitchen, then through the dining nook, waiting for the sound that had awakened her to repeat itself. She passed the closed door to Alma's bedroom and heard a quiet murmur. Did she have a radio in there? No, it was Alma's voice, gentle with laughter. Mired in solitude, perhaps she had begun talking to herself.

Next to Alma's bedroom, the linen closet door was ajar, a strip of red ribbon curling onto the hallway floor. Among the towels and sheets were gift-wrapped packages, some in Christmas paper, others in Happy Birthday paper. The wrapping job was perfect, the paper chosen to appeal to the gift recipient. Silky blue and cream-colors for a woman, rugged landscape scenes for a man, cowboys and Indians for a boy. Each package had a gift card dangling on braided gold thread. "To Jimmy on turning 9;" "To Jimmy, happy 11th Birthday;" "Merry Christmas to all of you;" "To Robert Happy Birthday;" "To my Daughter on her 31st Birthday."

At least three years of undelivered gifts. Three years of Jimmy's delight—or disappointment—denied. Three years of gifts that would reveal Alma's ignorance of Robert's character and interests. And three years of gifts for Jean—would they be unconscious reminders of Alma's disappointment in her, or subtle coaxes to improve herself? The wrapping paper was bright and new, no torn corners or yellowed tape. None of the gift cards was old or faded, and no matter what the year, they had all been written in the same bold, blue ink.

New wrapping, new cards. New gifts. In the speakeasy, Alma had held a pair of scissors in her lap. Was she giftwrapping down there?

Jean pulled out a package addressed to Jimmy on his ninth birthday. She plucked a shawl from a coatrack and used it to muffle her movements as she unwrapped the package. It was a set of Lincoln Logs, with plenty of roofing and plans for a western ranch. He would have frowned on it by his tenth birthday, but would have loved it on his eighth. It was a gift that demonstrated thought and care. She opened a heavier package addressed to "Son and Daughter on their Anniversary." *Son*, not Robert. But not son-in-law, or "that man" either. The gift inside was wrapped in gauze and carefully padded. It was cold to the touch, made of brown metal, glinting with chrome gears—a Revere 8mm movie projector. At the bottom of the box was a souvenir reel of film from the Grand Canyon. Years ago, in a wisp of conversation, Jean had mentioned to Alma how much she and Robert had loved the Grand Canyon and wished they could've filmed it.

"Just what exactly are you doing?" Suddenly Alma was

there, a housecoat over her night gown, wearing felt slippers that had covered her approaching footsteps.

"I thought I heard something, I came down to look around. Then I ..."

Through the open door to Alma's bedroom, Jean glimpsed a bright green telephone on the night table, next to it a dainty sherry glass, half full. Years ago, Alma had sworn she would never have a phone in the bedroom, and now there it was, shiny as a polished lime. Whistling, drinking, late night phone calls ...

Jean waved at the gifts. "What is all this, mama? What's going on?"

"Don't worry about that right now. You did hear something. I heard it too."

"It wasn't you? On the phone?"

"A car. Driving up and down the street. At least twice. I never get cars this time of night."

Jean hurried to the front windows, peered through a break in the lace curtains. The street was quiet, nothing moved. The streetlight flickered, as though about to short out. Some mongrel dog had decided that the cone of light cast onto the dusty shoulder was the perfect spot for a good night's sleep.

"Did you get a look at the car?"

"I heard it, it's not any of the neighbors. That's enough to know I don't like it, not two times up and down the street."

"Are all the doors locked?"

"Whoever it is, you brought them here, didn't you? With this mysterious, on-the-run business."

"Let's get out of here. Now. All of us. We'll go to a motel," Jean said.

"I will not be forced out of my own house by whatever nonsense you and your family have gotten into." Alma thrust her hands into the housecoat pockets, came up with the scissors.

Jean grabbed her mother by the shoulders, something she

had never done in her life. She was surprised by the taut muscles, the tensed strength. “This ‘nonsense’ is serious, mama. Someone has died. Do you read me?”

The hiss of tires, the low rumble of an engine. Jean turned back to the window. The car was a black teardrop in the night, headlights off, as it drove slowly past the house. The car stopped further up the street, then backed up, the driver taking care to avoid riding the brakes so there was not a glimmer of red to attract the curiosity of sleepless neighbors who might be gazing out their windows. The driver knew the car’s coasting distance down to the foot, and he let it drift to a stop, blocking Alma’s driveway. Blocking Jean’s car. Then he shut off the engine.

“What’s he doing?” Alma whispered, looking over Jean’s shoulder, pressing against her back—a body warmth she hadn’t felt from her mother in years. “Sittin’ there like a bump on a log. You know him?” Alma asked.

In the dim glow of the streetlight, Jean couldn't make out the driver's features, but he wore a dark colored fedora pulled down low on his forehead. It had to be one of the prowlers that Grandpa Tamarkin had seen. “No, but he knows me.”

“We could go ask him. It’s my driveway, after all.”

“No! He’s after us, that’s all that matters.”

“After you? What the blazes does that mean? What has that man gotten you mixed up in?"

That man. Don't jump at the bait, Jean told herself.

“We have to let them think we’re not at home, make them give up—then we’ll make a run for it!”

“You tell me what’s up, or no deal.”

“I can’t, I swear. For your safety.”

“My safety. My safety! You’re worried about my safety?” Alma said.

“Yes, damn you, yes!”

Alma looked like she had just been slapped, as though the idea of a daughter caring for her mother had never occurred to her. Alma glanced back out at the car. "He doesn't look like much, that fella. There's always some little runt stepping into things, overplaying his hand." With a whip-like twist of her hand, she thrust the scissors back into her housecoat. “Get Jimmy. I'll get the cellar ready. If the combined forces of the Modesto Police Department and the Stanislaus County Sheriff's Department couldn't find their way in there during Prohibition, that joker won't be able to either.”

Jean ran upstairs, shook Jimmy awake. He grumbled, pulled away from her, wrapped himself tighter in the blankets.

“Get up, get up. They're back. We gotta get out of here.” Jimmy's “training” kicked in. At one time a sleepyhead who never understood why the world had to start so early, he'd taught himself through willpower and manuals written for firemen to go on instant alert, all senses receiving, all muscles primed.

“He's getting out of the car!” Alma shouted from downstairs. Jean threw Jimmy his clothes, ran to the top of the landing, and made a shushing sound to her mother. “For God's sake, keep your voice down!”

“He's just standing there, looking the house over.”

“He alone?”

“So far.”

Jean turned back to Jimmy. He was dressed, putting on his shoes.

“Carry your shoes, we need to keep quiet.”

“What about broken glass? It's a very overlooked source of injury.”

“No one's breaking any glass.”

Jean pushed him out the door, onto the landing, down the stairs. Mr. Tough Guy was shaking, and her arms quivered when she held him.

“He's coming closer,” Alma whispered. Through the lace curtains, Jean couldn't see a thing. “He tripped over the ‘Bee’. Cursed a bit.”

"What if he breaks down the door?" Jimmy asked.

"If he thinks the house is empty, we'll be OK."

Alma herded them into the kitchen, yanked open the pantry door. Three walls of shelves, stocked with fresh supplies of the same staples they had always subsisted on—Corn Flakes, Bisquick, Quaker Oats. The hatch was difficult to make out if you didn't know where to look. Alma pushed down with her foot, a tiny door on springed hinges snapped open in the middle of the floorboards. Jimmy went in first, switching on his flashlight. Jean hissed, he turned it off. She climbed down three steps, then turned, reaching up to help her mother.

"I'll be fine," Alma said. Then she closed the hatch behind them. A deadbolt slid into place. Jean squinted through the peephole, but it went black as Alma covered it. She urged Jimmy down the stairs to the garden furniture, but neither of them sat. They stood there stock still, trying to contain their breathing as though an exhale could give them away, staring at the underside of the floor, like miners expecting a cave-in. Waiting for Alma to somehow handle this guy herself.

The whole situation seemed ridiculous. She wanted to laugh out loud, to slap Jimmy on the back, to tell each other terrible riddles until they made themselves sick. This is what fear can do, she'd read somewhere—make everything funny.

He would check their car, but she was pretty sure he wouldn't recognize it. Maybe he'd knock on the front door. Lightly, to avoid waking the neighbors. What if Alma stayed church mouse quiet? He'd check the back door, then the windows. And if he truly thought there was no one home? Would he give up and drive away, report to his bosses that mother and son had given him the slip? No, he'd tracked them this far, he would not relent. He would get inside somehow.

Then a more frightening prospect hit her. If he searched their room, he'd find their luggage, the maps of Nevada, the bowling scorecards—he'd know everything they knew and could predict their next move. Their only advantage would be gone.

They heard heavy footsteps in the house. He was already inside. He hadn't knocked, hadn't announced himself; he probably just picked the lock and let himself in. He made her furious—treating her childhood home, the trove of memories both mundane and tragic, but most of all private—as his own little piece of property. And then he started singing. "... if you ever go down Trinidad, they make you feel so very glad ..." The song accompanied the footsteps, as he edged through the house. "Drinking rum and Coca Cola, go down Point Koomahnah ..."

They tried to follow the sound of the footsteps through the living room—boots or work shoes. Jean imagined she could see the floorboards buckling with each footfall. They moved across the kitchen, then stopped. The pantry door opened. Jean and Jimmy held their breaths. The footsteps moved on, into the hallway, toward Alma's bedroom. Where was she?

"... help soldier celebrate his leave, make every day like New Year's Eve ..."

Like the men who had approached their house, this guy was not afraid of being seen or heard. And now he could be threatening her mother, while Jean hid in the damn speakeasy.

"... since the Yankee come to Trinidad, they got the young girls all goin' mad."

His voice was sharp and echoing, and she knew that he was climbing the narrow staircase to the second floor. Just before she heard the gunshot, Jean thought that he did a reasonably accurate male impersonation of the Andrews Sisters, and that he could really carry a tune.

10

She ran through the cellar, climbed the cement steps, fought the hinges and the locks on the secret panel, barking her knuckles. Out into the night, the fresh air slapping her cheeks, through the side yard, skidding on dewy grass, tripping on a coil of garden hose, glancing into the house —no lights, no movement. Onto the front porch, picking her way around the boards that she knew would creak, opening the door, squeaking, its hinges unoiled and stiff. She stepped into the front room.

A body fell, she could hear it writhing on the floor. By the time Jean reached the top of the stairs, the watcher, the muscular non-smoker, the singer, had stopped moving. Alma stood on the landing, clasping the balustrade for support as though the floor were pitching beneath her. Sticking out of the right pocket of her housecoat was the gray-metal handle of a pistol. The air was acrid and smoky.

"Mama, what did you do?" Jean knelt over the man's body. A bullet wound through the chest, maybe the lungs, blood spreading from beneath his back onto the floorboards, where it pooled up and congealed, rebuffed from seeping into the wood by Alma's obsessive varnishing. Jean felt for a neck pulse, held her ear to the man's chest.

"He's gone, believe me," Alma said.

Jean pulled the gun from Alma's pocket, it looked like a World War One antique, she was surprised it had even fired.

"It was your father's, a Savage. He bought it when he was building those cellars, for protection. We had our share of boot-leggers around here." Alma crouched and opened the man's brown, double-breasted jacket. He had a gun of his own, tucked into his belt.

"How could you ... How could you know?"

"I didn't, I just ... you didn't see his eyes. They were like a businessman bored with his routine day's work, an insurance man making another house call. I wasn't even a person to him."

The man's eyes were not all the way closed. Life had left him looking drowsy, about to fall asleep. His hat lay upended beside his head, empty now, like a beggar's bowl.

The phone rang. Jean glanced out her bedroom window—lights were on next door. "I'll go," Alma said, then headed downstairs, wobbly on her feet.

Jean had read her share of novels. She knew that at moments like these, her heart was supposed to be pounding against her chest, those famous hairs on the back of her neck should be prickling. She felt nothing like that; she was wrung out. But she could not weaken or wilt, not now. She searched the man's clothes as she heard snatches of Alma's phone conversation from downstairs.

"Oh, hello, Doris. Yes I'm sorry ..."

Just a handful of change in the left pocket, but in the right there were car keys and house keys. Two sets of house keys—for two different houses?

"My grandson ... he found Ben's old pistol ..."

Nothing in the shirt or pants pockets. Jean's hand was warmed with blood, but she dug into the left breast pocket of his suit. A billfold. Made from the same sort of hide that matched his belt, she noticed.

"No one's hurt. I didn't even know the thing worked ..."

Forty-three dollars. A California driver's license and Social Security card in the name of Gerald Hammond, 456 Alameda, San Jose, California. Beneath it, a Virginia license and Social Security card for Ralph Stowe, 94 Pike Road, Reston, Virginia. Both driver's licenses had the same picture—the dead man who lay at her feet.

"You know what they say about boys," Alma said. "If there's trouble around, they'll find it. Again, I'm so sorry we woke you up."

Lining the back of the wallet, Jean found a row of stitching that didn't match the rest. She tugged at the stitching, unthreading it to reveal a hidden pouch. Nested inside was a pocket-size photograph of Robert. It was annotated on the back with personal details: height, weight, age, hair and eye color, names of family members and relatives, addresses, phone numbers. It was a copy of his B.E. identification card.

They were still looking for him. Which meant he was alive.

Jean tucked Robert's badge and the driver's licenses into her pocket. She went into the bedroom, tore the blankets off the bed. When she returned to the body, Jimmy was standing over it.

"Go downstairs. Now!"

"What happened?"

"He threatened grandma."

Jean began to wrap the body in the blankets, blotting up as much of the blood as she could. Jimmy didn't move. A boy who had spent many afternoons playing cops and gangsters, Germans and GIs, killing imaginary enemies with toy Winchesters or falling in feigned agony, riddled with bullets, had no instinctive reaction. His body was not prepared for this. His mind, which had always been questioning and curious, was failing him.

"Jimmy, get out of here, I said!"

"No." Alma was climbing the stairs. She'd changed out of her slippers into gardening shoes and put on gloves. "We'll need his help."

"You want my boy to see this?"

"Seems to me he's already seen it. Listen to me, both of you. You can have your shell shock, later. Right now, we need to move him."

"The cellar," Jean said.

"And what do I do with him there? Let him start stinking like somebody's dead dog? We move him downstairs, just outside my bedroom. Doris is the neighborhood gossip. Sooner or later, everyone will call her, wanting to know what happened. She'll tell them about the gun, and I guarantee one of those prying little hens will call the cops and they'll come knocking."

Jean realized what Alma thinking. "But a widow who shoots an armed man about to break into her bedroom—no one will say a word," Jean said.

"And a widow who knows police Chief Randall, "Alma said. "He and his men used to drink in our little speakeasy."

Alma nodded. She went into the bedroom, returned with a pillow which she wrapped around the head, fastening it with a torn length of sheet. Jean watched, appalled.

"Well, we can't lift him," Alma said. "It's gonna take all of us just to drag him. You want to hear his head banging on every stair on the way down?"

"So let's turn him around," Jean said.

"Not enough room."

Jean positioned Jimmy at the legs, and he steered with the ankles as she and Alma shoved the body along the varnished floor. One leg splayed out and kicked over a small end table. Something crashed to the floor and shattered—Jean had a clear image of a ceramic cantaloupe from the Turlock Melon festival. At the stairs, they paused to catch their breath, then pushed him over the top step, Jimmy still at the feet, crouching as he clumsily edged down backwards. Alma and Jean lifted the shoulders as high as they could, but each downward step was a sickening jolt as the man's behind thudded, followed by the quiet thump of his pillowed head. At the bottom of the stairs, they let go of Gerald Hammond or Ralph Stowe or whatever his name was, and his arms and legs flopped to the floor. The descent had forced open his coat and his shirt rode up, exposing his bloody chest.

Out of breath, Alma wobbled, pressing her hands onto Jean's chest for support.

"What now?" Jean gasped.

“You’re going to have to tuck his shirt back in,” Alma said.

“What?”

“Well take a gander, how did it get that way?”

As Jean reached for the body, she could see every hair on his rounded stomach, feel every inch of his warm, sticky skin as she slid his shirttail back into his pants. Then they propped him against the wall opposite the open door to Alma’s bedroom, suggesting that the shot had driven him backwards from her threshold, a nighttime invader repulsed by a quick thinking, no-nonsense widow. How many thousands of far-off deaths had she witnessed in newsreels during the war? Bataan, Anzio, Normandy, time-fillers before the feature began? Her father had friends who hunted, who loped off in the morning, rifles crooked under their arms, returned in the evening with a deer or a passel of rabbits. Yet she’d never seen a bullet wound in a human being. It was an ugly, brutal, final thing. And her boy had seen it, too.

Jimmy shifted his weight from his left foot to his right, staring down at the body. It seemed like he wanted to reach out and touch it, to verify that it was real. His jaw vibrated, he blinked furiously. Jean smelled the tang of Pine Sol and heard the squeak of a rag. Alma was cleaning the stairs, which were streaked with blood from top to bottom.

She didn't recognize her mother. The overburdened martyr, disappointed by people, who she in turn made a point of disappointing, sealed off in her spic and span house because the world was simply too much for her—where had she gone? How had this take-charge, daughter-and-grandson-protector replaced her?

"We can't just leave him here," Jean said.

Alma looked up from her scrubbing, her hands flecked with blood.

"When the cops show up, you'll tell them your story—" Jean said.

"And they'll believe me."

"OK, let's say they don't arrest you. But we don't know who this guy is. He's probably not named Hammond or Stowe. Maybe he works for Braden Enright, or a rival company, or the government, or God knows who. No matter how well you know the chief, word'll get out. And then other men will show up. The men who really call the shots, who'll be more suspicious, more devious ... maybe more violent. And you know the worst thing—they probably have a clear conscience. Like this guy."

Alma sat on the bottom step. She dabbed Pine Sol on her hands to cut through the blood. Wiped off on the rag, exhaled in satisfaction. Another household chore checked off the list.

"And your suggestion?" Alma asked.

"We all get the hell out of here. Tonight. We find a safe place for you, while I try to get my husband back."

"Oh sure, a safe place. Maybe a nice rest home."

"I was thinking more of a hide-out."

Alma got to her feet.

"Jeannie ..."

Jeannie? She hadn't been Jeannie since she was ten.

"Jeannie, I have been hiding for years. Decades. From the past, from myself. I'm done hiding. You two get your things and go. You were never here. We haven't talked in months."

Alma went to the front window, peered through the

curtains. "It'll be light soon. You take the stranger's car, I'll move yours."

"Mama, you don't drive."

"But I know men who do."

"Men?"

"One gentleman in particular."

"Who? How do we know we can trust him?"

A faint, fast-vanishing smile crossed Alma's face. "We can trust him."

A gentleman in her mother's life? Twenty-five years a widow, relishing her misery, driving off anyone who came within ten feet of her front door. And now she knew a man who was capable of ditching a car somewhere it couldn't be? Jean's mind whipped back to the darkest year of the Depression, the railroad tracks with their hobos and Hoovervilles, the closing stores, the dying crops. To bring in extra money to supplement her job in the warehouse of an irrigation supply outfit, Alma had taken in a boarder. He slept in the speakeasy during January and half of February, complaining about the lack of heat, slogging out every morning looking for work. "You'd think my job would be safe," she could still hear him say in a forceful voice. "God and death, two most reliable businesses in the world and me out of a job." When he had appeared on Alma's porch to inquire about the room, he had described himself as an unemployed pastor and gravedigger.

"What was his name?"

"Who?"

"The boarder. Mark something, wasn't it?"

"He remembers *your* name," Alma said.

The smile again, still faint, but lingering now.

"As a matter of fact, he knows all your names."

Alma pulled Jimmy into a hug, crushing his cheek against her housecoat's quilted fabric,

"Les. Les Huntley," Jean said. Yes, it had to be him.

"It was his idea, you know," Alma said, nodding at the linen closet. She took out the package intended for Jimmy's ninth birthday. "Go on, open it, give it a real rip," Alma said. Jimmy did as she said, furiously tearing off the wrapping paper, revealing a box of Lincoln Logs. His face fell—he probably thought he was too old for Lincoln Logs—but he quickly recovered.

"Thanks. I'll build a fort," he said.

Alma tousled Jimmy's hair, gave Jean a kiss on her forehead, and then there they were, droplets of an exotic liquid that Jean hadn't seen for years, so few she could count them individually —a mother's tears.

JEAN SCOOTED the front seat forward so she could comfortably reach the pedals. It was a black, two door 1950 Chevrolet Fleetmaster with California plates. A top-of-the line model in like-new condition, despite its 45,329 miles. There was no registration on the steering column. No luggage, no traveling salesman's suits hanging from a clothing bar in the back seat. No business cards or maps in the glove compartment. The trunk offered no clues to ownership, just a jack and a perfect spare tire that had never been used.

"I found something." Jimmy had been busy in the back seat, stowing their luggage. Now he was on the floor, squeezed in between the seats, straining and grunting. "Move up a little more."

Jean slid the bench seat forward as far as it would go, until her knees scrunched against the steering wheel. Jimmy tugged a rubber floor mat out from beneath the front seat. Something metal and rectangular was affixed to the bottom of the mat with electrical tape. Jimmy used his pocket knife to slice through the tape and pulled out two sheets of metal.

Jimmy slid back into the front seat, holding two Nevada license plates, dusty and pitted. They were the same number—12-384—so probably for the front and back of the car. There was also a plastic pouch that held a laminated identification badge. The badge holder was Wallace "Wally" Marantz, Deputy Security Officer. He was five foot, nine inches, weighed one hundred and fifty-two pounds. In the picture he wore a loose-fitting sport jacket, flowered tie and he looked annoyed. His address was Sagebrush Court, no street number, no town, or state.

Jean looked at her mother's house, as the first gray streaks of light probed the porch. She pictured Alma inside, removing all traces of their visit. Walking past Wallace "Wally" Marantz as she cleaned and organized. Maybe treating herself to a weak cup of coffee in her favorite chair with its beaded arm rests and carpet-bag fabric. Turning off the end table lamp as the house brightened. Waiting for the police. Waiting for Les, her "gentleman," to do whatever he was going to do with their car. If I only knew how, Jean thought, I'd pray like hell for mama. Alma had always referred to prayer as "bullcrackey," but if Les Huntley had softened up Alma's family feelings, perhaps he'd squeezed a little God into her life, one cranky, reluctant amen at a time.

Jean drove through the side streets, meandering on her way to one more stop. Checking her rearview mirror the way she'd seen Widmark and Raft do it. By the time she reached the Silent City, the last of the streetlights had gone out and the tips of the trees were glowing with new sun.

The official name was Modesto Citizens Cemetery, but they'd always called it the Silent City. It was one of five cemeteries clustered in a parkland of the dead along Scenic Drive, a source of civic pride, and a teenage lovers' lane on Halloween midnights. Jean parked near the entry to the south cemetery. It was where the average folks were buried, no obelisks or mausoleums. Using Jimmy's binoculars, she counted the rows until she landed on the simple headstone for Benjamin Norris Maddux, born 1892, died 1934. No commentary or meaningful quote chiseled into the granite. Just a man who lived, who died. The headstone was water-stained. The engraved birth and death dates had darkened. But the grass surrounding the headstone was green and lush; Jean recalled walking on it barefoot as a teenager, cool, yielding, tickling.

The screech of brakes, the squeal of tires, the barking of dogs, the clash of metal and then the silence after the barking stopped. Yet not entirely silent; wind chimes tinkled on a front porch, and to this day Alma would not allow wind chimes in their home. A neighbor screamed, doors slammed. A hand grabbed Jean's skinny wrist and shook her; sawdust fell from her dress onto the weedy patch of dirt that bordered their front yard.

"Mom, are you looking for grandad Benjamin?"

"Yes," she said, passing him the binoculars. "Fifth row back, seven in from the right." Jimmy knew his grandfather was buried here, but Jean had never taken him to see the grave. To Jimmy, he was a remote figure from a distant past, and she had assumed her son was like he had been—uninterested, bored by family history.

"It's hard to read," Jimmy said.

"We'll give it a good cleaning next time we're here."

"Mom, what do you think happens when you die?" Jimmy asked, putting down the binoculars.

"I don't know. I don't think anyone does."

"Grandpa Tamarkin says some Russians think we go to another world. I don't know, I think we stay here. On Earth. It's just that—"

"What?"

"I bet soldiers go to a different place than other people. Not all soldiers, just the good ones."

Well, that's the trick Jimmy, she thought. Separating the good ones from the bad ones, and the in-betweens from everyone else. A trick you will work on your entire life, and never truly master. Was Wally Marantz, whose dead body Jimmy and his mother and grandmother had just dragged down a flight of stairs and propped against a wall like a bag of lawn fertilizer, one of the bad ones? Has he gone to a different place by now? Jean had no fixed thoughts about the afterlife; her father had not been religious, and Alma was a Christmas and Easter churchgoer at best, a "casserole Baptist" as she described herself, lured more by a hearty lunch than inspirational stories of birth and resurrection. God and his heaven had never come down to earth as part of their daily lives. She had no memorized Bible passages to pass on to her son.

Then she saw the smoke. Like a feather, pierced by a ray of rising sun. It came from behind a valley oak at the end of her father's row. Jean started the engine and drove forward a few feet until she could see behind the tree. She saw a guy smoking a cigarette, most likely the smoker who had watched their house in Los Altos. Marantz's pal. With a line of sight to Benjamin Maddux's headstone, waiting for her, on the off chance she would show up there. They had done their research.

It had been years since she'd visited her father's grave and today was not a good time to start.

JIMMY HAD NEVER HAD a problem sleeping in cars. He'd figured out early that his mind was a more exciting playground than the passing scenery, so during the few trips they had taken as a family, he would doze off into his dreams as Robert pointed out historical markers and humorously named rock formations.

Now, he was stretched out in the front seat, sleeping, a half-assembled Lincoln Log ranch on the floor mat. She hoped he wasn't having nightmares. He had heard a man killed, then helped drag his body down a flight of stairs, blood tagging his nearly twelve-year old hands. How would he be affected? Dr. Spock had skipped that part. She should never have given in to him at the Observatory. She should have taken him back to Helen's. Stowed him away at Lucy's Ladies Only Launderette with Jessie. Or gone straight to the airport, put him on an airplane to his grandparents in Portland. If there were prisons for bad mothering, she deserved the biggest of the Big Houses. So why did she keep going, keep driving? A hunch that gradually hardened into certainty; it would take both of them to find Robert.

She had driven south, passing through Fresno, her mind fixed on the deserts of Nevada, because that's where the blacked-out buses had gone, that's where the purring Chevy with the high miles was from. And maybe that's where Robert was. They had attached the Nevada license plates, hoping it would make them seem inconspicuous. Then she'd turned east, following the squiggles of back roads, working her way over the mountains, until the desperation of her mission crept up on her. She pulled into a filling station in a small town that was pinned between mountain and desert, a place where people could complain about the snow in winter, the heat in summer, and the lack of tourists all year around.

She had her maps of California and Nevada spread out on a picnic table that the station owner had set up in the shade of a lean-to where customers could self-wash their cars with a hose and tank of pink soap. There was a "Did you Know?" box in the lower left corner of the map, which bragged that Nevada was 110,567 square miles, the seventh largest state in the union. How were they going to find a non-existent town when they had no directions? She had narrowed their search to the southern deserts. She knew that in early 1951, an A-bomb had been exploded east of Death Valley. She figured that if B.E.'s secret site was nearby, they could draw from the technical expertise of local scientists. There might even be labs or other buildings already in place. It was close to the California border, which was another advantage. But it was still a long shot, and she hoped that once they crossed the state line, they could go to a library, ask around at diners and fire departments and the historical society. Calcite, anyone ever hear of Calcite? Was it far from here? How do we get there? Or would that even work?

Calcite would not exist in the public record. Lawrence Cutler would make sure of that.

She scrunched up the maps, too impatient to fold them, returned to the —a back seat nap was sounding good. And of course, Jimmy was gone. She checked the back seat—their luggage was still there. So, probably off on a scouting mission.

It was a one street town. The sun was directly overhead, scouring the sidewalks of shade. There was no one around. She passed a tavern, a one-room hardware store running a sale on snow shovels, and a grocery store with a red-aproned stock kid cooling off at the open refrigerator, chugging a Bireley's orange. Jean yanked open the front door.

"You see an eleven-year-old boy in here?"

The stock boy nodded, pointed across the street.

Rockhound's Paradise: Gems and Minerals for the Connoisseur, was a western storefront that could have been at home in Dodge City. Its show windows were crowded with colorful rocks and gemstones; strewn among the gems were mining tools and gold nuggets.

It was dim inside and hot. A fan on a counter at the back of the store funneled a breeze down the center aisle, which was lined with glass cases holding gems and minerals, individually labeled in beautiful calligraphy.

"The young man is with you, I presume," came a voice from behind the counter. As Jean approached, a man stood up into view—tall, thickly constructed, and very tanned. Make that burned. His hairline had receded, exposing so much scalp that he was as red as a stop sign. Wisps of white hair curled into his ears, and an arrow-shaped goatee descended at least six inches from his chin. He appeared to be in his fifties, but like many men Jean had met who spent their life in the sun, he could have been ten years younger. Or older. Like the rocks and minerals he sold, he seemed ageless.

"Adieu to disappointment and spleen. What are men to

rocks and mountains?" Every word was carefully pronounced as though he'd taken elocution lessons. "That's Jane Austen," he said. "You're familiar with her work, perhaps? Don't apologize if you're not, I'm not either. But I do appreciate an apt, well-turned phrase when it touches on my métier. Carl Shrake, professional gemologist, amateur hunter of the recondite and mysterious."

Before Jean could reply, Jimmy popped up from behind the counter, a fist-size, smooth gray rock clutched in his hand.

"Calcite!" Jimmy said. "They used it in lenses for bomb sights and gun sights. Because of its optical properties." Jimmy nodded at Shrake, as though they were already friends. "Tell her, Mr. Shrake".

"Your son seems to be a hunter too, Mrs. Vale."

"I hope he's not bothering you."

"Not at all. I don't get many visitors, so I make the most of those I do receive. Tea? Something stronger?"

Jimmy fidgeted and exhaled loudly. Shrake smiled and took the cue.

"There used to be a big calcite mine out in the desert. Not ore cars, like something from Snow White. Guys gouging into the sandstone, pummeling it with air hammers. A hectic place during the war, until they came up with a synthetic substitute. The mine was abandoned. Or so we have been led to believe."

"Where was this mine?" Jean asked.

"Western Nevada. Approximately 50 miles southeast of Death Valley."

Jimmy was excited, and with good reason. Let him wander on his own and there was no telling what he would uncover. He looked at her for approval and she nodded— this could be the lead they had been chasing.

"Mr. Shrake is gonna draw us a map," Jimmy said. "Scale of miles, everything."

"You said you'd been led to believe the mine was abandoned. What did you mean?" Jean asked.

Shrake toyed with his goatee, curling it around his index

finger. "The mine is situated in a high defile, partially encircled by a remote and unnamed mountain range with which I am quite familiar, thanks to my rambles. A foreboding, unattractive place to many, but a hundred million years of fascinating geology."

"A rock hound's paradise," Jean said.

Shrake smiled. "To camp there at night is to camp among the galaxies. But the last few times I've been up there, things have been different. Not in the mountains themselves, but down in the valley."

"Different how?"

Shrake sighed wearily. "Not far from the site of the abandoned mine, lights have begun to appear. More lights each time I go back. "

"What kind of lights?" Jean asked.

"Searchlights. Airplane lights. Car lights, truck lights. Man, despoiling all that beautiful darkness with light. Or rather, with what he imagines to be light. History teaches us differently, doesn't it? Where man first lights a candle, fire soon appears."

11

The soil beneath her back was cool. She was luxuriously barefoot, wiggling her feet in the lumpy dirt, so different from the powdery dust of her childhood. Things were alive down here, spiders skittering across the undersides of the floorboards just above her head, and sow bugs curled into perfect, protected circles; dead things too, the carcasses of two mice, lying together in an odd, last embrace. Sunlight leaked in through the screened air vents, creating a lattice pattern on her open palms.

Her hiding place. Hiding from what? Hiding from another ordinary day, perhaps.

Jimmy would be home from school soon; she couldn't let him find her like this, a cave dweller in an apron.

He found her anyway, he and his friends did. But somewhere else.

She squirmed out of the crawlspace through the trapdoor that gave access to below-the-floor wiring and plumbing. She needed to get a start on dinner. But once she'd emerged onto the patio, she couldn't force herself inside the house. She missed work at B.E, the clattering typewriters, the blaring phones, the deadlines, the burning smell of solder and malfunctioning test equipment; she even missed the nostril-killing stink of the Ozalid room.

She leaned their paint splattered ladder against the house's redwood siding, climbed up, grabbed the gutter—cleaned, she noted—hoisted herself up onto the roof, barefoot, but the shingles were freshly stained with creosote, splinter danger was low. She edged up to the peak, where Jimmy and Robert had laid out an X of electrical tape to mark the spot where a television antenna would stand. She curled her toes around the angled shingles, steadying her stance.

"Mom?"

Down on the patio, Jimmy and two neighborhood boys—Grady Gorman and Frank Burke, both sons of men who'd served with distinction in the war and had the souvenirs to prove it, who'd performed as two of the Three Stooges in the backyard circus on Jimmy's 9th birthday—were staring up at her. In about ten seconds, she'd go from the "neato mom" to the "neighborhood nut." She saw Jimmy cringe, as he endured the whispered jokes from his pals. Grady was the loudest, the boy with the cruel streak—there was always one. He mimed a drinking motion and staggered backwards.

She needed her lists. Maybe she should have filled that damned prescription for that stuff with the side effects.

"Anything yet?" Jimmy asked.

Jean shook her head 'no.' She didn't know what he was getting at, but No felt better than Yes.

"Probably not dark enough," Jimmy added. He was prompting her, he had a plan.

"Yeah, plus there's gonna be a three-quarter moon tonight," she said, trying to follow Jimmy's cues.

Grady had stopped his drunk act. Frank Burke looked up at her, a flicker of interest on his face.

"Although the Trent sighting was in broad daylight," Jimmy said.

"Trent. Sure."

"The guy with the rabbits?"

Now she knew. A couple years earlier, they'd seen the pictures in LIFE, *a flying saucer hovering over McMinnville, Oregon, spotted by the wife of a farmer named Trent as she was feeding their rabbits, then photographed by her husband. She and Jimmy had been fascinated: "Boy, I'd like to see one of those sometime!" She watched Jimmy, pivoting back and forth on his feet, waiting for her to pick up the clues, his friends coming closer. Burke looked thrilled to have a neighborhood roof jumper, possibly drunk at that.*

"Still, there are no ideal circumstances," she said. "As we discussed, the minute you think you won't see one, there it is. Do you have your binoculars?"

Jimmy smiled. "Ready to go. Should we synchronize watches? It's 17:00 hours." Synchronizing watches had done the trick, she was "neato mom" again, part of an operation that required the use of military time.

So, they had begun their private hunt, holding regular vigils on the front porch. It bound them at a time when Jean's "spells" were at their worst, and she saw Jimmy slipping into a caretaker's role, which made her ashamed and determined to bring him more adventure, more boyhood. What drew Jimmy to outer space were not blue giants or red dwarfs, not even the constellations and their impossible to picture mythological characters, but who else was out there and when were they coming here? They clipped sightings from the papers, pasted them into a scrapbook; they knew the names of the pilots and observers who reported the saucers, the various styles—discus, pie plate, doughnut, glowing dome, cigar-shaped. "I wonder, if rather than seeing me coming into the driveway some night, you'd prefer a flying saucer," Robert had joked.

"WE'RE ALMOST THERE!" Jimmy called.

She was seated against a large boulder, her fingers tapping its chalky surface, watched by a lizard doing his pushups. Her head swirled, she was unable to remember sitting down. She had taken an Isoniazid somewhere along the way, washing it down with lukewarm water from Jimmy's canteen.

"Mom, are you even listening to me?" Jimmy towered above her, haloed by a high, white sun.

"Go on back to the car I'll be right there."

She fingered another pill into her mouth, started to dry swallow, then stopped. This drifting into the past while wide awake—was it progress, or backsliding? Did it mean she was about to fall into one of her "states?" She spit out the Isoniazid. She stood up, ground it beneath her canvas shoes. Don't stare into yourself, she thought, don't fixate on the crossed wires, the crazy plumbing in there. Look outward.

Out there was the eastern edge of California, beyond it Nevada desert, flat as a skillet until it butted into a jagged mountain range. According to Carl Shrake's hand-drawn map, decorated with cartoons of vultures and men in rags dying of thirst, the abandoned calcite mine was burrowed into those mountains, and a small town had grown up below. From this distance, there was nothing ominous or strange about it, just five or six streets of houses at the end of a one-lane road, well-positioned at the base of the mountains to catch whatever moisture the desert skies reluctantly gave up. The town had a strategic advantage—they could see anyone coming from miles away. Most small towns were wary of strangers. But a town that didn't appear on any maps, whose existence itself seemed to be a secret could be ten times worse.

"Almost done," Jimmy called. He was working in the back seat of the car, inks and hobby knives and drafting templates spread out on the seat. "Grandpa Tamarkin's Forgery Kit" he called it.

Jean skidded down the shale slope to the turnout where they'd parked at the edge of the road. Jimmy slid out of the car, waving his handiwork for her to admire. He had altered Wally Marantz's Calcite badge to bear her name and a photograph of her he had found somewhere.

"It's terrific," Jean said. His craftsmanship was excellent, she couldn't detect a trace of forgery, but his deviousness was even more impressive. "Where did you get this picture?"

"Well, while you were cooking dinner, I had a look around. And found Nana's scrapbooks."

"In the drawer at the bottom of the mahogany hutch. The locked drawer. Which you picked," Jean said.

Jean studied the picture, her meticulous curls, the middy blouse, the smile, both brash and fearful, a fresh, untested graduate of the Modesto Stenography School, ready to take down whatever the men of the world had to say.

"You realize I was twenty-two when this was taken?"

"Dad says women always want to look younger."

Then he went silent. He gazed at the distant shimmer of Calcite. Perhaps imagining his father there, as she had done during the drive over the Panamint Range.

"Clean up the back seat," she said. "Stow away your stuff, maybe burn the Marantz photo with the lighter." She wondered if they had done enough back in Modesto to cover their tracks. They had phoned Alma from a booth outside the bus depot in Beatty, just across the state line, shouting into the receiver as dust devils pelted the glass with hard-grained sand. Alma had been calm and even a little cocky. The Modesto cops were there, they believed her story, but she couldn't talk long. Her gentleman had already handled "the matter of the car," saying that he would not let anything happen to Alma's family and that the "Lord helps those who help themselves." A man of God who helps to cover up a crime scene—a good catch, indeed.

"And I've been thinking. If they can't find Marantz, they'll be on the lookout for his car. So we can't just drive through the main entrance," Jean said.

Jimmy nodded his agreement, op to op. When he spoke, it was the voice of a second-in-command who understands that his role is to get the job done.

"OK, the situation has changed, roger. What do you suggest?"

"We walk."

They took off the license plates and dug them into the sand, topped by a pile of rocks, arranged to look random. They couldn't bury a whole car, so they drove the Chevy Fleetmaster a couple more miles down the lonely highway and parked it behind a two-story rock formation that was crested with hardy, twisted cactus. They stayed there waiting for dark, watching as the piercing desert blue faded from the skies, a pale new moon rose in the east and a hemisphere of a million stars took over the night. They compacted their belongings into the duffel bag, which Jimmy volunteered to carry, ceding the trailblazing duties to Jean. They set out at 20:30 to avoid the desert heat, their goal a collection of lights that was eight miles distant, according to Carl Shrake's map. They hadn't dared to drive to the intersection where the road to Calcite joined the highway, so they stayed to the northwest, walking parallel to the highway, passing the Calcite turnoff, then headed into open desert, intending to approach the town from the back. "Classic encirclement maneuver," Jimmy called it.

In the friendly glow of starlight, aided by occasional stabs of Jimmy's flashlight wrapped in a blackout cone, they made good time. They finished the steak sandwiches they'd picked up at a joint in Lone Pine. They'd need more food soon, and sleep especially.

"You think dad came this way?"

"No way to tell. But ..." She looked ahead at Calcite, then at the dark immensity that surrounded them. "Maybe we'd feel something, a trace in the air, if we just stood stock still."

They stopped. Flashlight switched off. Jean held her breath, sensed Jimmy doing the same. Then shut her eyes. She shivered. Now that they'd stopped moving, the night chill was creeping up her legs. They say the desert comes alive at night, she had expected to hear scurrying creatures, or catch the reflecting eyes of a jackrabbit. But not tonight, not this desert. No lizards crawled, no snakes slithered. It felt like dead, lifeless ground.

"What's that?" Jimmy whispered. He pointed to his left, away from Calcite to a column of slow moving, bobbing lights. Jimmy raised the binoculars to his eyes. "Soldiers, it looks like. Coming this way. But they look funny."

Jean took the binoculars and saw a column of twelve men marching toward them, two abreast, toting rifles and packs, lights strapped to their helmets. At first nothing seemed odd, but then one of the soldiers veered out of line, wandered off a few feet, stumbling as though he were drunk, before finding his way back to the column. Moments later another soldier drifted out of line and started to march backwards before he was shoved back into step.

Then powerful lights swept across the desert. They saw a desert-camouflaged truck roll out of the darkness, spotlights mounted on the cab roof, following the ragtag squad.

"Whatever the hell this is, they're getting closer. Let's scoot," she said.

Jimmy took off and was soon far ahead. She hurried after him, just as he stumbled, lost his footing, regained it, tripped again, then vanished into the earth.

She started to yell but stifled it; voices were sure to carry far in these soundless spaces. She ran forward, hissing Jimmy's name until her feet slipped out from under her, and she was on her rear end, sliding down a dusty incline, her elbows and knees bumping against sharp, metallic objects embedded in the soft sand. She braked to a stop, saw Jimmy a few feet below her, standing up, shaking dirt off his jeans.

“You alright?” she said.

“Yeah, I wasn’t watching where I was going. What is this?”

Jimmy clicked the flashlight, but it didn’t work. As he jiggled and tapped it, Jean realized that they were in a shallow pit, about the circumference of a Little League infield. She moved toward Jimmy but tripped over something that lay beneath the sand. She scraped at a covering of dust as Jimmy got the flashlight working. It was an animal of some kind, a coyote maybe, but it was mangled, missing a limb or two. The beam moved up the sides of the pit, which were pockmarked with holes, then illuminating the metal objects that Jean had struck on the way down. Twisted fragments of green or copper-colored metal, some scorched black. Different sizes, a few still recognizable as cylinders. One was nearly intact, sprouting with fins. They were artillery or mortar shells, she was sure. It was some sort of firing range, and like the coyote and God knew how many more broken and buried desert creatures, they'd wandered into the bull's eye.

Then they heard the "hut, hut, hut" of a sergeant or someone counting cadence. The squad of soldiers was outside the pit, just above them. The truck was louder now, engine idling. Jimmy switched off the flashlight, and they burrowed into ground as deep as they could. Jean felt matted fur scratch across her cheeks, something narrow and sharp jab at her—a bone maybe. She risked a glance up to the rim of the crater, saw the soldiers' haloed in the truck's searchlights. There were two figures in the truck cab, just watching the soldiers. She heard snatches of conversation: "Oh look, sarge fall down go boom;" "Fire your rifle, let 'em know where we are;" "Where we are, or where they are?;" "Just do it, the signal is three shots;" "I don't have my rifle anymore;" "Where the hell is it?;" "I mean I forgot it. No, I dropped it. No, I took it apart to find the cartridges. They were hiding;" "I can't read my compass. Can any of ya'll read yours?"

Jean heard chuckles, then barking laughter. What sort of soldiers were these? They certainly weren't running a disciplined drill, but neither did they seem like drunk boys will be boys out on a spree.

"The signal ain't three shots. It's a duck call. Like D-Day".

The truck horn trumpeted. The laughing conversation

subsided. She heard tromping boots as the soldiers presumably climbed into the truck. Tires skidded in the sand, and the mystery squad was gone. There came a final, delirious shriek and a cackling shout: “I just love how a full moon makes a man feel. Like he could live forever!”

The new moon was a mere sliver, barely bright enough to be seen.

Jean and Jimmy scrambled out of the pit on hands and knees. The blocky, black shape of a truck, no taillights, was receding towards Calcite.

"What was that all about?" Jean asked.

"Everyone knows they used cricket clickers to signal on D-Day. Maybe they weren't even soldiers."

"Then who were they?"

Jimmy cast the light around three hundred and eighty degrees, but instead of finding traces of the strange company of soldiers, they saw dozens of other pits, some small and deep, others wide and shallow, like moon craters. The desert floor had been gouged by a thousand impacts, Yucca trees had been ripped out and flung, charred and twisted, into rootless heaps.

“Creeping barrage,” Jimmy said.

“From how far away? And can they fire at night?”

“Ten, fifteen miles maybe. Sure, they can fire at night.”

“Then we keep walking.”

THERE WERE no barbed wire or guard towers, no B.E. guards fortifying themselves with ham sandwiches and thermoses of coffee. Just a freshly asphalted road that ended at a curb built to keep out drifting sand. Lining the road were basic ranch-style houses, compact and tidy, two bedrooms at most, hot off the assembly line. Painted shutters, a weather vane or two, but for the most part the homes were uniform in design and color. Jean could picture the unimaginative floor plans —she and Robert had seen similar houses as they gathered ideas for their own home. The front yards were mostly rock gardens, sensible in the desert climate, but a few stubborn homeowners—or were they renters?—were fighting to coax a new lawn to life. The back yards were not accessible from the desert, they were all fenced with solid but neighborly barriers. There were no garages, no driveways either. Cars were parked on the street. It was called Roadrunner Lane, and its one block ended at a T-intersection and another street of identical houses.

Dawn had come and gone. Jean felt they needed to get out of the desert before the fast-rising sun spotlighted them. She tucked the duffel bag behind a spiky yucca tree.

"Mom ..."

"OK, OK. Just whatever you can carry." Jimmy rifled through the bag, stuffing his pockets with batteries, chocolate bars, crumpled map pages, sliding pocket knife and compass into his belt, binoculars worn beneath his shirt. Jean covered the duffel with a layer of sand and dead branches. "We're not intruders. We belong here. We fit in. We're a mother and son who got nothing to hide."

Jimmy walked towards the curb.

"Stop. Stop," Jean said. "Look down".

"A dead rat, so? Yeah, OK, it's a big one."

"It's hung up on something."

They bent down and saw that the rat was entangled in a length of wire that lay just on the surface of the sandy ground, before it disappeared beneath the scrub bushes.

"Possible trip wire. Good eye, Special Op." The supreme compliment from Jimmy, but Jean could see he was scared. As they carefully stepped over the wire, she wondered how close they had come to blowing up the search for Robert.

Then suddenly, they were in the town of Calcite. As they walked up Roadrunner Lane, an engine approached. They fought their instincts to hide and kept to the sidewalk, a mom walking with her young son to the park for a pick-up softball game on another day of summer. A cream-colored milk truck from Silver State Dairies stopped next to them, and a man in white overalls and a matching, billed hat stepped out, lugging a metal carrier stocked with bottles of milk and cartons of eggs. He gave them a "Morning, folks," depositing his deliveries on one porch after another, moving with a practiced ease. As he headed back to his truck, he stopped. Gave them both a long stare.

"Just keep going," Jean whispered. Heads bowed, they walked on.

"You there. Young man." Jimmy turned around. "Don't recall seeing you before."

"Uh, we just moved in, we ..."

"Then you haven't seen me either, have you?" His voice was buttery, Southern-accented.

"Sir, my boy and I are late for—"

"Now what could you possibly be late for? Day shift hasn't even started yet." He lifted a carton of eggs from his carrier, set it down on the sidewalk, took out four eggs, three in one hand, one in the other. He tossed the single egg up in the air and caught it. Repeated the move several times, higher and higher until on the final toss, the egg caught the rising sun, glinted for a moment, then dropped into his open palm.

"Know what the national record is for juggling the most raw eggs? Four. Know what the record for most catches in a row is? Ninety-seven. Know who holds the record? No, not me, it's a guy from Buckeye Farms in Columbus, Ohio. But I'm gaining on him." The milkman launched into his juggling routine, first two, then three, and finally four, the eggs flying from hand to hand, in rainbow arcs, clacking together every third toss or so, never falling to the ground. "Thirty-three, thirty-four, thirty-five ..."

"Splateroonie!" An egg finally hit the asphalt, forming a perfect yellow puddle. "In about ten minutes Mr. Frazee will come out of Number 7, say 'hot enough to fry eggs this morning,' half an hour or so later, some local pooch will lap it up. Sorry, folks, no record today."

The milkman trotted back to his truck. Jean sighed in relief. He climbed up into the driver's seat, started the engine, then shut it off. "Where ya'll say you were headed?"

"The bowling alley," Jimmy said.

"We're going to meet with the manager. My boy here's hoping to land a summer job as a pin setter," Jean said.

"What'd you say your names were?"

"We didn't. But we're pleased to meet you Mr.—"

"Everyone just calls me the milkman."

She noticed the slight off-set of the milkman's jaw, as though he'd been punched hard, repeatedly and wore the deformation like a medal. He studied her and Jimmy with eyes that didn't seem to blink. There were no crow's feet or worry lines; maybe he had never seen anything that disturbed him.

"Well, better get back to my rounds. The company doesn't like me to deliver too late into the morning." He gave them another hard stare, drove to the end of the street, executed a U-turn at the curb, and drove back past them, offering a cordial tip of his hat.

Across the street, a taut looking man in a brown suit, carrying a satchel—padlocked, she noticed—stepped out into his yard. He nodded at them, leaned back inside, kissed the shadow of a wife, walked across his browned lawn, and turned on the sprinkler heads one by one. He inhaled the cooling mist, then he was on his way, striding up the street, joined by other men beginning their morning commute, sipping coffee from thermos cups, nibbling corners of toast; some grave, others doing their best George Burns or Kingfisher impressions from last night's radio programs; some dressed in blue work shirts and overalls; a few even wore shorts. Others in white shirts, sleeves rolled up, ties already loosened. Those are the engineers, Jean thought, guys who didn't have to answer to anybody. There were a few women, too, dressed sensibly but attractively, as Jean had dressed during her B.E. days, making just-so adjustments in their compact mirrors, flipping through reports that had kept them up all night (saving my boss from himself as they used to call it), delving into their sack lunches to make sure they'd packed the tuna salad sandwiches. The rituals of a suburban morning, compacted into a few square blocks in Nowhere, Nevada. Some people drove but most of these commuters walked.

It didn't take long to explore the entire residential area. There were only four streets, crisscrossing each other like a handwritten tic tac toe game: Roadrunner Lane, Quail Run Drive, Yucca Terrace, and Sagebrush Court.

Wally Marantz's street.

Which house was his? Thank God, there were no children's toys scattered in the front yards along Sagebrush Court. Jean hoped there was no wife in there, pacing with worry, wondering where her husband had gone and why she hadn't heard from him. Jean pictured Wally Marantz's drowsy death face, his upturned hat.

The hell with this, she thought; she smacked herself in the face with her anger. *He* broke into her mother's house. *He* carried a gun. He got what he deserved. She dragged Jimmy onward.

Sagebrush Court ended at Calcite Boulevard, the main drag. You couldn't really call it a business district. There was a post office, a diner, a chapel, a Western Union office, but only two shops—a grocery store named "Groceries" and a drug store named "Drug Store." They were buildings of whitewashed plywood with flat, tar-paper roofs; hastily built, barely sturdy enough to support the groaning desert coolers that were bolted to the walls beneath tiny front windows. Housewives and a handful of men drifted in and out of the stores, exchanging hellos. The citizens of Calcite for the most part seemed an open and friendly bunch, although moving among them Jean noticed a pair of casually dressed, unremarkable appearing men who carried no purchases, didn't speak to their neighbors, and seemed directionless, wandering up and down the block like bored teenagers. Was this what unemployment looked like in Calcite? Then Jean felt Grandpa Tamarkin's presence beside her: "Jean, there is no unemployment here. No men without purpose here." So, she smiled at them when they drifted past, and they smiled back.

The last building on the street was the library, a reconditioned Quonset hut, its corrugated walls decorated with hand-painted covers of current bestsellers: "The Caine Mutiny;" "My Cousin Rachel;" and "The Origins of Totalitarianism." Beneath the row of book covers, was a paragraph in cramped handwriting declaring that the library offered "Relaxed First Level Security Regs in our Reading Room."

Calcite Boulevard dead-ended at a T-intersection called Jackrabbit Road.

To the right, Jackrabbit Road led to a guard shack that was flanked by chain link fence, and beyond that, it met the thin black thread of highway. Straight ahead, the desert was criss-crossed with dirt roads that faded into heat haze. There were vehicles at work far out on those roads, kicking up dust storms, generating their own camouflage. To the left, two Quonset huts were joined end to end, marked by a revolving sign depicting a miner's pick and a prospector's pan of silver nuggets. Strike-It-Rich Lanes.

Jean realized she hadn't expected it to be real. Following a trail of hand scrawled bowling score cards had just been a move to make, something to do to break through helplessness.

"That looks like the kind of joint that would serve a bowl of chili. We need to eat, we need a motel. And I want a bath."

As they walked toward the bowling alley, a shadow started to follow them, big and boxy, spreading out from the asphalt onto the shoulder of the road. It was a police car, its silhouette magnified by the rising sun into something more intimidating than it really was—a funny little Rambler. They hadn't even heard it; it was the world's quietest police car. It parked in the center of Jackrabbit Lane and the swirling red light kicked on, its glow washed out by the brilliant desert morning. But the driver barely glanced at them. He took off his cap, wiped the sweat band off with his sleeve, rolled down his window and threw a cigarette butt onto the street. He picked up his radio microphone and spoke to someone, before reaching for another cigarette.

Then they heard a deep rumbling and a bus approached. By its shape, it could have been a San Francisco Muni bus painted over to blend in with the desert colors. There was not a word or number or identifying mark of any kind; even the license plates were gone. The windows had been covered with metal plating; an array of antenna and electrical equipment was clustered on the roof. The bus sounded its big city horn, the police car answered with a whoop of its siren. Then the bus crossed Jackrabbit Boulevard and tore into the desert roads with surprising speed, its oversized, cartoonish tires making it appear to float over the dust.

Calcite was not the end of the trail. Blacked out buses from the Bay Area brought their passengers here—engineers, secretaries, others whose roles she couldn't imagine —but the real work went on out there, where the desert floor yielded to rocky crags and concealing canyons. If Robert was part of it, would they tell her? If he wasn't supposed to be part of it, there were many places for a man to vanish.

12

"*If you wouldn't tell Stalin, don't tell anyone.*"

The slogan was hand printed in bold red letters on a banner hanging from the wall at the end of the bowling lanes, above an announcement for Ladies Night. Otherwise, Strike It Rich Lanes was a ramshackle version of bowling alleys everywhere—three lanes, a pool table, a row of cubby holes for street shoes, an empty five-seat lunch counter. There were no bowlers, just a bored cashier, eyes closed and dreaming, a smile on her face as she let a fan blow lukewarm air over her, and a man in a blue rayon shirt at the end of one of the lanes tinkering with what looked like a boy's erector set loaded with bowling pins, a toolbox at his side.

"OK, Muriel, hit the trigger," the man in the blue shirt called.

Muriel stirred out of her reverie. "Damn it, I had Montgomery Clift in a day dream, right where I want him." She picked up a small, antennaed, box-like device. She checked the wall clock, which was marked in 24-hour military time.

"Got to stay off the airwaves for another fifteen, Ernie."

"We're on a totally different frequency. No threat of interference, I keep telling ya."

"And I'm telling you I'm not gonna bust security regs so you can indulge your Rube Goldberg fantasies. And shouldn't you be in the field?"

Ernie, who was the embodiment of the demanding, petulant engineers for whom Jean had once handled purchase orders, slammed the lid closed on his toolbox and glared. "More boring run-throughs. My section is not needed out there today."

Muriel shrugged, then seemed to notice Jean and Jimmy for the first time.

"Yes?"

Jean hesitated—should she identify herself, come up with an assumed name? Why was she even there? What did she want?

"If you're looking for a game, we don't have any shoes that'll fit the boy," Muriel said. "Can he bowl in his socks?"

From her oversized pockets, Jean pulled out the bowling scorecards with the mysterious equations. "Actually, I'm looking for someone," Jean said. "I think he works here."

"It's just us gals working here," Muriel answered. "Except for Thomas Edison over there, who just stopped in to show off. And why aren't you wearing your badge. Restricted area protocols still apply, you know. Especially if you show up here asking questions. And double especially if I don't know you."

"Firing squad offense," Ernie barked. "How about a root beer float for those of us who are trying to improve what little social life we have around here." Ernie softened when he saw Jimmy approaching him. "Hey there, you wanna see something nifty?"

"Please, I need to see some identification," Muriel said.

Jean fidgeted as Muriel's interrogation face sharpened—lips down curled, eyebrows lowered. "I'm new here. Just got assigned. It's all a bit overwhelming," Jean said.

"I'll still have to call it in."

Jean watched Muriel's hand creep spider-like across the counter towards an extra-large phone with a grid of lights and toggle switches.

Jean reached into her purse for Jimmy's forged badge but stopped. Would it pass muster? Better go with the real thing, she thought. She handed Muriel her old B.E. badge, the plastic lamination slightly yellowed, which she hoped would make it seem recently used. Muriel's eyes widened and she smiled at Jean.

"Man alive, you're badge Number 88! Never seen one below one hundred."

"Please, don't make me feel any older than I am."

Muriel held up the badge to Jean's face for a side-by-side comparison.

"Honey, you got nothing to worry about. Although six months in this desert sun'll pile on a year or two. Anyhoo, you're gonna need a Calcite sector badge. Why don't you have one?"

"Calcite sector, right." Jean nervously flashed the Calcite identification, as Muriel gave it her hawk-eyed stare. "My oh my, getting younger by the minute, aren't we?"

Jean squeaked out an embarrassed laugh, quickly tucked the Calcite badge back into her pocket.

"And where are you billeted?"

Jean ran through the street names they'd seen, wondering if that's how "billets" were assigned. Would they have technical names or code words for their quarters? She glanced around the room, as though the answers would pop out from the bowling trophies and walls of photographs showing people cutting up, pointing slide rules at one another like six-shooters. She heard murmuring voices, saw that Jimmy and Ernie were in deep conversation at the end of the bowling alley.

"Come on, Muriel, just five minutes to go," Ernie called out. "Hit the trigger—the boy wants to see what I've got." Jimmy was crouched next to Ernie, examining the erector set contraption, hefting the bowling pins that were scattered across the lane.

"When the MPs come after you, don't pin it on me." Muriel aimed the boxy device at Ernie and pressed a button. The erector set began to move, lifting up the scattered bowling pins.

"Are the MPs really on their way?" Jean asked.

"Could be. They take radio silence seriously. So, you didn't answer my question —Jean. Where are you billeted?"

There was a whoop from Ernie and applause from Jimmy as the erector set smoothly lowered the ten pins back into place, ready for the next bowler.

"So, who just revolutionized the Calcite bowling league?" Ernie yelled. He slapped Jimmy on the back. "Nice talking with you, Skipper." Jimmy came back to the counter, tugged on Jean's arm.

"Skipper?"

Jimmy gave her a shifty look, then whispered. "Empty house on Yucca Terrace, end of the block. They're expecting someone to move in. Ernie wonders if it's us. I said I'd ask my mom."

Jean turned back to Muriel. She stiffened her spine and decided to go for a sense of privileged indignation. "I'm on Yucca Terrace. And Lawrence—sorry, *Mr. Cutler*—personally approve my billet."

"*Lawrence.* La di da. Well then, Yucca Terrace it is. It's sort of upper crusty. That means it's got a dishwasher. The rest of us make do by hand."

"Sorry, I didn't mean to pull rank, I—"

"Course you did. I'd have done the same thing."

"Mom, let's go."

Jean nodded, but one of the photographs had caught her eye. It was the picture nearest the door, crackled by morning sunlight. A group of men and women were bunched at the lunch counter, laughing, toasting each other with bottles of beer. The women were dressed like they always had at B.E., starched and rather stiff, but the men were not wearing standard engineer's get-up. Instead, they wore khakis, sand-colored vests, and heavy boots. The men's faces were blacked out with ink. Employee names, then bus windows, and now faces, concealed by wartime-level censorship. Jean looked closer. Though his face was obscured, Jean recognized the gangly, elbow-jutting stance of the man who'd crashed the Cutlers' garden party, and driven away in a panel truck.

"It was a good day, that day," Muriel said about the photo. "And if you were wondering, *they* know who they are, that's what's important."

Jean pinned her Calcite badge onto her lapel. Looked outside at the blazing heat.

"Say, how about a couple Cokes before we go," Jean asked. "Colder the better."

Muriel looked her and Jimmy up and down, still suspicious.

"Where there's Coke, there's hospitality," Jean said.

Muriel went to the icebox behind the lunch counter. Jimmy fell into a whisper again.

"The Sirks are here, mom."

"What? How do you know?"

"I asked Ernie. I said Mr. Sirk was helping me with a B-17 model, and I needed the original specs. You know, engineer to engineer."

Jean snorted, amazed at the shrewd little man who stood at her side, seeming to age a year every hour. Muriel returned with the Cokes. Jean handed her a dime.

"Guess I better pick up the house key. And I do that ...?"

"All in your orientation package."

"Of course."

They headed for the door. The knob was too hot to the touch, so Jean pushed on the glass, which was smudged with handprints. The heat slapped her in the face, and she staggered back a step.

"Weather courtesy of the devil himself. Welcome to Calcite, you two. Or three? There's a Mr. Vale, I assume."

"There is."

"Well, stop by on family night. First game's free. And sorry about Ernie's little improvement. I honestly didn't think he'd get it working. Guess your boy won't be a pinsetter, after all."

Jean stopped, looked back at Muriel. How did she know about her pinsetter cover story?

"It's a small town. Word gets around," Muriel said. "Well, it's not really a town, but you know what I mean. Toodleoo."

THE HOUSE at the end of the block on Yucca Terrace was anything but upper crusty. Concrete two step-porch, concrete walk way. A stingy living room bay window where there was no bay to be seen for hundreds of miles. The heat immobilized them as they stood on the sidewalk in front of the house, like prospective home buyers. Jimmy leaned against her, then suddenly twitched—he'd fallen asleep standing up.

"OK, Skipper, we have some decisions to make."

Jimmy rubbed his eyes, squinted into the blazing glare of the bay window.

"The house is at the end of the block, neighbors only on one side, which is good. The back yard's open desert, also good if we need to get out in a hurry. Question is, do we sneak in and try to keep our presence secret, or do we walk right up to the front door like we belong?"

"Front door will probably be locked".

"If that Ernie is right, and they're expecting someone to move in, maybe it's open."

Jimmy yawned, seemed about to keel over.

"We need rest and food. Come on."

Jean led Jimmy to the front door, trying to look like they belonged, homemaker and son, the advance guard for the engineer husband who would soon follow. There was a welcome mat, but instead of saying *Welcome*, a slogan was stitched into it with black thread: "If you get your information here, leave it here." She reached down to the mat.

"Mom. Stop!"

"What?"

"Pretend you're looking through your purse, like you can't find your keys. then look under the doormat."

She nodded. Rooted through her pockets for a couple seconds, then bent down.

"Wait—don't do that either. If that's not the hiding place, you wouldn't look there." Jimmy glanced over his shoulder and Jean spotted the cause of his worry – a figure drifting back and forth behind partially drawn curtains in the house across the street.

"So how do we get into the damn house?"

"Out back. Break a window. Nothing but desert beyond the backyard, right?"

The rear of the house was a lifeless yard that hadn't been watered in weeks, hemmed in by a wooden fence. Jimmy picked up a fist sized rock and was about to lob it through the back door window, when Jean looked up at the roofline. Galvanized gutters, sparkling and rust-free because there was so little rain. Where they'd always kept their "hidey" keys when she was little. Good enough for Modesto, good enough for Calcite.

"Can you give me a boost, or should I give you a boost?" Jean asked.

"I'll give you a boost," Jimmy said.

"You never have before, you know."

"You never asked."

Steadying herself on the downspout that was fixed to the wall, she climbed onto Jimmy's cupped hands, and for the first time in their lives as mother and son, he carried her full weight —straining, grunting, his breath sputtering between clenched teeth, but he held on as she reached into the gutter, scraped around, then found the key.

The interior was dim and pooled with gray light cast by desert sun filtered through roller shades. It was furnished with Penny's catalog furniture that Jean recognized from the layaway purchases she and Robert had made the first year of their marriage. There were nails in the walls, but no pictures hung from them. An empty bookstand. A radio, but no record player, no TV. The carpeting was sand-colored and thin. The kitchen floor was cheap, knotty plywood, a reminder of the temporary, almost military nature of the house —it was a make-do, Seabee version of a home.

They were both beat, both starving. They bumped shoulders as they pushed into the kitchen. Built-in cabinets, stove, refrigerator, and the famous dishwasher Muriel had mentioned. The refrigerator hummed—the power was still on. Inside was a paradise of packaged cold cuts, hot dogs, pickle jars, mustard, relish, mayonnaise, American cheese. The freezer was empty, but Jean figured it awaited the tastes of whoever the next tenants would be. Jimmy opened the cabinets —everything you could want, alphabetized: bread, white and wheat, Campbell's soup, Frosted Flakes, Jell-O, pork and beans, tuna, Vienna sausages. Thoughtfully bookended by Betty Crocker and Better Homes and Gardens cookbooks.

There was no thought of plates or utensils or sitting down at the kitchen table and its four plastic-upholstered chairs. They stuffed it all in standing, not caring what went with what or even how it tasted. "It all goes to the same place" Alma had always said when Jean got fussy, and now she understood.

"You know what this means, don't you?" Jean asked, flicking Ritz crumbs from her mouth, wiping mustard from Jimmy's face with her sleeve. "The new tenants are expected soon, otherwise the cupboards would be bare."

"No milk or eggs, can't be that soon."

"But how much time does that give us? A couple days at most, I'd say."

Jimmy nodded, and his eyes dropped shut. A hot dog

hanging half way out of his mouth, like a candy cigar. She had never seen him this done in.

"Come on." She led them into the first bedroom she came to in the hall, cramped and sparse, a bed and a dresser engraved with lariats and cattle brands—a room meant for kids, but no matter. It was cooled by an evaporative device, the kind of loud, ungainly contraption the better-offs in Modesto had, rumbling outside the window. She helped Jimmy drop onto the sheets, which were taut and unyielding, barracks style, a regular mother putting her regular son to bed.

"Mom ..."

"Nighty night Special OP, you're going to sleep."

"Just bring me the that big knife. Second drawer to the left of the refrigerator. If I need to defend us ..."

Before she could tell him no, he closed his eyes, and then he was out. But not all the way out, eleven and half year olds never are.

"Did you notice the phone?" he asked.

"Yeah. No dial."

"No dial on the radio either."

"Which means they want to know who we talk to and what we listen to."

THE SHOWER WATER WAS TEPID, veering toward cold, but Jean didn't care as it she let it stream the grit of the desert away. She had never slept well in strange beds anyway, and she thought back to the Vales' first family trip ...

A cottage-court cabin with blackout curtains that made her feel like she was trapped in a cave, pinned down next to a man whose body was there, so close, never, ever going away, and a one-year-old boy in a travel crib whose dreams were so vivid and loud, it was as if he already had an entire lifetime to draw upon. She had woken up in a panic, yanking open the curtains, glimpsing the mass of El Capitan that loomed above, like a slab of doom ready to topple over and smash them flat. Where was this sense of suffocation coming from?

Alma and her father had led separate lives, her father in his carpentry shop with his tools and his sketches for projects that would never be built —Colonial-style houses (In Modesto, imagine). Alma everywhere but *the shop, the garden mostly, pruning, shaping and planting; her dahlias could've won ribbons at the county fair if she'd ever worked up the backbone to enter. Evenings spent in their separate corners, with their own desserts and their own books. Every few minutes they would look up at each other, smile, then return wordlessly to their reading. Jean would be on the porch, counting moths, reading her Doctor Dolittles for the umpteenth time, straining to overhear snatches of "grown up" conversation, but hearing only the flip of pages from inside the house.*

So, over the years, a pattern had taken shape in her imagination of a husband and wife and baby living differently than how she had been raised. Not separate lives, but one *life, three equal parts. A solid block that should be held together, as though it were bound tight with baling wire, like the hay blocks she saw farmers tossing on and off truck beds all summer long. You're thinking too much, Jean, she had told herself. She had looked away from El Capitan to watch Robert and Jimmy sleep, curled smiles on their lips. She found it such a delightful sight, she went for their Brownie and took a sneaky snapshot. She thought of the posters and magazine covers with their wartime warnings: "Is Your Trip Necessary?" and she knew, yes, extremely necessary, they were doing just fine ...*

She toweled off, then went to stand over her exhausted boy, trying to recapture that moment of reassurance, but couldn't bring it into the present. She crawled into bed next to Jimmy, and held him, feeling how his weight deepened the mattress, reminding her of what his body had become and was on the verge of becoming, and quickly fell asleep.

As morning sun filtered through the blinds, Jean woke up more or less rested. She padded through the house, hoping to coax a history or a face or a name from its blankness. Every room was the same, a void, scrubbed clean after the previous tenants.

No trash below the kitchen sink. The dishwasher was empty. In the cabinets, basic pots and pans, so spic and span it was as if they'd never been used. The drawers held cheap utensils, a can opener, bottle opener, box of wax paper, paring knife, cheese grater, unopened pack of paper napkins. Even the contents of the refrigerator and the cupboard felt like supplies ordered by an Army quartermaster, probably in bulk and delivered pre-alphabetized.

It was a place that had taken the choices out of life. You moved in here, you accepted that someone else was choosing for you.

"Do you think dad was ever here?"

Jean jumped. "Jeepers, don't sneak up on me like that."

"Basic shadowing rules, mom. We don't announce ourselves. So, who do you think lived here?" Jimmy asked.

"Could've been anyone, I guess. But where are they now?"

She stared at the black phone on the kitchen counter. She longed to call Grandpa Tamarkin or Helen, or the phone booth at the launderette to leave a message for Jessie. But she was sure a B.E. operator would be listening in. She had another idea. She picked up the receiver, got a dial tone. Her fingers instinctively searched for the dial wheel that wasn't there. After a few seconds, a male voice came on the line.

"Switchboard".

"Yes, I'd like the number for Mr. and Mrs. Harold Sirk."

Absolute stillness on the other end.

"Hello? Are you there?"

"Ma'am, there are no phone numbers in Calcite."

"Yes, yes, of course, but I'm a new transfer and—"

"You should have read your orientation package."

"I know, silly me, what with all the movers and things I didn't get to it. Can you connect me directly to them, please."

Jean heard a series of clicks and the chirp of a ringing phone, followed by a loud buzz.

"That phone is currently experiencing trouble on the line," the switchboard guy said.

"Oh, well, it's late anyway. Can you give me the address so I can pop in to see them tomorrow. We're old friends from work."

She heard an aggravated sigh. "Ma'am, there are no house numbers here. It's in your—"

"Orientation package, yes, I know."

"Ask for dad," Jimmy whispered.

Jean shook her head no. "I think we've aroused enough suspicion as is."

"We've been looking for him," Jimmy said. "What if he's been looking for us? What if he really lives here now, maybe he's in one of these houses with a whole other family, another kid."

Jean's frown shut down that line of thinking. She hung up, stepped out to the front steps. She hadn't noticed it before, but there was no house number on the front door. No number on the mailbox, no numbers on the next-door neighbor's house, or on the house across the street.

At that moment, she missed Robert terribly. She missed the words he used, his tone of voice and facial tics, the ten songs he could sing by heart and the ten jokes he had memorized, the word origin stories he came up with—"Did you know that 'oscilloscope' comes from the Latin *osicllare*, to swing." She missed the occasional surprising twists of character, like the time he imposed a code of silence on the family for two days after reading an interview with some monk who was convinced that over-talking shortened the human life span. She even missed his rare rages, when he would hammer nails into the garage framing, pull them out, hammer them in again, pounding himself into exhaustion.

She wanted to scream his name.

Instead, she just spoke his name once, quietly, to whatever desert creatures were listening.

13

The Director didn't care for motor hotels, or, as the steadily abbreviating American language now called them, "motels". His tastes, which he knew were fussy and class conscious, tended towards New England inns, with ski tracks leading to wide porches, mediocre portraits of Revolutionary War generals on the lobby walls, and a welcoming grog served by a severe and judgmental Yankee couple.

He didn't like heat or dust or the threat of sidewinders. He didn't like the desert, certainly not *this* desert, with its bleached horizons and limited color palette. *This* desert was no one's idea of a national park, nor would America's great travel enterprises ever build spacious, timbered lodges here.

But as he checked into the Nevada Palms Motel—no palms in sight, but plenty of Nevada—he appreciated the opportunity that the blazing sunshine gave him to don his new sunglasses for the first time. He was self-conscious at first, but they were comfortable enough that he imagined getting used to them. Plus, the motel and the desert had tactical advantages. The Nevada Palms, one story, L-shaped, flat-roofed, was set on a rise, elevated just enough to offer a panoramic view of the surrounding country. One dirt road in and out. No one's gonna sneak up on you here, the owner boasted. He was one of those Zane Grey characters in modern dress who populated the west, and he was a welcoming host, a man who would unwittingly play a supporting role in history, if things went as planned. The view was one of the reasons the motel's "Big Blast" party had been such a success last year, when desert rats and interested citizens had gathered on the motel's white-rocked roof to sip whiskey and enjoy patriotic snacks such as Better Dead than Red Hots and Moscow Melts as they watched an A-Bomb test.

But now, the blank, endless vista was draining away the Director's renowned patience. If you could see forever, things could take forever to arrive. Like that harsh, distant glare on the horizon. It had to be a car, perhaps the car he'd been waiting for since dawn. But it never seemed to get any closer. He didn't think he could live in a place where time stretched beyond all reasonable measurement. Maybe when he retired, the slow pace of time would be consoling. A ridiculous notion. He would never retire. For better or worse, mostly worse, his services would always be needed.

OVER A BREAKFAST of cold Vienna sausages and Frosted Flakes, no milk, Jimmy and Jean discussed their course of action. They had two choices: stick out, or blend in.

"We've come all this way, and now I feel stuck," Jean said.

"What would dad do?"

"You know your dad. He'd knock on doors and introduce himself and tell a couple of bad jokes and pretty soon everyone in the neighborhood would love him. If this were a normal neighborhood in a normal town."

"Maybe that's what he did."

"I don't think so. By the time he got here, he knew the regular rules don't apply. And did you notice the mailboxes?"

Jimmy hadn't. "Finally, something Dr. Watson observed that

Sherlock missed— there are no names on them. And we can't just Peeping Tom our way block to block, hoping to get a glimpse of the Sirks. Especially since we don't know what they look like."

"You said we belong here. A mom and her son with nothing to hide."

"OK, but we don't have much time. I don't like that the phone operator knows we're here." And she wondered how long it would be until Lawrence Cutler learned that she was in Calcite. And what would he do about it. Surely, nothing violent because she was with Jimmy. Then she felt ashamed for thinking of him as her shield.

As they headed for the front door, the most annoying song she'd ever heard trickled into her head and began to nag: "If I knew you were comin' I'd've baked a cake."

So as perfect new neighbors, they brought ginger cakes, whipped up from a just-add-water Betty Crocker mix found in the cupboard, no eggs, no milk, but plenty of sugar. At best, Jean would be greeted as a friendly addition to the neighborhood; at worse she would be remembered as a terrible baker.

They used their first names only, and so did everyone else. Across the street lived Doris and Ronnie. Doris was Jean's age, deeply tanned, and sporting a showy neck scarf. Ronnie was a chemist who worked all the time, occasionally through the night which made Doris a bit lonesome, but he had bought her a television with his recent bonus. Doris noticed Jimmy perk up when she mentioned the TV, but she didn't take the obvious step of inviting him in to watch it. Next door were Peg and Frank. Peg was pale, quiet but not rude. Frank was a mechanic—she didn't say what kind. When she saw the cake, she said "My diet," then took three slices. At the next house, Jean flinched; it was Nancy Muldoon from the old B.E. secretarial pool. Her husband Bill had flirted with Jean and every skirt that sashayed past his desk. She wore a shiny red belt that would have been at home on a bullfighter, cinched tightly around a bulbous waistline, and was sipping from a glass of champagne. Luckily, she didn't recognize Jean. "Cake and champagne," she cooed, took a slice and shut the door.

And so it went up and down Yucca Terrace, over to Sagebrush, on to Roadrunner Lane, Jimmy furtively taking down names to compare to the decoded bomber crew list, but so far, no luck. There were men at home too: bachelors, a widower, and drowsy married men who worked night shifts while their wives worked days. A few kids streaked through darkened living rooms battened down against the heat, but out of habit or fear, they didn't acknowledge Jimmy. No one complained about life in the neighborhood, no one raved about it either. Jean and Jimmy were never invited in, or asked where they came from. There was a lack of, what was it? Curiosity? Nosiness? Emotion? Everywhere Jean had lived, neighbors gossiped about each other, traded secrets and jealousies. But not here. And if anyone was feeling isolated and trapped in this carbon copy of life, they didn't show it.

After the last piece of ginger cake had been courteously accepted, and the next to last front door closed apologetically, there was still no trace or mention of Evelyn or Harold Sirk. Jean punched her fist into a mailbox. It hit with a solid thump —it was a wooden dummy. The street didn't even get real mail.

Across Road Runner Lane, on the corner lot, a woman was crouched in the garden, armed with spade and watering can. One more chance.

"Come on," Jean said. "Neighborhood gardeners always know the juicy stuff."

The woman was in her late forties, a broad, laugh-lined face, her sensible hairdo bunched up beneath a blue cowboy bandana. She wore work pants with suspenders and was sweating freely as she gouged out a row of holes from the dry soil, plopping in dark, waxy succulents.

"Godforsaken Nevada dirt," she said. She tipped a watering

can into the plants. She stood, pulled off her right glove and offered Jean her hand.

"Betty Klingel. My real name, by the way."

Jean hesitated. But somehow she felt that a woman who complained was a woman who could be trusted.

"Jean and Jimmy. Just moved in."

Jimmy slipped his notebook into his shirt pocket, before accepting Betty's robust hand shake.

"Pleased to meet you. Will my name go in there too?"

Caught, Jimmy stammered for an answer.

"I'll just assume you're cataloging the natural flora and fauna for a show-and-tell report," Betty said. "Scorpion on your foot by the way."

Jimmy looked down, thrilled by the nearly translucent beast crabbing across his boot toe. He kicked it way, watching it skitter into the meager shade of a barrel cactus.

"Twenty species of scorpions live in Nevada. Some days it feels like we got all twenty of them on this block," she said.

"When you said earlier, that Klingel is your real name ..."

"Just being honest. Don't guess you got a lot of that traipsing up and down the street."

That made Jean squirm. Had Betty Klingel been watching them?

"What house did you say you moved in to?" Betty asked. "I know every yard here—I'm your gal for desert gardening tips."

"How are Evelyn Sirk's fuchsias doing in this climate?"

"I used to have one hell of a rose garden, but I had to learn a whole new way of working. But what the hey, what else am I going to do?"

She hadn't answered Jean's question about Evelyn Sirk.

"Do you know Evelyn at all? She's an old friend," Jean pressed.

"No weekends here, it's just 'go, go, go' and '*macht schnell,*' our marching orders set by one would-be general after another." Betty looked at Jean, as though prompting her to agree. "Makes you wonder what it's all for," she added.

Still nothing about Evelyn. Before Jean could answer, they heard a ragged growling from the skies as a plane chugged overhead, low enough to see it was painted solid gray with no markings.

"Rats, I don't have my airplane ID chart," Jimmy said.

The plane soon dwindled to a tiny cross as it faded into a blinding blue sky. "Thousand feet at most," Jimmy declared.

"Curtiss Owl," Betty said. "Scouting plane."

"I thought that was an Owl. We got 'em, and the Russians got 'em, too," Jimmy said.

"Scouting for what?" Jean asked.

"Whatever there is. Maybe me, maybe you. Bit much, if you ask me. But no one ever asks, do they?"

"I wouldn't know," Jean said. Grateful that she and Jimmy had survived their desert march without being seen.

Betty leaned closer, as though there were microphones hidden in the cactus monitoring their conversation. "What I'm saying is, can I count on anonymity here?"

"I guess ..." Jean saw Jimmy reach for his notebook, shook her head 'no.'

"I'm not a party line gal, as I'm sure you've gathered," Betty said. "So, I'm hoping a kindred soul has moved into the neighborhood at last. Things can be a little ... stifling here, and I don't mean the heat."

Jean wondered about Betty Klingel. She was the only person in the neighborhood who had voiced their dissatisfaction. Jean felt herself succumbing to the suspicious atmosphere of Calcite. Was Betty a complainer by nature, or was she trying to test Jean's loyalty to B.E.? Better to keep moving.

"Great to meet you, Betty. We'll let you continue to make the desert bloom," Jean said.

"Welcome to town," Betty said stiffly. Then she directed a

gusher from the hose into the tin watering can. In the morning stillness it made a clattering din.

Jean dragged Jimmy away, feeling Betty Klingel's good neighbor eyes drilling into the back of her neck. A wavering image moved slowly toward them through the morning heat. A boy about Jimmy's age, riding a squeaky, dusty bicycle, a canvas delivery bag slung over his shoulder.

"Paperboy, it looks like, "Jean said.

The boy slowed down, and Jean watched him and Jimmy exchange subtle nods. One professional recognizing another, maybe. Jimmy once had a paper route himself. The paperboy rode slowly past them, continuing along Roadrunner Lane towards its intersection with Calcite Boulevard. Then he stopped, looked back at them, a cloud of bubble gum billowing from his mouth. Jean thought she detected a wag of his chin, but maybe not.

"What's he want?" she asked.

"Search me."

There it was, the chin wag again. Then he rode off.

"He wants us to follow him," Jean said.

They trailed him up Roadrunner Lane, onto Calcite Boulevard for two blocks, passing a row of windowless Quonset huts and turned south onto Quail Run. Then they heard Rosemary Clooney singing "Come On A My house". The paperboy stopped in front of a beige cereal box of a house. There was a party in progress. Music poured out the open front door, people drifted in and out, fanning themselves, trading gripes about the heat. Women in their day-off clothes—pedal pushers, jeans, summer dresses—men in shorts and Hawaiian shirts, and a few who didn't take naturally to relaxation and wore regulation white shirts and ties. A poker game was in full swing at an engineer's work bench that served as a picnic table, a man in a chef's apron held a snake aloft with barbecue tongs before flicking it into the neighbor's rock garden. A group of kids had improvised a playground in the front yard. A Yucca tree topped with a black hat stood in for the bad guy, a girl and a boy armed with toy six-shooters, faced off with it, High Noon style. It was like any neighborhood get-together back home. Except for the shadows cast over the partygoers by the tall, steel supports of the Calcite water tower, which rose like a monster movie spider from a vacant lot in the middle of the block. Unlike most water towers, it was painted flat black. And there were two sentries armed with rifles, pacing the catwalk that ringed the tower.

They were about to head for the party when the paperboy shook his head 'no.' He hopped off his bike and entered the house. We've followed him this far, Jean thought. The boy says wait, we wait. But not too long, sonny; sticking out like this was not part of the plan.

Two men stepped out the front door. They had drinks in their hands, which they emptied onto a cactus patch. "God-damn B.E. company store and its diluted scotch," one of them muttered. "A fella can't even get plastered on his day off." A third man joined them—Jean recognized Ernie the engineer from the bowling alley. With a knowing wink to his pals, he passed around a camping canteen.

The paperboy came back out, got on his bike, rode up the street then turned into a narrow alley between two houses. They followed, dead-ending at the back door of one of the Quonset huts they'd passed on Calcite Boulevard. The paperboy knocked on the door. A moment later, a woman's thick-wristed arm reached out, handed the paperboy a dollar. "Mrs. Vale," a female voice said. The door opened a notch wider, it was dark inside.

"Just you, Mrs. Vale," the voice said.

"We'll go mess around," the paperboy said, speaking at last. "I know all the neat places."

"I don't know," Jean said.

"I'll be fine, mom."

"Are you really a paperboy?"

He reached into his delivery bag, handed her a copy of "The

Calcite Courier." It was five stapled pages of notices for Bingo Nights, discount coupons redeemable for an "Atomic Shake" at the Strike It Rich Lanes, an announcement for a rummage sale to benefit Radio Free Europe.

"How much is it?"

"They're a dime, ma'am."

Jean waved a ten-dollar bill at the boy. "OK, I'll take 'em all."

He grinned and reached for the bill, but Jean pulled it away, shaking it next to her ear, as though it were a sack of jangling coins. "Under one condition—you and my son stay here while I'm inside."

"Mom ..."

"No deliveries, no bike riding. You don't leave this block, or no sawbuck, got that?"

The paperboy and the ex-paperboy traded serious, men-in-charge looks.

"Deal," said the paperboy. "Say, I could fold them into envelope size for an extra dollar. Fit in a lady's purse that way."

"Don't push it, pardner."

Jean gave Jimmy a hug, and shook hands with his new pal, just a couple of deal makers. Then she poked her way into the darkness, and the door was quietly closed behind her. She heard a booming radio announcer's voice as a stout, compact woman in her thirties, wearing capris and a man's short sleeved, checked shirt took Jean by the arm with a grip a big-league pitcher would envy. "What are you doing here? Haven't you and your husband caused me enough goddamn trouble already?"

"What are you talking about? Who are you?"

"You know very well who I am. The paperboy overheard you asking about me."

"Evelyn? Evelyn Sirk?"

"Let's get ourselves away from the door. We'll attract less attention inside." She led Jean down a corridor into the Calcite version of a movie theater, five rows of ten seats each, a necking couple in each row. The man in row three was making serious progress as a newsreel showed Eisenhower on the campaign trail railing about "the mess in Washington, and aimless, bungling foreign policy." Evelyn and Jean sat in the back row, below the projector window, which was made from Saran Wrap. The clatter of the projector mixed with the excited newsreel narration made conversation difficult—and probably impossible to overhear.

"So," Evelyn hissed. "Your husband shows up in Buddy's life and now Buddy's probably dead. Explain yourself."

"I could say the same thing."

"Why are you here, Mrs. Robert Vale? And your enterprising little tyke. In Calcite, a town that doesn't officially exist."

She had a trace of a Southern accent, or maybe it was a small-town drawl, reminding Jean of the women who used to come door to door in Modesto, offering to clean the house, each with their patented mix of vinegar, lemon juice and Fels Naphtha. She had a narrow, pointy face that didn't fit on her solid, blocky frame. She wore her hair à la Veronica Lake, but it made her look distant, not glamour-puss. A bracelet jingled on her left wrist, and she toyed with it like it was a lucky rabbit's foot.

"Is it safe for us to meet here?" Jean asked.

Evelyn nodded towards the couples, entwined and fondling, as up on the screen, Betty Hutton entertained the troops in Korea. "All of 'em married, none to each other. They won't talk about us unless they want me to talk about them. You haven't answered my question. What are you doing here?"

"Looking for my husband."

"And how did you get here?"

"We walked."

"Impossible. You would've been seen at the checkpoint."

"We came in from the desert," Jean said.

"There are tripwires. They would have triggered a siren."

"We avoided them."

"You're lying."

Evelyn grabbed Jean's arm again, twisted until she grimaced. Suddenly, Jean wanted to knock this woman out of her seat, press her face into the popcorn strewn floor.

"Go to hell. We're done talking. Enjoy the show." Jean stood, Evelyn got up too, blocking the projector beam. No one in the audience seemed to notice as the Democratic candidate Adlai Stevenson was blacked out by Evelyn's silhouette.

"I still don't believe you managed to find your way in."

"It can be done, believe me. Or let's ask Harold. If he's still alive. He was a navigator, wasn't he?"

That's when the slap came. A loud smack, Evelyn's bracelet adding an extra sting. They both stood there in shock. Evelyn glanced at the screen. "Eisenhower and Stevenson, not a full head of hair between them." She plopped into her chair. Jean sat back down too. Angry wives who would probably fight to a draw and accomplish nothing.

"Evelyn ..." Jean began.

"No apologies. Apologies are for forgetting someone's birthday."

Evelyn lit a cigarette, offered Jean the pack. Though she didn't smoke, Jean took one, figuring it was better to share the peace pipe than push them into another confrontation.

Evelyn dug into her capris, the pockets overstuffed and bulging like a greedy squirrel's cheeks. Jean was expecting a bomb to drop—a photograph of Sirk and Robert in a furtive meeting or a threatening note to Sirk in Robert's handwriting. What she got was a square piece of paper that said, "Scotch Magnetic Tape," with a date written by hand below the printed headline—"7/8/52."

"What is this?" Jean asked.

"You don't recognize it?"

"Not Robert's handwriting—that's not how he makes his fives."

"It's my husband's writing." Evelyn turned over the paper so

Jean could read the brief note scrawled there: BS with RV. "This is the label from a box of recording tape I found crumpled in Harold's—Buddy's suit. No box, just a label."

"Was it a black suit?" Jean asked, recalling the black suit hanging from the tree,

"How did you know?"

"Not important right now. But I don't follow. Robert didn't have a tape recorder."

High drama movie music blared from the speakers on the wall above their seats. The feature had begun—*I Was a Communist for the FBI.* A shaft of sunlight from the opening front door streaked across the smoochy couples, who immediately pulled apart, the women smoothing their dresses, the men wiping lipstick off their mouths with their shirt cuffs. Two boys about Jimmy's age raced for the front row, hoping for gun-blazing, Commie-killing action.

"Buddy did. We're hoping to start a family, so he bought it to record our child's first words. He got us a movie camera, too. Top of the line, three lens turret. He was so proud of that thing." Her voice caught on the word 'proud,' her anger seeming to fizzle away.

"So, your husband and my husband, they made a tape recording together?"

Evelyn nodded.

"Have you heard it?" Jean asked.

"No. I don't even know where it is. After arrival here, we had to turn in the tape, they let us keep the recorder, but took the microphones. They gave us a couple of tapes they had lying around as so called 'compensation'—radio shows, Judy Garland, Mantovani."

Evelyn looked around the theater, making sure no one was eavesdropping. The couples were back at it, and the boys cheered the screen as Frank Lovejoy punched a bad guy in the kisser, knocking him onto the train tracks, where he was crushed by an onrushing locomotive.

"We civilians can't have that stuff. But *they* can. The MP station has recorders. Big ones. I caught a glimpse of their operation."

"Do they tape record your phone calls?"

"Maybe. Or maybe they just want us to think they do."

Jean shook her head at the twisted rules that seemed to govern Calcite.

"Our mortgages back home are being paid off, savings bonds for our kids, salary increases. And steak is a nickel a pound at the grocery store."

"But what's it all for? What the hell goes on here?"

"A lot goes on here."

"We came across an artillery firing range on the way in."

"Probably something they gave up on, who knows?"

Jean recalled Lawrence Cutler's discussion of the expansion of the business, of the need for new directions, new disciplines. And here she sat in a damn movie theater, Robert and the truth still far out of reach.

"You think our boys are OK out there?"

"Our boys?"

"The paper boy's not your son?"

"He's just a messenger." Evelyn turned away, the Veronica Lake hair concealing her face like a closing curtain.

"I just thought the Fort Apache tree house—"

"You were at my home?"

"Your husband's name was on a list that Robert hid in his desk at B.E. I wanted to talk to him, or you, or anyone. But the house was empty by the time I got there."

Evelyn gulped, trying to swallow the emotion that was rising up in her.

"I'm from a poor town in Arkansas you've never heard of," Evelyn said. "When Buddy and his training squadron came to town to practice at the airbase, he just plain hooked me. I was a bookkeeper at an electrical warehouse, and sometimes those flyboys would come in to rig up fixes to their planes, their equipment, and what not. He looked fine in that leather jacket, I don't mind saying. He went off to war, we wrote each other, he flew his missions, dropped his bombs, I did my work, counting the fuses and switches we sold. It made me feel strong and a part of things to know that some little doodad we sold was up there with him. After the war, when B.E. hired him, he sent for me, we picked up where we left off and got married—me, an Arkansas girl and Buddy, a Minnesota farm kid. we ended up in California. We planned a family, a big family, but—"

She was interrupted by a harsh, metallic blare, like a fire truck siren.

"That's not the movie," Evelyn said.

Jean looked up at the screen. Lovejoy was writing a letter to his son: "I am doing undercover work for our government, I'm fighting a dark and dangerous force ... if the truth gets out, it could mean the end of me ..."

The wailing siren was joined by a second, then a third, an unsynchronized chorus, increasing in volume. The theater lights came on. The couples pulled away from each other, traded shame-faced glances, then both the men and the women bolted for the exit.

"What is it?" Jean asked.

"That's a Yellow Code siren, but they've never used it before. At least not since I've been here."

Evelyn led Jean out the back door, along the alley, onto Quail Run Lane. Jean scanned the block, but there was no sign of Jimmy or the paperboy. She ran up the street, calling his name. The party was breaking up. A few people hurried toward their cars, fumbling for keys, guzzling their cocktails. Jean saw two men stepping into white jumpsuits, fitting what looked like doctor's masks over their foreheads, even as they wolfed down their hamburgers. Cars executed U-turns, swerving to avoid other cars parked along the street. The sacred turf of the street's one healthy lawn was mowed down by tire tread. Other neighbors rolled out barrels from their garage, and began to pry them open with barbecue spatulas, and garden trowels. Through open doors, Jean heard static and then a male voice speaking in low, stern tones—the single channel on the strange black radios had come to life.

"What's a yellow code?"

"Unspecified Emergency," Evelyn said.

"What is it, atomic bomb stuff?" Jean asked. "Why the masks? Mustard gas or something?"

"It's serious business, whatever it is," Evelyn answered.

A beefy fellow still in swim trunks lugged what looked like a window screen across his lawn, then climbed a ladder to his rooftop. At the roof peak, he fitted the screen over the top of the chimney and screwed it into place. A woman appeared at the foot of the ladder, as she quickly uncoiled a garden hose.

"Today isn't the day, is it, honey?" she cried.

"I sure as hell hope not."

"Well, we better shake a leg, just in case." The woman tested the high-pressure valve on the house, spraying the lawn and the driveway.

The man in trunks scanned the desert with the binoculars, then yelled to a neighbor on the roof next door, who was erecting a jury-rigged tower of equipment—measuring instruments of some kind. "How are the prevailing winds, Pete?" he called.

Pete flicked a switch and spindly devices that resembled fans began to whip in circles. "At nine out of the southeast. Light chop to them."

The sirens were louder here, and Jean realized they ringed the catwalk of the water tower, blasting their alarms in all directions. Then she saw Jimmy and the paperboy running down the curling water tower stairs.

"Two planes, dropping flares, flying really low," Jimmy said.

"What were you two doing up there?" Jean asked. She scowled at the paperboy. "What the hell did you get my son into?"

"This is Billy Larkin, and he didn't get me into anything," Jimmy said. "His father was ground crew in the 94th, Mr. Cutler's command. The Flying Fortress crew is here! Well, not here exactly ..." He waved at the distant mountains, craggy against the perfect blue sky. "They're probably up there."

A slightly tipsy straggler hobbled out of the party house to his car, hopping on one foot as he tugged a pair of rugged olive drab pants over his Bermudas. Then he strapped on a gun belt and a pair of sunglasses and got in the car. As he glanced over, Jean recognized him as the cop she had seen in a car outside the bowling alley. He gave a serious nod at Billy Larkin, who thrust his chest out with pride. "I gotta go." He straddled his bike, jerked the front wheel off the ground and spun it with his foot. "Speed limits are lifted during Code Yellow, and I have the fastest bike in the neighborhood. So I'm on patrol. See ya later, kid." He pedaled off, seeming to make a point of not looking back, leaving Jimmy to seethe at being called "kid."

"And I've got traffic," Evelyn said. "I have to report to the site." From her purse she extracted a folded up red vest and slipped it on. She had pinned back her hair and Jean saw worry in her eyes. "Maybe there was an accident, a crash or something. I pray Buddy's not involved. Not that anyone would goddamn tell me."

Now, all along the street, more neighbors inserted their hoses into the open barrels which were filled with some sort of liquid. Jean caught the smell of ammonia mixed with some other caustic, unidentifiable disinfectant.

"What happens here? This town, you, Buddy, all of it?!"

Evelyn started to march off, but Jean snagged her by the vest; they pulled against each other, a tug of war. "You're like the Army men Jimmy plays with, they take you out when they want to play with you, move you around without telling you why, then put you back in your boxes. All these little houses, they're just boxes full of toy soldiers."

"You have no idea what it's like for us. You're a stranger, an outsider."

"I'm Braden Enright badge Number 88. I was working for this company while you were pining away in Dogpatch, waiting for the perfect man to ride to the rescue."

"My *husband* ..." Evelyn said quietly "... is a hero."

She stalked off. Jean let her go, watching her red vest recede.

At the end of the street, where it met Calcite Boulevard, a small cluster of people was forming up into a line. The desert-camouflaged bus lumbered toward the waiting line, coughing ugly exhaust. Apparently, B.E. couldn't afford a decent muffler. Or maybe it was a literal smoke screen. The bus rolled to a stop. Its windows were blacked out. The door opened with a creaky whoosh, and passengers, led by Evelyn, pushed their way on board.

"We have to go with her," Jimmy urged. "If we can get to the crew, maybe they know dad."

"I don't think so."

"We fit in. We're a mother and son who got nothing to hide, remember?"

She watched the neighbors with their hoses and their masks, in crisis mode as they dealt with an unexplained emergency. How could she leave Jimmy here?

"Besides, wherever this bus is going, it could be even worse," Jimmy said. "So bad they won't even let you look out the windows."

Billy Larkin pedaled past at high speed, determined eyes peering out from above his mask. "Billy gets bike patrol and I'm supposed to sit around playing mumblety-peg?" He kicked at an unopened copy of the *Calcite Courier*. which lay in a front yard rock garden, tearing into the flimsy mimeographed front page.

She made a snap decision. "OK, get in. They aren't going to allow kids wherever they're going." She pulled a wad of Jessie

Harper's cash from her pocket, handed it to Jimmy. "I'll get the driver to drop you off at the bowling alley. I trust that Muriel gal."

"And now you're foisting me off on a babysitter? Will I get sodie pop?"

"That'll be enough of your lip, young man."

"You trust the bowling alley lady, but you don't trust *me*?"

"That's not the point."

"You trust me to hide your lists from dad. World's Ten Largest Islands, state flowers, canned vegetable brands—yeah, I made a list of your lists."

"Jimmy, please ..."

"You trust me to hide all kinds of stuff. I cleaned the dust off your back when you came out from under the house, you just didn't see it. There was a potato bug on your shoulder, you didn't see that either, but you trusted *me* to get rid of it before dad came home."

She tried to pull him into a hug. But he tore away, and his pockets spilled open. Two silver dollars, a piece of quartz and a small pill bottle tumbled to the sidewalk. Jean recognized the bottle, and she snatched it up.

"It's not to prevent TB. I looked it up at the library," Jimmy said. "So I kept that secret, too. But you don't trust me to be there when you find dad!"

"That's not what I mean, and you know it. Now get in."

As they climbed into the bus, the deriver squawked "No children."

"He's not going. Can you drop him off at the Strike It Rich? Please."

Her mother's plea worked. When they stopped at the bowling alley, Jimmy bolted to the bus exit.

"I didn't really want to come anyway. I got clues to follow. I'll find dad myself." Then he stopped and stared straight into her. "I bet he'd want to be found by me anyway."

14

When you board a Greyhound or a train, you jostle for the window seat. For the scenery, for the light, for glimpses into the backyards and windows of strangers' houses you pass. But when the windows are painted black it doesn't matter where you sit, you're all blindfolded prisoners in a claptrap cocoon, passing through unseen landscapes to an unknown destination.

Ten words. "I bet he'd want to be found by me anyway."

The boy who knew the byways her mind traveled on the dark days had mastered the art of wounding with ten words. She'd tried to sell the bowling alley as a great place to interview suspects, and he had just laughed. She was nagged by doubt about leaving Jimmy in Calcite, but the bowling alley was crowded, and he would not be alone. There was still a part of him willing to submit to motherly discipline, but she knew it would not stick around for much longer. As the bus headed into the open desert, and Jean disappeared into its blacked-out world, she felt newly ashamed that she had allowed Jimmy to slide into the role of secret keeper. She made a vow to change that. Back home in Los Altos, everything would be wide open—pills, lists, flying saucers at twilight—all of it.

Now perched on an aisle seat next to a woman she recognized from the plating department, whose name was Laura or Laurel, Jean wondered if this was the same bus she saw leaving the B.E. South Shop on Middlefield Road. Evelyn Sirk sat two rows back. Embarrassed by her below the belt attack, Jean gave her a wan smile she hoped carried a trace of apology, but Evelyn ignored her, fussing with the traffic vest, pinning her hair up into an all-business topknot. A tense atmosphere gripped the passengers, hushed voices traded rumors: *"I heard they're going to lock down Calcite;" "There's a bomb shelter below the bowling alley, you know. You access it at the end of the lanes;" "My Charlie says the MPs are being issued Tommy guns;" "I heard they're shutting down the water supply. Must be contaminated or some such."*

Laurel or Laura fished around in her purse, giving Jean a glimpse of what looked like a gas mask, before pulling out a laminated manual labeled, "CODE YELLOW—What to do in the event of an emergency." Jean thought about getting the bus driver to stop and let her out; she could hitchhike back to Jimmy. The bus lurched and slewed, as the tires tried to bite into the sand. Then it slowed down, the driver digging for a lower gear, and the bus fought its way uphill. It came to a stop. Through the front windshield Jean glimpsed dry, furrowed hills, and dozens of unidentified sparkles, like shards of broken glass, arranged in rows up and down the mountainside. Outside, she heard voices, radio static, car and truck engines. A uniformed cop entered, tense and serious, with narrow, questioning eyes that roved over the passengers as though each one were an enemy. His face was creased into a permanent scowl. And he carried a rifle.

"Oh hell," Laura or Laurel said. "Not 'Snead the Sniper'." Laura or Laurel leaned closer, lowered her voice. "He likes to show off by shooting lizards from a hundred yards away. I heard he was a POW guard out in Nebraska somewhere, and it was the happiest time in his life—until now."

Sniper Snead edged down the aisle, re-checking the passengers' identification, asking quiet questions, tapping his rifle barrel against the metal frames of the seats when the passengers' answers didn't make him happy.

"Wally Marantz is the usual guy, but he's on assignment somewhere," Laura or Laurel said. "Never thought I'd miss that mug."

The name *Marantz* shook Jean out of her Jimmy reverie and hurled her back to Alma's bloody stairs. Snead the Sniper moved closer, and from the way he drilled his gaze into Jean, it felt like he knew; he was back there in Modesto, watching, singing along with Wally Marantz—"Since the Yankee come to Trinidad, they got the young girls all goin' mad ..."

He gave Laura or Laurel's identification a squint, then studied Jean's B.E. badge. And kept studying it.

"Not to seem rude, but your photo is a little ... a little behind the times, isn't it Mrs. Vale?"

"We women all have our vanities."

"Vale. I know the name."

"I doubt it."

"Few people doubt me, Mrs. Vale. Those who do are usually proven wrong. After a nice, private chat."

"You sound like a character from a Sam Spade novel. Do you read Hammett?"

"Not a lot of time to read novels on this job." Snead the Sniper thumbed through a stack of papers on his clipboard.

"Mr. Vale not joining you today?"

"Mr. Vale?"

"That's a nice wedding ring. I assume there is a Mr. Vale. A generous, loving husband, I'm guessing."

"Yes, Mr. Vale does quite well. As one might expect from a senior B.E. executive."

"I know the executive masthead by heart and there's no Vale

on it. I'm afraid I can't let you off the bus until I contact your husband."

Jean ran through a stream of potential lies, wondering which, if any, Snead would swallow. The door opened and the passengers got up, pressing down the aisle, which was blocked by Snead.

"There's a reason Mr. Vale is not on the masthead at this particular time and in this particular place," she said. "His duties include monitoring personnel performance during a Code Yellow, so anonymity is somewhat of a necessity." She hoped to unsettle Snead, but he didn't bite, and he didn't move. Impatient murmurs rippled along the aisle.

"And by the way, I don't blame you for not knowing," Jean said.

Most men could not resist a challenge to their insider knowledge, but Snead was different. He smiled. "There's a world of difference between what you don't know and what I don't know. So if you'll just take your seat—"

"I'll vouch for her."

Evelyn craned her head into the crowded aisle. "Her husband works with mine. They're old friends."

"Yeah, come on Snead," a passenger said. "We got to get on station."

Through the open door came the sound of clipped orders being issued and running boots. Snead handed back her identification badge, hanging on to it for several seconds after she'd taken hold of it. "Try to keep out of everyone's hair," he said, then spun around and marched off the bus.

"Thank you," Jean said to Evelyn as they pressed toward the exit.

"Having you in the hands of the MPs doesn't help anyone," she snapped.

The site wasn't what Jean had expected. Set in a natural bowl scooped out of the desert, it benefited from the shade of a high, steep mountainside; it seemed twenty degrees cooler than the streets of Calcite. It appeared more improvised than master-planned. There were no guard towers, no steel-reinforced command centers. Just a few quickly thrown-up buildings that looked like miner's shacks, three Quonset huts, plus a row of Airstream trailers painted in desert colors, linked together by phone lines and electrical cables that wound through the sand in thick, black bundles. The entire site looked like it could be torn down and moved in a couple of hard-working hours. Workers, some in civilian dress, others wearing medical whites or MP uniforms were busy and hurried, determined faces that broadcast weighty concerns, urgent agendas.

The passengers disembarked and dispersed to the Quonset huts and trailers. Others milled, unsure of what to do or where to go. Evelyn hurried to an intersection where three dirt tracks met, but there wasn't enough traffic for her to direct. Then Jean noticed Snead the Sniper and one of his fellow MP's eyeing Evelyn from the front seat of a jeep, their heads bent in conversation.

A crew of men in white smocks appeared, carrying round cylinders on their shoulders connected to spray guns. They tugged surgical masks over their mouths and began to hose down a row of camouflaged military trucks. Jean smelled something sweet and spicy, almost mouth-watering in the air, not the sting of ammonia she was expecting.

She pushed into a knot of people, where she felt less conspicuous. She heard anxiety in the women's voices: "Was there a crash, an accident? Why don't they tell us anything?" A stern reprimand from one of the men: "You'll find out what you need to know, when you need to know. You're on coffee, so hop to it!" Followed by a blistering hiss from another: "This is like Army shit at its most haywire. I'm in maintenance, but I don't see anything to maintain."

The crowd began to shove and elbow. Finally, tempers turned into action and the group surged toward the last Airstream trailer in the row, which seemed to be an administrative office of some kind. Pulling Jean along, passing two trailers that were linked by an improvised corridor of translucent plastic. Jean saw a figure dressed in white, moving like a shadowy wave behind the plastic, which billowed in the breeze generated by the hurrying crowd. Jean could swear the figure was watching her.

Twenty feet from the administrative trailer, the crowd skidded to a stop. Jean squirmed to the front and saw a squad of armed men trooping out of a large tent that was perched on the hillside. The squad moved down the steep slope with practiced ease. They were mostly dressed in blue jeans and t-shirts instead of uniforms. A few wore shorts, but their boots were Army issue, and their faces were serious and set. Once in position, they didn't move, didn't make eye contact. She thought of the stumbling mystery soldiers she and Jimmy had run into—these men were another cut entirely, a crisp, well-trained unit.

None of the sentries issued a command, no one in the crowd spoke up. The anxious calm was broken by the rattle of a rusted iron gate rolling down to bar the Airstream's front door. Then, in a series of clangs, metal shutters dropped shut on all the trailer windows. As though they didn't want anyone to know who was inside. But Jean knew. As the last shutter closed, she'd seen a face peering out, heavy eyebrows lowering like black-out curtains. Lawrence Cutler.

Had he seen her? And if he had, what would he do? Toss her into the Calcite clink? For what? She didn't know anything, but what she didn't know felt important. An entire secret town had been planned, built, and populated by the company that had hired her and her husband, a company that had paid for Jimmy's birth. A company she used to recognize and respect, with clear-cut rules and business goals set out neatly in monthly reports.

"May I have your attention please." Cutler's voice boomed from a bank of loudspeakers set up on top of the administrative hut. "I would like to offer hearty congratulations to all personnel who responded to this Code Yellow alarm. We are gratified by your dedication and preparedness. Had this been a true emergency, we are certain you would have effectively carried out your assigned jobs. And rest assured, if it were the real thing, you wouldn't have detected the scent of cinnamon mulled wine coming from our disinfectant team. You may now return to the bus to be transported back to town. Again, our thanks to all of you."

Jean's first reaction was relief. Jimmy had not been exposed to chemicals, or mustard gas, or radiation, or whatever other deadly inventions the minds of these men could dream up.

The bus started up, exhaust plumed into the air. The workers seemed divided—some moved toward the bus, others gathered around Nancy Muldoon, who slapped her red matador belt against her palm like a hickory switch. "We've been fed so much goddamned malarkey for so long, how do we know this is a really a drill?" Another group, led by neighbor Peg and Ernie the bowling alley engineer got into a verbal scuffle with the Muldoon faction—Jean heard the words "loyalty," "house payments," and "career" spat out like hot curses.

The loudspeakers hissed and a different voice tried a firmer tone: "You must clear the area now. Our work here is ongoing, and time is of the essence, as I'm sure you all understand."

The sentries' postures stiffened, their grips tightened on their rifles, held at port arms. Muldoon and her clique grumbled, but finally edged away. They joined the others retreating toward the bus, knocking carelessly into one another. A rude figure in a dusty overcoat jostled against Jean, and she jostled back. The figure faded into the crowd, but Jean thought she recognized the face. She was about to go after him, but Evelyn was there, prodding Jean by the elbow.

"Come on, that's that."

"Now that I'm here, I'm not going anywhere."

"You can't stay. You're not authorized."

"I'm staying, nonetheless" Jean felt that she was close to the heart of the B.E. secret world. Maybe Robert was here among the labs and Airstreams.

"You'll get in trouble, and by association, I will too," said Evelyn.

"In trouble? With who? I have a right to be here!" Jean's rising tone was attracting glances.

"Keep your voice down. Now let's go."

Jean didn't budge. Evelyn was starting to fume and even turn red, like a cartoon character. Jean laughed, expecting steam to start venting from Evelyn's ears.

"This is funny, is it? Funny?"

"Tell me what's going on here. Is it a bomb or something, some secret new airplane?"

Evelyn's gaze shifted away, back towards the Airstream trailers.

"Please, Evelyn, you know. More than I do, that's for sure."

Evelyn just shook her head.

"You said Buddy could be dead, and that contact with Robert led to it. What do you think happened to him?"

The line of sentries pivoted slowly towards them, a clear signal for the workers to board the bus.

"We're in the same boat here," Jean said. "Both our husbands missing or dead."

"Buddy was promoted. To a higher echelon. More pay, better benefits. And increased watchfulness from everyone. And then ..." The bus was filling up. The driver punched on the horn, the shave and a haircut rhythm. "If I say anymore, I could go to jail."

"Oh come on ..."

Evelyn reached into her pocket, yanked out two folded sheets of paper and handed them to Jean. "Read this!"

Legal documents of some kind.

I, Evelyn Sirk, assignee to the Calcite codicil of the Braden Enright Employee and Spousal Acknowledgements, do swear and affirm that all operational details including but not limited to engi-

neering, mechanical, chemical, electronic facts and data that I may be instructed on or become aware of during the term of this agreement, shall be treated as privileged and confidential to Braden Enright. Such information shall be considered in the national interest of the United States of America, and I will be subject to specific penalties, as discussed in Rider A-6, including asset forfeiture and imprisonment should I violate this agreement.

The driver kicked the bus into gear and drove right up to them. He glowered through the open door. "I wouldn't mind being the fellow you gals are fighting over, but we really have to git. Now."

Evelyn snatched back the document. "Good luck to you, Jean. In the civilian world we would be friends, but here, you're a dangerous person to be around." Evelyn climbed onto the bus. She stopped on the third step and looked back. She didn't speak, but mouthed the words slowly and precisely so Jean could easily lip read: "It's not a bomb."

The bus spun its tires and Jean jumped back, sprayed with sand. As she dusted herself off, she felt something in her pocket that hadn't been there before. Something she immediately recognized—a bowling scorecard from Strike It Rich Lanes. No arithmetic scribbles like on the scorecard she and Jessie found at the South Shop on Middlefield Road, but a note in the same handwriting: "Hide until dark. Other side of the hill west of the trailers. I'll find you. An admirer of your husband's."

15

When the bus pulled away, Jean hid next to it, using it as a moving shield as it climbed the hill to its turnaround spot. It was slow going, she could easily keep pace; the sentries couldn't see her through the black-out windows. As the bus executed its turn, she slipped away and took cover behind a steel shed, which she realized was the men's latrine. The uneven spray and trickle of water on metal—there were two in there, and they were distinguishable by their different styles. This was surely the most ridiculous situation she had ever been in.

She worked her way to the corner of the latrine, where she had a clear view of the Airstream row and the hill behind it, as described in the note from the guy who had jostled her. Best to look like I belong, she concluded. She marched purposefully along a gravel path that wound behind the Airstreams, pausing at the alleys between each trailer, peering out at the site, which had returned to normal, whatever that was. The sentries were gone, workers drifted in and out of the Quonset huts, some carrying armloads of supplies, others coffee cups and sandwiches.

She veered off the gravel path, climbed up to the ridge, then looked back. The shadows cast by the mountainside were lengthening, draping over the site like a cape. A few lights came on in the huts, a generator coughed to life, reminding her of the power mower Robert had so proudly purchased a month before and which Jimmy had eagerly commandeered. She skittered down the far side of the rise, out of the Airstream row's line of site. She found herself in a little valley, a dry wash running through it, prickled with sagebrush and cactus. Lining the wash were huge, box shaped boulders that had withstood the rounding and polishing of centuries of flash flooding. They had indentations and protrusions which formed natural canopies. They were the perfect hiding place.

She chose a thrusting, triangle-shaped boulder and tucked herself under its concealing ledge. Only now, hidden safely for the moment, did she realize how fast her blood was running. Her breathing was clipped and painful, like thumbtacks being pinned into her lungs. She shut her eyes, leaned against the cool surface of the boulder, and imagined herself home in bed, with the afternoon light fading in the hour before Robert came home, the nightstand electric clock with its gentle hum, and the cawing of seagulls who frequently worked their way across the mountains in advance of a Pacific storm. She'd always loved the gulls' unexpected appearances—they signaled change.

She reread the note. "Hide until dark. Other side of the hill west of the trailers. I'll find you. An admirer of your husband's." Why should she trust the anonymous writer? Maybe it was a trap? She considered Evelyn's words—"It's not a bomb." But what was it? She reviewed her years at Braden Enright—they had always made electronic testing and measuring equipment. Lawrence Cutler had loved to quote some famous English scientist: "When you can measure what you're speaking about, you know something about it." She'd ordered the parts herself, components for oscillators, attenuators, audio signal generators, volt meters. She knew the company lore, how they'd assigned big numbers to their earliest equipment, such as the 209-A oscilloscope, implying it was the latest in a line of electronics, and the first of a new series. Trying to make a bigger impression than the one hundred employees in their cramped headquarters presented. The unglamorous looking products they manufactured seemed harmless, even cheery: a control mechanism to operate the telescope on Mt. Hamilton and an electronic harmonica tuner. Their first big sale had been to Walt Disney, something to do with theater amplification for the voices of cartoon characters. How the hell had working for Mickey Mouse led them here? How had she ended up alone, cowering beneath a rock ... except she wasn't alone.

She heard the chirps first, then saw them—two mottled brown and black crickets, perched on the rock wall, getting ready to hunt as night fell. She'd always felt crickets were good luck and now, Jiminy Cricket—Disney's Jiminy Cricket of all people—was here reminding her of her son. Maybe B.E. had helped bring his voice to the world, too.

She wanted to touch the crickets, encourage them to alight on her arm, but she couldn't raise it, she was too tired. She couldn't keep her eyes open, but her ears kept going, broadcasting each comforting chirp, even into her sleep.

The crickets woke her with their silence. Jean peered out from her hiding place. It was well after dark. On the low hill on the opposite side of the wash, a fringe of white light appeared instantly, as though a giant light bulb had been switched on. Her instinct told her to stay put. Robert's "admirer" had said he would find her. But her curiosity was stronger than caution, so she emerged, joining the mice and lizards she could sense scuttling around her in the darkness. The light drew her on, seeming to grow brighter as she climbed the hill, spreading out as though it were the glow from a small town. At the crest, she stopped. Squinting, trying to put together the puzzle pieces of the panorama below.

She missed Jimmy. He would be thrilled to see things he

was not meant to see. There was a long runway down there, a black asphalt stripe cutting through the flat scrubland. At the center of the runway, surrounded by light towers, basking in illuminated glory as though it were a museum piece was an airplane even Jean recognized: America's "Wing and a Prayer" war-winner—a B-17 Flying Fortress. A small group of men wearing overalls was clambering over the wings, climbing in and out of the cockpit, clutching toolboxes. Unseen hands protruded from the belly of the plane, lowering cables and electronic equipment onto a forklift. Mounted in the turrets where the gunners had once sat—like in the photographs that decorated Lawrence Cutler's home office—was a tangle of pipes and hoses. Jean scrabbled down the slope for a closer look. The light towers were so bright and intense, she hoped they would blind the workers to anything that moved in the darkness above them. She edged to within a hundred feet, and squatted like she had seen Jimmy and his friends do—holding their breath, not moving, trying to become part of the landscape, like Apaches.

She recited the crew list she and Jimmy had memorized, wondering if Neal Clark, Will Yancy, Harold Sirk, Randall Ravetto, Morris Gupman, Roger Duval, Frank Alvarez, Delbert Connelly, Preston McHale, Max Prentice were at work down there.

Then she saw "Robert's admirer." The man who slipped her the note. She recognized the loose-limbed way he moved, arms and legs seemingly at—he was the unwelcome guest who Lawrence Cutler had argued with at the garden party.

He stepped out of the darkness behind and paced to the copilot's side of the cockpit. He carried a satchel in his rubber-gloved hands. Two other workers were probing through the cockpit, wearing surgical masks and gloves. Even behind the mask, Jean recognized Betty Klingel's wide face and piled up hairdo. The admirer climbed a stepladder so he could get access to the cockpit, issuing orders and gesturing. Like a surgeon's assistant, Betty Klingel handed him a series of bottles and chemistry flasks, which he gingerly placed into the satchel. As he secured it with a padlock, the admirer looked straight at Jean, as though he had night sense. He nodded once in her direction, backed down the stepladder, vanishing into the shadows beneath the belly of the bomber.

He knew she was there, but now what? What did he mean by the nod—stay put, or go back to her hiding place? Think like him, she told herself. But since she didn't know who he was, how could she know his thoughts? The work crew continued to box up equipment removed from the plane. She circled behind the darker end of the runway, pushing into the desert, kept going until she was out of range of the light towers, which from a distance reminded her of Hollywood movie premiers she'd seen in the newsreels. She found herself in a maze of waist-high barrel cactus. As she picked her way through it, her clothes stuck on the needles, slowing her down. She twisted her body, but the maneuver only drove more needles into her.

"Elmer's Glue-All," a low voice said. "Apply a layer with a popsicle stick, wait half an hour, then peel it off. Unfortunately, we don't have half an hour." He stood at the edge of the cactus field, as though he'd sprouted out of the ground.

"Is my husband alive?"

"Walk straight toward me, Mrs. Vale. Let our shadows blend, they'll only be looking for one shadow."

"Are they watching you?"

"Always."

"Are you a prisoner of some kind?"

"Quite the contrary, I'm a commodity. A valuable commodity."

"Is he *alive*?"

"As of three days ago, yes."

Jean wanted to collapse in relief; instead, she squirmed through the cactus, and was greeted by a firm handshake and an appraising stare.

"My name is Quentin North. I'm a chemist by profession and a conflicted human being by nature and experience."

"Jean. My resume is not as impressive, but here we are."

North lit a cigarette, and waved it around, scattering the embers. "They let me have cigarette breaks, although I don't smoke ordinarily, so they'll be expecting the sparks. I get bathroom breaks out here too, because they know I'm repelled by the communal latrines. Heresy for a lapsed socialist, but as you said, here we are. They also know I treasure moments of solitude, and they allow me my indulgences."

"Why are you telling me all this? I don't know you. But I saw you at the Cutlers' party. What's your connection to them?"

"You and your husband have blundered—no, that does you a disservice—you've insinuated your way against great odds and at potential risk into my world, a world that has been locked down for the last two years." His voice wasn't Californian. It wasn't southern or eastern, undistinguished except for the language. College boy, as Robert might have said.

"Get to the point, Mr. North. Where is my husband?"

"And because Robert has come to share some of my beliefs, and I hope that you may as well."

"What beliefs are those?"

"You're married to him. Surely you know."

"And you don't know my husband if you think that's something he discussed with me." Or I with him, for that matter, she thought.

"Perhaps that's for the better. Uncertain beliefs can be healthy. The world has seen too much unwavering conviction, too much profound belief."

"Actually, I'm wondering if you saw him at all, or even talked to him."

North handed her a snapshot. Blocking her body with his, merging them into a single shadow, he flicked on a lighter and Jean recognized a photo Robert usually carried in his wallet. Jimmy wearing a homemade Foreign Legion cap, armed with pick and shovel, excavating a backyard "archeology site." The light went out before Jean could examine it closer.

"Why would he give you this?"

"Pride, I expect. Like father, like son—unearthers of truths."

"I assume you're a bigwig at B.E. You could've gotten hold of Robert's wallet somehow."

"Your son Jimmy's favorite snack is Junior Mints. Then come Fritos and if he can't get those, he'll settle for frozen potatoes, of all things, California Golden brand."

"That's not Robert at all. He wouldn't suddenly start rattling off things like that."

"He didn't just 'rattle them off.' It emerged in the course of our discussion."

"Discussion about what?

"Chemistry, actually. A bit of brain science and biology thrown in as well."

They heard a truck drive onto the runway. One of the light towers refocused its beams.

"OK, they'll be needing me. I have to get back." He grabbed Jean by the shoulders. "I need to know, Mrs. Vale."

"Know what?"

"Are you truly your husband's wife?"

"What in tarnation does that mean?"

The light tower flashed on and off. The truck blared its horn.

"Don't play hausfrau games with me. Are you?" He kept one powerful hand on her shoulder, flared the cigarette lighter with the other. She sensed he wanted her to see his eyes, sharpened slits, slicing into her. "Are you willing to go against what everyone believes? What Cutler believes, what his bosses in Washington believe, what the country believes? Because if you aren't, there is no penalty. I will call my *minders* and you will be escorted without repercussion back to Calcite. And since I'm an excellent bowler who has the only perfect score that has ever been recorded at Strike it Rich Lanes, and certainly the only perfect game within fifty miles of an atomic explosion, you will be awarded five free games and endless ice cream sodas for your son. What'll it be?"

Static and amplified microphone howls. "Mr. North. You're needed at the end of Runway 30." Then, late night laughter, men who were overworked and had gotten hold of booze. "You got some Nevada cowgirl out there? It can be a lot of work to get those boots off."

"You asked me up here, to what? Make me pledge my loyalty to you? What have you dragged Robert into?" She pulled against his grip. He let her go, though she sensed there was a reserve of physical strength there that he had not called on. "Why did he come here in the first place?" she asked.

"I can't tell you yet."

"America's security? The hell with that."

"It's in your interest to be in the dark—for now."

She suspected she would get no further with him. He had the easy superiority of the "big picture" men Lawrence Cutler used to bring in to explain "B.E.'s long term thinking" to the engineers, who then explained it to the bench workers like Robert who in turn explained it to the secretaries and purchasing agents.

"Just what do you want with me? Why do you even care about me if you and Robert are so buddy-buddy?"

"Because I may need to call on Robert for help. For something important, even urgent. And now that you're here, I need to know where you stand."

"I stand with my husband. Not with you, and not goddamn B.E."

"You stand with your husband. That's good enough for now."

They heard the truck backing up, turning, headlights sweeping.

"They're coming," North said. "Take that hillside up through the sticky pan array, there's a footpath so the maintenance workers can access them." North pointed toward the dry hills she'd seen on the way in, with rows of strange rectangles that resembled baking pans mounted on stakes.

"What are those?" Jean asked.

"Fallout collectors. Usually coated with an alkyd-resin toluene solution for easier data collection."

"Fallout? Like atom bombs?"

"From a previous B.E. project. The company doesn't just measure electronic signals hurtling through the airwaves. They had a team out at the atomic test site last year as well."

"What? B.E. was involved with all that?"

"On the periphery, a single government contract. But it helped to lay the initial infrastructure for Calcite. Although by now, they may have a dozen new contracts as well, but I'm not privileged with that information."

"You keep saying 'they', not 'we'."

"I wasn't part of the atomic project. It's a delusional game I play with pronouns so I can live with myself. Now go, please!"

Jean looked up at the rows of sticky pans. "Isn't it dangerous?"

"The area is clean. Those are dummies. To fool low flying aircraft, should any pilot be reckless enough or sufficiently off course to overfly us."

It was almost comical, something out of Tom Swift. They were pretending to work on the A-bomb to deflect attention from the true nature of—of what?

"What was the Code Yellow all about?"

"It means the day of reckoning is getting close."

"You are an extremely annoying man, Mr. North."

"So I've been told. Once you pass the array, you'll hit the path leading down to the main road. You can easily walk back."

"It took at least a half hour on the bus."

"Half of that was backtracking and diversion, so the workers who hadn't been up to the site before would become disoriented. You'll see the lights of Calcite once you reach the road. I'll find you if I need you."

They heard charging footsteps and saw backlit silhouettes flitting towards the cactus field.

"When you saw Robert, how was he? Normal seeming?"

"I don't have a working standard on his behavior, so I can't judge."

"He's usually calm, sort of blindly sociable, not a guy you'd expect to cause trouble. Harmless."

"He was none of those things. The opposite, actually."

"Do you have another meeting planned?"

"Depends on circumstances. We may meet in a chapel out in the desert. A splintered cross on the roof. Now get yourself out of here." He waved her off, then strangely, he unbuckled his pants and dropped them to his knees.

Jean ran, wondering what North had meant about going up against everything she believed in. But he had met Robert, she was pretty sure. And he was using Robert for something. Whatever it was, it would be just another damn secret, like everything else in Calcite. She climbed, weaving between the sticky pans on their spikes, like car speaker stands at a drive-in movie. She stumbled, reached out to steady herself on a sticky pan, then yanked her hand away. What if North was lying about the array, and the pans were truly collecting fallout? She'd heard the civil defense sirens blasting from the Los Altos fire station on Fridays at 5 o'clock, seen the magazine ads for family Geiger counters. What if she were surrounded by atomic radiation now; it worked silently, she'd read, infiltrating the blood system.

"After a hard day's work, a man can't take a satisfying midnight shit?" North's annoyed voice carried up the hillside.

Jean crested the ridge, and as promised the lights of Calcite beckoned a couple of miles away. The main road, empty now, led razor straight to the main gate. Jean had always been a walker, even her father's affection for automobiles and distaste for pedestrians, couldn't stop her. As a girl, she'd walked across fields, meandered through orchards, splashed barefoot through shallow stretches of the Stanislaus and the American rivers, marched down Modesto alleys and main streets, strolled through the new State Theater while it was still under construction. She could do this walk in her sleep.

She didn't know what to think of North, but she had no choice but to believe him. To trust him? She wouldn't be sure unless he came to her in desperation. But he'd met Robert, and he was alive! She tried to picture Robert at a furtive rendezvous in some remote chapel. The man who had been surprised to learn that San Francisco was named for Saint Francis. As a married couple, they hadn't been church-goers or talked much about God or Jesus or the Bible. But then she realized that in his own way, Robert *was* a kind of church. The church of acceptable striving, the church of good dads and breadwinning husbands, a church without cunning. That was her husband. Or had been her husband until he'd vanished. And that didn't sound like the man who Quentin North had met.

By the time she got to the road, a sliver of moon was rising, the stars were sharp as needle points, the Big Dipper was easy to spot. She stepped up her pace, avoided the deep sand along the shoulder and made good time on the asphalt. A coyote loped across the road, glanced at her, then bolted off, attracted by unseen prey. It was a good omen; all creatures have their missions. That sounded sort of religious, didn't it?

She heard the truck before she saw it, an engine approaching from Calcite. No headlights. She darted off the asphalt, and crouched in the sand, but the truck sped up, veering across the road, driving on the wrong side, heading straight for her. It was boxy and cream colored. The milk truck. Its headlights flashed on, the beams were arrows, searching. If she stood up, she would be a fat target. She sat unmoving on her haunches, as the back doors of the milk truck swung open, and two men in civilian clothes climbed out. One she didn't recognize; the other was the guy they used to call "The Bloodsucker," a combat medic who had supposedly hit Omaha Beach, but who was better known for running the B.E. blood drives where he was enthusiastic and hands on. She sifted through the sand, it was deep, she could probably outrun the truck, its tires would sink as they gouged for traction. The bloodsucker and the other man reached into the milk truck, pulled out what looked like a flagpole. They each took an end and unfurled it into a stretcher. She was empty-handed. They would have to drop the stretcher to pursue her. She was alone, there were three of them. They would have to confer while all she had to do was run. If she took off now, she could build up a lead.

The milkman slid out from behind the wheel.

Jean took deep breaths, ready to bolt.

With his left hand, the milkman switched on a flashlight, painted his face with light, a self-portrait so that she could see his determination, then ran the beam down the length of his arm to his right hand and the gun it held. He was in his pristine white uniform, and Jean couldn't find the will or the energy to run. Who runs from the milkman?

He shook his head, as though he were disappointed in her, as the Bloodsucker and his pal lifted her onto the stretcher. Their arms were thick as redwood logs, and she was just a handful of kindling to them. She felt a needle puncture her arm and she watched the sickle moon drop behind the mountain, dragging the stars with it.

16

There was no milk or cream, no eggs or butter, no cottage cheese.

Just thirst, which made no sense because saliva was trickling down her chin. Her face was hot, her arms were shaking up and down, slapping her torso, then collapsing, only to spread the jittering to her legs. She felt herself moan, sensed the movements of her throat, but didn't hear her voice.

She couldn't see but maybe that was because her eyes were closed. Or maybe she lacked the strength to lift her eyelids. She was lying between two crisp sheets. When her legs and arms spasmed, the sheets stayed true and stiff, like a restraining outer shell. The twitching in her limbs spread to her toes and fingers, then abated, leaving her drained and groggy. There were pillows beneath her head. Warm, so she'd been there awhile. She could feel light through her eyelids. Had the sun come up? There were no day sounds, but there were no night sounds either. Or maybe she was deaf now?

She opened her eyes. Heavy light weighed down on her from hidden fixtures above. She was alone in a sparsely furnished room with one window, shade drawn, and one door.

The bed was metal framed, no headboard. There was a nightstand to her left—no, not a nightstand, a stack of cardboard boxes. With labels she couldn't read. No clock, no lamp. A pitcher of water and a glass. She poured a glass, guzzled it sloppily, then flopped back down.

She was dressed in the same slacks and blouse. Desert sand gritted the sheets, shaken off by her convulsions. She examined her body by hand. No wounds or scars or broken bones. But she was still hot, still sweating. Her hands found a folded washcloth next to her pillows, which she used to blot the perspiration from her forehead and neck and wrists. Whoever had done this to her—whatever they had done to her—they had anticipated her symptoms. Which meant they had caused them. She gave herself a mental hurrah—she could still think.

Should she get up? There was a throw rug on the concrete floor next to her bed. Not until she knew where she was or how much time had passed. But the only way she could determine that was to get up and raise the window shade.

Then she realized that of course she could hear. She had heard the pitcher clink against the glass and the glug of water as she poured it. She shut her eyes, because somewhere back in her girlhood, she had come to believe that the tighter you clamped your eyelids the better you could hear. She detected a dull electrical hum, like an icebox doing its duty. Then more rumbles and hisses, exhalations of pipes and pumps. Were there other rooms with other beds and other ... what was she, a patient, a prisoner?

She forced herself to her feet, wobbled towards the roller shade, yanked on it, but it wouldn't snap up. It was nailed into place. Not just at the top and bottom, but along the sides, a nail every inch, so she would have to cut the shade apart to look out the window. Why have a window at all? To keep her from looking out? Or to keep others from looking in? She scratched at the shade fabric, hoping the sun had turned it brittle. But she couldn't break through and didn't have the strength to tear the shade free from the nails. She dragged back to bed.

The door opened and two men marched in. One was the Bloodsucker, the other was a short, mild-looking man with wavy, fussed over hair who wore a doctor's white coat, and carried a tray glinting with medical instruments which he placed on the night table. The doctor coughed, the dry retch of a desert cold, which he seemed quite willing to spread around.

"Where am I? What's happening to me?"

The Bloodsucker held Jean in place on the bed as the doctor rolled up her sleeve, dabbed at her wrist with a cotton swab, then filled a syringe from a red capped bottle labeled U-20.

"What is that? I'm not sick. There's nothing wrong with me!" She twisted her hand, managed to slap the syringe out of the doctor's hand onto the floor. The Bloodsucker pinned her arm to the mattress as the doctor calmly readied another syringe. He jabbed her, pushed the clear chemical into her veins, and it spread like a stream of warm bath water. Then her lips began to tingle and the room spun around her in Merry-Go-Round circles. She began to shiver.

It felt like only ten seconds had gone by, then they were back again. She was weak and her extremities were fired with pain. The doctor carried a thin tube connected to a funnel. He slid the tube into her nose and began to pour from a white coffee pot into the funnel. She choked, mucous jetted out of her nose. She jerked up like Frankenstein's monster electrified into being, slumped back against the pillows, twisted onto her side as pain spread from organ to organ, shooting up her neck into some newly created vacancy behind her eyes where it pricked and punched until she was certain her eyeballs would pop out and roll onto the floor. Would they rattle like marbles? Or were eyeballs soft and squishy?

Then, like a storm running out of rain, she wilted into the

sheets and was at rest. The doctor was studying her with a nodding, satisfied gaze.

"Where's the suck blooder?" she asked.

"Who?"

"The suck blooder. The other man."

"Not needed right now. You're responding well to treatment." He hacked into a handkerchief.

"Why did you go away and come back seconds later?"

"It was an hour, Mrs. Vale. Hour and ten minutes to be exact —a bit longer than we prefer."

She found herself staring at the backs of her hands, which were white as paste. She scratched one hand with her other, trying to draw color and blood to the surface.

"Pallor is one of the side effects. It's not permanent." The doctor reached into his pocket, causing Jean to flinch as she expected another needle, another tube. He came up with a pack of Stik-O-Pep LifeSavers, unwrapped a handful and crunched on them. Jean noticed the ceiling was a corrugated metal arc about a yard above the tops of the walls.

"A whatsit hut."

The doctor laughed. "Yes, Mrs. Vale, it's a Quonset hut all right. I believe it did duty in Korea. So, will your husband be checking in on you soon?"

She blinked rapid fire, as though it would summon her husband into the room. She couldn't picture him. He was a noun—*husband*—not a human being.

"How would he know I'm here?"

"We can contact him, let him know where you are. We allow select visitors, depending on the phase of your treatment."

"Treatment?"

The doctor tugged an ink-scribbled memo pad from his pocket. "Just tell us where we can get in touch with him, and we'll rush him here. I'm sure he's concerned."

"I don't—I don't know where he is."

"Oh come. I know where my wife is at this very moment. Home with our two-year-old. Watching 'Love of Life'."

The doctor readied another syringe, then knocked on the door.

"No, keep the sucker blood out. I won't fight you. I'll go to sleep. Promise."

The doctor smiled and nodded, as though they were the words he had expected to hear.

Another injection. Ten seconds later, another tube in the nose, writhing anguish followed by calm. Same questions from the doctor, same answers from Jean. She didn't know where her husband was. Another injection. Another ten seconds. She lost track of how many times she went under, how many times she was brought back to consciousness.

THE ROOM WAS DARK NOW. No nose tube. She felt a towel stretched across her upper body like a bib at a barbecue. Wet and sticky with whatever had drizzled or sprayed from her mouth and nose. Hands pulled the towel away, replaced it with a fresh one.

"You still don't know?" A different voice. Not the doctor's.

"His name is Robert," Jean said. And now she could imagine him perfectly, in his blazer and gray billowing slacks, his harmless smile and his harmless cocktail that had no booze. The out of staters party in a third-floor gabled apartment in Palo Alto that her friend Gwen had organized, with Jean the honorary Californian. It was a get-together for outsiders trying to become Golden Staters, drawn by jobs and the threat of war that promised to create more jobs. She and Robert talked, clumsily at first, then easily. He was serious and wanted to do serious work. He'd taken classes—nights and correspondence —in electricity, radio repair, weather prediction, world history. And as history led to war, it led him to California where he had a sense that big events were about to happen, events that would bypass him back home in Portland. But he was stuck working as a bank teller and she was already at B.E., closer "to the heart of things" as he called it. He had a flair for fun and laughter, too. "Bounce Me Brother With A Solid Four" on the radio. Everyone knew the words to "Boogie Woogie Bugle Boy," no one knew the words to Bounce Me Brother. Robert did. He asked her to dance. He was graceful and perfectly sculpted for her, the nook below his collar bone that fit her head. He seemed to caress her with his breathing which he somehow timed to the music. "Am I moving too fast?" he'd asked. "You look harmless to me, brother," she said, intending a complement. He wasn't a wolf like other Peninsula men into whose dance floor embrace girlfriends had pushed her. He wasn't a hunter desperate to get in his shot before war came which, even in the summer of 1941, everyone knew was on its way.

"He's harmless," Jean said, to whoever was in the room with her. Her voice floated around the room, then came back to her.

"Then why is he not at his desk, doing the job for which I amply pay him?

Why did he come to Calcite? Why has he been meeting with former crew members of my command? Why is he compiling lists and dossiers on them?"

Eighth Air Force. Not Clark Gable, but Jimmy Stewart. Jimmy ... where was he? Why hadn't she thought of him until now?

"Lawrence? Is that you? Can you ... can we ... light please?"

"No Jean, I cannot turn on the light."

"My boy. Is he OK?"

"We're discussing Robert now."

"I need to see Jimmy!"

"Why is Robert attending secret funerals for B.E. employees?"

"Who ... who told you all that?"

"You did, Jean."

"No, I didn't. When?"

"After the fifth session."

"Fifth what?"

"Coma. That's what the insulin induces, that's what helps you break free, helps you talk to me."

She could smell his breath in the dark.

"El Zarape." Jean said. "Enchiladas from El Zarape in Palo Alto?"

"Do you think I'm enjoying this, Jean?"

"But why are those enchiladas here? Or am I back there? Can I have one?"

Jean felt a spoon slide into her mouth, and the slippery cheesy glistening of an El Zarape enchilada on her taste buds. She was reluctant to swallow, to surrender the familiar, comfortable sensation.

She had the thoughts but couldn't round them up into a speakable bundle. "Naps. Not coma."

"I've been told that it's a very effective treatment for someone with your condition. We're just trying to help you. To heal you."

"Hunger, thirst? My conditions. Why so dark here?"

"Well, your mental state, your psychology. The reason you were let go from B.E. I'm just a businessman and an ex-soldier —and a caring friend, I like to think. I don't pretend to understand. I have experts for that."

"The doctors. Experts."

"So I'm told."

"By who?"

"Other experts. Another bite?"

Jean could sense the spicy forkful hovering just beyond her lips. And Lawrence her interrogator, a bad one at that. He kept it dark so she couldn't read his face, couldn't gauge his reactions as she answered his questions.

"I asked Robert to stop. But he didn't," Lawrence said.

Don't answer, she told herself. Make him keep going, make him reveal.

"His damn digging into B.E. business that wasn't in is department. It became his obsession. I offered him the promotion he'd been pestering me for, the promotion he thought that fair play and hard work had made his right."

He *did* deserve it, she thought. He soldered the wires that made B.E. successful.

"I offered him a special class of stock, a private issue that few in our company can hope for. And you know what 'harmless' Robert Vale told me? He said 'go get fucked, Larry'".

"Robert said that? *My* Robert?" She shivered, then realized it was a giggle. A giggle of pride.

She felt Lawrence lean closer, his breathing labored. "So we need to know where he is. I'm as concerned about him as you are."

Jean turned over on her side, like a wife who'd had a spat with her husband and didn't want to be touched or apologized to. She heard Lawrence walk to the door and open it. The murmur of low-voiced disputes. Someone came in, loomed over the bed. He took her arm, shoved in the needle ...

She had worked on the model house for seven weeks. Framing it, siding it, constructing windows out of broken bottle glass she collected in the alleys during her walks. It was two story, with two chimneys, dormer windows, a porch capped with trim that she'd carved out of Lifebuoy soap. She prayed it would never rain on this house. Mostly, she'd used kitchen knives to cut and her mother's tweezers for the more delicate work, but when she needed planes and saws, she'd slip into open sheds and garage workshops, or skulk down to the Southern Pacific yards and borrow tools for an hour or two. Never needing to go into her father's workshop, never needing to use his tools. She worked in secret, always alone, on a rocky shore of the Stanislaus River when it was sunny, or a cement nook beneath one of the irrigation canals when it rained. Never in her room, never at home, never where her father or mother could see her. She shook the sawdust out of her clothing before coming home after a day's work, taking a bath to remove the unmistakable smell of freshly cut wood —her father's smell. During construction, she hid it in her closet, a jumbled, secretive place that her mother knew never to clean, and her father avoided because it was a girl's closet. She thought about adding a closet like it to the house, but limited patience and materials prevailed. When she was finished, she varnished it and rode through town with it tucked under a blanket on her bicycle basket to let the shellac fumes waft away before bringing it home. The night before "presentation day," she couldn't sleep. She got up every hour and checked on the house, afraid to turn on the light, but reassured by its bulk and the smooth finish which felt like a melted Hershey bar. The next day she couldn't eat. Her mother would set something on the table; her appetite was not in her stomach, but in her heart and head. It was late summer, school was out, the heat was heavy, the wind was still, and the day was endless. She had planned what she would wear, but when the time came, everything happened so fast that she didn't notice. It was probably the same dingy brown dress she always wore in warm weather—"It doesn't show the dirt," her mother said. She gingerly picked up the house, draped it with a pillow case, then rushed down the stairs, balancing it in her arms like it was a thousand dollars of breakable China, not bothering to clutch the banister for support, not needing to, she was riding on her own rails now and would never fall off. Through the front room, out onto the porch, the house where she lived making way for the house where she wanted to live, its roofline and chimneys bulging beneath the pillow case, her sneaky two months of craftsmanship soon to be revealed to the most demanding, most appreciative audience in the world. She was too young to know what it meant to be supremely alive—life was just there, living was what you did. But in years to come, she would recognize that moment as a pinnacle of expectation and pride—to have created something you loved for someone you loved. She heard the horn, and then the Maxwell Touring car turned the corner onto their street, as much a part of her father as his carpentry, the eye-catching symbol of what his handiwork had achieved and brought into his family's world, one side painted baby blue, the rest dull black, awaiting new paint because her father was not going to have a car that looked like every other. She ran across the yard to the shoulder of the road, the pillow case blew off the model house, which now gleamed in the sun that refused to set or even cool down that day of all days.

And then she made the biggest mistake of her life.

She couldn't wait for him to park, to come to her, to ask professional questions as he peered into the tiny windows and admired the flush fit of the roof. She ran into the street, lifted the house above her head, grinning, and saw her father's eyes burn with pride—one second of pride, the longest and the shortest, the most important second of all time—and then he swerved to avoid her. Somehow, the violent jerk of the turning car knocked his hands off the wheel, drove his foot onto the gas and he careened toward the valley oak across the street, that dead, ancient tree with its thick, thrusting naked branches, the tree that hadn't provided shade for years, the tree that no one cared for, whose limbs were sharpened by wind into perfect, natural claws. As the Maxwell collided with the tree, a giant limb snapped off from the trunk and pierced the windshield, shattering it into shards that the neighborhood kids would collect and trade with each other. The limb kept going, spearing into her father's neck, pinning him to the back of his seat as the engine revved under the pressure of his foot then slowly faded to idle.

ALL OF THAT was recalled in the twenty-five seconds between the return of consciousness and the return of Doctor Nasal Tube. He performed his messy liquid task and was gone again. There were shadows now, which meant the sun was coming up. She could feel its heat warming the Quonset hut roof. The sheets were no longer so confining, but she didn't have the energy to sit up. Walking seemed like an impossible challenge.

"You've been crying," Lawrence Cutler said, standing in the

corner furthest from the bed, as though he were afraid she might jerk her way towards him and somehow hurt him.

"What's in the tube, what's in me now?"

"Glucose. To reduce the danger of an aftershock from the insulin. Why were you crying, Jean?"

"Memories."

"Of Modesto, I assume. Your girlhood. But I wonder if more recent Modesto events came to the surface."

He's hunting and pecking, Jean thought.

"Sure, the big flood. Way back when sometime. High water marks everywhere, the San Joaquin especially, but every river ..."

"Stop. Stop. I'm trying to help you here and your evasiveness isn't productive."

"Neither is yours, Lawrence. I asked you where my boy is. Tit for tat."

"I don't know where he is. Not specifically. Your turn—where's our security officer, Marantz?"

"Who? Is he the galoot you hired to snoop around our house?"

"Whatever measures we've taken were for your and Robert's protection."

Why was Lawrence clicking over there in the corner? Click, click, click.

"Because if Robert knows certain things and acts on them," he said, "it could be bad for B.E. If he told you those things, it could be bad for him. And you." Click, click, click. "You two are very close, aren't you?" he continued. "Like Frances and me. Peas in a pod?"

"You and Frances aren't ..." She couldn't finish the sentence, although she knew what she wanted to say: Frances has the slide ruler mind, the true engineer's gift, she corrects little Lord Larry's homework. Frances wears the pants, or at least one leg of them. But that's only fair, isn't it? One leg each? She and Robert were partners. They saw themselves as a team. Had been. Still did? Still were? He admired her practicality, liked that she had carpentry skills. He could wire, she could hammer. He found her beautiful, when others didn't. Was amused that she was a terrible dancer, and he could teach her.

"Aren't what?" Click, click, click.

"What's that noise?" She saw Lawrence's shadow arm rise like a salute, and his shadow hand shook something wooden and rattling.

"Cribbage. I learned it during the war. When I was down on the ground and my men were up there in the flak. It calms, it focuses. I play against myself which means I usually lose."

"Am I up there now? While you're down here?" she asked.

Click, click, click ...

"I just want to talk to Robert. Again, I'm asking—where is he? We've searched Calcite, no sign of him. But you're here, aren't you. So it makes me wonder ..."

Lawrence opened the door, Doctor Nasal Tube strode in with his syringe tray. As she went under, she heard the doctor whisper to Lawrence, "She's worse than Sirk."

HER FATHER's neck was so big, so solid. She had curled her arms around it so often and it seemed as thick and imposing as a Sequoia. How could it be so easily pierced? In the midst of her screams, she ran her hand across the blood that was spouting onto the upholstery, and she found the box of taffy that he often brought her as a treat, the treat no one could stand so she always got all of it.

She didn't remember her father's funeral or the burial, events which she heard people refer to as "saying goodbye." But he was right there, under that ground. He hadn't gone anywhere. He was still in Modesto, still within sight of at least one house he'd built. Why would you say goodbye to someone who hadn't left?

But she could perfectly recall the three other funerals.

The first was for the 1924 Maxwell. It sat in the driveway for three weeks. Neither she or Alma dared to approach it. Finally, it was sold to a scrapyard under the condition that it be demolished, but Alma didn't trust the scrap dealer's word. The car was still in running condition and she feared they would sell it and she'd have to see it trundling around the county. So one afternoon, cooled by a rare summer drizzle, they watched as the doors were torn off and consigned to an infernal crushing machine, the engine lifted out, the hood crumpled into an accordion, the tires burned, and the steering wheel that her father had let her hold on to so many carefree, destinationless drives, straightened and pounded into a tube then chopped into sections and thrown into a bin. As they walked away, she dipped her hand into the bin and grabbed one of the steering wheel sections, squeezing her hand around it until the burred metal edges cut her and drew blood.

The second funeral was held for the tree. She watched men chop it down and saw it into pieces. It was dry oak, perfect firewood, so it ended up in a chimney or a woodstove or maybe a campsite. A fat, gray, ugly stump remained. It seemed to get uglier and rattier by the day. A few hardy neighbors tore into it with axes and shovels but couldn't dislodge it. Finally, on a day when a green shoot of something miraculously began to peek out from the stump's dead core, a grubber crew was hired and they dug it out, root by root—one of the roots was called the heart—and drove it off to parts unknown. She was the only one who said goodbye to it because it was truly gone.

The third and last funeral ...

ANOTHER TWENTY-FIVE SECONDS OF MEMORIES. Jean thought she had heard something important earlier, right before she went under. What was it? Then the familiar dizzy swirl and joint pain and sweats. Her head was higher; there were more pillows now, enough to almost sit up properly. She decided not to open her eyes. To slow down her breath, to pretend she was still under. Comas make you sneaky, comas make you sly. The door opened and Jean heard both men step in, felt them hover. A finger snapped in her ear, she didn't flinch. A thumb and a forefinger pinched her left palm, she didn't move. A light passed over her eyelids, which held strong, stayed frozen.

"Shouldn't she be coming out by now?" Lawrence asked.

"Oh, she's quite out. Quite the game player, too."

She heard the snap of a lighter and smelled a burning cigarette. Someone held it beneath her nose and the smoke rose into her nostrils and her head jerked away just as her eyes opened. The room was different. A chair had been placed in the corner where earlier Lawrence had stood. There was a gray metal desk lamp and a telephone on the stack of boxes. Now she could read the writing on the label: "Dickens to Fitzgerald." Books.

Doctor Nasal Tube readied his tools, but Lawrence shook his head no. Raised Doctor Nasal Tube eyebrows. Still no. The doctor shrugged and left. Before he could close the door, a woman's white-sleeved arms passed in a dinner plate to Lawrence.

"Tamales this time. We have them delivered once a week. We go through a lot of ice getting these babies here." He brought the plate with knife and fork and napkin to the nightstand. The smell was wonderful and tangy, but there was no room in her stomach or anywhere else in her body for food.

"Calls to mind the gals' lunches I'd take us to. Just me and the ladies. My peacetime crew."

And there was no space in her head for a cheap, sentimental bribe. She kept silent.

"We're not getting anywhere, are we Jean?"

Lawrence sighed heavily. Leaving the tamale platter on the nightstand, he retreated to his chair. "You know, I used to give flying lessons back in Indiana to pay for my engineering studies. Curtiss Jenny. So, when the war came along, it was the Army Air Force for me. Not because I wanted to bust off into the wild blue yonder, climbing high into the sun, at 'em boys, give 'er the gun. But because I was qualified. If I'd been a hunter, I'd have joined the infantry as a rifleman, if I'd been a weekend sailor, I'd have joined the Navy. We go where we're qualified, where we fit in, like these cribbage pegs. I thought I could fit in here with you, Jean, because of our friendship, because of our working together."

THE THIRD FUNERAL *lasted a minute at most. Funeral for the House That Jean Built. It was still in her hands as she crawled across the front seat towards her father, set it down on the floorboards then grasped the oak branch, figuring she could pull it out like an Indian arrow. Alma had snatched the house out of the car. Before saying a word, before crying, before touching her father, she'd taken it and swung it against the front porch river rock wall, rocks that Jean had helped her father gather, swung it again and again until it was only splinters falling through her fingers.*

MEMORIES ARE for the near dead. She didn't want them. She needed to develop a strategy for dealing with Colonel L. Cutler, group commander. She felt a shift in the air, a prickly tension she couldn't identify. Cutler was glancing anxiously at the window shade that could never be raised. He went to the phone that had appeared on the nightstand, raised it to his ear, checked for a dial tone.

"As I said, we're not making any progress here. So, when this phone rings, it will be for you."

17

VALE PRIVATE INVESTIGATIONS – Discrete, Dedicated, Deadly

From: Field Operative (F.O.) James Vale

Subject: Search for Missing Person XYZ.

14:30: Stakeout at Strike it Rich Lanes. Crowded, but no one will answer my questions about what's going on. Top secret, they say with a wink. I hate it when adults wink. Conversation is hushed, difficult to eavesdrop. Muriel gives me root beer floats. She asks if I have found any new friends to play with here in town. Crimіny—a friend to play with? Despite my status as an operative, she treats me like a visiting nephew or somebody.

An all-clear warning sounds. It was just a drill of some kind. People go back to work.

16:30: Bill Larkin arrives. On so-called bike patrol, showing off like a big cheese. Making sure the bowling lanes are safe—makes me laugh.

6:45: Informed Larkin of hunt for missing person XYZ. He is excited and wants to deputize me to Bike Patrol. I say no, it's other way around, I will deputize him. We do both. Here is the Vale Oath of Service: "I swear to uphold the traditions of Vale Private Investiga-

tions, to renounce fear and weakness and to pursue malefactors with all due action, including force if required."

Larkin Inventory: Mercury Fleetline bicycle equipped with light. Razor—for cutting bundled newspapers but fine defensive weapon. No identification. Says not necessary, all know him.

17:15: We move out. Cover story—rock collecting. Muriel doesn't want to let us go. Op Larkin stomps feet. I plead, kid style. It didn't work with Senior Op Vale, but it does the trick here. Muriel gives in.

17:30: Proceed southbound. I'm on foot, Op Larkin on bike—it will be a getaway vehicle if needed.

18:00: We meet at picnic table in park to plan search for Missing Person XYZ. But Larkin asks questions about Senior Op Vale. I say that is secret. He keeps asking about her. I want to do a door-to-door search. It is possible that XYZ is held here against his will. In a shed or back room. As kids, we will not cause suspicion. Op Larkin stalls. He asks if there's a girl I like. I say no. He keeps nagging. I make a deal—I tell the truth and he helps in the door to door. Monica Herndon, I say. Her mother is in Calcite, he informs me. She is a bigwig.

19:10: We begin our search. Not being tailed. But Op Larkin doesn't stop until last house on the street. Op Larkin refuses to state whose house we are at.

My antenna are up. I want to leave. The door opens and two men step out and lead me inside. More later.

When the phone rang, she was sitting up, maybe asleep, maybe awake, the sheets clenched in her right fist, sweat drenching her back where it leaned against the two pillows that had become sticky and hot. Without releasing her grip on the sheets, she picked up the dull black receiver.

"So, you were talking about salt," said a voice with a faint English accent. More accurately, English-inspired. Chilly and precise. Vann Claridge.

"I don't know where Robert is."

Jean assumed it had been a few hours since her last round

of injections and comas and dreams and glucose. She felt in command of her thoughts in a way she hadn't for several hours. Or was it days?

"The evaporation of salt as a matter of fact. I found it a surprising topic to say the least," Claridge said.

"I don't remember talking about salt. What the hell are you after? Robert is—"

"Put Robert aside for a moment. Let's turn to Jean Vale, builder of houses, daughter of a father taken tragically too soon …"

They weren't just memories or thoughts, they were words. *Her* words. She'd been talking to them, before sliding into the coma, or in those disorienting seconds when she was coming out.

"I'm thinking about the institution of marriage. Individual marriages are often secretive lairs where couples curl up like hibernating bears. Deepest fears and ambitions are exchanged, never to be shared with the outside world."

Bears? What was he talking about? Is that what an Ivy League education does for you?

"I'm thinking of Julius and Ethel Rosenberg, for example," Claridge said. Husbands and wives share secrets—I'm wondering what Robert shared with you."

"Sure you're not thinking about your own marriage? At the garden party, you said your wife died three years ago. Under what circumstances, I wonder."

"A sadness that I live and breathe every day."

Claridge didn't feel a drop of pain, Jean thought. There was no quaver of sadness in his voice. He sounded empty.

"Assume for the time being that Robert is beyond our reach. He's not here, but you are. So, the question becomes: what does Jean Maddox Vale want? Why is she in Calcite? Why is she in this room, enduring this?"

"I didn't do anything to deserve this."

"I've been in many rooms questioning many people, beginning in Germany in 1945. Transit camps. The Luftwaffe Institute for Aviation Medicine, the Göring Aeronautical Research Center at Volkenrode—their progress was beyond ours. As victors, we had to set arrogance and pride aside, and realize we could learn from others. While the good Colonel Cutler was back home being feted as a war hero, a few of us were positioning our country for the coming conflict. Looking for an advantage, talking and absorbing, and in that process, I gathered many insights. Chief among them is that people put themselves in places. Out of their own volition. They stew, they lash out, they complain about the injustice of their predicament, but …"

Claridge's voice cut off. The phone line was still active. Jean heard shuffling papers and the pad of footsteps. The door opened and Vann Claridge stood there, his frameless glasses pinching his hawkish nose, his gray eyes lacking expression, a cigarette holder without a cigarette in his left hand, a buff folder thick with documents, held in his right. He wore a tan-colored double-breasted suit, his way of adopting the colors of the American West, and pristine desert boots.

"You're amused by my camouflage, Mrs. Vale. As I've been intrigued by yours."

Then the spasms began. Her body jerked towards the edge of the bed, forcing Claridge to step back as she fell onto the throw rug, grasping at it, curling into it. She reached for a hand up, he withdrew as though revolted by the prospect of touching her. Doctor Nasal Tube and a nurse she hadn't seen before—slender, fawn-like, too young to be in charge of patients surely—rushed in and knelt next to her. Jean's nose began to bleed, spit cascaded out of her mouth onto the cement, forcing Claridge to edge further away. The doctor readied the glucose tube while the nurse applied alcohol to the injection sites, rubbing rougher than was necessary, her girlish face relishing her brief moment of power over Jean.

"No," said Claridge.

"She could be going into hyperglycemic shock," Doctor Nose Tube said.

"Let's take her out to get some air," Claridge said.

"You're asking me to violate—"

"Whatever shred of tired civilian medical ethics you haven't already discarded by working for us?" Claridge said.

Doctor and nurse exchanged glances, then all-in-a-day's work shrugs, the doctor grabbed Jean's shoulders, the nurse her legs and they helped her up.

"I can walk," Jean said. She threw off the blanket and wobbled to her feet but couldn't remain standing. She wanted to seem solid in front of her tormentors, but she felt like a wisp, something a rat's breath could blow away. She perched on the edge of the bed—at least she was half way to her feet. She wiped the blood from her nose with her hand and zeroed her gaze on the handkerchief in Claridge's suit pocket.

"May I have that please?"

Claridge shook the handkerchief free from its neat fold and handed it to her. She blotted her nose, then—the hell with blotting—she jammed it into each nostril, gouging deeply, and tugged out a sticky, semi-liquid crust of nastiness, then handed it towards Claridge. He let it drop to the floor.

"So how did your wife die? Anne, wasn't it?"

"My marriage is not at issue here."

"You brought it up. The hibernating bears nonsense."

"Offer me something valuable about Robert. I need to understand him. Then we'll see what I am able to say in return."

Jean knew Robert was alive and had met with that North character. She knew about a chapel out in the desert. Had she told them that? Judging by their questions, maybe she hadn't. But she wanted to repay his cruelty, to see if the high and mighty suffered too, if they experienced pain. So she had to give him something.

"Robert might have had an affair," she said.

"When?"

"Years ago."

"How many years ago?"

Then it struck her—what if Claridge the former OSS man knew something she didn't? What if his agents had uncovered a secret best left alone? She shouldn't be playing these games. Shut up, gag yourself, Jean. But she went on.

"Your turn," Jean said

"Well, Mrs. Vale, I don't accept that you believe there is a firm foundation to support your suspicion about your husband's infidelity. Nevertheless, I appreciate your stab at honesty. It's a start."

"Tell me, you goddamn monster," Jean hissed

"Anne took her own life," Claridge said quietly.

She nodded because she could picture it: the pill bottles and the empty glass of something French, Anne Claridge lying gracefully in state on their bed, the nightgown bought in Paris or London during one of Claridge's diplomatic tours, pearled lightly in perspiration, cloaking her in a tasteful shroud.

Claridge took off his glasses, no doubt to show Jean that tears would not be on his agenda. With his handkerchief out of action, he buffed the lenses on the sleeve of his tan suit. "Shall we?" Claridge offered her his arm. She rose, managed to stay on her feet. Residual shakes rippled through her body and settled in her toes, which began to shudder. She realized that they had removed her shoes, but thank God they hadn't stripped her and forced her into some hospital gown while she was out—she was still in her same clothes.

"My shoes?" she asked.

"You'll be fine in your socks."

Claridge led her out the door into a long room that seemed to run the length of the building. Boxes of books were stacked against both walls, labeled by author: Carson–DuMaurier, Steinbeck–Stevenson. They kept walking, past an Army cot with a copy of "Eisenhower" by John Gunther lying face down on the pillow, an ice chest serving as a nightstand. A young, nervous looking man was seated at a metal desk squeezed between more boxes, wearing earphones until he looked up to see the subject of his eavesdropping wavering over him, nose bloody, arms pricked with injection marks. She pulled away from Claridge and slapped the guy on the shoulder. "Loose lips still sinking ships? Howzabout a kiss from the girl with the star-spangled heart?" She bent down to kiss him and he recoiled. "What's the matter with the men in this jerkwater outfit, anyway? Never seen a real woman before?" She looked at Claridge who seemed annoyed by her messy unmanageability. She saluted him. "Left? Right? Straight? Which way?"

Claridge led the way, then nodded to the right. Jean opened a door between two filing cabinets and found herself underneath a black, starry sky. A soft desert wind caressed her face, and she wanted to weep from the sensation, gratefully embrace the openness of it all. She was in a small patio enclosed on three sides by a head-high brick wall. Brand new, she noticed; she and Robert had laid a brick walkway last year and she recognized fresh mortar, smelled it even. There were two benches, both shaded by umbrellas. A shiny Coca Cola machine with a hand printed note: "Every Nickel Goes Directly to Crusade for Freedom." And no doctors. This is how the game is played, she thought. This is how prisoners are broken, the tough guy turns nice guy, brings you an ice-cold drink before he lowers the boom. Claridge was still in the storage room, talking quietly, with the eavesdropper probably. That wall intrigued her. It wasn't part of the original Quonset hut, so it must jut out into the street. She stepped onto a bench and peered over the wall. No street, no yard, just open desert. But there was a strange, lumpy shape out there, not boulders, not a shack.

"I knew the fresh air would do you good," Claridge said, walking onto the patio and shutting the door behind him.

Jean's instinct was to jump back down and sit, like a shamed schoolgirl, or worse, a prisoner caught trying to escape. But she stopped herself, and gave him an innocent, "who, me?" smile. "Cassiopeia, clearest I've ever seen it."

Claridge looked up at the stars, then shook his head as though the heavens disappointed him. "I never understood stargazing. Dreaming of objects millions of miles away. Although I imagine it can be comforting to wonder if our loved ones are looking up at the same skies. Is Robert? Is Jimmy?"

A cheap tactic, she thought. He cared for no one, she would pretend to care for no one. She didn't follow his skyward gaze, she didn't even want to share the view with him. As she got down from the bench, she realized what she'd seen. It was a car. In the middle of the sea of sand, where no car should be.

Claridge sat on one bench, he motioned Jean to take the other. Her legs were still shaking, and she tapped her foot furiously on the ground, Gene Krupa style. There was another knock on the door, and Lawrence Cutler's face appeared, furrowed with concern. Claridge waved him away, and Cutler withdrew.

"He's loved, our Lawrence. Loved by his men. But it can be a curse to be loved, the expectations are high and mount steadily. Eventually you move from basking in love to needing to be loved, and that can be a trap. It can make you ignore obvious peril. America was loved. When we liberated Sicily, Paris, we were loved. Beautiful while it lasted. But it's not what America needs right now."

She heard a rhythmic tapping and saw that Claridge was drumming the handrail of the bench with the cigarette holder. Almost in time with her feet.

"In six or seven minutes, you'll experience another attack. More will follow. You will be ravenous but there will be no food, you will experience a fierce dizziness, but we will deny you solid ground, your heartbeat will accelerate until the feeling that it is about to burst from your body becomes unendurable and you will beg to faint. But we won't let you faint."

Jean felt a tremor of terror, but then told herself that Claridge was just trying to scare her.

There they were, passing a pleasant evening on side-by-side park benches. A man revolted by a bloody nose, yet unperturbed by convulsions and pain. Or women passing out.

"No wonder she killed herself," Jean said. Claridge didn't take the bait. Jean lolled her head against the back of the bench, closed her eyes. She couldn't stand Claridge's gray, bloodless presence.

"Everything you've been through emotionally ..." He pronounced "emotionally" with spitting contempt. "Witness to a dying father, your son the same age you were when he died. Who could not be moved? We are a forgiving society and there would have been a place for you in it. Insulin shock therapy is a different beast I'm afraid. There exists the small possibility of aftershocks or minor convulsions. Employers don't appreciate absences necessitated by one's medical condition. If something were to happen to Robert, you would become Jimmy's sole provider."

"I'll sling hash. No greasy spoon west of the Rockies will care about my so-called condition."

"That would be a shameful waste of your talents. But there is an alternative."

"What?" She was starting to feel woozy again, her vision clouding.

"Do you know about the National Security Act of 1947?"

"No."

"But you've heard of the CIA, yes? The Security Act established it and other agencies devoted to our safety. A different kind of war is coming, Mrs. Vale, and a different kind of warrior and tactic will be required to fight it. There are no distinct front lines anymore. The front lines are in our homes, our schools, our television and radio broadcasts. Or more pointedly, in here," he said, tapping his forehead. "In our own minds and in the minds of our opponents." Claridge slid with a hiss of gabardine across his bench until he could lean over the arm rest into hers. "I brought many former enemies into our fold. Men who Lawrence Cutler's bomber boys no doubt pummeled mercilessly. Often, people who have lost a war—or in your case a skirmish—want to do the right thing. I imagine even Julius Rosenberg is having second thoughts. Or perhaps they just want to be on the winning side for a change."

"My husband is not a Russian, not a Rosenberg ..." Her speech was slurring, the attack that Claridge promised was prowling towards her.

"But I believe he's working for the wrong side. He's on a personal quest of some sort, which tells me he cares more about his own self-aggrandizement than about providing for his family."

"Robert never missed a mortgage payment. Ever."

"It's one thing to respond heroically when life and war thrust the opportunity upon you. But to strive to be a hero in peacetime—that's a bit selfish, it strikes me. Almost 'narcissistic,' to quote the jargon. Still, he made his decision and once we find him, he will be dealt with."

"I'd like to go back to bed now." Jean tried to push to her feet, but it felt like she had gained five hundred pounds.

"But you have a choice. To embrace the side of right, the patriotic side. To work for us."

"Back to B.E?"

"A higher calling—we the people. The government who funds and encourages B.E. The company is way beyond capacitors and oscilloscopes, as I'm sure you have divined. You're smart, ambitious, a swift learner. How many women have scraped their way out of the dust bowl of the Central Valley and renewed themselves in the San Francisco Peninsula? We would of course train you further, with appropriate salary increases, access to some of the higher ups in government who it's my privilege to know."

The dustbowl came to *us*, Jean thought. Claridge didn't

know or care about America beyond Washington. He hated being here, in the empty spaces of the west that couldn't be controlled or even understood.

"Work for you? When you probably killed my husband? Last night, maybe. Or this morning, for all I know." Jean laid down on the bench and curled up. She began to imagine how her father would take care of Vann Claridge. With nails and a hammer. Slowly, one ten penny nail at a time, the final nail driven straight into his ear so the last sound he heard on earth was steel spearing into his brain.

"We did nothing of the kind," Claridge said. "We want to know what Robert knows, what sort of game he seems to be playing. He is obviously no use to us dead." He stood, smoothed his trousers, buttoned his jacket. "I finally understand what they mean by dry heat. If we were back in the District, I would be foul with sweat by now. I think it's time for the next phase of your treatment."

"I'm loyal. To you, to B.E., to the country."

"What about those salt evaporation ponds, then? What about the red and green lights?"

"I don't know what the hell you're talking about."

"*I'm* not talking about it, Mrs. Vale. *You* were. Pre-coma, post coma. Red and green lights ... salt. Code words perhaps? Cryptic phrases that could unlock deeper secrets. I think I'll recommend increasing your dosage."

Future pain shot through her, imagined pain that her mind was supplying to her organs and limbs. "No, please, I can't take another one."

But he was out the door and gone. Leaving her alone with the stars. As she lay there, something played around in her mind, something she had heard as she drifted in and out of her coma state. But what was it?

. . .

<u>VALE PRIVATE INVESTIGATIONS</u> – Discrete, Dedicated, Deadly

From: Field Operative (F.O.) James Vale

Subject: Search for Missing Person XYZ

Time: 21:45

Status: I am in Calcite. Being questioned by persons unknown. I am using the Grandpa Tamarkin Technique to fight interrogation—do not let them make friends with you; do not accept food or drink or offers to watch Dragnet; do not tell one truth because you will become used to it and will no longer be able to lie. There are two groups of men here and they argue a lot. In low voices which I can't pick up.

Need to contact Senior Operative Vale. But how? Where is she?

18

As kids, the Director and his sister, Anne, were inseparable. Mischief partners, keeping each other's secrets from their parents. His—he broke into their neighbor's house just for the thrill of being bad. Hers—she had obtained covert access to their parents' address book, and sent naughty, anonymous letters to the diplomats, minor politicians, suffragettes, and temperance movement leaders who formed their starchy, well-meaning social circles.

They had quarreled and wrestled until their bodies went their own ways and he started to like girls and she started to like boys—especially strong, quiet, powerful boys who didn't bully or raise their voices to get their way. "Quiet boys grow into powerful men," she told him. Yet she was powerful and confident in her own right; she thrived at St. Mark's and on to Brown where she studied English history. The Director found himself thoughtlessly following some forgotten, Jefferson-admiring ancestor into the University of Virginia, where he took a law degree, moved to Washington, DC, and went to work for Carter, Ledyard and Milburn (founded in 1854, as the partners never tired of reminding him).

She nestled in academia, he mired in securities law. Bored, appalled even, by the pointless commercial lives led by his fellow lawyers. All through these years, they talked long distance. They marked their parents' anniversaries with home visits—it's our twenty-fifth, twenty-nineth, thirtieth, can you believe it, their mother would marvel—as though years of marriage generated compound interest like a savings account.

Their paths rarely crossed professionally unless, as Anne once joked, they attended the annual convention of the Most Boring Jobs in The World, which would no doubt be held in the Most Boring City in America, but the convention planners were too bored to decide on what that would be. When they met for dinner or cocktails in Washington, they were always unescorted, no girlfriends or boyfriends or fiancées. "We're simply too dull for all of that," she said, and he agreed.

And then one evening, that changed. At a retirement party for their father Edmund, a low-level State Department official with unpopular liberal views, held at an undistinguished Manhattan hotel through whose doors no presidents had ever passed, in whose bar no titans of empire ever conspired. Just a hotel with an affordable rental ballroom. It was there, as the Under Secretary for Balkan Something or Other, in the falsely tremulous voice of an aspiring actor, read aloud the final stanzas of Wilfred Owen's "Dulce et Decorum Est," that Anne met a pale, trim and tailored, forward tilting tower.

The irony was too painful to digest, an anti-war poem read loud in the presence of Vann Claridge.

And thus began her years of descent.

The Director knew that Claridge would still recognize him, so tonight he wore a fedora pulled low over his face—a ridiculous disguise, but it was something—and he slumped low in the passenger seat. Miss Jessie Harper had parked her DeSoto in the sand, away from the streetlamp and they watched the two lights that burned in the Quonset hut.

Their path to this night and this place had been roundabout, marked by diversions and roadblocks but also by pure, blessed luck. Forgery, bluff, and disguise had gotten them past the main gate—providing they went immediately to city hall to obtain new Calcite Area Passes. City Hall was a tiny Wild West structure that promised a folksy mayor and a crew of cranky council members. But it was also the MP headquarters and the policemen that came and went looked stern and diligent. Afraid to press their charade further, they drove through Calcite, up and down the preposterously named streets, unable to knock on doors or ask questions of the few pedestrians they encountered, their only strategy was hoping for a sighting of Jean or Robert or Jimmy Vale. They grew irritable. They were stuck.

It was cocktail onions that changed their luck. As the Director prowled the three aisles of the grocery store for sandwiches and Cokes, he overheard a conversation between a male customer and a female clerk in which the clerk expressed surprise at the quantity of gin being purchased. "Second bottle, isn't it, Eddie?" When the Director moved to the end of the Notions aisle (he had never been sure just what *Notions* were) he saw a young, earnest man in his twenties, buying a bottle of gin from the appealing brunette clerk. "Not for me, for the boss," Eddie said, clearly smitten by the clerk and anxious to disabuse her of the idea that he was a drunkard. "Pimento olives come in yet?" he asked. "A real martini has onions, so I'm under a bit of pressure here."

Though very little tracking prowess was required, the Director was proud of their ability to shadow Eddie to the Calcite library's book storage facility, housed in a rust-stained Quonset hut set at the edge of the desert. *I've become a spy after all*, he thought, recalling his "pep talk" to his team back in D.C. Eddie entered the building with the gin, stayed an hour or so, and exited *sans*-gin, but never intoxicated. The process was repeated a couple days later. Aside from Eddie and his gin deliveries, the only other visitors the place welcomed were the daily changing of a single MP guard, and a wavy-haired man carrying a leather satchel, accompanied by a young woman wearing a belted, hooded overcoat, standard issue for a U.S. Army Air Force nurse. A medical team, the Director decided. They timed the doctor and nurse visits, learning their schedule. They seemed to be on 24-hour call, but never spent the night. But someone else did stay very late, and judging by the martini consumption, the Director surmised it was Vann Claridge.

The Director and Miss Harper "staked out" the Quonset hut for two days and nights, retreating into the desert during the day, keeping watch with binoculars in the cramped shade of the Desoto, returning to their sandy private parking spot after dark. There was no radio reception, so no Bing Crosby or Inner Sanctum, not even the grisly but riveting spectacle of Walter Winchell publicly destroying himself. One night, then two, with no sign of Claridge. He began to fear that his deductive instincts had been baked out of his brain by the unaccustomed Nevada sunshine. But on their third night, at 2 a.m., they saw a wedge of light as the front door opened, and Claridge stepped out. Despite the late hour and lingering heat, he was immaculate, wearing a suit, sipping from a martini glass, comfortable and confident, as though he were back home plotting and strategizing at the Willard Hotel bar. He seemed to be talking to himself, but they soon realized he had an audience; Eddie the gin delivery man joined Claridge and refreshed his martini. The Director couldn't follow the thread of the conversation, but he picked out the phrases "Dogwood chain," "Venona," "mule turds"—the names of secret operations—and he knew that Claridge was telling war stories. Eddie was thrilled by every word, awed by the honor of being privy to "secrets" revealed. Vann Claridge had always been thus, a shadow hero who needed a degree of limelight, a silent service icon who thrived on admiration, adulation even, yet bestowed little of it on others. And then it became clear: Claridge was an interrogator at heart. No, heart had little to do with it. He wasn't truly interested in what made people tick, such as a psychiatrist might be, but he would still pride himself on his ability to plow through marathon sessions. He would sleep an hour here or there, require little nourishment other than Gordon's Dry and perhaps a good book. Sooner or later, he would get the answers he was seeking.

"If I were a betting man, I would wager that either Robert or Jean Vale are in there," the Director said.

"And I have a plan," Miss Harper answered.

JEAN WAS LYING on the bench in the outside patio, her head on the metal arm rest, thinking about the stars, trying to remember which season was best for flying saucers. The symptoms Claridge had promised were knocking at her—dizziness, fatigue. Then she heard someone fiddling with the lock on the door, and Jessie Harper slipped in. Jessie's strong arms lifted her up, propped her onto her feet, propelled her across the patio. The welding scars on her left wrist seemed to glow, as though they were lit from within.

"Jessie? Here? That can't be you, can it?"

"Yeah, I don't believe it, either. Time to go, Mrs. Vale."

She was wearing her B.E. janitor's uniform, feather duster dangling on her wrist by a leather thong, rubber gloves protruding from her back pockets like pale, dead hands.

"You're ... you're working for them?" Jean asked.

"Well, they think so, whoever they are. The MP is on a cigarette break while I clean. He warned me away from this door, but I have my ways around a lock, you know. Can you walk?"

"Maybe."

"Show me."

Jessie pulled her supporting arms away and Jean managed the five steps to the door, her legs loose and flailing, not working in unison.

"It's sort of like the Scarecrow from the Wizard of Oz, but he made it to the Emerald City, so you'll do OK. You don't have any shoes?"

"Guess not," Jean said, assuming it was just another taunt from Vann Claridge.

Jessie gave a coast-is-clear peek through the door, and they went into the long book storage room, Jessie reaching her hand behind her like an older sister, trying to pull Jean along in her stumble shuffle. They walked by a large, heavy door, secured from inside with a deadbolt, then passed the eavesdropper's station. He was gone, his headphones curled around a chrome cocktail shaker. From outside, they heard the popcorn crackle of tires on gravel.

"He's ready. Let's get a move on," Jessie said,

Jean kept going, her mind racing, compiling: Evelyn Sirk in the movie theater, Evelyn and the recording Buddy Sirk and Robert had made. Just beyond the door, stood a filing cabinet. Jean stopped. Three drawers, alphabetized. First drawer: 'A–G.' Second drawer: 'H–O.' Third drawer: 'P–Z.' All locked. No time for finesse. She snatched a fire ax from the wall. She swung the ax above her head, but Jessie grabbed the handle and for a second, they were both paralyzed, like a statue of two soldiers in hand-to-hand combat.

"We go through four shades of hell to get here, and you want to catch up on your filing?"

"It's in here, it has to be."

"What's in here?"

"Tapes, I'm betting."

Jean guessed she must sound insane, but she didn't care. Her eyes were starting to swim, and the fire axe weighed a thousand pounds, but she needed to find that tape, even if they had to carry her out of here.

"OK, OK. I know this model," Jessie said. "Put down that damn tomahawk and let's be smart." Jean dropped the fire ax. Jessie pushed against the cabinet, tilting it against the wall, raising the bottom six inches above the floor. "You hold it right there," Jessie said.

Jean leaned her weight against the cabinet, keeping it in position. Jessie dropped to her knees and slid her hand beneath the cabinet. "There's a rod in here, it controls the locks ... if I can get my thumb on it." The cabinet wobbled as Jessie probed around. Something clunked inside the filing cabinet, and all three drawers ticked open a smidgen. Jessie pulled out her hand and Jean let the cabinet thud back into place.

"Get what you need, pronto," Jessie ordered.

Fists were pounding on the heavy front door. "Hey, lady, there ain't that much to clean in there. Come on, open up."

"I locked it, but that door won't hold forever. Let's move!" Jessie barked.

Jean pulled out the lower drawer. Inside were dozens of files. Jean had searched a thousand file drawers in her career. The trick was a double technique—the moistened left hand flicked through one file while the right hand jumped to the next. Never two hands on a file; it was too slow and her bosses had always prized speed. Three quarters of the way to the back of the drawer she found it: SIRK. A folder holding just a tape box. She opened the box—the tape was there.

Then she remembered what she had overheard: "She's worse than Sirk." Meaning her? Did "worse" mean better, stronger?

The pounding continued on the front door. But then a timid tap-tap knocked from somewhere behind them. An old wooden door creaked open, and a man stepped in from the night, back lit by car headlights. He wore a Fedora and baggy, oddly fitting janitor overalls similar to Jessie's, a name patch above the breast pocket identifying him as "Rose." He had a stubble of a beard that he scratched with his fingernails, probably a man used to beginning each day with a clean shave. He looked late forties, maybe fifties. A calm face, slightly sunburned, a face that seemed to smile often, but wasn't smiling now.

"Close the drawer and re-lock it," the calm-faced man said.

Then he turned back into the night, his gait precise and unhurried, as though he had practiced it until he felt it would inspire level-headedness in others.

Jean flipped through to V, but there was no file on Robert. Prompted by Jessie's scowl, she grabbed the tape, and they hurried out the back door. They were behind the building, just outside the patio wall Jean had peered over, Jessie's DeSoto parked at the edge of the desert. Jean and Jessie made for the car, the gravel scratching at Jean's feet. The calm faced man nudged Jean into the back seat, instructing her to lie down under a thin, ratty blanket. He got in the passenger seat, Jessie slid behind the wheel. Jessie passed Jean a canteen over her shoulder. "Drink plenty of water, hell, empty it out," she ordered. She jammed the DeSoto into gear and drove along the gravel alley that ran behind the Quonset hut.

As they turned at the corner of the building, Jean snuck a glance and saw Vann Claridge and the eavesdropper following an MP to the front door. Claridge's left hand shook, and his trademark cigarette holder fell free. As he bent to retrieve it, the left side of his body seemed to wilt. Did he have some sort of condition, maybe the aftermath of a stroke? As he stood back up, he saw the car, and locked eyes with Jean. It was too late for her to duck down ... and she wanted him to see her in mid-getaway.

"We need to go. Now," Jean said.

Jessie punched the gas, gliding through the gears like a racing car driver. She sped them in a beeline away from the Quonset hut, steering them into the open desert. Jean glanced out the back window, saw Claridge and the MP running.

"We need to find my boy. I left him at the bowling alley."

"We'll take care of it, Jean," Jessie said.

"We have to get you to safety first, Mrs. Vale," the calm-faced man said. "And a phone that's not monitored."

"Who are you?" Jean said, trying to sit up.

"Down!" he snapped. Back down she went.

"I'm guessing Rosie isn't your real name," Jean said, referring to the name on his overalls.

He didn't answer. Jessie swerved and bumped through a series of rapid turns. Jean looked back, didn't see a pursuing car.

Jean pelted Jessie with questions. Jessie explained that after waiting a week for Jean to get in touch via the laundry, she'd remembered that she had an old address book of Connie's. When they first got to B.E., they felt in need of new friends, so they had traded address books one night over a few beers. Gossiping, laughing in approval or disapproval at the names in their books. Jessie had forgotten to return Connie's, so she went through it alphabetically, making calls, trying to get any information she could about what Connie had been up to, walking the delicate, painful line of keeping the news of Connie's death to herself. When she got to D, she found a curious listing for someone named Director. The Director answered on the first ring—it was an emergency number known only to Connie and a select group. After Jessie proved that she knew Connie, she told the Director about her death in the test chamber. He had been worried that he hadn't heard from her, and now he sounded sincerely shocked. He explained that he had been developing what he called "multiple sources" for a couple of years. Calcite was still just a rumor, "a whisper on the breeze." A place he hadn't truly believed in until Connie the Crusader, from her "listening post" inside Braden Enright had fleshed out the rumors into facts with notes, memos on overheard conversations, and the occasional document or receipt copied and passed on to the Director. He and his team spent weeks trying to collect enough corroborating material to convince him Calcite was real. A conviction that propelled him into action.

"He needed help, someone both you and Connie trusted. So guess what? That meant me," Jessie said.

"How did you get past the main gate?"

"Just being myself. They need janitors everywhere, don't they? Got our friend here a pair of overalls courtesy of Lucy's Ladies Only Launderette, which explains the roominess in the bust. And the trunk's chock-a-block with mops and buckets. White man's still in charge, of course."

"But the identification badges and all?" Jean asked.

"Roman Tamarkin. He helped phony up the badges based on mine, and information Connie had passed to the Director. But sweet Jesus in the Georgia pines, can he talk up a storm."

"You used my neighbor? Don't you have any spies of your own. Mr. Director?"

"Not to speak of. Ours is a small operation, manned by rather bookish citizens," the Director, aka Rosie, said.

"They miss you," Jessie said. "I supposed there's no way for you to call them?"

"All calls are monitored here. On their end as well, I'm sure. I miss them, too."

The Director turned on the radio, nothing but static, He switched if off and they rode in silence for a minute.

"My boy, please. We need to get him."

"We'll take care of it, Jean. I promise," Jessie said.

Jean felt sleep coming on, genuine sleep, no injections or fits or interrogators. About to sink into dreams, where her body could reclaim its natural pace and breath.

"Why? Why did you come here at all?" Jean asked.

"We came for you," Jessie said. "After what happened to Connie, no way in hell was I about to lose another friend."

Rescued by a friend. She felt the shudder of approaching tears, but nothing came; maybe she was dried out, but she dabbed at her eyes anyway, working the frayed end of the blanket in circles. They kept driving. Dirt roads, it felt like. No lights anywhere. Jean didn't know where they were going and knew not to ask.

19

When Jean woke up, before she opened her eyes, she vowed never to sleep again. Sleep had once been her escape, but now it loomed as a time destroyer. How many days did I lose, she wondered? How many thoughts were choked off? How many hours of Jimmy's life did I miss?

She was in a motel room, twin beds, the other still made. Her right arm ached. It weighed a hundred pounds as she dragged it from beneath the covers. The injection sites were ugly black-red stains deliberately left untouched. There would be scabs, then scars, permanent reminders of her "treatment."

She saw a change of clothes that Jessie had brought, draped across the foot of the bed: a woman's uniform of some kind, green-striped seersucker pants and a short-sleeved blouse. Looked like it would fit and was cool enough for the desert.

She picked up the clothes, trudged into the bathroom, undressed, and stepped into a cement floored shower. She was still slightly dizzy, so she sat on the cold floor. The shower had one temperature, lukewarm, but it felt like all she'd ever wanted. She emptied the bottle of Prell into her hair, which was stiff and gritty, knotted by the dry heat into a handful of corn stalks. She pictured the magazine ads: Radiantly Alive! It was true. She turned her face to the showerhead, squatting in the cascade, trying to keep her eyes open, letting the water in wherever it wanted to flow. Enough water to swallow a thousand Isoniazid pills, maybe enough to drown her nervous "spells." She ran her hands over her soap-slicked belly and along her diaphragm, pressing, searching, but felt only stillness—the knives inside were resting. Sharpening up perhaps, but not stabbing.

Then she heard a voice from the next room. She turned off the shower, pressed her ear against the mildewed tile wall.

She couldn't make out the words, but the voice was Robert's.

She put on the seersucker uniform and went outside, picking her way across a gravel driveway, her footing a bit unsteady, but improving. It was still dark but creeping towards dawn. She knocked next door. Why the hell was she knocking? She barged in, heard a mechanical squeal, then Robert saying "OK, I'm here with Harold 'Buddy' Sirk, B.E. Badge number 397."

The man she had called Rosie was monkeying with a tape recorder that was set up on the dresser, a cigarette pressed between his thin, blistered lips. He no longer wore the work overalls; he was in khaki pants that had never seen a speck of dirt and a perfectly pressed, button-down blue shirt. He looked more like the Director he claimed to be. But director of what? Jessie Harper was there too.

And Evelyn Sirk.

"Jean, welcome back to the land of the living," Jessie said. "There's a thermos of coffee and sandwiches for you. We're almost ready to go here."

"Is that Robert and Buddy Sirk's tape?"

Evelyn nodded. She made some more adjustments to the recorder. "Thank you for bringing me this, Jean." They exchanged a brief hug. Evelyn seemed smaller than the last time Jean had seen her ... how many days ago? Her hair was lank and unwashed, Veronica Lake long gone, her cheekbones seemed rubbed away, so her face had no angles or definition.

"Mrs. Vale," the Director said. "I trust the change of clothes suits you? A Marine Corps Women's Reserve uniform, I believe."

"Jimmy, did you find him?"

"As you suggested, we talked to Muriel at Strike It Rich Lanes. She said your boy is safe with friends.

"Safe where? With the paperboy?"

"Paperboy?"

"Billy, Billy Larkin."

"His name came up, we called around, can't get through on the phone."

"Then we need to get to town—*now*."

"I'm afraid that's impossible at the moment. With you gone, they're on high alert. They'll have changed the windshield stickers, all kind of things."

"He's right, Jean," Evelyn said. "Extra scrutiny at the main gate."

"Well, we can't just squat here and cool our heels," Jean said.

"I assure you, we will not just be cooling our heels," the Director said.

Jessie handed Jean a sandwich. She chomped into a glorious combination of tuna and Wonder Bread, dribbling mayo onto the bedspread. Two chairs were arranged side by side, facing the dresser, which was topped by a scratched mirror. Her reflection was awful—pale, ancient looking, like something Boris Karloff would excavate from a tomb if they ever made "Bride of the Mummy."

"Thank you, thank you. For everything back there. I don't mean to be ungrateful." She turned away from the mirror, opened the thermos, and sucked black coffee from it like a lush drinking straight from the bottle. She would stay awake for the rest of her life if that's what it took.

Suddenly, it all roiled up and burst out of her. "What the hell happened to me? I was kept for days, injected with things, interrogated like in a nuthouse by my old boss, and by his boss apparently. I pay my taxes, I work, I don't complain, I'm not a Red or any other color."

"You wandered into their gun sights, to stretch a metaphor. You and Robert as well. Getting into Calcite was no small feat. How did you—"

"Don't you start in on me too with your damn questions."

"I apologize, you're quite right. You've been on the receiving end of Vann Claridge for three days, you have a right to expect some relief here. Such as it is. If you don't wish to talk, I'll respect that."

"Oh, I want to talk all right. A storm." She looked at Evelyn, hesitated, but then spit it out. "I think they held Buddy there too. Any word from him?"

"No. Still missing, too." Then Evelyn took Jean's hand. "But we have them both right here," she said, giving the tape recorder a possessive pat.

Jean looked out the window, where dawn was slowly drawing up, a faint fringe of orange behind the mountains. She saw Jessie Harper's DeSoto, and a Chevy two door, probably Evelyn's. "So where are we? Still in Nevada? Far enough from Calcite that I don't have to look over my shoulder every waking moment?"

"Thirty-five miles outside of town. You're fine here for the time being. I paid the manager to take the day off."

"So, Mr. Director. Are you a cop? Or do I need to call the cops? The state police? G-Men? Bring hell down on that place."

"I have no law enforcement authority. I'm sorry. But rest assured our interests are aligned."

"And they are what exactly?"

The Director mused for a moment. "Short term, to find your husband and of course, your boy Jim. Long term, it's more complex."

"You men," Jean said. "Everything too complicated to explain. 'Beyond capacitors and oscilloscopes,' 'hibernating bears.' If I were president, I'd make a law so you had to talk the way I grew up around in Modesto—no nonsense. Don't muddy it up in a mishmash of horse manure. You sound like a damn Washington politician."

"Guilty, I'm afraid. The Washington part, I mean."

"Can we get started here? Please," Evelyn said. "I don't give a damn who he is, but he and Jessie here were smart enough to keep calling, then hanging up if I sensed the operator was listening in. When we got a chance to speak freely, they gave me directions to the motel."

Jean looked out at Evelyn's Chevy, picturing herself roaring back into Calcite, come what may, because this was unbearable, Jimmy unaccounted for.

Jessie placed a hand on hers. "Jean, you can't go back there. Next time, you won't get out. They're looking for you, not Jimmy."

The Director turned on a portable fan to a low hum. "Keeps the electronics cool," he said. The Director motioned for Jean and Evelyn to take seats.

"You're not going to listen?" Jean asked.

"I listened to it while you were sleeping. They say this is the most beautiful time of day in the desert, so I think Miss Harper and I may take a walk."

Evelyn and Jean took their seats. To Jean, the tape recorder suddenly seemed a monstrous thing, the twin reels like accusing eyes. Just a machine, she reminded herself. Evelyn pressed the play button. There was a crunch of static, a buzz as a microphone was adjusted, and then Robert's voice.

ROBERT: OK, the date is August 14, 1952, and I'm here with Harold "Buddy" Sirk, B.E. employee badge number 397. Mr. Sirk, can you say a few words so I can get a proper level.

SIRK: What should I say?

ROBERT: Here, read the box scores:

SIRK: Uh ... Philadelphia Phillies vs. New York Giants, Polo Grounds. Phillies five runs, nine hits, no errors, Giants two runs, six hits, one error.

Buddy's voice was friendly with an aw-shucks flavor to it. A man Jean pictured petting a big, happy dog with floppy ears. Jean glanced at Evelyn, whose expression was flat and distant.

ROBERT: OK, let's discuss the events of August 14, 1943, as you told them to me when we first met.

SIRK: Well, sir, at the time I was a navigator assigned to a B-17 with the 94th Heavy Bombardment Group based in Bury St. Edmunds, England. I'd applied for pilot training, but because my math was aces, they enrolled me in nav school.

ROBERT: And what were your duties as navigator?

SIRK: Plot our course in each direction. Work out a flight plan with our captain. Calibrate the instruments pre-flight: altimeter, compasses, airspeed indicators, astrograph, and so on. Be the pilot's eyes and ears, you might say. Get us to the target, get us home. In addition, I had to know exactly where we were every mile of the mission.

ROBERT: What number mission were you on that day?

SIRK: It was my fifteenth. Twenty-five, and you went back to the States, but only one man in four survived to twenty-five. Those English girls in town, they didn't do so well with the guys who were superstitious; everyone knew which gals had been with men who'd died. Anyway, ten more to go and I was done. Back to the States. Back to Evy. Hey, baby, if you ever hear this, I petitioned to name our plane after you, believe me. But the captain's mom was named Alice, so Dallas Alice became ours, and I grew to love her anyway.

A quick glance at Evelyn. Stone-faced.

ROBERT: How many were in your crew?

SIRK: Ten. Captain Neal Clark, we called him Captain Straight and Level; Will Yancy, the copilot; Randall "the Scandal" Ravetto, the bombardier and nose gunner—he knew the Norden bombsight inside out, the scourge of British maidenhood when he was on liberty. Max Prentice, radio officer and nose gunner; Roger Duval, the engineer/top turret man; Frank Alvarez and Del Connelly, the waist gunners; Preston McHale, the tail gunner; and down in the bubble we had Morrie Gupman, tallest guy in our unit so naturally they stuck him in that little ball turret, where he dwarfed the .50 cal.

Jean recalled the list of bomber crew members that she, Jimmy and Grandpa Tamarkin had studied—the same names.

ROBERT: What was your mission that day?

SIRK: The target was Schweinfurt. The industrial zones, specifically the ball bearing factories. We knew we were in for a rough time when Group Commander Cutler handled the briefing himself.

ROBERT: Why was that?

SIRK: Because he briefed us personally before the worst runs. He was like a dad with dozens of adopted kids—he gave us an extra edge of belief and courage. He had faith in our abilities. He was tough on us and on the ground crews, but wasn't a shitbird about it, you follow? And he always sweated the mission, up there in the tower, counting every plane as it landed. Plus, he's a detail man. So the maps, the briefings—they were accurate down to minutes and millimeters. And it was going to be a big show, a hundred of ours, linking up with a couple other full-strength groups. Too many up there was my initial thought, too much to go wrong. I don't mind saying, all ten of us took the chaplain's blessing that morning, whether we believed a word of it or not. Sometimes before a mission, you'd get the "clanks," you knew today your number was up, and you couldn't shake off dread. I had 'em bad that day.

ROBERT: How did the mission go at first?

The conversation lost direction, focusing on technical facts: bomb payloads, airspeed, wind direction. But then Jean realized it was Robert's way of making Buddy comfortable, getting him to talk about his area of expertise, subtly encouraging him to brag a bit.

"He won an Air Medal, you know," Evelyn said. She took one of the Director's cigarettes and lit up. "On his very first mission. For plotting an alternate route back to England after they'd lost an engine. Buddy could always ... always find his way home." A couple tears glistened as her face plumed in smoke.

SIRK: ... climbing through the clouds was nerve-wracking, you can't see, but you knew there were dozens, hundreds of bombers in the soup with us, basically flying blind. You burst out of the clouds, and suddenly there they are, all those ships, all those guys. It's an overwhelming sight. We formed up into our box, nearly wingtip to wingtip. Funny thing you learn on your first formation, the sky isn't as big as you think it is. But Captain Clark, he had the touch.

ROBERT: So after you'd formed up ...

SIRK: I got us to our initial point, but the flak started up where it shouldn't have been. It was intense. The thing is, it looks puffy and harmless, but the Krauts had our range. Those 88 shells exploded at altitude and threw a storm of metal at us. I'd seen it puncture the hull. I'd seen it tear off the arm of our tail gunner back on my fifth mission. First time I saw flak I figured, hell, they're shooting at us, just dodge. But you don't, you fly right into it. I couldn't believe it, I thought it was a joke. I wanted to rush into the cockpit and yell 'go around this stuff.' But straight in, those were the orders. We couldn't be cowards even if we wanted to. Infantry, you can run, every man for himself. Not in the bombers. The pilot ran the show, unless he chickened out, and they never did, so we were along for the ride. Which is why everything that happened was such a—I don't know the word, not a shock, but a ... violation.

Buddy's voice caught. He seemed to be searching for words.

SIRK: And then it started.

ROBERT: What started?

SIRK: It. The thing, the change. The reason I'm here, the reason you're here talking to me.

ROBERT: Go on ...

SIRK: These strange lights, they just popped up around us. Out of nowhere. Reminded me of Christmas ornaments, bobbing and weaving as if someone had shaken the tree. We all saw them, chatter clogged up the interphone until Captain Clark had to shut us up 'cause we were approaching the target.

ROBERT: Could it have been a new German weapon?

SIRK: That's what I thought, maybe a new-fangled type of shell. But nothing exploded, nothing shot at us. They just buzzed and flitted around us. Duval up in the top turret said they swung around up there too, sort of pulsing. Morrie Gupman, who spoke a little German, called them "Feuerbälle"—Fireballs. We were guys who didn't panic, who'd learned how to shut it off. But there it was—unashamed fear. No one warned us about this, not a word from Colonel Cutler in his briefing. I could hear Captain Clark cutting in and out as he tried to raise other pilots. We kept waiting for the bombs away signal. We weren't the lead plane, so Randy didn't use the Norden. He just sat there, waiting.

ROBERT: Did he ever drop the bomb load?

SIRK: We didn't bomb anything that day.

Neither Robert nor Buddy spoke for a few moments. There was the sound of ice dropping into a glass, a sip that turned into a gulp. "Kentucky bourbon," Evelyn said. "Buddy's 'happy drink' he calls it, as opposed to scotch and soda, which he never could stomach".

"Robert doesn't drink. Sometimes I wish he did."

There was another clink of ice in a glass, a glug of bourbon being poured. Evelyn raised an eyebrow at Jean. "First time for everything."

ROBERT: How long did it last?

SIRK: No idea. The lights went away, like flashbulbs burning out —gone, just like that. But everything was different then. You have to imagine, the flak is pummeling us, we're all in our early twenties, gung-ho, coiled up like springs, we trained for months, and it all just went away. I could feel us changing course, I checked my nav aids and the compasses, but by then I didn't care. I knew we were climbing above our ceiling limit. I stared at the altimeter but did nothing. My muscles seemed like they were gone, I was loose. I was light-headed, that feeling of all's well with the world that you get after two drinks, before you ruin it with a third.

ROBERT: What did you think was happening?

SIRK: I didn't think. That's not how it was. I didn't analyze, no one did. We were just in it. Everyone slowly went crazy. I remember tearing open a chaff packet—little pieces of tin that we would scatter to fool enemy radar—and running them over my hands as though they were poker chips. Duval disconnected from his oxygen, strolled around the plane with the bottled O2. It's a narrow, cramped space in the Fortress, and he kept bumping his head and his elbows. Alvarez unplugged his flight suit, and sort of danced over to the bomb bay doors with his arms spread like he could fly. He would be dead without that heated suit—it was thirty below up there. So, I walked him back to his station, pretending I was a salesman—"This one is you, sir. Fits you to a T." I got him plugged back in. Then Will Slansky came back from the cockpit, pissed a river out the pee tube, the angle wasn't right, the prop wash blew it back onto the ball turret Plexi bubble, where it goddamn froze. At that moment, an ME 109 appeared, but it came from below, which they didn't do so often—they liked to attack straight on to keep up their airspeed. I thought I should yell down to Maxie in the turret to blast away, but I didn't. Maxie didn't shoot, no one did. Neither did the Messerschmitt. This here is important now: you need to learn to hate in order to fight a war, it's not a natural state of mind. And it's harder to develop that hate at twenty thousand feet when you can't see the enemy's face, can't pick out his uniform or the glint of his rifle. So, our hate came slower. But it came as more and more of our planes didn't return—it came and came hard. All the Krauts deserved it, their factories, their roads, their churches, houses, even their wives and grandkids. And then it—the hate I mean—it just died, like someone blowing out a match. Captain Clark began this Glenn Miller medley. He had a good voice. Some of us started singing along—"Pardon me Boy, is that that the Chattanooga Choo Choo." Or just nodding to the music, lost in their own thoughts ... or lack of thoughts.

ROBERT: Were you in contact with other planes in the squadron during this?

SIRK: I later learned from the captain that there was some chatter between the pilots, but their words didn't make sense to him. More likely he *didn't make sense to* them. *Our ship was lost in a private dream. We strayed out of the formation box, we left the flak behind and just seemed to drift. Like we were already in heaven, where we wouldn't have to bomb anybody, and no one would ever shoot at us again."*

"Your husband doesn't talk much, does he?" Evelyn said.

"Not much. He never has. He likes to listen, though."

"Before he was transferred out here, Buddy mentioned that he had found someone to talk to. I guess I never appreciated how much he had to say."

SIRK: Finally, we all came out of it, kind of dazed, like walking out of a movie matinee into sunlight and realizing the world kept going while you were sitting there in the darkness. None of us looked at each other, we just went back to our stations. Captain Clark came over the interphone: "Buddy, get our position and give me a course home. Potential drop areas. I'll bring her in heavy if I have to, but I'd rather not. And two alternate airfields. Everyone else, stay sharp, we're still over enemy territory. And when we land? As the Captain, mission failure is my responsibility." We didn't want to put it all on his shoulders, we thought about sabotaging the compass or the bomb bay doors, blaming the whole fiasco on mechanical failures. But that seemed wrong too, and everything was so wrong already.

ROBERT: And you all made it back. Your crew, your ship.

SIRK: Yeah.

Again, the interview came to a stop. They heard the rustle of fabric, an exhale of satisfaction from Buddy.

SIRK: It's a relief to get that tie off.

ROBERT: So, when you returned to base?

SIRK: The minute we touched down, jeeps were all around us, MPs, Colonel Cutler and his staff. We were led off like prisoners. We saw some of the guys in the ground crew—they looked like they were in shock. Everyone looked away from us. Back there on the flight line, we saw a couple other ships who'd gotten back. Some were pretty banged up, lot of tail damage and ... this I'll never forget ...

More ice, more bourbon.

SIRK: Jersey Girl had taken a big hit in the hull, the port side of the plane was torn open, and you could see clean through a ragged hole on the other side. All the way to the little chapel they had out there, beyond the wire, green pasture as bright as anything. I guess it had been a bad time, but we didn't know how bad yet. Is there another bottle? Because this last part, it's ... I don't know, maybe this wasn't such a good idea ..."

"It's a grand idea, maybe the best idea you've ever had," Evelyn said to the tape machine. She was shivering. Her handkerchief was used up with tears, you could probably wring it out and leave a puddle on the floor. She jangled her bracelet urgently, then tightened it on her wrist as though she were afraid it might fall off. Jean noticed that blocky, styled letters dangled from the thin chain: USAAF.

ROBERT: It taste OK? We're out of the Harper but the counterman at the liquor store told me this is just as good.

SIRK: Anyway, they loaded us into a deuce and a half, drove us to a part of the base that had always been off limits—Barracks X they called it.

ROBERT: What did the brass think happened?

SIRK: They only knew we hadn't dropped our bombs. To their way of thinking, we'd abandoned our mission. But we hadn't flown to Switzerland or somewhere; we'd come home. But it wasn't home anymore, it never would be. They basically locked us in. Told us there would be debriefings. From the MPs we picked up the full story of the run. We'd been part of Black Thursday, one of the deadliest raids of the war. Our raw numbers were not as high as some units, but the loss percentages were about the same—twenty-five percent. ten planes lost, a hundred men gone. The flak was bad, but the Luftwaffe did the real damage. They'd put together a huge swarm of fighters, 109s, Focke 190s, dozens of them. We only survived because we didn't proceed to the target. We went to bed that night, to a man, wishing we were dead. They held us in there for four days, and afterwards, we couldn't speak to anyone about it. Not even to ourselves. You won't find our story written down anywhere. Nothing in the official unit histories. After they let us go, some of the guys felt so guilty they volunteered for more missions, the more dangerous, the better. But the Army saw that for what it was, a suicide wish. We were all grounded.

A chair slid across a floor, someone stood, paced.

SIRK: A couple of the boys hit their twenty-five that day. They were sent home. The rest of us were eventually reclassified as "surplus crew; manpower needs sufficient at this time," and we were processed out of active status and came home too. Paperwork in order. Heroes. But Randall Ravetto didn't feel like a hero.

ROBERT: I wish I'd met him. As a mourner, I felt like an invader.

Jean recalled the black jacket hanging on a tree, the black clothes in the trunk, the black boutonniere in the street in front of the Sirk house. It had been Randall Ravetto's funeral that Robert and Buddy Sirk had attended, and they had probably made the tape shortly afterwards.

SIRK: He went out on his own terms. Far be it from me to judge.

On the tape, glasses clinked in a toast. To Randall the Scandal. A man Robert had never known. A minute of silence followed. Jean realized that Robert was waiting for Buddy Sirk to fill the empty space, to come to him, the way he'd dealt with Jimmy. He never scolded or ranted, his face always told his son, "You know what you did wrong. You'll tell me when you're ready." And Jimmy always did.

ROBERT: What about Barracks X?

SIRK: Stalag X, we called it. That first day, Colonel Cutler visited us. Angrier than I'd ever seen him. But as he talked to us, he could tell we'd experienced something no aircrew ever had. We felt like cowards, but he sensed something deeper in us. He calmed down, became the concerned father. And then they yanked him away. We never saw him again until he handed us our final paperwork. No more Army personnel, no more uniforms. The men that dealt with us from then on were in civilian dress.

ROBERT: Who were they?

SIRK: Army Counterintelligence maybe. We never found out. They debriefed us individually and in groups, hours at a time, looking for overlooked details or discrepancies in our stories, they tore apart every minute of the mission, from wheels up to landing. We'd go to sleep exhausted, then start in again after breakfast. And they were smart guys, engineering backgrounds, they knew the latest in German weaponry and flight advances, but we had nothing to tell them, really. They were just lights, you saw all kinds of sunlight tricks up there on a mission. They even ran one interrogation in German, trying to trick us. Digging for the so-called "Wahrheit," but none of us knew what the truth really was. They had a job to do. But there was this one guy for whom it seemed like much more.

ROBERT: Who was he?

SIRK: We didn't know. Pale as a ghost. Tall, like a skinny steel girder. Strange.

ROBERT: What do you mean by that?

SIRK: He had no facial expression. He just made notes in his files. And, boy, did he have files. On each of us. He knew our biographies down to the day. He knew details about our wives and kids, where they'd gone to school, the names of our pets. A couple of the guys broke down, but it didn't affect him. He never smiled or anything. Morrie Gupman even trotted out the old "scheisse bomb" joke.

ROBERT: Scheisse bomb?

SIRK: There was this guy in another outfit, probably a rumor, but he'd save his morning crap in a paper bag, take it up to altitude where it froze, toss it out when he crossed into German air space. Morrie knew how to tell that joke, believe me. But no reaction.

ROBERT: You said he was fascinated by your mission.

SIRK: After lights out, we'd see him on the runway, pacing, cigarette glowing at the end of his FDR holder. We'd wake up before dawn and he'd still be there. Staring at the planes, at the sky—at the barracks. After he'd called in the doctors and they were working us over, you'd see him through a crack in the door, watching, making his infernal notes.

ROBERT: Can you talk a bit about the doctors.

SIRK: Physical exams. Blood, piss, everything. Skin samples, fingernail clippings, hair. They seemed obsessed with our brains, our skulls, X-rays or whatnot from every angle. Needles inserted in places I'd never imagined. Ever had a spinal tap? I don't recommend it. Things got sucked out of me I didn't dream were even in there. I think they injected some sort of chemical in our blood, so they could see our veins, they said. They'd have taken our shit to their microscopes if we'd let them— that was our one successful rebellion in Stalag X. Then the psychologists showed up. With their tests. Memory quizzes, kids' colored blocks we were supposed to arrange into patterns we saw in our mind's eye. What animal does this phase of the moon remind you of? Draw yourself as you think others see you. Some of us had a little fun—I drew myself as Tojo, a couple of the guys went for Göring. Or Mae West to really confuse things.

Buddy Sirk laughed, big, hearty, loud. Evelyn smiled.

"That's the famous Buddy laugh. Had it since he was a kid, I guess. When he was happy, when he found something funny, he could make a whole room laugh."

That tore at Jean a bit, reminding her of Robert and his open-faced, casual sociability.

SIRK: They ripped Dallas Alice apart too like it was the scene of a crime. They'd moved it to a closed hangar, but we could hear the ground crews working on it all night. Engine tests. Rivet guns, taking it apart bolt by bolt, then reassembling it. Word was they were going to fly Alice back to the States.

Jean thought of the bomber she'd seen out on the runway, Quentin North and Betty Klingel crawling over it.

SIRK: After four days, they had everything they were going to get. We had to sign agreements never to discuss the mission, which none of us wanted to talk about anyway. And the steel ghost—that's what we called him—he had the addresses and phone numbers of our wives, our parents, our brothers and sisters.

ROBERT: He wouldn't tell them, surely?

SIRK: He wouldn't have to. A hint in a phone call, an anonymous letter—your husband isn't what you think he is. That's enough to eat away at a marriage.

Vann Claridge would do it in a second, Jean thought. He would even enjoy it.

SIRK: Will Evy hear this?

ROBERT: Do you want her to?

SIRK: Depends on what we do from here on, I guess.

ROBERT: Well, I know what I want to do.

SIRK: I do too.

There was a click, and the sound cut off. They let the tape keep running, but there was nothing left to hear. Buddy's voice was gone, but his presence stayed, as though he had checked into that motel room too.

"Can I get you something, Evelyn?" Without waiting for an answer, Jean poured her a cup of coffee from the thermos, then brought a glass of water from the bathroom. The sun was blazing into the room now, so intense it felt like it could burn holes into the carpet. Outside, she saw Jessie and the Director hiking down a ridge behind the motel, on their way back.

"He never mentioned a word about this," Evelyn said. "In nine years, not one hint. Sometimes, I wish our men would tell us all the awful things, the horrors and the rage and the murderous things. I would've listened, I would've accepted. I wouldn't blame him or question him like they did, like that monster did. Buddy's still a hero and a good fella, no matter how you slice it, no matter what happened on that one, single mission."

Jean couldn't tell Evelyn the details of what she—and probably Buddy—had been through. After what they'd just heard—

his honesty, his laughter. Evelyn didn't know that the "steel ghost" had returned to finish the agenda he'd set in motion during those summer days in England, with its churches and shiny green meadows. Evelyn stared out the window, but Jean knew she was peering into the past, looking for clues, or missed opportunities, imagining conversations they could've had, the years in which they could have lived in truth. A future with all its shapes and variations and joys—if only Buddy hadn't been on that bomber in July 1943.

"You brought me this part of Buddy. Thank you," Evelyn said.

Evelyn pulled her into a hug and Jean wanted to run away. But she hung on, letting Evelyn's emotions churn. Finally, Evelyn broke the hug, lit another of the Director's cigarettes. There was a discreet knock on the door and the Director poked his head in. He tapped his watch. "We have a time limit, and we have some decisions to make, so ..."

Jean smiled blandly and shut the door on him.

"A couple years after he got home, Colonel Cutler called," Evelyn said. "For old times' sake, he said, veterans swapping stories. A week or two after the call, Buddy was hired at B.E. He started on the assembly bench and, as it turned out, a couple other guys from his unit were already there, a few more hired a month later. Buddy felt good, like the old gang was back together. And he loved the job, even though he was just another guy at a workbench."

"When my Robert started at B.E., he rode the benches too. He showed up before everyone else in assembly and turned on the test equipment."

Evelyn gave her a comradely nod. "Then he and the men in his crew started getting promotions, one after another and Buddy told me, see, this is how it works, the training pays off, the unit sticks together, we help each other in peacetime. This is the future that we fought for."

The promotions Robert didn't get, Jean realized. Not the

transfer to white collar which had passed uneventfully, marked in her memory by the appearance of shoe trees in Robert's closet, metal stretchers designed to keep his new office shoes in shape. This was something else, the advancement through connections and shared experience into an exalted brotherhood from which Robert would always be excluded.

"But it didn't go the way you thought, did it?" Jean asked.

"No. As I say, we planned on a family and the promotion came with a better salary, mortgage assistance. We were, as Buddy said, "shitting on silk." But then somehow, Buddy lost interest, he didn't want kids. And the tree house, well, on foggy mornings I swore I could see a little boy and a little girl playing in it. Pushing and shoving each other, like a real brother and sister would do."

The tape continued to play until it ran out and the take-up reel clacked. Evelyn started to rethread the tape.

Jean tried to assemble a coherent picture in her mind: Connie Latimer had died in a test chamber of some kind. The crew of Dallas Alice, the same men on the list that Robert had tracked down and mailed to himself, had experienced something over the skies of Germany that was so far beyond their understanding that a practiced navigator like Buddy Sirk felt they had been briefly lifted to heaven. But when they came back to Earth, Randall Ravetto, battle-hardened bombardier, had found only a personal hell.

Why had Buddy and Robert made the tape? Surely there was more to it than Buddy unburdening his soul or confessing; he could've done that over the phone or in a bar. And why had Buddy chosen a civilian to hear his story, breaking every code of military honor Jean had ever read about? Most significant of all: what would Robert want her to do now?

The tape squealed as Evelyn rewound, punching Stop, punching Play until Buddy's generous laugh filled the room. Evelyn played the same ten seconds again and again ...

Jean couldn't be in there anymore.

Outside, she drank in the morning air, the pungent waft of creosote bushes stinging her nose. The heat was slowly building; it would be a scorching desert day. She heard the buzz of an airplane, saw it approaching from out of the low sun, high winged, glistening silver like the Spirit of St. Louis.

"Mrs. Vale. Over here!"

The Director knelt in deep shadow at the end of the motel, an Auto Club map spread out in the dirt beside him. She ran to the shade, pressed herself against the wall.

"They may not have seen us yet. Miss Harper is moving the car around back, hiding it in a junk pile. Mrs. Sirk has to get out of here. The minute that thing is gone." They heard a door opening. The Director leaned around the front corner of the motel. "Mrs. Sirk. Stay inside. Please."

"Is everything OK?" Evelyn asked.

"Fine. Just please stay in there for the moment."

Jean heard the door slam shut, as the single engine droned closer.

"Are they from Calcite?

"Perhaps our escape was too easy. We improvised, but maybe they did too, taking advantage of the situation to set us on the run, so they could follow us."

"*Us*?"

"Mr. Claridge and I have a past. I suppose you could call it. I do wish it was only me he was after, and I could be your personal Audie Murphy, holding him off with bon mots and barbed tongue as you made good your escape."

"Since I don't have any idea of where I'm going, that plane'll run out of gas if it tries to follow me."

"Be that as it may, we can't stay here, they may have ground units on the way."

"We, us. We, us. Why are you really here, Mr. Director Man Without a Name?"

"I won't insult your dignity by claiming friendship or concern for your well-being as my primary motive."

"Well, that's a start."

"A man named Quentin North and I have business to conclude."

"North. The chemist."

"You continue to impress me, Mrs. Vale. You wouldn't know his current whereabouts, by any chance?"

"Don't you know it? Since you're in business and all."

"Since our last discussion, the location of his activities has changed."

"Don't spies have—what are they—fallbacks or backups?"

"I'm not a spy, as I've explained." The Director studied the map, his mouth furrowing into a frown. The airplane engine was an insistent growl, it seemed to have descended and was circling above them. "Damnation. I don't even know what I'm looking for." He began to fold up the map, when Jean stopped him. He had marked Calcite's location with an X, but something caught her eye just a few miles to the west, in box G 10: St. Xavier's Wayfarers Chapel. Below the cross, in tiny print, one word: Abandoned.

VALE PRIVATE INVESTIGATIONS – Discrete, Dedicated, Deadly

From: Field Operative (F.O.) James Vale

Subject: Search for Missing Person XYZ.

Time: Uncertain

Status: Was given a quiz to prove that Missing Person XYZ worked for Braden Enright. Told them his bench number, what kind of solder he used. There are men here whose names I recognize but for this report, I can't say them. They are certain that Missing Person XYZ is not in Calcite. This is a setback. The men are arguing. A big event is coming, but I don't know what.

Time: 00:00: Op Larkin has a few final questions for me. He has built his own lie detector. He attaches a garden hose to my arm, connects it to a ham radio and a voltmeter which I bet comes from the Gilbert Atomic Energy Lab. He asks questions; my age, what grade I'm in, favorite ball player. Then he asks more serious ones: "Am I a Communist?" "Do I hate J. Edgar Hoover?" Some men are watching from the kitchen door. Drinking what I think are highballs. Larkin's father is proud. He even gives his son the list of questions. Then, because I am just a boy, I hear what I should not have heard.

Case Notes: *I may have solved a big mystery. I need evidence and I know where to get it. This mission could be dangerous. But a true Op looks danger in the face.*

20

Jean found it surprisingly easy to assuage a guilty conscience. She owed Jesse and the Director so much—her rescue, her freedom—yet she did not want them to accompany her to the remote church in the desert. If Robert was there, she wanted their reunion to be private, husband and wife. Her emotions were in such a tangle, she had no idea how she would behave or how Robert would react. She did not need an audience. She told them she wanted to go alone and apologized.

"You don't owe us an apology," the Director and Jessie chimed in unison.

"You got us closer to those bastards who cranked open the valves that killed Connie," Jessie said.

"And I still have my reckoning with Vann Claridge," the Director said. "We can't allow him a victory he doesn't deserve. Especially considering what you've been through, Mrs. Vale".

As she applied mercurochrome from the motel manager's first aid kit to her scabbing injection marks, Jean described the test site above Calcite with as much detail as she could remember. Nearby mountain formations, roads leading in and out, the angle of the sun, anything that could help Jessie and the Director get a picture of its scale and location. Were they going to try to infiltrate it? The Director wouldn't say. "Ignorance is bliss," he said, especially if she fell into Claridge's hands again. For once, Jean valued his secrecy.

She and the Director pooled their remaining cash and bought the Nevada Palms' 1945 Ford pickup. Her ownership wouldn't be registered anywhere, but it was Jean's to drive. "Run it into the ground, if you feel like it, ma'am. I won't miss it," the manager said. Now Jean sat behind the wheel, its big engine idling next to Jessie Harper's DeSoto. Evelyn leaned in through the driver's door like a carhop. She would return to Calcite, until she had a husband to hold or a body to bury.

"Listen, maybe Robert pushed Buddy, drew him into this somehow and I know there's nothing I can do to change that." Jean said.

"I didn't hear any pushing. Don't take away from Buddy's decision. He always found his course, I told you."

"The steel ghost, the man Buddy mentioned on the tape. I saw him, Evelyn. He's here."

"I caught the recognition in your eyes. I saw you scratch at the marks on your arm, saw you squirm and try to hold yourself still. I appreciate you trying to keep it to yourself, but you didn't have to."

The Director strode up to Evelyn, and handed her a rock, brown and gray, bumpy. But when she turned it over, its interior flashed bright blue. "Nevada fire Opal," the Director said. "Seems a rockhound forgot it in a room. If anyone questions you, you were on a nature walk."

Evelyn nodded her thanks. She backed away from the truck window, looked up at the cloudless sky.

"What do you think happened up there, Jean?"

"Everything that Buddy said. That's what happened."

"I guess only God know what it means."

Jean never knew how to continue a conversation once God

was introduced. "Maybe some time we'll find that liquor store where Robert bought their drinks, and buy the place out," Jean said.

Evelyn got into her Chevy and drove off. The Director climbed into Jesse's DeSoto, Jessie honked the horn several times, her version of goodbye and good luck. As Jean pulled out onto a dirt road, she watched the painted palms on the motel sign in her mirror as they were washed out by the sun, the only palms she'd seen so far in Nevada.

She drove over unnamed, unpaved dirt roads that led to sand-blown intersections, the map flapping on the seat, a hot cross breeze drifting through the open windows. It was only thirty miles, but the drive took all afternoon. She had to pull over every hour or so, parking in whatever meager shade she could find, falling into dreamless naps, waking up groggy, fortifying herself with sandwiches the Director had packed, then pushing on. Missing turn-offs, backtracking as she watched the sun go down ahead of her. This was no slow nightfall, the skies were blue and seconds later they were bursting with stars. She steered the truck up a low hill, stopped, checked the map, kept going. Beyond the hill, another flat plain, stretching into blackness.

Then she saw the light at twelve o'clock high.

It looked how they'd always thought it would, all those twilights on the porch with Jimmy, trying to summon the flying saucers. It didn't cross the sky like an airplane, it rose vertically, a white-green light, brilliant and fast moving, as though Venus the evening star had been shot into motion. Jean had never believed in signs and omens; her father had trusted in his tools, her mother in balanced household accounts; you were on your own, there was no one to show you the way. But even Alma might have been awed at that moment. Then Jean realized she was looking at a flare, very manmade, that someone had fired from deep in the distance. As the light settled and dispersed, it lit up a small, wooden chapel, topped by a small belfry. It looked to be about a mile away.

She drove up to the chapel and parked next to a teetering fence. The church looks lonely out here, she thought. Run out on. Its builders and their intentions long gone. No "one if by land, two if by sea" lanterns in its belfry. Its cross was off kilter and missing one arm. She switched off the truck headlights. She found a flashlight beneath the seat and probed her way up the three sagging front steps. The door dangled on one hinge, and when she tugged it open, the hinge pulled out of the frame and the door dropped onto the steps like a gangplank. *Well, there's an invitation.*

It was more stalwart than it looked from the outside. Kept alive by the dry desert air. Stars peaked through rips in the ceiling, the altar was knocked on its side, the pews were a little rotted but still aligned in rows, the chapel's pine walls were perforated by insects and maybe a few gunshots left by busted-out silver miners who'd found their way into church looking for one last piece of Providential guidance. But the spirit of the place had not departed. It was still there, untouchable but available, even to a doubting, plain-as-nails Valley gal like her. Or maybe it was something else ...

"Robert? Are you there?" she whispered. *Had Quentin North and Robert plotted here? Plotted what, exactly?*

She passed the flashlight light over the pews and beneath them, up to the preacher's lectern, a cactus poking up through the floorboards, leaning on it for support. There was no trace of Robert, but what had she been hoping to find? A page torn from a Bible with phrases marked as some sort of code? But still, it felt like he had been there. Felt? So, she was "feeling" things now. She thought of her pills again. Isoniazid. I *sono*, you *sono*, they *sono*. The idea of them now filled her with revulsion. After everything that had been pumped and squirted into her, she would never take so much as an aspirin again.

She sat down on the front pew. Closed her eyes. So tired all of a sudden. But that fallen altar bothered her. She stood it upright, then took her seat again, waiting for the Good Word, waiting for the ghost parishioners to gather. She heard the squawking of crows, then the faint rat-a-tat of beaks pecking on the roof. Crows were morning birds back home; here they roamed the night.

BRIGHT LIGHT SWEEPING down the center aisle woke her up. *Are Elizabeth Taylor and Nicky Hilton getting married here?* was her first fuzzy thought. Then the light cut off and she heard car doors, whispering voices. Footsteps cautiously stepped onto the fallen door.

"Thunder in the east," a voice called.

Sign, countersign.

"I don't like this," the voice said quietly. Two pairs of footsteps entered the church, tromping heavily. She peeked around the end of the pew and saw a good-looking but stooped man wearing a cardigan buttoned to the neck, prodding at the darkness with a gun.

"Thunder in the east," the voice prompted again.

She could keep hiding, draw it out another minute or two, but sooner or later it would become clear if they were friend or foe.

"It's Jean Vale. I'm going to stand up now, so please lower your gun."

More whispers.

"It's Will Slansky, Mrs. Vale, I think you know who I am."

Jean stood up to meet him, and he shook her hand enthusiastically.

"The copilot," she said, and he seemed to unbend, as though he'd been told by a parent to stand up straight. He didn't let her hand go until another man took it. He was compact, densely built, his hands bumpy and scarred. His smile was wide and welcoming. "Frank Alvarez," he said.

'Mr. Alvarez, you were the waist gunner."

"Port side," he nodded. A light bobbed in the doorway, and two more men came in. One carried a kerosene lantern, which he placed on the altar, casting a friendly glow over the battered pews. "And this lamplighter," Alvarez said, "this ugly ol' Mick here is my better half." Del Connolly was bald, but cultivating a sparse, manicured moustache and a goatee. His face was speckled with red bumps. "Mosquito bites," he said. "The middle of the desert, and they still find me." The second man towered over the others by at least a foot. He wore a leather flying jacket with a fleece collar and sported shiny black, matinee idol hair. He wasn't content to shake her hand, he enveloped her in a crushing embrace, but quickly backed off in embarrassment. "Morrie Gupman," he said.

"Down in the ball turret," Jean answered.

It felt like a reunion, although Jean had never met these men. They were happy to see her, she was happy to see them. Then, one by one, they turned their glances out the front door, where a shadow wavered, moved closer up the gangplank, then stopped in the doorframe. It was Jimmy. She ran to him and clutched him tighter than she ever had. He let her. She told him that he was her champ, her Jim Hawkins, her David Balfour, her Martin Kane. He let her. She pulled away, but only to better align herself to kiss his face, his hair, his hands. Then she saw the cuts and bruises.

"What happened to you?" she asked, shooting a scowl at the aircrew, as though they had somehow failed to protect him.

"I got in a fight." His voice cold, but proud.

The fighting years, she had called them, ages eight to ten, when Jimmy had wanted to get into fights, an unnamed, unexpressed anger humming just beneath the skin. He'd pick fights with other kids, but they wouldn't turn on him or lash out, as though they sensed he didn't really mean it. He bragged that someday he'd come home bruised from a real "duke-fest." One afternoon she'd heard grunts coming from his bedroom and she caught him punching himself in the face in the mirror to get a shiner. She had to wrestle his fists to his sides, taping an oven mitt to his "left hook," while sitting with him as he paced it off. It became another of their secrets. Robert was only told that his son had taken a tumble sprinting for home in a tied-score kickball game.

"With who?" she pressed. "Are you OK?"

"With Larkin. And I'm fine."

He unzipped a tan field pack he wore strapped to his waist, pulled out a packet labeled "Sulfa Powder." Jean looked at Will Slansky who hovered behind them. He winked at her and mouthed the word "sugar" as Jimmy dusted his cuts and bruises. First aid administered, he walked back outside to one of two cars that were parked facing the church, opened the trunk and hunched over, just a shadow to her again. She knew to leave him alone, and she turned back inside, where the crewmen huddled in a knot, like anxious uncles.

"Thank you—thank you all for bringing him to me."

"The boy's got spirit, it's the least we could do," said Connelly, running a hand over his bites. "Could use a bit of the real sulfa myself."

"Plus, he knew all our names, ranks and crew positions. Kinda flattering," Alvarez added.

"Where did you find him?" she asked.

The men exchanged serious looks, as though trying to decide whether to trust her. She saw that Connolly, Alvarez and Gupman were deferring to Slansky. After many years as civilians, these men were still loyal to the concept of leadership, still accustomed to a life marked out by rank and procedure.

"We found him twice, actually," Slansky said. "With the Larkin kid, at Tom Larkin's house. Going through a bit of a, what would you call it ...?"

"Interrogation?" Jean guessed.

"Well, yes. With baloney sandwiches and Twinkies but a questioning, nonetheless. We picked up the gist of his story, how you came here looking for your husband. A real Sherlock, that kid."

"Have you seen him. Robert Vale?"

"No, but that doesn't mean he's not here," Alvarez said.

"Anyway, we pried him out of that situation. He took a shine to us, and the feeling was mutual. We felt that the boy should be with his mom or his dad, but we didn't know where either of you were. So, we came up with a plan. And like most plans, it went off the track. First off, we drove to your house—well, the house on Yucca Terrace you commandeered," he smiled.

"You can come and go as you please?" Jean asked.

"For the most part," Slansky said. "Paperwork to wrestle with of course. But we're kind of the lucky ones."

"The guinea pigs," Gupman snorted.

"The house was under guard. Locked up tight. We didn't know what had happened to you, couldn't risk asking."

"By that time, he was feeling cocky," Alvarez added. 'I'm just a kid,' he bragged 'They'll trust me.'"

"It was at that point that he disappeared," Slansky said. "Took off straight into the desert, like he knew where he was going."

"So where did you find him the second time?"

"This is where it gets a little tricky. When we found him, he was scared to death. Pawing through the dirt, up to his elbows." Slansky looked out the door, Jean tracked his glance—no sign of Jimmy. "Looked like he'd been crying. Maybe for his dad. He wouldn't want us to tell you that, the stoic warrior and all, but this really isn't his war." Slansky paused in thought. "Or maybe it is."

"*Where* did you find him?"

"There's an artillery range. It's seen sporadic but intensely targeted use, heavily cratered. They were testing it in 155 millimeter shells at first."

"It?"

The crew exchanged uncomfortable glances. But no one answered.

"I've been there, goddamn it!" Jean said. "We saw soldiers, they seemed out of their minds, behaving oddly."

If Slansky was surprised. He didn't show it; he just nodded, still the unflappable pilot. "Well, then maybe you can guess what he was afraid of."

"That his father was buried there." Jean noticed a hymnal lying open on the floor, the left page rat- or bird-eaten, the right side intact: 'Blessed Assurance.' She almost smiled; courage pops up from unexpected corners. "Was he?"

"No," Slansky said. "At first your boy thought maybe he was but ..."

"There's more to it, isn't there?" she asked.

Slansky nodded. "But I don't want to step on Jimmy's toes. He can show you."

Jean walked to the doorway. Sand and scrub glowed beneath the rising moon. Jimmy was a silhouette standing next to the overturned fence, a solitary watcher. Her brave little boy, now one of the bomber crew.

"Why did you bring him here?" Jean asked Slansky.

"We've been coming here to meet," he said. "Those of us who—what's the right way to say this?"

"Who disagree with certain aspects of the program," Del Connelly prompted.

"We meet here because it's safer than back in town. We've been taking extra precautions, so we only meet at night."

"July 9, 1943. I know what happened," Jean said.

"You ... *you know?*" Alvarez said.

"All of it. Pretty much."

"And you're not running for the nearest foxhole? We're quite possibly deranged lunatics, you see."

"Lawrence Cutler doesn't think so. Van Claridge doesn't think so. And neither do I. As far as being a lunatic goes, you can sign me up as well. I'm on your side."

"You don't know what that side is, Mrs. Vale," Will Slansky said.

"Claridge held me for three days, gave me the works. My own private Barracks X. What other side could I take?"

The men nodded, studiously. She figured that by now, nothing, not even a housewife in distress locked up in a makeshift clinic concealed in a library could shock them. She was grateful they hadn't tried to shower her in worry and apology. Up on the roof, the crows started again, hopping on their talons, pecking, cawing.

"Something probably died up there," Slansky said. "It's a strange place here, but then, most of us have become used to strange. We thought we could put it behind us. But once we got hired on by Colonel Cutler and started up the ladder at B.E., promotions, salary increases, Christmas bonuses ..."

"You're all here? All ten?"

"Not all. Roger Duval's in bad shape, drinking problem, a few other things. We lost touch with him."

"Although I'm sure *they* haven't." Connolly said.

"Pres McHale didn't accept the offer to join B.E. He had a good civilian life going and ..."

"Was well compensated for turning the Colonel down. And keeping quiet." Connolly said. "Begging your pardon. Captain."

That drew a glare from Slansky. "Neal Clark's still the captain in my book. He's with Northwest Orient now, in charge of pilot training. His cadets are in good hands. Probably wouldn't share our views, anyway. The fellas bumped me into the left seat, ceremonially speaking. I don't approve, but Army habits never die. Then there's Sergeant Ravetto." Slansky's chin jerked, and he made the sign of the cross on his cardigan. "And Lieutenant Sirk ..."

Jean had an urge to say it aloud—*Buddy*—because she felt she knew him, but she didn't want to presume a familiarity the crewmen might find intrusive.

"... missing in action, I guess you could call it." Slansky finished.

"Captain," Connolly said, tapping his watch.

Slansky nodded. Alvarez, Gupman and Connolly went through a parade of personal tics: Gupman tightened his belt and knelt to knot his shoelaces. Connolly stuffed his mouth full of Beeman's, ran in place for a few seconds. Alvarez lit two cigarettes, took one for himself, passed the other to Gupman. Will Slansky watched with amused indulgence, too squared away to need ritual preparation for whatever was to come.

Through the arched window facing the last pew, they saw another flare going up, scattering its white-green light across the sky.

"We gotta run, Mrs. Vale. That's the signal," Slansky said.

"For what?"

"Dress rehearsal guess you'd call it. For test day."

"A different kind of war is coming, Mrs. Vale, and a different kind of warrior and tactic will be required to fight it. The new front lines are in our own minds and in the minds of our opponents." Vann Claridge's words.

"It's our Trinity Test, you might say," Slansky added. Jean knew he was referring to the first detonation of the A-bomb out in New Mexico in July 1945. The war-ending weapon that still wasn't big enough, so now they were building the "super bomb" as Truman called it. Somewhere she'd seen it called the "hell bomb."

"But it's not a bomb they're testing, is it? Or some new cannon or airplane. Those strange acting soldiers I saw, were they the first guinea pigs?"

"I'm just a businessman and an ex-soldier. I don't pretend to understand, I have experts for that." Lawrence Cutler's words.

She saw the outlines now. Lawrence Cutler recruiting his original crew to work for Braden Enright, his ambition fired by the idea of designing the future, maybe seduced by money, or flushed with the pride and peacetime self-respect that came with winning the approval of a man who had the president's ear. And to prove himself beyond the call of duty to his wife, Frances Braden Cutler. It was Lawrence's ball, but it was Claridge's game.

"No, it's not anything like that. What sets everyone on edge, is that no one, I mean truly deep down, knows what it is. Even the chemists and biologists and engineers with their formulas and their equipment can't really say," Slansky said.

"And because of our unique experiences, we're the only ones with first-hand, real-life knowledge," Connolly said. "Reunited for one final mission. Lab rats in bomb jackets. 'Is this what you felt? Is this it?' No, it's not euphoria it's more of an acceptance ..."

"No, I tell them, it's more like we ignored our surroundings, mentally molding them into something else," Slansky added. "All our experiences up there, they were different, it's tough to get a scientist to grasp that."

"I thought you were opposed to this whole thing?"

"The testing will go on and it's not our role to stop it," Slansky explained. "And it's certainly not within our power. We have a job to do, families to support. But if anything happens, anything goes wrong, odds are it won't get all of us. Someone will be able to tell the story."

"And they won't be able to bury it," Connelly said. "Like a lot of other things out here."

"As far as the future goes," Slansky said, "that's for the American people to decide, I suppose. That's a fine son you have there. Mrs. Herndon will be on site tomorrow, and afterwards she'll be heading back home to your Bay Area. We figured to send Jimmy with her."

"Tousle his hair for me, would you?" said Gupman. "We know he hates that."

The four crew members walked out into the night, and Jean pictured them back in 1943, stepping from the summer-green English countryside into their cramped warship of American-made steel. She could see Del Connelly, just nineteen the first time he sat behind the .50 cal at the waist gunner's window; Frank Alvarez, grousing about the fit of his flight suit; Morrie Gupman straining and failing to get comfortable in the ball turret. And she saw Will Slansky, not as he was now, carrying a weight that he didn't know how to get rid of, but as the co-pilot, fitting on his oxygen mask as they hit ten thousand feet, scanning his instruments, glancing out at the cloud cover, then giving the high sign over his shoulder to Buddy Sirk, with his charts, chronometer, and his calculations. Buddy, who always got them home.

Their two cars U-turned and drove up to the rise, headlights doused. They stopped on either side of Jimmy, who stood still as a sentinel. They spoke briefly, Jimmy pivoting from one car to the next. Then the cars rolled on to the ridgeline, Jimmy waved, and they disappeared. He stood his ground, showed no sign of returning to the church.

Go out there and grab him! Get him as far away from Calcite as you can.

Drive like hell to the California border. But it was naïve to believe that crossing an imaginary line on an Auto Club map would automatically make them safe. Vann Claridge could reach over the horizon, and when something was too conspicuous or low level for him to handle personally—like dealing with those spineless Los Altos cops— he had Cutler to do it for him, and Cutler had little night crawlers like Wally Marantz.

She went to the truck, grabbed two cushions stinking of gasoline and a Nevada Palms blanket from the cab, then threw them onto the pews. She dragged one of the pews from its row, the weathered wood creaking, swung it around and slid it back so that two pews faced each other. She pushed them together, their bed for the night. Jimmy would come in when he was ready.

21

The Director insisted that all staff members take a first aid refresher course once a year. Perhaps he had been inspired by the Civil War tent hospital that had once occupied the organization's grounds, caring for casualties from the Army of the Potomac. He could treat scrapes and avulsions and burns, control bleeding, improvise splints and slings. They hadn't covered bullet wounds. Or snake bite.

He crawled into a dry wash, hidden by twisted stands of scrub and by sunset-lengthened shadows. One shot had gouged a path through his thigh, another pierced his left wrist, scraping the bone, leaving his hand limp and useless. The shots had knocked him down, onto a sleeping snake who woke up in a rage and struck him just inches from the rifle wound. He didn't think it was a rattlesnake, he hadn't heard the clatter they say accompanies an attack. It stung, whatever it was, and his vision had started to blur, another reminder that these climes were not for him. During his preparatory reading on the conditions that might await him in the Mojave Desert, he'd learned to not clean the bite. For now, focus on the gunshot wounds. He was bleeding from his thigh—*direct pressure!*—he could still hear the first aid instructor's commands. Or maybe that was the wrong move. If he restored his blood pressure, the snake venom would flow more quickly through his system, wouldn't it? But what if it wasn't venomous, just a mean son of a bitch? He couldn't see invisible poison, but he could see fresh blood. With keys, teeth, and his right hand he tore a length of sleeve from his shirt, and pressed it into the leg wound. He improvised a splint from a dead Yucca branch, and laid it across the wrist joint, tying it in place with a ripped off shirt sleeve. He settled his breath and tried to slow his heart rate. The moon was sinking, and soon the blood trail would be tricky to follow. Wait it out. Think, don't feel. Choke off the pain.

Anne came to him then. For some reason he recalled the myths they'd believed in as kids: Santa Claus and the Tooth Fairy, of course, but local legends such as the White Witch of Saratoga who would drop out of trees onto the cars of unsuspecting lovers, and scratch the roof to ribbons with her steel fingernails; the boy who ate his family's Bible and became a millionaire fortune teller—the Director had to take their Bible away from Anne, who had already chewed her way through ten pages of Genesis. As an adult, the Director had become more skeptical, more selective in his beliefs. But Anne ...

... Anne had believed in Vann Claridge early on, and by the time he had reached his peak, so did most everyone. OSS hero, European linguist, science and engineering advisor to FDR and Harry Truman, the only man to sit on both the President's Scientific Intelligence Committee and the Joint Intelligence Committee. She had believed in the same big picture things he had—country, church, democracy, in studying the tides of history and the markers they carried that could illuminate the present, and help to guide the future. And she had believed in a certain way of conducting herself. Diligent work, fair play and charitable giving, the power of words and ideas; fists were for Irish brawlers and prize fighters. She believed in consommé to begin a meal, honey dew melon to end it, grilled steaks and fresh oysters in between. She believed in seasonal wardrobes, conservatively cut, one strand of pearls, not two, matching gold wedding rings, the husband's slightly bigger. She believed that it was inappropriate to ask questions about her husband's secret work, and unnecessary to share details about her own. She believed in the value of one's status, but not at the expense of treating shabbily those who weren't of their social or professional castes.

She believed in love. But Claridge believed only in the utility of his fellow human beings, including—maybe especially—his wife.

Near the end, the Director, sensing in Anne a longing for fresh perspectives, had offered her a position in the organization. She had declined, declaring that she was going to embark on a path of self-examination, correct her flaws and failings, and emerge as a new person. That had never happened. She ended up believing only in brutal, slow death. Hanging herself from the heavy stem of the ceiling fan, the blades motionless as she twisted and choked. Her last glimpse of life perhaps the minor Winslow Homer which hung above the fireplace. Dying slowly.

In her wedding dress.

The Director's blood flow had slowed from a stream to a seep, but the improvised bandage was soaked through. He ripped another length of sleeve, pressed it to the wet, sticky flesh. He imagined hawks circling up in the sky. Or did that only happen in westerns?

The Director had always been a desk and telephone man, a facilitator, a gentle tugger on diplomatic strings, a debater of philosophies designed to lure people into his corner. A liaison to sister organizations in Europe. And although he had exchanged letters with Mohandas Gandhi, for the most part he was a reluctant exploiter of connections; such reticence made him effective, and he was not above deploying false modesty. But when Connie Latimer was murdered—and he had no doubt that was the case—the first of his “troops” to die in the line of duty, his distanced, squeaky clean approach began to disgust him. He had come here to act, to get dirty. To get blooded. And though it reeked of the eye-for-an-eye cynicism which ruled and threatened to ruin the world, he had come for hands-on revenge.

It had gone well at first. To his surprise, he had become crafty and clever, a rescuer of imprisoned women, even. The coded Western Union cables exchanged back in D.C. with Mr. North when he made the “beer run” to Las Vegas had established their rendezvous point. Even when the test site had been unexpectedly moved, Jean Vale’s hints had been helpful. Studying wind patterns, matching them to elevation and landscape, he and Jessie Harper knew they were closing in on the test site when they heard muffled PA announcements echoing off the rock walls. They had split up, Miss Harper in the car, searching for a backroad access, the Director on foot. And then ... a jackrabbit hunter, of all things. Half blind, firing at anything that moved. The Director hadn’t seen the hunter, but he pictured a prospectorish fellow who lived alone, ate beans out of cans. The hunter had assumed he missed, bellowed a loud “Fuck you, scwewy wabbit,” hadn’t even bothered to check on his prey, just moved on.

Now, he could barely walk, and the blood loss would soon impact his ability to think rationally. The swashbuckling Light Brigade role he had imagined for himself would fall to others. That’s more appropriate, he thought. Perfect, even. To paraphrase one of his father’s heroes, Senator Albert Beveridge, it would “come from the grass roots, grown from the soil of people’s hard necessities.”

No hawks. No blood-scenting wolves. Just silence. And dizziness. But he had to keep moving. He could not die out here; Anne would not let him.

. . .

Jimmy stood in the doorway, but didn't come in. Like a temperamental housecat waiting for a treat to be offered. She met him at the threshold. She rolled up her shirtsleeves. *See, nothing up my sleeves.* She turned her pockets inside out, tossed the truck key and a few stray coins onto the pews. Empty now, except for a trickle of sand that fell to the floor. "No pills, see? No more secrets for you to keep."

He took two steps into the chapel and stopped, looked around. Jimmy noticed the makeshift bed, and his eyelids drooped shut momentarily. One thing that had always set him apart from other kids—when he was beat, he had no trouble admitting it. He would climb under the covers and fall asleep with a comic book in his hand.

"Billy Larkin thinks that dad's dead."

"That why you fought?"

"No. That was about other stuff he said about dad."

He walked to the bed-pew, perched on the edge. Then took out two Hershey bars from his pack, handed one to her.

"What stuff?"

He waved his arm, batting away the question. She tried the Robert approach, letting Jimmy come to her. She ripped open the Hershey bar and dug in, chewing slowly, gratefully. Waiting for more from him. But he turned his attention to his supplies —maps, compass, pocketknife. He polished his field glasses with a dusty sleeve.

Suddenly, she felt like shaking him. She wanted to knock all of this military poise out of him and mother him again. She wanted him sick with a soaring temperature and a runny nose, she wanted to keep him home from school, to serve him Campbell's tomato soup with a plate of peanut butter and Saltine sandwiches so she could watch him squeeze the crackers together to force the peanut butter out through the holes, like tiny worms. She wanted him to make a mess, maybe spit up, just a little, so that she could clean up after him. She wanted him nurseable.

His eyelids fluttered, closed, then opened. Closed again. Still sitting up, but he was slipping. She itched to press him on those ten words: *"Dad would probably want to be found by me anyway."* But she decided it could wait; maybe some things were not meant to be understood all at once. Why did she need to know everything that was in her son's heart? Did he know what was in hers? He laid down, squirming to avoid the fissure where the two pews butted against each other. She covered him with the motel blanket, and as she tightened it around his shoulders, she had the impression that he had grown in the days they were apart—his body was tougher, his bones seemed stronger.

"What did you find out there, Jimmy? In that pit?"

He rolled onto his side, scratched at his face with hands. His nails were crusted with dirt from clawing and digging in the artillery crater. She recalled how she used to nag him for his dirty fingernails. She'd grown up with her nails permanently caked in black and, for some flimsy, forgotten reason, she had wanted something different and cleaner for Jimmy. He tugged a metal object out of his shirt pocket, handed it to her. Though smudged and dusty, it glinted in the pale lantern light—it was a tie clasp, big enough for the widest, showiest necktie.

"Made from aluminum strips, longitude stiffeners or something," Jimmy said.

Soldered roughly to a three-inch-long metal bar were five styled, metal letters: USAAF.

"The letters were cut from the fuselage skin of a Flying Fortress."

The same style letters on the bracelet worn by Evelyn Sirk.

And then he slept, and she stood watch.

THE FIRST SIGN that they'd blundered into the middle of history was a sudden wind. It came up quietly, as dawn was rising, wafting through the broken windows on the west side of the church. It accelerated in tempo and intensity, until powerful gusts were rifling through the empty window frames. She had nodded asleep sitting sentry at the pew nearest the window, and the wind slapped her awake, kicking over the lantern, spilling kerosene onto the floor. Then, as abruptly as it had begun, it stopped.

Jimmy flashed instantly into alert mode, threw off the blanket, infantry-crawled to the window, peered over the ledge.

"Mom, something's going on, something big."

A commotion outside—engines, construction clamor, shouted instructions. Jean risked a look over Jimmy's shoulder and saw a line of trucks formed into a circle like a wagon train. A man was running toward the chapel, a man in black and white—black pants, black shirt, white lab coat. Quentin North tromped up the door gangplank into the church. He looked like he'd been through the ringer—red-eyed, face grimy, hair awry. He smelled like gasoline and stale coffee. He wiped his face with the sleeve of his lab coat, turning it black.

"Exhaust from our generators, sorry. And you must be Jimmy. So, listen here—the test site has been relocated, you're right in the middle of it. We're doing a live run through with the blowers in a few minutes, once they get the towers set up. We need to get you out of range."

Through the front door Jean saw two mammoth flatbed trucks rattle by with what looked like POW camp guard towers lying flat on their load beds. The trucks were followed by a caravan of Airstream trailers and a few civilian cars, dust swirling behind them.

"Look, it's Mrs. Herndon!" Jimmy said.

Beverly Herndon slid out of one of the cars. She was in full war-correspondent gear, khaki shirt and olive drab tie, combat pants rolled up above the ankles, a WAC cap perched on her head at the perfect, jaunty angle. She reached into the car and lugged out a movie camera topped with two giant film reels like Mickey Mouse ears. She propped it on her shoulder, yelled to someone in the back seat, "Harvey, the headlights are perfect, natural lighting. Let's not fussy it up." She darted among the trucks and trailers, camera rolling, as though she were reporting on the D-Day landing. Jimmy seemed hypnotized by Bev Herndon, then Jean realized he was squinting into her car, wondering if Monica were with her.

"I think there's another way out," Jean said. She led them past the altar, to a narrow door that was just a few slats of rotting wood. North and Jimmy kicked it open.

The scene outside was astonishing.

There were three wooden platforms about a hundred yards to the west. They'd been invisible in the darkness, unattended, although there had probably been a guard out there somewhere. Giant motorized fans taller than a man were positioned on them, the source of the wind that had suddenly switched on and off. A maze of pipes connected to each fan, leading to what looked like tanks of propane gas. She recognized the Administrative Airstream trailer—workers were filing in and out. On a hill behind the trailer, crews were erecting the preassembled towers, levering them up to their full height, at least fifty feet, the transport trucks' load beds serving as the foundations. Other workers craned more giant fans onto the crow's nests on top of the towers. Beyond the towers, the landscape was dotted with moving lights. Jean couldn't tell how many. The lights were filing slowly across a wide plain, but then they split into two groups, turned away from each other in opposite directions.

"Trinity," Jean whispered.

"Trinity Two, some call it. But destruction is the exact opposite of what's intended," North said.

"Do I get the truth now? All of it?"

North nodded, then shot a concerned look over Jean's shoulder. She turned to see two MPs in their small-town police uniforms, walking toward the Ford pickup. They opened the doors, probed the front seat with flashlights.

North took off his lab coat, told Jean to put it on, then led them past the fan platforms to a plateau where two more Airstream trailers were parked end to end. Workers wearing miner's headlamps were sliding blocks under the axles to level them out. They reached the middle trailer, as someone called out to North.

"Get inside, now!" He pushed Jean and Jimmy through the door, shutting them in.

No vacationing families had ever vagabonded across the country in this Airstream. The windows had been blacked over —no one could see in, and they couldn't see out. The interior had been converted into a laboratory that seemed too complex to be useful. It was like being inside the workings of the human body, if the body were made of metal and glass. Galvanized pipes and iron supporting rods connected vertical glass columns that stretched from floor to ceiling, linked together by smaller glass pipes, like veins and arteries feeding into capillaries. Meters and valves and pressure gauges calibrated and monitored whatever flowed through this geometrically aligned network. Jean recognized a B.E. hydraulic indicator, Model B-9. There were shelves lined with beakers and flasks and stoppered bottles. An array of electronic equipment hummed and blinked on an aluminum work table, connected by bundled cords. A kitchen shelf with industrial solvents hung above the sink. Next to it was a hat rack. Giant insect heads, with bug eyes were hanging on the rack—gas masks. Jimmy reached for a mask to try it on, but Jean stopped him. "Let's not touch anything in here. The whole place feels deadly to me."

North came in, checking his watch. "My team will be here in a few minutes. We're starting at dawn. I argued for later in the day when the winds will be more unpredictable, which would give us a better idea of how to correct for unexpected dispersal patterns, but there are a lot of military guys invested in this, and 'we strike at dawn' seems like a line of scripture to them."

"Why was the test site moved?" Jean asked.

"They say it was penetrated, infiltrated. It's a big desert, we can do it anywhere." North spun some dials and valves, and a clear liquid began to circulate through the pipes and glass tubing, passing through filters and strainers. North opened a sliding panel in the blackout window above the sink, did a quick scan, then pulled it shut again. There was a thump outside, and the Airstream seemed to jump up and down. "Just the main conduit connecting to the reservoirs on the trailer's undercarriage." North went to the door, yelled out some instructions, shut the door again.

"We have a few minutes, what do you want to know?"

"Everything."

North knelt on the floor facing a smaller network of pipes and turned on a faucet which fed water into a row of potted plants, laid out in single file like a greenhouse. "I've got baby Ocotillo, chuparosa, and this deceptive little beauty. Jimmy, take a look at this." North brushed his hand inches above a beautiful, delicate white blossom. "Datura, it can be highly poisonous."

"Mr. North, *please* ..." Jean snapped.

"You're right, I'm sorry. After the war, American companies turned their attention to the important things in life—how to sterilize orange juice without heat, developing run-proof ladies' hose, and so on. I wound up working for an outfit called Consolidated Mills. They were desperate to expand into the snack food market, and willing to pay chemists like me to help them get there. Looking for the ideal blend of crunch and texture."

An electronic trill beneath the sink. North pulled out a walkie-talkie, raising his voice to cut through a cloud of static. "Set the blower baffles to accommodate the new wind conditions. I've got the soup on now. It should start flowing to the tanks any moment ... They are, huh?" He signed off the walkie-talkie. "The VIPs are here—Cutler, Mrs. Cutler, Claridge and his acolytes."

"Frances is here?" Jean asked.

"Why shouldn't she be? With her formidable background in mathematics, she can run rings around Lawrence—on paper at least. And in many ways, her ambitions for B.E. outweigh his. Where was I? Oh yes, God knows how, but Vann Claridge found me; being an OSS veteran has its advantages. What drew Claridge's attention to me was private research I'd been conducting into different chemicals that plants and animals synthesize. I thought they might shed light on the inner workings of our own brains, believe it or not. So, he knew I was not scientifically rigid in my thinking. He showed me the medical tests from the bomber crew at Bury St. Edmunds. Their blood was different than ours. There were chemical traces in there I hadn't seen before, although some were superficially similar to my own studies. Even the men's spinal fluid had been altered. The Nazis had been obsessed with a miracle war-winner—the V1, the V2, guns that could shoot around corners, electro U-boats, jet planes. So maybe this was along those lines, a new energy source designed to function at high altitude. Maybe an accidental by-product of chemical warfare experiments. Claridge and his staff went through thirty thousand German patents hidden away in the salt mines of Merkers, but they found nothing helpful."

North wouldn't stop talking. Jean realized he had been living behind a barrier of secrecy for so long, sequestered in his lab and bound to silence, that he hadn't been able to talk openly with anyone. For years, perhaps.

"So, I abandoned my search for the 'ultimate taste bud tang' and joined the project. They got Dallas Alice out of mothballs and flew it back here from Europe last year. We went through it but couldn't find anything evidentiary. Only the men had been altered, not their combat environment. Have you ever heard the term 'neurotransmitter?' It's a fancy word for the chemicals that fire the human brain into activity or slow it down. They may even have a relaxing effect on the nervous system. Discovered by an Austrian scientist, Otto Loewi, back in the Twenties. And get this, the idea came to him in a dream. I felt immeasurably relieved."

"Why?" Jean asked.

"A trained bomber crew had become docile, unable or unwilling to fight. Their bodies and blood presented a chemistry I had never seen before. Where had it come from? Why not from a dream? Why not from those mysterious lights they saw dancing around their bomber?"

North's voice had softened, his face lost its lively, storyteller's gleam. Whatever had transformed the Dallas Alice crew, he seemed changed by it too.

"My job was to isolate the chemistry and synthesize a compound that could be reproduced in quantity and deployed in battle."

"For Korea?"

"They don't give a damn about Korea. This is bigger, the next war in Europe, against the Soviets. I had unlimited funds at my disposal, a small but brilliant team of experts—a biologist, a physiologist, an anatomist, a clinical psychiatrist from the Walter Reed Army Institute of Research. All approved by Claridge and sworn to secrecy, under penalty of prison. Just as I am. Using the men's altered biology as a roadmap, I believe we've succeeded in the task. I called it 'the peace drug' to assuage my conscience that had become tainted by careerism, but they see it as a weapon that could be used to disable enemy forces without firing a shot."

"But that doesn't sound bad. To the contrary."

Quentin North swallowed heavily, twice, like something was caught in his throat that wouldn't go down.

"We held many of our early tests in a controlled environment that mimicked the conditions present on the plane on

July 3, 1943. In the altitude compression chamber at the B.E. facility on Middlefield Road."

There was a knock on the metal skin of the trailer. North waved for Jean and Jimmy to fold themselves into a corner, behind the lab table. North opened the door an inch and argued with two MPs. Jean only half listened, her thoughts running back to Crusader Connie as the photographer pulled away the blanket to reveal her blood-wrinkled face.

"No, you cannot come in. We are at a critical phase, and I can't have extra people in the lab."

"We don't report to you, sir. Our orders are to search the lab."

"Check back with Lawrence. Have him call me with the authorization."

North slammed the door on the MPs. He motioned that the coast was clear. "We knew we had to take the tests airborne, get the bomber in the air. So, we outfitted Dallas Alice with probes, monitors, flew that damn plane over half the state of Nevada. Testing our compound on guys who'd never been exposed to it, using the original crew as a control group. They got bonuses, as if that could make up for forcing them to relive the war. I asked Mr. Cutler to pull these men off the project, I even barged into their garden party, but I couldn't get near Claridge. Cutler is still protective of his men, but I honestly don't know where his true loyalties lie."

"Was Connie a test subject?" Jean asked.

"No, she found her way into the chamber somehow, accidentally triggered it to set for twenty-five thousand feet."

"Accidentally?"

North frowned. "I'm quoting from the official explanation."

"So it's not a space gun, or a supersonic plane or a rocket tank?" Jimmy asked.

"No, son. Just this." North ran his hand along the grid of pipes and conduits. He was possessive, Jean thought. But not proud. "We established that the compound works at altitude.

We've run small ground tests on small groups. Now, we're about to conduct a widespread trial on a simulated battlefield."

"Why do you keep working for them? If you don't believe in any of this?" Jean asked.

"In my younger years, I was quite the active socialist. Claridge knows every minute and movement of my actions. Today, that makes me a Red, a target for every congressmen on the warpath. Prison if I don't testify against others from back in those days. No company in America will touch me." An alarm clock rang. North switched it off and attended to his valves and gauges. "And I didn't say I don't believe in it."

He opened the blackout panel, a pale, pre-dawn light on his face. "They're getting set out there. I have to be on the western tower with the meteorologist. My assistants will handle things in here. I need you to keep moving, they've brought in the head watchman and his team, and they'll push hard to root out the infiltrator, imaginary or not, test or no test."

Jean peered through the hatch and saw the milkman stepping out of a car. No sparkling white uniform now—he wore fatigues, a black, complicated looking rifle slung over his shoulder. Two bulky armed guards in dark blue overalls got out of the same car, and the milkman began to lecture them, like a football coach on the sidelines of the big game.

North grabbed another canvas-wrapped walkie-talkie, flipped through a series of switches. "This is a receiver-transmitter. Range is about a mile, maybe more out here. Do not call out because others can listen in. Wait to be contacted."

North nudged Jean and Jimmy out the door as two assistants approached the trailer, a man and a woman, gas masks around their necks, both impossibly young, the woman lugging a metal suitcase in each hand, the man dragging a dolly loaded with a free-standing safe. "Let's start with batch 39," North told them. "It's given us the least trouble. I've got it loaded into the lines and its flow rate is good, coagulation points stable."

The towers had all been erected, hoses and electrical

cabling in place, generators coughing to life. Across the plain, the moving lights were winking off, and Jean could make out two companies of armed soldiers facing each other, fifty strong perhaps, separated by a hard-baked no man's land.

North unlocked the trailer next door, nodded for them to enter. Inside, it was part bookworm's paradise, part file clerk's nightmare. Shelves sagged beneath the weight of fat technical manuals. Documents were stacked floor-to-ceiling, leaving a narrow pathway in the center of the trailer. "Our archive storage. You'll be safe here while the MPs work their way through the more obvious targets."

Then a series of roars thundered outside, growing louder until they combined in a continuous, mechanical drone. Unlike the lab, this Airstream had windows, and they saw that the giant, motorized blowers atop the towers had all kicked on. There was a cluster of people on the nearest tower. Jean spotted Lawrence Cutler, Frances by his side, snapping away with a Brownie camera. A glint of sun sparked through a notch in the hills behind them and seemed to highlight Frances' bright animated features and luxurious hair. Even here, she looked perfectly put together. Some people never frayed or ruffled; Frances Braden Cutler was one of them. Climbing slowly up the ladder to the tower was Vann Claridge. Cutler bent down like a servant to give him a hand up.

She and Jimmy needed food and water. There were bags of plant food on a shelf displaying more samples of North's desert gardening prowess, but no sink or refrigerator. Then Jimmy found a small icebox in the leg space of the desk. Inside were two apples, a package of cheese crackers, and a Tupperware container of homemade egg salad—a secretary's lunch was the same everywhere. They used the crackers as spoons to scoop up the egg salad. Jimmy crunched on the apples as he peered through his binoculars.

A deep rumbling tone carried over the roar of the blowers. Jean recognized it as the spotter plane that had been searching for them. "It's circling above those soldiers," Jimmy said.

The walkie-talkie squawked. "OK, we're going to move you again," North said. "You'll hear three knocks at the door—it will be an ally. Follow her." They heard a truck engine approaching. Seconds later, three knocks and Jean opened the door to a woman's eyes. Her hair was covered with a shower cap, a surgical mask over her nose and mouth, her body draped in white overalls. Those eyes—did they recognize her? Did they belong to one of the neighbors Jean and Jimmy had met during their get-acquainted rounds? The woman gestured with a gloved hand toward the bed of a canopied truck that had backed right up to the Airstream door. Jimmy and Jean climbed into the truck, and the woman patted Jimmy on the shoulder, as though she had seen him before. Then lowered the canvas flaps to conceal them. They sat on a wooden bench and the truck jerked forward.

Five minutes later, they stopped. Jean peaked through the flaps. They were closer to the "battlefield" as the crow flies, but higher above it. Half of the soldiers wore gas masks, the others did not. Something odd was happening to the weather. A soft mist sparkled in the rising sun, not thick like fog. There was no lake or pond, no river to generate early morning condensation, but there it was, vaporous and wispy, as though heaven-high cirrus clouds had descended to Earth.

This was Trinity Two, Jean realized. North's miracle chemical that had flowed around them in his lab, transformed into visible air, the soldiers maneuvering through it.

The walkie-talkie crackled. North spoke four or five words, and they were moved again. Then two more times, escorted by the masked mystery women. To an armory, finally into a tent that stored canned military rations, the labels faded. Jean and Jimmy plopped down on the tent's plywood floor, leaned against the stacked cans. I'm still a prisoner, Jean thought. And now my son is too.

The walkie-talkie cawed yet again, and she felt like smashing it against the wall ... if only there were a wall. "What is it?" she asked, the anger rising in her. "You said this was our last stop. You should've just left us in the armory, and we could have mowed down the milkman and his boys right then and there."

It wasn't Quentin North.

"Jean?"

His voice sounded hollow and distant, like an echo of an echo.

"Robert? Is that really you? Not a tape recording, not a Lawrence Cutler trick?"

"It's me. How's Jimmy?"

He was already reaching for the walkie-talkie, she was already wiping the sudden tears from her eyes with a sleeve, which only rubbed in desert grit, producing more tears.

"He's right here. We're both here! My God, if you only knew what we'd been though to find you. And you OK? I imagined a thousand things that could have happened to you. But where are you right now?"

"I have to be quick, get off the air. Behind the tent is a hillside, leading up it is a narrow dirt path, maybe they used to use it for the mule teams. It veers through a sandstone canyon. When you come out of the canyon, you'll cross a dirt road and find a clearing. You'll see a hole, like a cave. It's a Calcite mine. See you in five minutes." And then he was gone. She hit the call button, desperate to talk, but Jimmy shook his head. Stay off the air.

They lifted the back tent flap, saw the hillside and the road, a chalky slash climbing through the pale brown badlands. As they hiked straight into the rising sun, Jean realized neither had said "I love you." That just wasn't the Vale way.

22

He walked from the back of the cave into the morning sun, like a nocturnal creature risking the daylight. She thought he'd be jumpy, maybe hunched a bit, a fugitive making himself a smaller target; he'd be dirty and unshaven, his hair matted with dust. But he wore a white shirt, sleeves rolled up, and his favorite gray pants which she'd ironed a hundred times while he watched and waited in his boxers. He'd shaved, combed his hair—not the way she preferred it, a bit mussed but with the ruler-edged part that was the "B.E. look" favored by the photographers in the monthly newsletter.

"Your place or mine?" he asked.

Jean and Jimmy ran to him. He pulled them both into a bear hug, the first time the three of them had hugged together in years. She kissed him hungrily, tasting sand, smelling creosote.

"I thought you'd left us. I thought you'd run away. I thought you'd been killed. I thought you'd killed someone and were on the lam," Jean gasped. "No, I didn't think any of those things."

She pounded on his chest with her fists, wanting to knock

him to the ground and keep punching once he was down. "Goddamn you, goddamn you!" She kept up the pummeling until her fists burned and her arms grew jittery. She went limp, he held her tighter. "Or that my problems had become too much. That you wanted someone who was a clean slate—you know, paper white. Someone who wasn't messy in the head, who didn't need a kid to take care of her." Then the tears came, bone-cracking sobs that she felt would break her in two. He held her still tighter. She wanted to live in that embrace. For the next five minutes, she did, as her shuddering was absorbed by Robert's arms and chest.

"How did you find me?" Robert asked. "I can't imagine what you two went through to get here?"

"No, you can't. That I am sure of."

Jimmy started rooting around among the boxes of U.S. Army rations that were propped against the cave wall. "Where are we? What is all this stuff?" he asked. "Any weapons?"

It was more cave than a mine. No rusting ore cars, just flaky sandstone walls and jutting rocks. Wooden shipping crates marked with numbers and letters were stacked next to the ration boxes. Jean noticed a metal suitcase similar to those carried by Quentin North's lab assistants. A bedroll of army blankets, a leather jacket for a pillow. A flat boulder served Robert as a nightstand, tin cup, plates and utensils arranged next to a lantern. Empty ration cans were piled next to the boulder, as though Robert were expecting a cleaning lady.

"Here, let me show you something," Robert said. "The angle of the sun is just about right." Jean and Jimmy followed Robert to a niche gouged out of the cave wall. Seconds later, a ray of morning light streaked in and shined on the niche. A cluster of rocks gleamed like prisms. "Calcite crystals," Robert said. "The light strikes them at a different time each day; it's sort of my personal sundial."

Jean had no patience for his private enthusiasms. "Why? That's all—why?"

"It started out as one thing and led somewhere else so quickly, I could barely keep up with myself," Robert said. "I didn't tell you because I thought it would be too dangerous to involve you. I never expected you to turn detective and come looking for me." He turned a look of admiration on his son.

"We had to, dad. We followed clues, and maps," Jimmy said. "Then we went off the maps, navigating across the desert. We even fell into an artillery crater!"

From another niche in the cave wall, Robert took out his walkie-talkie. He switched past the static and the agitated voices until he found a music channel. "Somewhere out there is a guy who breaks the rules. Mostly at night, but he's been active this morning. He sits in his truck, turns on the radio, holds his transmitter up to the speaker." A dance band played a slow number she didn't recognize. Robert pulled her to him, and her head fell naturally into its spot, and he began to lead, butter melting in a pan. "Back there, at work, every month, men were being promoted, men I scarcely knew moved up without warning or explanation. Yeah, I was jealous, who wouldn't be? But then, as I dug into it, I began to suspect great things were being done. These men were at the center of it, and I was on the outside, just another tie and a shirt at a desk."

The music cut off, replaced by a gruff military command. "Section Blue reporting. Dispersal complete."

Robert looked straight into her eyes, which he seldom did. They were not a couple given to fond, dreamy gazing. "I wanted my family to know that there's more to me than they can see or sense."

No, this would not do. Jean pushed Robert away. She would not be smooth-talked or smooth-danced. She would not be placated with his agonized inner workings, not after what she'd been through.

"What the hell does that mean? Words, that's all. Jimmy, any ideas here?" Jean asked,

"Not if you and dad get all mushy on me," he said.

"Jean, don't put him in the middle of this."

"*You* put him in the middle of it. If you'd come home that evening like you did every other evening, he wouldn't be in the middle of anything. None of this would be happening. I wouldn't be standing in a cave with a man I used to sleep beside who I now barely recognize."

Jimmy moved to the mouth of the cave, unsure of his role, unaccustomed to seeing them argue in front of him. He set up an observation post on a packing crate, focused his binoculars. Observe anything other than his parents. Robert gazed out at his son, with a fondness and focus she'd never seen on his face, but she didn't trust her powers of understanding anymore. Not where her husband was concerned.

"How is he?" Robert asked. "He *looks* fine. And you? Any ...?

"Any ...?

"I mean, are you feeling worse? Better?"

"Can we stick to the point? Please? The point being we got through the war together, when the whole world came apart, and now you—"

"I what?"

"You've come apart, too. I got hired on at B.E., and because my shorthand was prizewinning, I finagled Lawrence into interviewing you. Of course, you charmed him. And your natural mechanical skills made you the perfect bench man."

Could that be it? Was Robert so tender and prickly that he resented her helping to get him hired?

"We had good salaries, but we didn't go crazy," she said. "Kept our noses to the grindstone all through the war, didn't even splurge for champagne on VJ Day—hard cider as I recall. We saved and saved to build that house, enough to raise our boy. Have you forgotten all that? While you were rambling around on your ... your crusade, I was ... I was ..."

She couldn't tell him what they had done to her. Not to spare his feelings, but to avoid the precision she would need to put the ordeal, with its needles, its descents into oblivion, and its groggy climbs back to the living, into clear, chronological language. If she told him, maybe he would let a hint slip to Jimmy, and she wasn't ready for him to hear it.

"And how did *you* get here, anyway?"

Oh, and her mother Alma had killed someone, but that could wait for another day. Or century.

Robert shrugged. "Rode the bus. Like everyone else."

"The bus."

"I had been at this thing awhile. I knew where they made the badges. I prowled the waste baskets for scraps. I'm an assembler in my bones. Still."

She could picture Robert on the blacked-out bus, telling jokes, making friends with the co-workers he didn't already know, turning it into an outing, just another Braden Enright hayride.

"I listened to the tape you made with Buddy Sirk."

Robert scratched at his upper lip, scraping across the shaving lines, his trademark gesture of surprise.

"You made it right after the Ravetto funeral. Yep, we've gotten pretty damn good, Special Operative Vale and me."

"It took me awhile to track Buddy down," Robert said. "Even went to the Los Altos police, showed them his photo—no help at all. Out of all of them, he's the one that needed to get it off his chest. But why he talked to *me* ..."

Because you're harmless, Jean thought. Like I told them after coma number five. Or was it six? "And you drink now apparently. Or at least sip. Bourbon, isn't it?"

"I'm not coming apart, Jean. It's the opposite. Pieces of me are finally beginning to fit together."

A violent thought drilled into her head, between the eyes, the spot that movie gangsters always aimed for, and the pictures never showed because it was too upsetting to see a dark blot of blood spring out of a character actor's forehead, Elisha Cook, say, or Brian Donlevy. A thought that terrified her, but why should it? She was different now. And maybe Robert wasn't so harmless after all.

"If I asked you to kill a man, would you do it?"

"What man?"

"A very powerful man."

"What man?"

"Not the man you told to 'get fucked.' His boss—Claridge."

Robert smiled, but it was not the room lightener he'd beamed at her that first night at the out-of-staters' party. It was a leer, like a boy seeing his first dirty magazine, or the back-row student who'd come up with the answer that baffled the rest of the class.

"I guess North didn't tell you everything," he said. "Jimmy, you should hear this. I'm going to need your help." Jimmy rejoined his parents, glad to be brought into the huddle.

MR. NORTH and the Director didn't have a fallback for emergency communication. The Director had wondered what Quentin North's would be, mentally reviewing his written correspondence and telegrams—their phone calls had been rare because they assumed North's phones were monitored—and come up with nothing. The Director's ideal fallback didn't exist. There were no outdoor restaurant patios, cooled by Atlantic breezes, staffed by efficient waiters serving potted shrimp. But they did have an agreement that if things became "discombobulated"—his father's favorite, if slightly inaccurate word for a confusing situation—the lack of communication was a form of communication in itself.

He and Miss Harper *did* have a fallback, a traveler's outpost where they had stopped on their way to Calcite. It came into view now, across a lonely stretch of asphalt, as the Director hobbled out of the sand, blood trickling down his leg, the splint bristling with cactus needles. A Signal filling station, a cafe: "Hot Meals at All Hours." Miss Harper's DeSoto parked outside, gas tank presumably topped off. And a small casino stinking of muffler fumes and Ethyl gas. He staggered across the roadway as a slot machine whooped, coins clanked, and the lucky winner cheered drunkenly.

THE WALKIE-TALKIE BUZZED AGAIN, three times, some kind of signal. Robert put on a pair of gloves, grabbed a stair dolly which leaned against the cave wall. He began to load the packing crates onto the dolly, ferrying them to a flat spot just outside the cave, restacking them neatly. "Your observation platform goes too," he said to Jimmy.

Jimmy huffed and puffed like a weight lifter and added his "observation platform" to the stack.

"Robert, what is it? What's happening?"

"Those files and papers—could you stow them in an empty box? Jimmy you're good with a hammer and nails."

Jean saw piles of documents, laid out alphabetically on top of one of the crates. She smelled fresh mimeograph ink. Had these documents recently been copied from North's archives?

"Are you stealing this stuff?"

"Stealing? No."

"What then?"

"I'll explain everything. But we're under time pressure right now."

For the moment, action seemed preferable to argument, so Jean did as he requested, taking a professional's care not to smear the documents and to maintain their alphabetical order as she set them into a crate. She fitted on the plywood cover, and Jimmy hammered it closed. Robert lifted it onto the dolly, rolled it outside, the last of the crates. Jimmy climbed onto the stack, scanned the desert. "They're loading the soldiers into trucks. They're driving off. Looks like it's all over."

"This is North's research!" Jean said. "It's B.E. property, Robert. What are you doing with it? Why is it stored up here?"

Robert's gaze jumped from the desert below, to his watch, to the walkie-talkie, then back to the desert. "Picture your neighbor, Joe Doakes, a neighbor you don't like, who keeps you up all night, is cruel to his kids, throws trash into your yard, maybe he even threatens you. For protection, you get a pistol, he gets a rifle. You get a bigger rifle, so he gets a Tommy gun. Eventually you're both armed to the teeth and neither of you dares fire the first shot."

"Like us and the Russians with the A-bomb."

Robert nodded. "But if you had a way to put your neighbor to sleep before you snuck over the fence to rob him, what would you do?"

"Nothing, because I'm not a robber."

"But maybe you're certain that Doakes is a guy who covets your jewelry and is secretly just waiting for *you* to fall asleep so he can break in and rob you. Wouldn't you want to stop him first?"

"I'd probably move."

"Countries can't move, Jean."

They heard an engine cough and a grinding of gears, as a gray panel truck with sun visors lugged up the road to the clearing where the crates were stacked. The same panel truck she and Grandpa Tamarkin had seen at the Cutlers' house party, which seemed like decades ago. Quentin North was at the wheel. He climbed out, holding two champagne bottles, one of which was half empty. He took a long slug, poured the rest out onto the ground. "Dispersal rates normative. Aerosolization 91 percent active saturation. Non-protected troops suffered 86 percent impact, although elapsed time to battlefield self-removal seemed to vary according to body size and ability to recognize wind direction. Debriefings and full medical exams scheduled for 23:00 hours, which will no doubt prompt minor modifications to the formula and further testing. But for now, ladies and gentlemen, Trinity Two is a qualified success." He held the full champagne bottle above his head like it was a golf trophy. Then he hurled the bottle into the ravine, it shattered against a boulder into green glitter, its spray white and frothy.

North looked at the assembled crates with a nod, marched into the cave. "I see the family reunion is complete. Robert, you're lucky to have her." Then pointing at Jean, "and *you* are lucky to have *him*. And you ...," nodding at Jimmy, "are fortunate to have them both, and *they...*," a wave that took in Jean and Robert, "are lucky to have you. Have I covered it all?"

"Will Slansky, Alvarez, Morrie and Del, are they all right?" Jean asked.

"We'll know after their physicals. They had a baseline of exposure already, so they're the control group, perhaps they'll react differently. They were wired for sound, commenting on what they were experiencing, how it compared to 1943. They'll undergo a battery of psychological tests as well." A shadow crossed his face, not a darkening of sunlight but a darkening from inside. "Most of our subjects from the early testing are fine, but a few have experienced disturbing, even disabling mental memories."

"Claridge wouldn't care about that," Jean said. "It would probably make him gleeful."

"True. Anything that disables enemy troops temporarily is gold to him. Long term incapacitation is ... whatever's more valuable than gold." He pointed at the panel truck. "I said I'd get you out of here, that's how. Robert, you got my signal?"

"Two short, one long."

"Are you still committed to this plan of action? Without commitment, you will be caught."

Jean clutched Robert's shoulders, pressed their foreheads together, and said quietly, "Please give me the truth. I need to hear it from you. What plan?"

"We're going to end Cutler and Claridge's dream," Robert said.

"Mrs. Vale, I didn't plan it like this," North said. "I had

always intended to take a more physical role at this point, but the net of suspicion has been tightening around the site ever since Connie Latimer stumbled onto bits and pieces of our project. And security measures steadily increased as testing day approached. I'm under scrutiny like never before; I can't leave right now without bringing it all tumbling down. Your husband is an ally I never saw coming."

"But it's your dream too. You created it," Jean said.

"And on the surface, it seems a meaningful creation, a humane development. Especially when contrasted with the world-ending weapons being tested fifty miles from here. It promises to remove the urge to violence, to promote a sense of well-being, or at least, silly distraction in the enemy. Without bloodshed. But everything we think makes it compassionate, makes it immoral."

"Jimmy, I want you to listen to this," Robert said.

"Robert, isn't that a bit much to lay on his shoulders?"

"My shoulders can carry more than you think, mom," Jimmy said. He flexed his muscles, and Robert slapped him on the back.

The "men" were right. She'd broken the old operating rules of being a mom, just as Jimmy had shed the confining skin of being "just a kid."

Robert took a folded sheet of paper from his white shirt, smoothed it on his thigh. "These are Buddy Sirk's words—he says it much better than I can: *Anything that makes war humane, makes war easier. This thing, it doesn't kill. It doesn't shred human bodies, doesn't maim or create cripples in wheel-chairs. There's no shell shock that we know of. It doesn't destroy cities, bury women and children under rubble, so it will be tempting to use. Up there at twenty thousand feet, they were trying to kill us so we killed back, but from a distance, like I was a doctor in a hospital, administering medicine. We had a job to do, and I don't regret it, but I don't wish it on anyone else. You develop this thing, it means we'll go to war again. Soon. A hundred Koreas will follow. And Trinity Two will not be the only weapon used, believe me.*

Robert refolded the paper and slipped it back into his pocket. He was suddenly stiff and formal. It was how Robert masked internal passions, those rare storms that blew through his blood every few years, whose origins Jean never asked about or understood, knowing he preferred that she not acknowledge them. Though he had let another man's words speak for him, this was a first for Robert, letting her feel what was in there.

She took his hand, walked her fingers up and down his palm; she'd done it the day of their city hall wedding, as she said "I do," hoping her touch would give them a long life line together.

"I think Buddy Sirk is dead," she said.

Jimmy handed Robert the USAAF tie clasp. "I found this, dad."

"Tin-lead solder, looks like," Robert said,

"Evelyn Sirk has the same letters on a bracelet," Jean said. "Same size, same style."

"Men stationed overseas would make their wives and girlfriends jewelry out of whatever they had at hand—mess kits, bullet casings, German coins. Where'd you find this, Jimmy?"

"Out there, the artillery test range. That crater."

Robert stared at Jimmy, knowing there was more. Jimmy stared back, broadcasting again over the private, father-son radio frequency. Robert handed the tie clasp back to Jimmy. "We'll have to make sure Mrs. Sirk gets this." And that was that. No shaking of heads, no expressions of sorrow. That's how it was now, in father-son land. Probably how it had to be.

"Thank you for reading that, Robert," North said. "One hopes to be worthy of Mr. Sirk's words."

"So you're going to sabotage it?" Jean asked, looking from Quentin North to Robert.

"That would be impossible," North answered. "There is a

select group of scientists following everything, plus Vann Claridge's colleagues, and paid advisors to the Joint Scientific Committee. Pieces of our research are forwarded to them on a weekly basis, they verify it or offer suggestions. They would spot sabotage immediately. In addition, Lawrence Cutler has committed significant B.E. resources to the project, with the understanding that if trials are successful, the committee will steer lucrative manufacturing contracts his way. After today, he can't be fooled either."

"You're not planning to steal it? You're not going to sabotage it?"

"No. We're going to share it."

WHAT SHE WANTED to say as they waited for North's evacuation team to show up: *We've had causes shoved down our throats for years, Vann Claridge threatened me with causes and historical certainty and battlefields of the future; we fought for causes in Europe and the Pacific; we're on a crusade for democracy or something in Korea. Quentin North has a cause, Lawrence Cutler has a cause, the Director or whatever his name is has a cause, Buddy Sirk had a cause and now you're hitting me with* your *cause. I came out here with my son to find my husband, and now I have him back and we're a family again; our lives can be restored to their boundaries and routines, dedicated to no cause greater than waking up after a good night's sleep to freshly perked coffee and buttered toast on the table. Why does life have to expand to be worthwhile, why do we have to strive for goals that are bigger than us?*

Aren't we big enough just being people?

What she thought: *Robert read me so well. I was waiting for this or something like this.* She didn't know the reasons but suspected they had been inside her for years. Since the day she married? Since the hour Jimmy was born? Since the day he spoke his first word, though she couldn't remember what it was. Since December 7, 1941? Maybe earlier, watching Alma crash her model house to splinters. Earlier still, the day *she* was born. Or the day her great grandfather abandoned his house in Americus, Kansas and fled west with his family, on the run from debts and a life blown to pieces by struggle and misfortune.

What she said: "Your biggest mistake, buster, was not asking me to join you."

23

"To paraphrase the Danish physicist Neils Bohr, who won the Nobel Prize for elucidating the structure of the atom: 'In the coming war, humanity will not be safe unless secrecy is banished,'" Quentin North said.

There were four sets of documents describing the day-to-day progress of the work on "Trinity Two," including that morning's test. Four sets of documents written in the international language of science for four scientists from England, France, Germany, and Russia—private citizens *not* government representatives, North emphasized. Trusted, brilliant men and one woman, including one Russian, who shared his belief that if all were equally armed with equal knowledge, no one would attack first. "Their origins stem from peace committees, from disenchanted scientists who were involved with the Manhattan Project, and are now worried by the urgency of the super bomb. It is my belief that atomic secrets cannot be kept by a single country, because physics knowledge is worldwide, the underpinnings are known. Trinity Two is different. It's ours, it's America's. Exclusively. And, therefore, the temptation to use it will be overwhelming. In my lifetime. And certainly in your son's."

"Does this mean we're smugglers, mom?" Jimmy asked. But there was no trace of the boyish enthusiasm the idea of a "smuggler" would normally have sparked. She could see him struggling with the complexities of the situation, his role in the "adult world" he was not meant to understand.

"No Jimmy. It means ..."

What did it mean? There were four vials of "the stuff" in its final chemical formulation resting in a padded metal suitcase secured with a combination lock. The suitcase was then placed into a shipping crate marked "Plumbing Supplies" and the name of a fictitious hardware store in Vallejo, California. The documents and the "stuff" would be driven out of Calcite in the panel truck, which made regular trips to Las Vegas to stock up on staples that kept the test site workers fed, clothed, and supplied with beer. No one would dare interfere with the beer run. But it wouldn't be going to Las Vegas this time.

"Where?" Jean asked.

"The original plan was to meet in the small San Francisco office of a sympathetic organization. Whose director never flirted with communism and is therefore not tainted, a man who forged the links between me and the outside world, because I've been kept nearly prisoner here, my calls monitored, my correspondence opened."

"Does this director have a name?" Jean asked.

"Oh, I'm sure he does. At his request, I've just always referred to him as Owen. Probably after the anti-war poet Wilfred Owen.

Owen. Her rescuer.

"That's out the window now. I have been forced to improvise. Fortunately, I have an unexpected associate in your husband. Only Robert knows the location of the new handover because I asked him to choose it himself. He's memorized the contacts' phone numbers and when he's in place he will call one of them, who will let the others know."

"But won't B.E. have Robert arrested? For theft? Or worse?"

"They can't prove anything. No documents are officially missing. All the chemicals are accounted for in my bookkeeping. And those on the receiving end won't talk. Plus, an arrest would attract attention, and Claridge or Cutler won't want to admit what happened. Can you imagine Vann Claridge falling on his sword in front of the president—'Well, sir, we lost the stuff.' Assuming the president even knows about it."

"The world will be safer, but won't know that it is," Robert said.

"Exactly," North agreed.

Jean had traveled so far from "normal" life, that riding along with her husband as he committed what her "normal" friends would call treason didn't feel shocking, or wrong, just inevitable. *Do I really care about world peace?* she asked herself. *Sure, I do, but this much? Do I care about borderless science? Where did Robert get this sudden conviction, this crusader's drive?* There was something deeper that she didn't understand, that maybe she never would. Unless she saw this through to the end.

"What about you?" Jean asked North.

"I'll stay here and supervise whatever further testing is required. Join the brain trust for a celebratory dinner tonight, then back in the lab tomorrow. Everything has to keep going, just another day at the office."

"Eventually they'll know it was you."

"Maybe. If they do, my career will be over. But Claridge's leverage will be gone because my true convictions will no longer be secret, my past will be an open book. I expect my eventual unmasking to come as a great relief. It's you and Jimmy I'm concerned about."

"There's another supply truck," Robert said. "That one *will* go to Vegas—with you and Jimmy. From there, we've made arrangements for you to get back home."

"Hmmm. I see," Jean said.

"What's wrong?"

"Your plan is hogwash. All your eggs in one basket. What if you have a wreck? What if Cutler puts out an alert to local cops or sheriffs?"

"He wouldn't do that. It would risk revealing the project."

"Or they'd stage an ambush, run you off the road, light the truck on fire, burn every last file and make it look like an accident."

"But how would they find out our route?" Robert asked.

"Someone could talk. Who else knows about this?"

"My assistants Laura and Tom. Loyal to a fault, I would trust them with my life," North said.

Neither North or Robert had been locked in a room with Vann Claridge and his mad doctors. Nor had Laura or Tom. But that was not a subject she would bring up.

"Divide the material into two loads," she said. "Two vans traveling different routes. If one gets stopped, they'll think they've got everything and the other will probably get through."

"I can't let you do that," Robert said.

"A little late for your concern, dear. Are we married or not? We're either going to share this thing or we're not. And by the way, where is our son?"

He was not in the cave or manning his sentry post. Jean headed down the dirt road, followed its steep, downward path, and spotted two figures below. She couldn't identify them in the lengthening shadows but one was tall and one was short. She began to run, scuffling in the chalky dust. Then she recognized the milkman, wearing fatigues and a black knee length jacket, binoculars dangling from his neck as he towered over her son.

The milkman—the beast who had delivered her into the hands of Vann Claridge.

She charged. Caution, self-preservation, fear—all of it gone. She rammed straight into him, taking him by surprise, knocking him backwards. He tumbled, tried to get up. Jean called on hidden muscles and sinews she never knew she had and kicked him square in the face. His head fell backwards onto a sharp boulder, blood sprayed, he groaned, then struggled to turn his head.

Mother and son just stared, aghast, even proud of what she had done. She tasted something sweet in her mouth; or did she just imagine it as the welcome taste of revenge?

"Mom, the left side of his jacket is heavy—bet you that's a gun!"

Jean found the pistol, held it at a distance as though it might explode in her hand. The milkman began to stir as Robert ran to join them.

"What the hell's going on?" he asked. "You OK?"

"Mom hit this guy—hard. He went down."

Robert was stunned, his eyes shifting from Jean to the gun in her hand to the milkman.

"That's quite a woman you got there," the milkman said, wheezing, spittle coating his lips. He brought his hand to the wound on the side of his head. "Head wounds always look worse than they are. And that kid of yours, eagle eyed."

"How did you find us?" Jean asked.

"What do you think I do in that plane up there? Sightsee? I memorized every hill and gulch and abandoned mine for a hundred square miles when Mr. Claridge hired me. It was only a matter of time. I served with him in occupied Germany, so I know what he expects." The milkman pressed his elbows into the dirt for leverage and wobbled to his feet.

Jean pointed the pistol at him and backed several feet away. He wasn't the kind of man who was afraid of an armed woman. He looked unsteady, but a guy confident enough in his skills to entertain young boys as an egg juggler might make a move at some point.

"Mom, ask him."

"Ask him what?"

"You know what."

"Did you kill Buddy Sirk?" Jean asked.

"Mr. Sirk was committing treason."

"This guy killed Buddy?" Robert asked.

"I think so. I don't know. Maybe the doctors did, and he just buried him." Jean waved the pistol at the milkman. "Out in the firing range, into the pit. That's where you dumped him. We've got proof!"

"Check his truck for a walkie-talkie," Quentin North yelled down.

"No need, it's right here," the milkman said. He took out a walkie-talkie from his other jacket pocket. "I already called it in. Now I need to head into town, make it official for the bureaucrats." The milkman smirked. Robert grabbed the walkie-talkie, which buzzed with static.

"Is someone on their way?" Robert asked.

"He's bluffing," Jean said.

"Right, I'm probably bluffing," the milkman said, smiling.

"Keep the pistol on him, Jean," Robert said.

Robert hurried to the truck cab and pulled the keys out of the ignition. He lifted the hood, pulled out a fistful of wires and the distributor cap. He looked down the steep dirt road, then reached back into the cab and released the emergency brake with a clunk. The milk truck jerked forward, then rolled downhill, accelerating as it went, veering wildly, until after a couple hundred feet, it slid off the road and collided with a boulder. The front end crumped, steam geysered from the radiator.

"We gotta get going, *now*. Someone may be coming!" Robert yelled up at North. "Jimmy, go help finish up."

Jimmy ran back to the cave. Jean waved the gun in a circle at the milkman, as though honing in on a bull's eye.

"What do we do with him?" she said. "Tie him up or something?"

"With what? And what for? The damage is already done."

"Take off your shoes," Jean told the milkman. He refused,

she fired a shot in the dust. "And your socks." The milkman obliged and handed her his shoes and socks.

"Start walking, pardner," she said. That drew an admiring look from Robert.

"I have a daughter your son's age," the milkman said. "Just doing my job, which is to keep her safe. From people like you." He took a handkerchief from his pocket, pressed it to his scalp wound. Then he turned, and headed down the road, barefoot,

"I'm afraid this accelerates our schedule. Who knows what he may have seen?" North said, when they were together back in the cave. "It's not going to be like I'd hoped, with main gate clearances and a paper record." He grabbed his walkie-talkie, punched in a series of buzzes, long and short. "We'll cross over to Jackass Flats Road. They won't know our route. Tom will lead us to the other panel truck. We're going with your plan, I think, Mrs. Vale. I presume you can handle a floor shifter? And by the way, excellent work, the three of you."

THEY DIVIDED up the material at a desolate crossroads. The moon was a sliver and the Milky Way seemed impossibly close, almost like a blessing of some sort. North sensed it too.

"This is the first project I've ever done that I can't explain fully. I understand the 'how' of the science, but I don't understand the 'why'. Why those men? Why in those skies? Why on that mission? After Cutler's party, I took my time getting back here. I drove, wandered, parked at the base of the John Muir Trail that ascends to Mount Whitney. I walked until I was exhausted, emptied. I slept outside that night, within sight of those peaks, a dazzling night exactly like this. And then it struck me—this is a formula handed down from God."

"I thought you didn't believe," Jean said.

"This is a God I'm still in the process of constructing. You know we scientists, always experimenting. This God is more like a twinge of starlight, a flicker of the atmosphere, a spark of dew—it contains everything in the universe, including the *stuff*." Then he slapped Jean and Robert on their shoulders. "So don't goddamn lose it."

Tom, North's lab assistant, turned out to have been a talented commercial artist before taking up biological chemistry, and within an hour the sides of the gray panel truck read "Sierra Nevada Septic Tank Service" in dripping, sludgy letters, the mascot a skunk holding a wrench in one hand and his nose closed with the other. Which probably made it the least likely truck on the road to be pulled over by a curious cop, so it was assigned to Robert. Jean would drive the other truck, midnight blue, pockmarked by long miles on gravel roads; Jimmy would ride with her. Jean gave the gun to North; he might need it, and she didn't want it in the car with Jimmy.

"I'll leave a message for you at Terravox," Robert said. "Under the parts delivery bin attached to the north wall. I'll give you a status update. "

Then, if all went well, they would meet back at the house. The three of them, home at last.

"If I don't see you again ..." North said shyly, approaching her with a round package wrapped in foil, reminding her of glittery silver bells she saw hanging from streetlights at Christmas time. She opened it and found a plant with thin spiky leaves the color of string beans. "*Eriodictyon Californicum*, also known as Yerba Santa," North said. "A healing plant, sacred to the Indians. You can make tea from it that is a balm for tired eyes. Bees spin it into flavorful honey. This is from my private little nursery, but there is a rich concentration of them out at the A-bomb testing range. I have no way of knowing what long term effects they may suffer. I want this one, at least, to survive."

"It's beautiful, thank you," Jean said.

With both trucks loaded, Robert led Jean into the darkness beside the road. "When we're done, I obviously won't be working for Braden Enright anymore."

"I wouldn't want you to."

"So I was thinking ..."

He looked down at his feet, as though hoping they would walk off on their own and take him where he needed to go.

"We could build houses. Not for us, for other people. Affordable, comfortable family homes."

"Burglar-proof. With phones that aren't monitored and mail that's not opened?"

"You've got it in your blood. Jimmy and I are pretty good with tools. I bet I could swing a loan for us to get going. We'd be working for ourselves. *That's* gonna be the ticket from now on."

"I think that's a splendid idea."

They kissed. An old-days kiss. A parked-above-the-lights-of-the-Bay-Area-kiss, a honeymoon behind motor court curtains kiss. More than they'd ever kissed within Jimmy range.

"Where are you going to do the hand off?" she whispered, masking her words by gliding her lips from his ear to his smoothly shaved chin.

"Think about it. You'll know," he whispered back.

Robert looked at Jimmy, who stood upright and stiff-legged, as though coming to attention before a commanding officer. For a moment, Jean was afraid they would do something horribly corny, like salute each other. But Robert said, simply, "I love you, kiddo."

"Me too, dad."

Then they got into their trucks and drove off in opposite directions. In her rear- view mirror, Jean saw Robert's tail lights wink on and off three times. She one-upped him, signaling four times. He answered with five, she went for six, then saw four flashes of Robert's seven before his truck dipped into a wash and was gone.

She didn't know how large the Calcite Test area was, where its borders lay, how they were patrolled or guarded. But since Robert was going to continue along the west-bound gravel extension to Jackass Flats Road, Jean took the unnamed, paved crossroad, heading north. Slowly bumping their way back to the Bay Area, Jimmy at her side with his compass and maps. They would close this case the way they began it, together, Field Operative Vale reporting to Senior Operative Vale.

Jean felt fine handling the panel truck with its squeaky brown vinyl seats and stubborn shifter. She was on the road, and somewhere out there in the night, so was Robert. She could picture him behind the wheel, driving lefty, his right arm draped across the seat back as though reaching for her, the cool-as-the-breeze technique he'd deployed when he'd taken her to see their lot for the first time, the one-third acre with its apricot trees and golden foxtails pressed flat into the soil by Robert's boot steps, where he had paced out the dimensions of the home they would build together. The home they were returning to now, after an adventure they would share with each other for years to come, theirs and Jimmy's alone. No family she could imagine would have run such delirious, heart-embracing risks. She tuned through the radio, searching for a song that Robert might be listening to if he had reception. Mostly static, then "Mockingbird Hill", a definite no. More static, then she heard it—"Musetta's Waltz" from La Bohème. Robert had the .78, would sometimes drop it onto the Crossley player after dinner and conduct while reclining on the chesterfield, translating roughly from Italian, something about hidden beauties and the scent of desire. Jimmy began to hum along; he knew it too, perhaps from those father-son nights on stakeout at Spivey's drive-in. Jean found it miraculous: opera, out here in the darkness of the Mojave desert, a powerful AM station, from Las Vegas maybe. Neither she nor Robert knew where the other was, but it felt like they were together, closer than they'd ever been.

Puccini eventually drifted out of range, replaced by a nagging hiss. She switched off the radio, let the swish of the tires tick off the miles.

"Mom!" Jimmy yelled, pounding the dashboard. A football

field length ahead, she saw two jeeps parked on either side of the road. She stopped, slammed into reverse, and backed up over the lip of a rise so that the truck wasn't visible to the jeeps. She turned off the headlights. She nodded at Jimmy, and he took the caps off his binoculars, got out, climbed onto the roof. "Jeep on the left is empty, two guys in the front seat of the other. Smoking." Jimmy snorted in derision. "What a couple of lolly-gaggers. Even a blind mortar man could pick them off."

So they turned back, Jean coasting down the gentle slope before turning on the headlights. She drove back south. But they saw no more jeeps, no guard towers, no barbed wire. Jimmy navigated them along a potholed, zigzag route until they merged into a westbound road that widened, the asphalt suddenly smooth as though it had just been poured, the roadbed crowned for drainage, sporting a newly painted center divider that glowed poppy yellow. This has to be California, Jean thought. No one knows how to lay down a highway like we do! She began to sing: "... where bowers are flowers bloom in the spring, each morning at dawning, birdies sing and everything ..."

But there was something lying on the road.

Stretching across both lanes. A hose or cable, maybe a downed power line. She braked to a stop, and they got out to inspect it. Jean saw no electric towers or telephone poles. What was it? She didn't want to touch it, afraid it might snap or spark at her.

"Maybe it's one of those things they have at a service station. You drive over this, and a bell rings," Jimmy said.

"Yeah, but where does it ring?"

She traced the black, arrow-straight cable across the pavement, onto the shoulder until it disappeared into the ground. She knelt and dug through the sand, exposing several more yards of cable. It had been deliberately buried. Who knew how far it stretched, or who was waiting at the other end for it to ring?

They got back in the car, frustrated, fuming. No wall, no machine guns. Just a taunting thread, an inch around at most. After all they'd been through, it seemed cruel in its insignificance.

"I'm not turning around," Jean said.

"And we can't lift the car over it," Jimmy answered.

Jean curled her hands around the steering wheel. Revved the engine.

"Fuck it."

It took a second for Jimmy to get over the shock of hearing his mother say those two little words that had never crossed her lips in his presence. More like half a second.

"Yeah, fuck it!" Jimmy said.

Jean punched the gas and the panel truck surged forward, leaping in joy, as though it were happy to help. Let the damn bells ring, Jean thought. Wherever they are, let 'em ring.

"A sun kissed miss said, 'Don't be late!', that's why I can hardly wait, open up, open up that Golden Gate ..."

But as the night wore on, as Jimmy fell asleep with the California map pulled up to his chin like a blanket, as she refueled the thirsty truck at the world's loneliest filling station, her mind began to seethe with worry. Could they really trust those scientists that the Director/Tennyson and North had contacted? What if Claridge had infiltrated the scheme and turned them into allies; maybe they'd be armed. The milkman probably assumed they had seen the field test and would follow whatever orders his hero and boss Vann Claridge gave him.

What had Robert meant by "Think about it. You'll know?"

She nudged Jimmy awake. He snapped up, all business, checked the map, glanced out at the dark highway landscape.

"Where would your dad do the handover, do you bet?"

"I don't know."

"Put some brainpower into it, come on."

"Maybe the old artillery pillboxes at Baker Beach. Hard to

see in, but easy to see out. We went there for my birthday, remember?"

Somehow, that didn't feel right, more Jimmy than Robert.

"Any other ideas?"

"Somewhere else he knows, I guess."

What places other than home and work did her husband really know? He had no weekend getaway spots, no favorite parks or beaches. On their Sunday drives they did just that, they drove, and he never expressed a strong desire to return anywhere they'd been. They'd never vacationed in the same place twice. Yet something stirred in her, rustling the rafters, as Alma used to say whenever she had a troubling thought. A memory pushing to the front of her mind.

What about those salt evaporation ponds, then? What about the red and green lights?"

I don't ... know what the hell ... you're talking about.

I'm *not talking about it, Mrs. Vale.* You *were. Pre-coma, post coma. Red and green lights, salt. Code words perhaps. Cryptic phrases that unlock deeper, more intricate secrets ...*

Eventually, the milkman would report what he had seen. Claridge would never let the handover go through. They would kill Robert, close-up or from afar, whatever method was most efficient. Depending on Claridge's mood and yen for personal glory, they could bring in local police or federal officials to arrest the four scientists for spying. No, Claridge was securely beyond the need for glory and had been for years. The calculations of warfare were all that concerned him, that sustained him. Killing Robert was the simplest calculation of all.

Jean pounded the gas, pushing up the Pacheco Pass, the rolling, grassy hills black as a starless sky. The truck swerved and shuddered as it hit the new four lane expansion, and the speedometer needle swung toward eighty.

"Mom, what's going on?"

Jean didn't answer, peering into the night, hoping for a

mileage sign to whip past, waiting for the turn off to Highway 101.

She switched on the radio, spun through the dial until she heard Dick Crenna's high-pitched nasal squeak on a late night repeat of "Our Miss Brooks."

"A show about teachers, who cares?" Jimmy said. "You know where, don't you?"

"I have a hunch, let's say."

"This is a Vale operation, mom. I need to know too."

"This is between me and your dad. There are some things that need to belong to us, and only us."

"Like you and dad planting those arrowheads out back for me to find, the junior archeologist."

"Yes, like that."

"It's not like that at all."

"Jim, enough is enough. I realize we can never go back to the natural order of life, but I'm asking us to, just for tonight. I'm still the adult, still your mother, and you are still a boy. No, you're more than that, you're an age unto yourself."

She waited for the anger and rebellion. But he surprised her. He managed a reluctant, fleeting smile. He switched off the radio. Years from now, maybe they would swap one-upping stories, their adventures embroidered into family folklore. Jimmy would be old enough for a beer and she found herself wondering what he would be like if he were just a little sauced.

An hour later, Jean and Jimmy waited on an empty cul-de-sac in an industrial neighborhood in Mountain View. She had called Helene Gillett from a phone booth, and she was on her way in a rented car. She had checked beneath the parts bin outside Terravox, but there was no message from Robert. Terravox was a B.E. supplier whose employees she'd talked to dozens of times. How many of them knew who they really worked for, or what their companies did beneath the surface; how many operated simultaneously in the secret world, contracted to men like Claridge?

When Helene and Grandpa Tamarkin pulled up next to the panel truck, Jimmy handed Jean his kit bag, a serious sacrifice for an op so professionally equipped.

"You'll need my binoculars. Good to have a first aid kit too."

He hauled out his treasured U.S Army flashlight, with its handwritten Morse Code key taped to the handle. He flicked it off and on, testing its beam for strength and range. "One last thing," he said as he got out of the truck. "Dad and I have code names. His is "Red Team One, mine is Green Team One." Then he walked to the car that would take him to Helen's—a final precaution before they reunited at home. Jean thought that he had grown up more in the last hour than during their entire adventure.

VALE PRIVATE INVESTIGATIONS – Discrete, Dedicated, Deadly

From: Field Operative (F.O.) James Vale

Subject: Search for Missing Person XYZ

Time: 03:15 Aug 19

Location: Los Altos HQ

Case Status: Missing Person XYZ found alive and in good shape. As of this writing, case is closed.

Team Evaluation: Both Senior Operative Vale and Field Operative Vale performed outstandingly. Recommend additional shadowing training and that we find secure communication channels for use in future cases.

Further Research: I have learned that the mysterious lights the crew spotted over Germany were called Foo Fighters. Named after the comic books "Smoky Stover." Suggest Team Vale acquires a collection of these comics.

Personal note: S.O. Vale is tying up loose ends. F.O. Vale knows that S.O. won't be able to tie them all up herself. Discussion with person XYZ is crucial.

. . .

THE EVAPORATION PONDS of the Leslie Salt Company were an eye-popping patchwork of red, green, orange, and yellow water, colored by little living creatures, miles of them, stretching around the bay from Redwood City south to San Jose and east to Newark and Fremont, traversed by mud levees, railroad spurs and one lane access roads. Exactly as Jean had described it to Claridge as she emerged from a coma. It had always reminded her of a giant, natural jigsaw puzzle, the borders between the pieces constantly shifting under tidal pressure, the colors changing as the invisible amoebas grew and the salt level increased. As every local schoolchild learned, salt was one of the oldest industries in California, harvested from the bay long before gold was discovered at Sutter's Mill. During the day, it was a hectic place, as bulldozers scooped up crystallized salt from the reddest of the ponds, dumped it into flatcars on Leslie's train, which transported it to the processing factory. Behind the factory rose white hills of salt, five stories high.

Jean had parked the panel truck in a dirt clearing on the shore of the ponds. Wearing a pair of boots a size too large that she'd found under the front seat, and carrying a tire iron, she squished into the shoreline marsh. She had Jimmy's field glasses and a flashlight. She ventured onto a rickety wooden foot trestle which traversed a stagnant slough. Forests of reeds pressed in on both sides, scratching at her with their wind-whittled edges. Tucked among the reeds, spaced evenly as though planted by a landscaper were tall white and gray birds, flashes of black on their heads like tiny caps. Motionless and silent. Her footsteps didn't disturb them; tiny crabs scuttling through the mud didn't tempt them. It felt like they were standing guard.

The trestle broke out of the reeds, to give a clear view of the evaporation ponds. By night, the colors had faded into shades of black and gray. The factory night lights were sparse, the salt mountains looked cold in the moon light, like dunes of ice. It was a vast, dim landscape, but there was one spot where red and green lights winked back and forth at each other from tall, spindly towers.

The lights that would draw Robert here.

Erected on an embankment, the lights marked the approach path to the runways at Moffett Field where adult Robert had indulged his fantasies of flight, watching planes he would never pilot taking off and landing. Knowing that Jean loved movies, he'd taken her and infant Jimmy to the airfield's front gates on their one-year anniversary, weaving through giddy girls and women, all hoping for a glimpse of Corporal James Stewart who was undergoing flight training at Moffett before heading off to Europe. They hadn't seen Stewart face to face, but from the back, they'd spotted a tall, lanky fellow in a uniform, who loomed over his fellow crew members, as they slipped into the shadows of a hangar. It was color-blindness that had broken Robert's dreams of flight years before—he was unable to distinguished between red and green—and the navigation lights on those towers were a taunt he couldn't resist; maybe if he gazed at them long enough, one day he'd have perfect vision. One day, in his mind, he would soar.

Then she sensed, more than saw, a subtle blotting out of a patch of stars as a flight of black wings soared overhead, circling upwards, even though there was no warming breeze to lift them up. It felt like a sign to get moving.

Using Jimmy's flashlight, she walked to the end of the trestle. A hundred yards ahead, she saw a railroad spur. An idle flat car offered an ideal protective vantage point. She tested the waters of the salt pond, dipping her ankles into them as she had once tested the Stanislaus spring run off on the first day of swimming season. It reached almost to her knees, but her feet touched a solid bed of packed salt. She slogged forward, releasing a strange odor as she moved. It wasn't really salty, but it was pungent—maybe the little critters or algae that lived down there. She felt almost as tiny, surely the only person wading through those eight thousand acres at four in the morning of ... whatever day of the week it was. She stepped up onto the track and crouched. Using the flatcar bed for support, she scanned the ponds with Jimmy's field glasses. She didn't see Robert and she didn't see any men with rifles stalking the levees. Was she too early? Too late? Should she signal with the flashlight, code name to code name, as Jimmy had said. No, that would call attention to herself.

She left the cover of the railroad car and loped along the tracks to where they intersected with another footpath which led closer to the navigation towers. Another scan, still nothing. Then she saw headlights, pointing straight out across the bay, dissipating into darkness. She ran the footpath to a crossing, wide enough for a car, and veered left toward a metal shed that probably held the power supply for the navigation towers. The headlights were streaking out from behind the shed.

From the Sierra Nevada Septic Tank panel truck.

It had skidded off the road into the pond and was sunk in salt water higher than the tires. There were round, dark spots dotting the sides and doors of the truck. Bullet holes. She went to the passenger door, which was nearest the road. She peered into the cab; there was no one on the seat, but there seemed to be a figure slumped on the floor by the pedals. She pounded on the window, got no response. She risked a blitz from the flashlight, but it just reflected back off the glass. She tried to pull the door open, but it was blocked by the curb of the levee. She waded into the pond, sloshing around the front of the truck. She couldn't get the driver's side door open either, the weight of the truck had caused it to settle deeper into the salt bed, and the pressure of the water held the door closed. She pounded on the driver's door, the figure didn't move. Finally, she couldn't stand not knowing. With a two-fisted downward thrust, she slammed the tire iron at the window, and after three goes, the glass shattered. Now she could see that the figure was not a person, but a blanket stretched lengthwise, wrapped around something that lay on the floorboards. She boosted herself into the empty window frame, teeter-tottering at the waist as she reached for the blanket and tugged. It covered two cement blocks that had been propped against the gas pedal. The handbrake was not set. The steering wheel was tied into a fixed position by a battery cable.

Something roared overhead and bursts of light turned everything white. Jean lost her balance, dropped the tire iron, and fell backwards into the pond, gulping salt water and whatever lived in it. When she got to her feet, dripping and crusted in salt, she had a thought that if someone poured a bucket of pepper on her, she'd be ready for the oven. The intense light was gone, as the plane landed at Moffett, a Panther, a Neptune, a Fury or something, Jimmy knew all the names. He would have loved it, closer to the action than he'd ever get at the Memorial Day air show. She probed around in the water until she grasped the tire iron. Feeling like human seaweed, she waded to the rear of the panel truck. She knew what she'd find, but she gave the two small back windows her best DiMaggio swing, and they fractured until all she had to do was push and they dropped away, breaking into pieces. She stepped onto the bumper and peered into the truck.

No wooden packing crates. No metal suitcases containing samples of "the stuff." They'd shot an empty, driverless truck full of holes.

Robert had beaten them.

But was the shooter still out there? Or was there more than one shooter?

She ran back along the foot path to land, as more planes swooped over, lower and louder, trying to slip into the airfield before the visibility closed it down. She took a last look at the marooned truck, its headlights still beaming out across the bay. She wondered how long it would take for the battery to drain, for the truck to be shrouded in darkness.

When she got to her truck, she noticed there were two sets of tire tracks in the dirt road. She tracked them with the flashlight beam: one led to the salt pond embankments, the other onto the paved road. She spotted a scattering of plywood splinters in the dirt and smiled. He'd done it here. The scientists recruited by the Director—Jean wondered how many had shown up—had taken possession of the documents and "the stuff" and driven off. Then Robert had set the truck on its decoy run. The shooter had probably been positioned out on the ponds below the navigation light towers and blazed away at the onrushing truck, as Robert slipped off into the night.

But why hadn't Robert left a "Mission Accomplished" message at Terravox? And she had another worry; if B.E. knew about the second truck, they would be looking for it.

She drove to the dump in Palo Alto at the edge of the bay—it was closed, but Jean had broken so many rules, she drove around the wood-railed barrier without a thought, onto a road bordered by heaps of trash. Jean and Robert had been here many times, disposing of damaged wood, shattered tile, empty paint cans, the leftovers from their construction site, and she experienced a brief longing to be back with him in their home-building years, painting the redwood sidings, as he laid the bricks for their walkway. She parked the truck between the two tallest mountains of trash and took the keys. As she walked off, a grim smile crossed her face—the "stuff," and all those pages of chemistry formulas and math calculations, those years of B.E. endeavor, coming to rest amidst the garbage from hundreds of homes.

She found a phone booth near Bayshore and called the house. No answer. She called Helene; she hadn't seen Robert either. Jean felt a fresh surge of fear. What if Robert wasn't done? He had been betrayed by the company and the people he trusted. He had lost a new friend, Buddy Sirk. Would "destroying Claridge and Cutlers' dream" be enough?

"... would you kill a man if I asked you to?"

"... what man?"

Had he taken her seriously? Had she been serious herself? At the moment, maybe. She hadn't told Robert the details about what Claridge had done to her, and she probably never would. But Robert sensed something awful had happened, she had read it in his face ...

"I wanted my family to know that there's more to me than they can see or sense."

The way to Claridge led through Lawrence Cutler.

DAWN DID NOT FLATTER the Cutler home. It was designed for sunset, when its wide- open expanses welcomed rosy skies and wispy, back-lit cirrus clouds. Eastern light was chilly and distant, as though the horizon were reluctant to yield up a new morning, and it seemed to turn the glass walls dull, murky. Shadows cast by the miniature cypress trees were meager and spindly

Jean stepped out of the cab, waved it away. She saw Lawrence Cutler staggering through the yard, a whiskey bottle in one hand, crumpled sheets of paper in the other. He was disheveled, shirt tail hanging out and ripped, hair wild and speckled with—was it blood? He was rambling to himself, then he spotted her and raised his voice.

"In Europe, the Army had a couple of hangmen, Jean, did you know that? They traveled around, executing soldiers—American boys, who crossed the line. No one in my unit, mind you. I think one of them was the same guy who went on to drop the Nazis at Nuremberg, gave the works to Keitel and Ribbentrop. Though Göring, that fat bastard who shot down a hundred of my men, cheated him with cyanide."

"You're talking nonsense, Lawrence. What the hell are you going on about?"

"If I had the hangman's number, I'd call him. Now. Make this night right some way. For you and the boy ..."

Jean couldn't follow him. Was he confessing to something?

"I never wanted it, Jean. But it came to me by osmosis, you marry a Braden you get buckled in to the Braden dreams, the Braden ambitions. I was a good commander, a damn good commander ... back there. Where I knew what the mission was. Not here. Here I let everything go horribly wrong. Frances stayed true blue during the war, you know. No Dear John letters like some of the other fellas got ... made me love her all the more, made the fear of losing her the deadliest thing in life.

"Lawrence! Look at me, listen to me. Is Robert here?"

"For a while I was perfect for her, the engineering background, the Army Air Force uniform that I kept pressed and tailored even as I gained weight so I could wear it when the oil of social advancement was called for. The medals, spit-shined, the oohs and aahhs from so-called admirers. This is why we fought—to succeed, to thrive, to "conquer."

Lawrence took another swallow of whiskey. Even drunk, his words were precise and clear. "I'm sorry, I'm so, so sorry ... I tried to, but you can't stop a Braden. In no man's lifetime has that ever been ... or will ever be ... goddamn possible." He waved the papers, tried to read them aloud, but he couldn't focus. Jean grabbed them. The first sheet was in Robert's handwriting: *I hereby resign from my position as Manufacturing Specifications Deputy Manager, effective this day, August 29, 1952.* The other was the stock certificate he'd been given after he moved from the assembly plant into the main office. "I've got Robert's check here, too." Lawrence rooted through his pockets. "It's for the amount B.E. paid towards Jimmy's birth. 'Settling the accounts,' he called it."

Jean brushed past Cutler and ran along the stepping stones.

"Don't go in there, Jean!"

"Robert, are you here? What's happening?"

The front room felt desolate without carefree partygoers to populate the scene. She heard a saxophone stumbling through "Begin the Beguine," accompanied by orchestra. One of Cutler's homemade practice tapes was spinning on the tape recorder in their hi-fi system, filtering out from hidden speakers. Jean ran through the house, but no one was there. She slid open the back door, stepped onto the porch, the lawn—no one there either. Then she remembered the outdoor entrance Frances had shown her the day of the garden party. As Jean edged around the side of the house, she heard the saxophone again. Cutler's practice tape had moved on to "Take the A Train." She found the steps that led down to the below ground door, pushed it open as Cutler honked into the chorus. Jean edged along the concrete hallway, the music growing louder until she came to the metal door to the bomb shelter. Unlike her last visit, it was wide open. Cutler's sax continued; they'd even installed a speaker down here. The smell of Old Dutch cleanser was strong, overlaying another, less familiar smell.

The overhead lighting was flickering and ugly, like Death Row in a prison movie. Frances Cutler sat on a camp stool, a framed photograph resting on her lap. She wore gardening overalls that seemed to never have encountered a trowel of dirt, her hair was done up in a sensible bun, wrapped in a silk bandana. She wore rubber gloves. In her left hand was a gun, the old service pistol from the display case in Lawrence Cutler's office. Jean's eyes moved from the gun to bunk beds that were bolted into the concrete walls. The top bunk was empty, but on the lower bunk ...

"No, no, no, what in God's name have you done?"

Jean pulled back a City of Paris comforter from Robert. His eyes were closed. She screamed his name over and over but couldn't hear herself. She pressed her face to his, there was no breath. She tried artificial respiration even though she had no idea how to do it, but she could not coax a flutter of life out of him. She tore the comforter off entirely, revealing a dark, blood-ringed wound just above Robert's heart. She felt for his pulse, her wedding ring scraping across his as she clasped his wrist. Nothing. His blood had pumped out of the wound, then stopped. It had all stopped, every moving part of Robert had been shut down. Everything had left him. When the soul departs, it does so quickly and directly, as though it does not want to linger. It wants us to see: *THIS is the body without a spirit.*

Frances raised the pistol with a slack wrist. "It wasn't supposed to be loaded. It's a souvenir, an artifact ... sort of like Lawrence." Jean lunged for the gun, but Frances bolted to her feet, backed toward the bomb shelter door, the pistol pointed at Jean's heart now. "But that doesn't mean I'm going to hand it over, Jean. It was just intended as a threat."

"Why, Frances? What is there inside you that could make you do this?"

Frances held up the framed photograph. "Look at this," she commanded.

Jean was shaking, her skin crackling, her blood threatening to overflow the banks of her arteries.

"*Look at the photograph, Jean.*"

"Have you called an ambulance?" Jean asked. "Maybe something can be done, I've heard of people being brought back even after their heart has stopped."

"Someone is on the way." She thrust the photograph into Jean's face and ground the gun barrel against her neck. The picture showed a man she recognized as Carl Braden, standing next to his wife and a little girl Jean assumed was Frances. It was a ribbon cutting ceremony for a small office building.

"I wanted Robert to see what he was about to destroy; all that we built since that June day in 1938. My father, who overcame things none of us can imagine. My mother, the slaughterhouse foreman's daughter who gave him everything, gave *us* everything, dead of the cancer before she saw a stick of roof laid onto the building, before she saw Walt Disney spin a single dial of the 9100 acoustic generator. Before she saw me in a cap and gown ..."

Jean looked around desperately, as though she were hoping

to find the lever that could reroute the last minute of life back onto its proper track. The big band saxophone continued to blare mercilessly.

"Lawrence has been something of a disappointment, never quite ready to do what was necessary. He always underestimated me, just as my father did. Which makes the senseless destruction of Braden Enright even more painful."

Jean couldn't look at Robert's body, but she sensed it behind her, still flesh and blood.

"Trinity Two is everything for this company and for its future. And for the future of my children."

"You don't have any damn kids."

"Those plans were temporarily set aside as we carved out our path. But now, seeing Lawrence as he truly is, I don't consider him a prospective father. Maybe I'll adopt—better not to tie my destiny to one man."

"How dare you talk about children? My son has no father!"

Jean glanced around the bomb shelter, looking for anything that she could use as a weapon. The absurdity of it was cruel—Commie bombs could fall tonight, and Frances Braden Cutler would survive, Jean trapped in here with her, alive. But the Family Foxhole Model 2 would be Robert's tomb.

Frances had said *about* to destroy.

Trinity Two *is* everything for this company.

Frances didn't know it was over, didn't know she'd lost. She had shot Robert for nothing, not even for the purity of revenge. Should Jean keep it to herself? Or appeal to whatever minimums of human guilt stuck to the edge of Frances' true character, the character that she had probably been molding since childhood. No, that might not work. But the knowledge that she'd made the wrong move and made it too late, *that* would gouge at her. Frances was like Vann Claridge in that way, the mechanics of life motivated her, not the sentiments.

"Trinity Two is gone, Frances. It's the world's now. You missed the future by just a couple of hours."

Frances was a blank, as though she hadn't heard.

"My husband whipped you. And if he hadn't, I would have." Jean edged closer to Frances, keeping her eye on the gun. "I didn't care about Trinity Two at first, or the great causes and the nobility of sacrifice. I'm not sure I do now. I only know that we took it from you ... the one thing you value most in the world. How does it feel?" *How does it goddamn feel?"*

"You didn't—you couldn't."

"We did. Ask your husband."

Lawrence had appeared in the doorway to the shelter, no whiskey bottle. He had stopped weaving and was back in charge of his body. He simply nodded at Frances. Frances turned a smidgen pale, her famously blushing, perfectly-maintained complexion showing signs of wear and tear. Lawrence entered the shelter, switched off he overhead speaker, taking care to avoid looking at Robert's blood-marked figure. The silence, which Jean thought would come as a relief, was worse than the music.

"Did you call them? Are they here yet?" Frances asked.

Jean was waiting for a chance to grab the gun, but Frances kept it pointed at her.

"Called who?" Jean asked.

"A team from the office," Frances said. "To take care of things here."

By "things," Jean knew she meant Robert.

"He'll get all the life insurance and death benefits due him as a long- term employee, Jean," Cutler said.

"You're already writing his goddamn obituary?"

"And we'll take care of Jimmy, too."

"Leave us alone, Lawrence," Frances said. "Let us girls to settle accounts."

Cutler nodded. "I've got a memoriam notice to write, anyway." He edged out the door.

"Well, Frances, it looks like it's time to shoot me now," Jean said. "Should I crawl up into the top bunk? That way you won't have to lift my dead weight up there."

Frances didn't answer. She was both focused and absent, her mind churning like the spinning wheels of an overturned car.

"It's sound proof down here, so another shot or two won't be heard," Jean said, trying to needle her into a distracted moment in which she could go for her gun.

"I'm never going to smell those South San Francisco meat-packing fumes again."

"Oh, please. Joan Crawford doesn't suit you at all Frances."

Jean ducked to the floor, crawled to Robert. She searched Robert's pockets, her hands sliding through his blood-slicked coins and keys, until she found his engraved B.E. pocketknife: "To Robert V. for 5 years of service." As Frances raised the gun, Jean prepared to charge with the knife, to thrust into her as though she were separating the tendon from a porterhouse.

But then, Colonel Lawrence Cutler, group commander of the 94th Heavy Bombardment Group of the 4th Bomb Wing, United States Army Air Force, came back to life, reaching around Frances from behind, snatching the pistol out of her hand. "It's over, Frances. It's over."

She whirled around, shock on her face, as though she were preparing to attack her own husband. But then, so quickly Jean could barely follow it, Frances Braden Cutler, always in charge, always well-turned out, always the imperious boss's daughter, wilted to the floor. Her back fell against the concrete wall, she closed her eyes—her way of shielding herself from the horror of what she had done? Or just a cowardly, internal escape?

Two men in dark suits appeared in the bomb shelter doorway. "The team is here, Mr. Cutler," said one. The other picked up the gun that had killed Robert, subtly brushing his suit jacket open to show that he was armed. Jean was depleted; worse, she felt numb. She allowed the suits to lead her upstairs, across the yard and into the house. With its gracious *Sunset Magazine* living room with its easy traffic flow, the perfect-for-seasonal-entertaining kitchen with its matching avocado-colored countertops. She glimpsed herself in the mirror; still covered in muck, her overalls blotched with crusty patches of salt.

The rest of the "team" arrived. They worked for B.E., which was now in effect a subsidiary of Vann Claridge's secret world, and Claridge was not a man who Cutler could simply "call off." The front door opened, admitting a doctor carrying a medical satchel and a B.E. janitor toting a drum of industrial cleaner. They were followed by a man and a woman in business attire; the man freshly shaven, redolent with Old Spice, the woman with office-appropriate make-up, hair brushed and pinned—what sort of people looked so go-getting at 6:30 a.m.?—who identified themselves as legal counsel affiliated with B.E. and the President's Joint Scientific Committee. They sat Jean down at the dining table with its harvest theme place mats and spoke in drab phrases and unemotional tones. Despite Jean's brandishing of a knife, no assault charges would be filed against her—charges that could lead to her being separated from her son. There would be no murder charges, either. As a matter of fact, Robert Vale had not been there at all. The body that wasn't there was now being prepared for transport by a skilled and discreet doctor who specialized in post-mortem grooming, and would be released to a local mortuary, with whom B.E. had a close relationship. Mrs. Jean Vale, who hadn't been there either, could claim custody of it in the morning.

Jean nodded numbly, signed several documents she didn't read. She just wanted to go home to Jimmy.

24

All the lights were on in the house. Jean stepped out of the private car that Lawrence Cutler had arranged for her, the driver a silent and compliant B.E. employee, who didn't need directions. Jimmy flew out the front door and rushed toward her, skidding to a dead halt as he saw that Jean was alone.

"Where's dad?" he asked.

Jean had felt herself falling back into the coma state during of the fifteen-minute drive from the Cutler house. She hadn't prepared an explanation or an excuse, hadn't formulated any expressions of grief or consolation. The truth felt unworkable, and she had signed it away into silence.

"What happened to you? You're all muddy and stuff?"

"Jimmy, let's go inside."

"Did you do it? Mission accomplished?"

She nodded. Jimmy came at her like a base runner charging to first, enveloping her in the least Jimmy-like embrace she had ever experienced. She was covered in muck, and he didn't care. He edged away and pulled something out of his pocket. She recognized the green leather jewelry box from her dresser. It had once held a necklace passed down to her from some distant relative that had fallen to pieces when she tried it on. Jimmy opened it with a flourish—resting on the red felt was a ribbon or award of some kind.

"I knew you could do it, I knew it! Well, not at first, but in Calcite. Anyway, I made this for dad."

He plucked out the ribbon, a narrow strip of cloth, hand-inked with red and blue vertical stripes, tapering to a silver dollar dangling from a tiny chain. It was a commemorative coin from Robert's collection, depicting a prospector panning for gold. Jimmy had affixed a strip of paper to the coin and coated it with airplane glue to preserve the caption, written in scrolling script: "California Medal of Heroism."

"So, when's he coming home?"

"I DON'T REALLY WANT to see him," Jimmy said.

"No one is going to see anything. Certainly not your father reconstructed, like some sort of mannequin. I saw it with *my* father. It's a lie, and I won't allow it."

They were sitting in Robert's Plymouth outside the California Mission-style Chapel of Chandler's mortuary. Jean had decided not to "take custody" of Robert, had declined the offer to view the "deceased" in the privacy of their "caring, family-run sanctuary." Robert was in there now, being "prepared" for burial, the expenses covered by B.E., whatever they were. For some reason, Jean had wanted to see the place, and Jimmy had insisted on coming along.

Late the previous night, she had told Jimmy everything, sparing no detail if he asked. After what he had been through, she decided he had earned the truth. The secret with which she was entrusting her son formed a heavier weight than most twelve-year-olds were asked to carry, and as she told the story, she felt the words darken with guilt, thinking that one day, she would be punished for her honesty. Yet concealment would have been worse. She couldn't imagine sitting down years from now with Jimmy and saying, 'Well son, I think you're finally old enough to know the truth about your father's death'." So there would be one last Vale family secret, the "big boy of secrets," as Jimmy called it. Not a secret that divided them, but a brutal, even gallant knowledge that united them.

He had not wanted to be cradled or held that night. He emerged from his room the next morning— this morning—at dawn, crying, shuddering, climbed onto the bed next to her and enveloped her, consoling her. *He* had consoled *her*.

"I've seen enough," Jean said, turning away from the funeral home. "How about you?"

"He's not really in there, anyway. Not the real dad."

"No, he's not."

There was no funeral. She'd hated her father's and didn't want to put Jimmy through it unless he insisted. He didn't. Of all the formalities, the most difficult was having to decide on a public cause of death. Helen and Grandpa Tamarkin, Robert's parents, his co-workers from B.E., all held conflicting assumptions and suspicions about the last few weeks of his life. She could not satisfy them all. So tragically, unexpectedly, an undiagnosed heart condition had claimed him while he was away on a business trip.

Robert's parents Henry and Marie came down on the Shasta Daylight and stayed at a motel on El Camino. Jimmy was surprisingly welcoming to them, the first time she had ever seen him express affection for his grandparents. Alma drove in, with Les Huntley, her "new gentleman, an Elks pal of mine." He was the boarder Jean remembered, the grave-digging reverend, now with thinning hair, thinning everything really, and a slight stutter that kept him out of the conversations about Robert. But he had what he called "pride of ownership" when he draped his arm around Alma as she boasted how she'd handled the Modesto cops who had come calling, along with the ambulance that had toted the invader away. Sticking with her story about a widow, threatened in her own house. A few days later, the police had paid a second visit. They asked a few lazy questions about a missing B.E. employee, but they refused to be intimidated by the mucky-mucks from over in the Bay Area who had pushed them into the case. Valley pride mixed with dry, hard stubbornness had won the day.

No one mentioned the name Wally Marantz.

Robert was buried in Alta Mesa, the headstone picked out by his parents, who supervised its carving and its installation. Jean thought headstones were for Civil War soldiers and people who had made it to one hundred. But for the rest of us, she couldn't imagine a less human memorial than a block of stone set among acres of similar blocks. But she felt too exhausted, too grief-stricken to object. Surprisingly, Alma took an active part in the headstone design, even going out with Henry and Marie for smorgasbord at Dinah's Shack after meeting with the stone mason. Setting a task—that was how Alma grieved for a man she had never warmed up to and barely thought about. Her opinion would probably never change, not even on the day her own headstone was cut and laid.

Most days, Jimmy stayed in his room, and she stayed in hers (how quickly it had changed from "theirs" to "hers"), but they left their doors open so they could keep an eye on each other. One day, he'd be sorting through a shoe box of bones and artifacts he'd excavated from the backyard, the next day he'd have his baseball cap on, working on his Bob Feller wind up. At night he'd lie in the darkness, practicing Morse code with a fork or a knife, tapping out his and Robert's code names. Her Morse was good enough to recognize Red: dot-dash-dot, dot, dash-dot-dot; and Green: dash-dash-dot, dot-dash-dot, dot, dot, dash-dot. It kept her awake, but after a few nights, the rhythmic tapping became comforting, like a ticking clock and it lulled her to sleep. Eventually Jimmy stopped, first dropping Red Team One, then Green Team One.

They ate simple meals out of cans, or the high falutin'

dishes that Helen and Grandpa Tamarkin cooked up. Franco-Russian cuisine Helen called it; Tamarkin insisted it was Russo-French. Of course, they knew the heart condition was a lie—they had been her earliest allies in intrigue. Over Stroganoff and Boeuf Bourguignon, she brought them gradually into her confidence, day by missing day, not telling everything, but enough so they knew Robert had died for a cause he believed in—or at least a cause he'd taught himself to believe in—not during an out-of-town mission to increase sales. If anyone could keep a secret, it was Grandpa Tamarkin, former servant of the Czar.

She and Jimmy cried at different times, living beside each other in quiet pain. She tacked her lists up around the house again, reciting them as the mood struck her, and though Robert wasn't going to come home to find them, she took them down every night at 5:30. Maybe there is consolation and continuity in our ailments and their treatment, she thought. Either that, or death and grief are the ultimate medicines.

And she plotted revenge. Bombing raids in a Piper Cub over the Cutler house. A campaign of threats until Frances had a breakdown and hung herself from the Lana Turner propeller. She, Jean Vale, would have to take vigilante action because the courtroom scene that played every night in her dreams was always the same: "In the matter of the murder of Robert Vale, how do you plead Mrs. Cutler?" "Not guilty, your honor." "The court agrees, you are hereby exonerated and free to go. The court would like to add that it considers you a patriot of the highest rank." But there was nobody around to kill; Lawrence Cutler had taken a leave of absence and Frances was out of state, in high level meetings, and had delegated the day-to-day operations of B.E. to "trusted associates."

She'd learned this in dribs and drabs from former co-workers who phoned or dropped by with food. Their concern seemed genuine—well, falsely genuine, the way people who share no true bereavement feel obligated to act. Jean was not ostracized or treated with suspicion, she heard no under-the-breath hints of treason or betrayal. The Claridge-woven cloak of secrecy had been draped over it all, from the main office to the South Shop to the streets of Calcite.

The calls and visits from colleagues, friends and neighbors were brief but laborious and Jean was grateful when they tapered off. Neighborhood boys, immune to the rituals of adult mourning, thank God, came over to mess around—Grady with his comic book collection (two girlie magazines tucked among them, she noticed), Frank Burke with his Daisy Red Ryder air rifle. Tommy Miyaki helped to set up a tetherball pole in the backyard, mixing the concrete himself before pouring it into a tire that served as the base. But Jimmy just watched, evaluating which pieces of his youth he wished to keep and which he was ready to leave behind. Even Monica Herndon stopped by. Her excuse was they were going to be in the same class when seventh grade started at the end of the month, and she wanted to bone up on geography, which she knew was one of Jimmy's strong suits. But he way they sat Indian style across from each other on the back lawn, drinking Cokes and plucking dandelions, told Jean that Monica had something else in mind. Jessie Harper was a frequent visitor. She and Jimmy took walks, telling their war stories, which Jean was sure the neighbors found a sight to behold. "You've finally arrived Jean, you got yourself a colored baby-sitter," Jessie said. She'd found another job as a janitor at Palo Alto High. "They call us custodians now, and I'm sure I'm the first gal those kids ever saw mopping down a gymnasium." She was taking a correspondence course in police work. "Ever since Connie, I've been so angry and fit to be tied. I got a real taste for it now."

There was one visit Jean made herself. Evelyn Sirk had moved back into the house in Redwood City. B.E. hired Bekins to bring their furniture home from Calcite, but she refused to take delivery of it, redirecting the moving van to the nearest Goodwill store. She and Jean sat on the front porch on a spanking new turquoise swing set, sipping bourbon in Robert's and Buddy's honor, Evelyn wearing the USAAF tie clasp on her lapel, the two of them holding hands like teenage best friends. They knew that no body would be found, no gravesite for Buddy Sirk would ever hold his remains. He would stay a casualty of peacetime, his death unremarked except by Jean, Jimmy, and the crew of Dallas Alice. Evelyn said she preferred it that way, rather than have a "passel of excuses, lies and old fashioned butt covering" dumped into her lap. *She* knew the truth, and she would cling to its slender comfort.

`"We're just a couple of peace widows, I guess," Evelyn said.

"I don't think that's all we are, Evelyn. We're survivors. And sooner or later—"

"The survivors win?"

Jean smiled, nodded, then topped off their glasses.

WHEN YOU DON'T GO LOOKING for a man's secrets, that's when you find them.

There were tasks you took on when your husband died. You cancelled his monthly haircut with his barber. You went through his clothes and shoes, deciding which to donate to the Salvation Army, which to pass on to relatives or children. You threw away his razors, his after shave, his hair clippers. You unsubscribed from his magazines, sold off his fishing tackle (which Robert had bought but never used). If he collected anything—coins or stamps, say—you had them appraised; if low value, you passed them on to the local Boy's Club. Jean did none of those things. She didn't want to go rooting and categorizing, she wanted his things to simply continue to be his. You took his name off bank accounts, off the Christmas Club, off the car registration, off the mortgage. She didn't do any of that, either. If someone had business with Robert, they could call.

Someone did.

A young man named Barry Thornhill, assistant branch

manager from a bank Jean had never heard of. He sounded nervous, as though she were his first official customer call, and his boss was listening in. He wanted to know "in light of your husband's passing," if she would like to continue the semiannual payments to John and Vivian Traynor and to the estate of Corporal Carl Vilette.

"I'm sorry," Jean said. "I'm not sure I understand. What payments?"

"Well, they are usually around $75, although the payments to the Vilette estate are ten percent higher. Because they have a daughter, I expect."

"Payments for what?"

"Well, that's a private matter between the parties involved here."

Jean stared at the phone as though it were an implement she'd never seen before, spinning its curlicue cord. "This is the first I've heard of this. How long have ... we ... been making these payments?"

"Since February of 1946, it appears. I wasn't here at the time, and no one who is currently employed here was. But the instructions are quite clear. I could send them to you for review, then you can drop by the branch, and we can sort this out."

John Traynor. Could that be Johno, Robert's legendary hellion best friend that Jimmy had once mentioned?

Jimmy stood in the doorway to the front room and Jean realized that he had overheard her end of the conversation. He was holding "The Story of King Arthur and his Knights" by Howard Pyle, the book he'd have Robert read to him on his birthday, one knight at a time, long after he could recite it by heart.

"Do you know anything about this?" she asked. He nodded.

"It's a simple story of three friends; three musketeers. We were restless, roamed around a lot. Living out there in Gresham, sort of small-town Portland, we figured the world was passing us by. None of us had much money. But the three of us had fathers who got around. My dad drove an ice truck. Carl's dad was a motorman on the Broadway Line and Robby's dad, he ran that elevator up in the Yeon building. To us, it was like driving a vertical racing car, and we'd make him run that thing until he threw us out. You could see both rivers from the top of the Yeon, too. And that's where the Bridge Jumpers Club formed. We got it into our noggins to locate every bridge across every creek and stream in Multnomah County and jump off 'em. And we did it —shallow, deep, didn't matter. Sometimes we'd bring a couple of girls to show off for. One of them took a liking to me—hard to imagine, with the face God's given me now—but mostly they were bored silly and of course we didn't recognize that. We spent more time with each other than with our families, and that didn't change, not when we landed our first jobs, first girlfriends, lost our first grandparents. We didn't change and we didn't want the city to change. We wanted the ice trucks to keep going and the streetcars to keep running and the elevator operators to hang on to their jobs. We wanted to be Bridge Jumpers forever. Talking about it now, it sounds like we became old men, but that's not it. We were just smart enough to recognize when things were good and adult enough to know they wouldn't be good forever. Farming, the shipyards, sawmill work, it all went away after the crash. Hoovervilles everywhere, even beneath the bridges we'd jumped. I stocked shelves at Fred Meyer. Carl got hired on with a salmon packer in Astoria. Working beside those big lug Scandinavians, he learned how to swear a blue streak in Swedish, Norwegian and Danish. Robert ended up down here and wrote to us that he'd met a beautiful woman with real backbone. And he sent us her picture, and true, she was beautiful. Still is, if you don't mind my saying, and here's the picture, if you want to see it ..."

They'd driven over from Fremont in a four-door Mercury that was especially equipped to accommodate "Johno"

Traynor's wheel chair, his wife Vivian unloading him with practiced ease, and pushing him up the driveway to the front door. Jean had invited them in, but they preferred to stay outside. Vivian rolled her husband onto the lawn, and Jean brought out three kitchen chairs and a pitcher of lemonade. Jimmy crouched on the grass, monkeying with the hand controls of the wheelchair, asking "what kind of speed can you work up in this baby?" It sounded like he was acting fresh, but he wasn't. Jimmy had known about Johno for years, had his address and phone number, and Johno had known about Jimmy, although they had never met or spoken. "I hear they're working on a powered model," Johno said. "That thing will roll like a bat out of hell, I'll bet."

John Traynor was lean, with a butch haircut and a handlebar mustache, a combination that made him seem half teenager, half Western outlaw. The left side of his face was scarred and blotchy with burn marks, which had aged into a brown and tan patchwork. His blue eyes were alert and roving, his upper arms powerful from years propelling the wheelchair. He wore a gray turtleneck sweater, blue jeans, and expensive-looking, brilliantly-shined dress shoes. "Everyone's eyes go straight to my legs then to my shoes, so I try to give 'em something spiffy to look at." Vivian Traynor was a woman whom men often dismissed as "handsome." A permanent wave that looked home done, healthy cheeks, strong hands, a stature that was solid and rested firmly on both feet. She had clearly been through a lot but seemed designed to bear up.

Jean looked at the photo of herself standing on the San Francisco side of the Golden Gate Bridge, bundled in a car coat, the camera capturing her in mid-shiver. She remembered the day, a fog-date they'd called it, but she hadn't known Robert had taken her picture.

"When the war came, we all had the same thought: this is tailor-made for the Bridge Jumpers. We all registered, you had to if you were between twenty-one and thirty-five. They weren't desperate then like they were later, when if you had two functioning eyes, and said yes to the question "Do you like girls?," you were on your way to training the next day

"So, Robert flew up to Portland the second week of February '42, supposedly to attend his parents' anniversary," Jean said.

"Yep. We thought if we registered together, and if we were drafted, we could serve in the same unit. And that's when we went in for our physicals. A hundred bare asses, going desk to desk, getting our paperwork stamped. Teeth examined, lungs, foot exams, reflex tests. You had to wait around awhile for the results, but we were pretty strapping, especially Carl from the packing plant. He and I were classified 1-A, but Robert said he didn't make it through. We never got the whole story, he didn't want to talk about it, and we didn't nag him. He just walked to the bus stop, said 'make us proud' and rode off. Those were the last words I heard him say."

The sun had passed over the roof and was baking the lawn. Johno put on sunglasses, poured himself and Vivian fresh glasses of lemonade.

"Can I ask what happened to Carl?"

"He died in April '45, on an island you probably never heard of, a long way from the history books."

"And you?"

"Maybe you saw in the newsreels during the war, how the Japs honeycombed islands like Iwo and Okinawa with tunnels and bunkers, where they were going to make a suicide last stand. How we had to clear 'em out with flamethrowers."

Jean nodded.

"Those were men, on both sides, scorched by the devil himself, men who endured what no man should ever have to endure, who died the way no man should ever have to die." Johno slapped his burned face, then plopped both hands on his spindly, paralyzed legs. "You heard of the million-dollar wound? The wound that doesn't kill you, but sends you home? Well, I got the fifty buck and a Kewpie doll wound."

Johno pushed down on the armrests, fighting to lever himself to his feet. Vivian tried to ease him back into the chair, but he struggled against her. "I want to stand now, Viv." He rose, shaky, but securely supported by Vivian who planted herself like a tree stump. "So, after I joined, I was driving a fuel truck, seven hundred and fifty gallons, making a delivery to Camp Abbot, out there along the Deschutes River. They had a combat engineering school, and I had a wild hair to join it, so I asked my CO if I could make that day's delivery, sort of get the lay of the land. A mile from the main gate, a white-tailed deer ran across the road and I swerved, the truck tipped, dumped me out, front end fell on my legs, the metal skidding triggered a spark and the damn thing ignited. If there hadn't been a fire crew practicing out there, I'd have burned to cinders and taken a thousand acres of Ponderosa pine with me. I never made it to the Pacific; never even made it out of Oregon."

Out of breath, but looking relieved, he slumped back down in the wheelchair.

"Would you like something stronger, Mr. Traynor?" Jean asked.

"Johno. And yes, if you wouldn't mind."

From beneath the sink where it had long been stored for "medicinal purposes," Jean retrieved a bottle of Old Granddad and splashed it generously into Johno and Viv's lemonades.

"I never thought of myself as a hero," Johno continued. "And I certainly never thought of your Robby as the coward he seemed to think he was. When the first checks arrived, I thought it was a mistake, called the bank, but they said the money was above board, fully approved payments from Robby. I sent 'em back because I was angry and proud. I didn't want any darned charity. Then we heard that Carl's widow Peg was getting them too, a bit more 'cause she has a daughter, Rhonda, about Jimmy's age. I called Robby at work, said thanks but no thanks, and he said I was gonna have to live with the extra income, that I'd have done the same for him. So maybe I couldn't find work as a steeplejack or a mail man and the twenty bucks a week in GI Bill unemployment dough didn't last long, but I still had a brain. Viv and I set up a little accounting service and ..."

Johno seemed to run out of juice. He gave a wave at Vivian over his shoulder, cueing her to take over.

"What I got John to finally see is that the money was a way for Robby to keep them all together," Vivian said.

"Did he ever visit?"

"We moved down here to be close to my sister, so he could have come by any time," Vivian said. "But no. That's not the kind of 'together' he had in mind, I don't think."

"It was more in here," Johno said, pressing a flag-saluting hand over his heart. "Or maybe here," tapping his head. "But I don't know, I never truly understood the man."

Jean could feel the waterworks about to turn on. She poured herself a shot of Old Granddad-ade, downed it, relishing its sugared, lemony burn.

"I imagine that he didn't tell you, Jean," Vivian said, "because he didn't want you to think that he was denying you and your boy anything. Many's the time I thought about ringing you up myself, but I didn't because that felt like it would be a violation of Robby's privacy. And so the years drifted by, and sometimes the money was a blessing, sometimes we'd send part of it to some battlefield commission in Washington trying to get a marker set down for Carl out in the Pacific. They had a graves registration unit in Europe, thousands of men were dug up and sent home, but Carl is still out there somewhere."

Vivian and Johno exchanged nods. "But now, John is the last Bridge Jumper left ..."

"And I can't even jump off an overturned bucket," he laughed, taking another snort.

"... so, we all agreed, Peg and John and me, that we will pay you back every dollar because, well, shit ..."

"No! Never. If Robert wanted you to have it, well ... well, shit ..."

And then they were crying, a flurry of hands reaching for other hands, Jimmy scooting across the grass to shoulder slap Johno man to man, the lemonade pitcher toppling over, strewing bright yellow lemon wedges across the green grass, the Old Granddad, empty now, rolling under the wheelchair.

The rest of the afternoon passed in companionable chat or relaxing silence. Some off-color Army jokes were told, Eisenhower vs. Stevenson debated, but with little interest or passion. There was no storytelling, no "remember when," or "how about that time he ..." With the sun slipping towards the summer-dry hills, Vivian pushed Johno to their car, got him squared away as he griped about front seat adjustments and wheelchair settings. No details were worked out, no plans made, no promises exchanged.

As they drove off, Vivian honked and Johno flashed a signal with his hand out the window, scissoring his index finger and middle finger into a pair of legs, leaping up, then dropping to the imaginary water below.

Neither Jean nor Jimmy moved to clear up the lawn. They sat together on the fence, waiting for the street light to come on. A half hour went by.

"He was 1-A, wasn't he?" she asked Jimmy. "But he didn't tell the guys." Jimmy nodded. "And once he got to B.E., he was deferred from the military because he was providing an essential government need. We'd signed a big contract with the Navy for hundreds of those oscilloscopes, and no one knew them better than your dad. He helped to assemble the first one and he signed off on the last one."

Jean felt she was homing in on the shame that had lain so heavily on Robert's heart.

"Why did he tell you and not me?"

Jimmy shrugged.

"Jimmy!"

"He heard me talking about Grady's dad's Nazi flag, the dagger and helmet he brought back. He thought I was ashamed of him. So did that little rat Billy Larkin." Jimmy rubbed his cuts and bruises, which were healing slowly, probably because he refused to treat them. "The real reason he didn't join up with Carl and Johno was because he was afraid that he'd let the fellows down where it counted most. In the war. But ..."

"But ...?" Jean asked.

"He told me because he wanted to teach me a lesson. I memorized it: 'A man honors his debts. Mine are to the men who died in my place and to their families. Yours will be different, but I know you'll honor them too.'"

THE DIRECTOR COULD NO LONGER pace corner to corner in his office as he critiqued rough drafts of his correspondence; he limped. His left arm was in a sling, so his typing had been temporarily curtailed. But his handwriting had always been excellent, and his voice was firm and clear as he read aloud the letter he had revised half a dozen times.

Dear Mrs. Vale,

I hope this letter finds you and your son in good health. There are no words equal to the task of expressing my condolences and it would be insulting to you for me to try. I'm writing to inform you that we have created an annual prize which carries with it a modest stipend, and have named it the Vale Prize, in tribute to you and your husband's contribution to the cause to which our organization is dedicated, the promotion of peaceful co-existence among the world's peoples. The international participants in Robert's recent undertaking share my conviction that the good you have done, while never to be made public, will save lives, perhaps just one or two, perhaps thousands. Early next year, we will be naming the first honoree and would be privileged if you, your son, and Miss Harper could attend.

It will be a simple ceremony held here in our somewhat cramped offices. There will be no trophy or engraved certificate; the honoree will not know the name of the prize or the story that lies behind its creation. That will stay between us. We will cover the costs of air transportation and lodging, and I hope that you will take the time to tour the sights of our nation's capital, seeing them not just as edifices of stone, but living ideals that endure in large part because of citizens like you and Robert and Jimmy and Miss Harper and Connie Latimer ...

God, what a hideous writing style, he thought. Pretentious, bureaucratic, devoid of character and directness. 'Good health?' They'd lost a husband and father. 'Living ideals?' Lord preserve me. These are not the words of a human being connecting to another human being. He trimmed the purple prose, then added a postscript to the letter and permitted himself a flash of appreciation.

Vann Claridge has been appointed National Intelligence Counsel to the Atomic Energy Commission (a self-created position no doubt) so his influence on our nation's war footing and weapons policies will continue and likely expand in the near future. But thanks to you and Robert, we've wounded the bastard. How can I tell? He visited his wife's grave for the first time that I know of. I was at the grave myself, bringing zinnias to my sister Anne. He was not grieving, he was not remorseful, he did not seem contemplative. But he was there, which speaks volumes to me. His armor is chipped, his martinis will need to be stronger and more numerous from now on. His stroke symptoms seem to be advancing, which I know bothers him not only physically but mentally—he has more battles planned and every cell that degrades within him is a cell that can't be thrown into the fray. In his darker moments, I imagine he is experiencing the first faint flickers of mortal fear, which pleases me to no end.

Yours Truly

Rosie

. . .

TWILIGHT.

Neighbors arriving home from the plant, the office, the shop, the school. Kids grousing as they break up their ball games and fights. With school scheduled to start in a week, every minute spent washing up for dinner or changing out of dirty clothes was a minute lost. The Black Mountain beacon blinking on. The sky purple and deep blue.

"Porch?" Jean asked.

"Naw."

"I think I'll sit out here awhile."

"Roger. Oh, and mom? I put the medal case on your dresser. I think it's yours too."

"Jimmy?"

"What?" he asked.

"Thanks for taking care of me."

He rolled his eyes. And went inside.

Jean headed for her familiar spot on the porch. If she timed it right, she'd catch the blur of the southbound SP commuter train as it flashed by at the end of Echo Lane. But ... If I sit down now, I may never get up. I'll still be sitting here, waiting, when Jimmy finds his first girlfriend, suffers through his first romantic catastrophe, writes angry, weepy poetry about it or maybe a song, comes home drunk for the first time, careful to avoid tripping over me. I'll be here as the widow hunters start to circle—the war created thousands of widows, Korea maybe thousands more—fighting off their concerned advances. I'll be there as Jimmy moves out, loads up his car he bought from a summer job and heads off into the working world. I'll still be there as gray streaks my hair and I study the Miss Clairol ads.

No. Do *not* sit down. Keep moving.

Robert had denied her the purity of grief, her mourning would always be tarnished by Vann Claridge's words: "To strive to be a hero in peacetime—that's a bit selfish, almost narcissistic." Anger and pride battled it out in her stomach, in her head.

In her wispy premonitions of the future, she sensed there would be no victor.

So be it, then. The months and years ahead would be a step-by-step search for those damned navigation lights. Robert hadn't found them, maybe she wouldn't either, but Jimmy would. Red, green. Red, green. He would slip artfully between them and land safely.

A car drove by slowly, the engine so quiet it seemed like it was muzzled in cotton, two men in the front seat she didn't recognize, making a point of not looking at her. The car stopped three houses down, just out of the streetlight's glow, lingered too long to be checking an address, then drove off.

They would keep watching. But she would not watch them back.

And one day, when the time was right, she would make them pay.

VALE PRIVATE INVESTIGATIONS – Discrete, Dedicated, Deadly

From: Field Operative (F.O.) James Vale

Subject: Search for Missing Person XYZ.

Time: Late

Comments: I can now reveal that Missing Person XYZ is Robert Jensen Vale. My father. Fallen in the line of duty.

HISTORICAL NOTE

On November 1, 1952, at 7:15 a.m. local time, 2:15 a.m. and a day earlier on the West Coast ...

... as Jessie Harper burned the midnight oil preparing for her rules of evidence exam; as Vivian Traynor helped Johno to his feet in his quest for a late night snack; as Quentin North lay sleepless in a Mexico City hotel room, wondering when he would hear from the personnel office of Grupo Monterey C.V., a fast growing food company; as Evelyn Sirk sat in darkness, listening to Buddy's tape; as Jimmy Vale dreamed of Halloween and the costumes he and Monica Herndon would wear; as Jean Vale sensed for the first time in months that Robert was beside her, his breathing measured and healthy ...

... on Eniwetok Atoll, the United States detonated "Ivy Mike," a thermonuclear fusion device the size of a small factory, yielding the equivalent of 10.4 megatons of TNT. It was seven hundred times more powerful than the Trinity Test in New Mexico.

BIBLIOGRAPHY

Stephen E. Ambrose. *The Wild Blue: The Men and Boys Who Flew the B-24s over Germany 1944-45*. Simon & Schuster, 2001

Travis L. Ayres. *The Bomber Boys*. New American Library, October 2009

Timothy Good. *Need to Know: UFOs, the Military and Intelligence*. Pegasus Books, 2007

Annie Jacobsen. *Area 51: An Uncensored History of America's Top Secret Military Base*. Little Brown, 2011

John Marks. *The Search for the "Manchurian Candidate": the CIA and Mind Control*. Norton Paperback, 1991

Trevor Paglen. *Blank Spots: the Dark Geography of the Pentagon's Secret World*. Dutton, 2009

Kevin Starr. *Golden Dreams: California in an Age of Abundance 1950-1963*. Oxford Press, 2011

Richard Rhodes. *Dark Sun – the Making of the Hydrogen Bomb*, Simon & Schuster, 1995

Philp Taubman. *Secret Empire*. Simon & Schuster, 2003

Evan Thomas. *The Very Best Men: The Daring Early Years of the CIA*. Simon & Schuster, 1995

ACKNOWLEDGMENTS

Thank you to my early readers: Vicky Mlyniec, Peter Hankoff and Yasser El-Sayed. Wonderful writers all, you kept me on course with your suggestions and encouragement.

When my creative doubts surfaced, Sue Perry, Richard Opper and Ann Poppe responded sharply: "Get over it, get it done."

Ich bin Cornelia Feye sehr dankbar. As my editor and publisher, her careful reading of the novel uncovered plot holes and inconsistencies, while leading to sharper conflicts and greater emotional depth.

All my best to the librarians, pub owners and coffee shop baristas who didn't know they were there for me on a journey that took longer than I expected.

ABOUT THE AUTHOR

David Madsen is the author of *Black Plume: the Suppressed Memoirs of Edgar Allan Poe, U.S.S.A.* a speculative mystery set in the American-occupied Soviet Union, which was a Book of the Month Club selection and *Vodoun,* a thriller that blends voodoo with American politics and the Haitian revolution.

He is also a produced screenwriter, with credits that include *Copycat,* the Warner Brothers thriller starring Sigourney Weaver and Holly Hunter.

A third generation Californian, he grew up in the San Francisco Bay Area, one of the main settings for *Under a Secret Sky.* While researching Secret Sky, he traveled to the back gate of Area 51. Although he didn't gain admittance, his license plate is no doubt in a secret data base, which he accepts as a badge of honor.

You can find the *Under a Secret Sky* playlist on Spotify

The author doing Cold War research during an air raid drill
April 1960

ALSO BY DAVID MADSEN

Black Plume: The Suppressed Memoirs of Edgar Allan Poe

U.S.S.A.

Vodoun

L.A. Adventures: Eclectic Day Trips by Rail through Los Angeles and Beyond -- with Elisa Makunga

www.ingramcontent.com/pod-product-compliance
Lightning Source LLC
LaVergne TN
LVHW091617070526
838199LV00044B/829
9798990818101